D1522135

Praise for *Road to Omalos*

"*Road to Omalos* is an engrossing detective story, romance, and adventure that takes the reader inside the mind of a sociopathic criminal. I enjoyed it immensely!"

—Harry Markopolos, the "Madoff Whistleblower," author of *No One Would Listen: A True Financial Thriller*

"Jax expertly weaves this gripping narrative from the opening paragraph. Meticulously drawn details entice and enthrall, consistently employing the five senses to bring her literary vision vividly to life. Vibrantly depicted characters often struggle with conscience as they vacillate between virtue and obligation, in an array of interlacing subplots that serve to enhance this spellbinding tale."

—US Review of Books

"Marilyn Jax has done it again! The suspense, interplay, and conflict between the characters will keep the reader on edge right up to the brilliant, unexpected, and explosive ending. A Greek thriller!"

—Dr. Thomas Rumreich,
Forensic Odontologist

Praise for *The Find*

"*The Find* is a gripping suspenseful murder mystery from beginning to end. Modern criminology is joined with Aztec history to solve a murder decades old and to give flesh and narrative to a skeleton found beneath the rubble. Throughout the novel, there is much to uncover. Written in a crisp style, *The Find* is quite a find!"

—Michael Berenbaum
Author, Lecturer

"*The Find* fully engages the reader with its elaborate and well-executed plot. Jax does a formidable job populating her novel with a bevy of rich and appealing characters, each painted in remarkable and vivid detail. Accordingly, the settings are painstakingly drawn, engaging the five senses with each thorough description. The parallel story lines tug at the reader, enthralling not only with the unexpected snakes and turns of a masterful mystery, but enchanting as well with its real and sympathetic heroes and villains alike. Jax's in-depth knowledge of World War II history, law enforcement, and investigative techniques lend credibility to an already mesmerizing tale, one that is sure to satisfy to the end."

—*US Review of Books*

"From the Caribbean to Miami to London and back, the plot has more twists than even the most addicted mystery buff can handle. Just when you think you've solved the case, a new suspect takes you in another direction. Marilyn Jax has written a thriller that will keep you guessing to the very end."

—Ron Meshbesher
Past President, National Association of Criminal Defense Lawyers

ALSO BY MARILYN JAX

The Find

Road to Omalos

. . . and watch for *Never In Ink*

SAPPHIRE
Trails
a novel

MARILYN JAX

ISBN 13: 978-1-59298-506-7

Library of Congress Catalog Number: 2012910807

Printed in the United States of America

First Printing: 2012

16 15 14 13 12 5 4 3 2 1

Author photograph by Patrick Broderick.
Cover and interior design by James Monroe Design, LLC.

Beaver's Pond Press, Inc.
7108 Ohms Lane
Edina, MN 55439-2129
(952) 829-8818
www.BeaversPondPress.com

To order, visit www.BeaversPondBooks.com or call (800) 901-3480.
Reseller discounts available.

Dedicated to the memory of my
cherished Uncle Arvid

You showed us how to live a life of high honor
By your constant example, you taught us all the right way

ACKNOWLEDGMENTS

As always, I would like to offer a profound thank-you to my readers. You are my encouragement to pen each succeeding novel.

A special note of gratefulness to my cherished Daniel. You are the apple of my eye.

To my family and friends, your continuous support means everything.

Also, a colossal note of gratitude to the Lake County Sheriff's Office, the Whitefish Police Department, the Flathead County Sheriff's Office, the Montana State Crime Lab, and Mountain Lake Lodge, for valuable consultation during the crafting of this mystery.

And to my impressive managing editor, Amy Cutler Quale; my mega-talented designer, James Monroe; my remarkable editor, Angela Wiechmann; and to the always-helpful staff at Beaver's Pond Press—together, you're the *crème de la crème*. The best of the best.

To the beautiful state of Montana: Your ever-present big blue sky, fresh air, clean glacial lakes, majestic mountains, towering ponderosa pines, breathtaking scenery, and prevailing spirit inspired me to write *Sapphire Trails*.

PROLOGUE

Whitefish, Montana

A RECENT RASH of burglaries rocked the residents of the quaint town of Whitefish. Homeowners living in the pricy and prestigious Iron Horse community, located on Big Mountain and overlooking Flathead Valley and Whitefish Lake, had fallen easy prey to the mysterious thief. Striking within this remote residential locality, the intruder had absconded with valuable art and a mix of cash, watches, and jewelry. The victims' losses totaled a handsome sum.

The burglar hit in the dark of the early-morning hours, presumably between 1:00 a.m. and 3:00 a.m., and each time when no one was home. Many of the victimized homeowners maintained primary residence in San Francisco, where they were employed, and traveled to their Iron Horse community homes only sporadically—some just a single weekend a month. And because the stately homes sat vacant so much of the time, the area had become ripe pickings for the housebreaker.

The time elapsing between break-ins was erratic, making it impossible for the local Whitefish Police Department to formulate any sort of pattern or predictable movement on the part of the culprit. Mercifully, no one had been physically injured in the capers, but lives had been disrupted in a powerful and dramatic way. The victims—and the community at large—no longer enjoyed peace of mind.

Although the intruder escaped with a variety of high-end items during the heists, the Whitefish police determined that the thief's primary focus appeared to be the authentic pieces of artwork within each majestic home. Some of the paintings were quite large in dimension and required extra time and effort to remove from the walls and tote away. This factor baffled law enforcement. Perhaps an extra set of hands was needed to carry out the acts? As time went on, more questions than answers bombarded the local authorities.

The Iron Horse community was targeted for a reason. The mostly custom homes peppered throughout the private golf club enclave were superior properties. And it was a well-known fact that many contained art collections or at least valuable pieces of art. Highly in-demand Native American warrior and Arabian horse head oil paintings by CJ Wells, and notable pieces by famous Montana artists like Charles M. Russell and Ace Powell, were among the works that disappeared into the night, leaving behind gaping empty spaces on the cavernous interior walls of the impressive rustic dwellings.

The Whitefish police chief was quite certain about one thing. The thief seemed to have an extensive and admirable knowledge of art—selectively targeting the priciest pieces within each home entered. And that was the only clue his department had to work with. To date, no DNA, fingerprints, or other traces of the burglar had been recovered.

Residents of the charming town of Whitefish strolled the streets as before, going through the motions of daily living and pretending nothing had changed. But a closer look revealed introspective expressions on sad faces and eyes filled with bewilderment, for the burglaries had disrupted the normalcy of Whitefish in a profound manner.

Since 1904, when the Great Northern Railroad was being constructed through the northwest section of Montana, the townsfolk had always grasped fiercely to the small-town ambience of this early Western settlement. But slowly, over the many years, the town of Whitefish had melded into a mixture of both old and new. General stores and Western bars mingled with art galleries and boutiques, and a miscellany of eateries—from small-town cafés to upscale restaurants—popped up on its attractively old-fashioned streets.

Located on the northern edge of Flathead Valley, gracefully nestled between the high peaks of Glacier National Park and Big Mountain, Whitefish quickly became a welcoming place for visitors of all ages and of varying outdoor sports interests.

But now, for the first time, the long-standing old-town friendliness of the delightful railroad town was on hold. Things seemed out of focus and hopelessly out of control.

Customarily calm and unruffled, the hardy people of this picturesque community appeared on edge and even bad tempered. *Where will the culprit strike next? Is anyone really safe? Could he be one of us?* These were some of the questions overheard time and again from the mouths of Whitefish residents. Many had lost the ability to sleep through an entire night, and brooding was widespread. Despite security systems in place to ward off intruders, the burglar had amazingly outwitted even the most complex of home-monitoring devices.

Countless weeks had elapsed with the Whitefish Police Department attempting to track the individual or individuals responsible for the recurring crimes, and all efforts had failed miserably. The thief remained one step ahead and on the prowl.

The situation was reaching a climax. Inhabitants of Whitefish were demanding their town back. Unrest was palpable. Something had to be done, and fast.

The deep feeling of melancholy that had flowed over the picture-perfect town seemed to have hardened in place. The gloom would not lift, nor could the town return to its normal stride, until law enforcement apprehended the mysterious criminal and put an end to the madness that had invaded this magical place.

1

Office of Caswell & Lombard, Private Investigation
Miami Beach, Florida

CLAIRE CASWELL RIVETED her eyes on Gaston "Guy" Lombard, transfixed by what she did not see. Who was sitting there in *his* chair, wearing *his* clothes? Where was the Guy Lombard she knew so well? He looked the same, but he was different in an inexplicable sort of way. He was going through the motions of being Guy Lombard, yet something was missing. Something significant. She could see it in his eyes. The eyes always gave it away. They looked vacant. And while others did not notice the change, she had for some time.

"Thoughts of Crete keep flooding my mind," Claire said. "Months have passed, and here we sit, working in Miami as if the whole thing never happened."

"I know," Guy said. He looked up from a file that had held his attention for the past two hours. "Every time I think about what I . . . what *we* . . . went through in Crete on that ill-fated case, it infuriates me. I've gone over it a thousand times in my mind. Maybe more. For a while there, I didn't think I'd get out alive. And I was even more concerned about you." He exhaled a deep sigh. "But here we are, and the case that took us to the Greek island is now only a foggy memory."

"Is it?" Claire asked. She walked over to the man she loved, her life and business partner, and kissed him tenderly on the cheek. "Are you okay, sweetheart? I mean, are you *really* okay? Maybe it would help if you talked to someone. A professional."

Guy shot a half-angry look her way. "I don't need help. The wind is back in my sails, and I'm doing fine. I think about it less and less these days."

She continued to look at him with concern, not at all convinced by his words.

"I'm healed now," Guy said, "and I only have a handful of scars to remind me of that horrific ordeal. So all in all, I'd say I'm pretty much back to my old self—my mean, old self, and my rage is burning hotter than ever." He paused momentarily, appearing deep in thought. "Actually, I'm thankful we both got out of that investigation in one piece. I realize it could have turned out much worse." His eyes glazed. "But I'm okay. Really, I am. I'm fine."

The expression on his face did not match his words. He appeared distant and profoundly troubled. And full of anger.

"I don't know, Guy," Claire persisted. "Seems at some level you're still enraged about what happened to you, and you have every right to be. But you must find a way to let it go, to get past it and move on. It's hurting you . . . and us." She paused. "You seem melancholy most all of the time, and you wear this desolate expression on that handsome face of yours, and it worries me. I've never seen you like this before. You've been this way ever since we returned from Crete, and from what I see, it doesn't seem to be getting better."

"Okay. Okay. You've made your point. Now give me a break, Claire, will you? The bastard almost killed me! What do you want from me?" He got up and stormed outside.

Claire gave him a few minutes to cool down and then went out to look for him. She found him leaning against the trunk of a towering palm, finding shelter from the heat of the blazing Miami sun under its sprawling green fronds. He had folded his arms over his chest, and he wore the face of someone buried deeply within his own thoughts.

"Guy?" Claire said softly. "We saw the case to conclusion. We can be proud of that fact. Justice found George Zenonakis in a strange way, I'll admit, but he did pay for his crimes. We did our job, and we survived. It's time to put it behind us now."

"Yeah. Right," Guy said. "I realize that. But I keep thinking about that good-for-nothing and what he did to me. I can't seem to shake it—that feeling of utter helplessness . . . of thinking I was going to die. The entire time I was a Miami-Dade state attorney, I dealt with nefarious people. I've been threatened by the deadliest of criminals anyone could conjure up in the mind. But I've never been captured and battered to within inches of my life. And the worst part of it all was that I couldn't fight back. *I couldn't fight back!* I had to take whatever that monster doled out on me. You can't possibly comprehend the feeling of not being able to defend yourself." He hung his head.

Dispirited dejection seemed to devour him. It was as if he'd seen death and come back to talk about it. Being kidnapped and severely beaten by the criminal they had gone after had taken what seemed to be a permanent toll on Gaston "Guy" Lombard.

"Some days are worse than others," he said openly. "This happens to be a bad one." He looked at Claire with deep-seated sadness penetrating his eyes.

"I'm so sorry, Guy. It was a tough case. Driving the road to Omalos to rescue you almost did me in, too. I quiver just thinking about it. I had to face my fear of heights head on, and for you I did it. I had no other choice. But I would never, *ever* travel that road again! I still have nightmares about it."

"Claire, I'm sorry, too. I had no idea it was still bothering you." He stood up straight and took her in his arms. "There was no way to foresee what that case would demand from us." He breathed in and out deeply. "Again, I'm happy the whole thing is over."

"Me, too," Claire said. "But I want *you* back."

How she hoped the former Guy would return—the man he'd been before the case that had taken them to the Greek island of mystique and intrigue. How she wondered if the glimpses of perfect hopelessness embedded so deeply in his coffee-colored eyes would one day be gone.

Claire's mind drifted. She was turning thirty-eight this year and Guy forty-eight. The ten-year age difference had never been a factor in their relationship. In fact, since their first encounters—back when she was a government fraud investigator for the State of Florida and he was the lead Miami-Dade state attorney, back when the two joined efforts on certain cases to put lawbreakers away—there had been a special, inexplicable connection between the two of them. Exchanging calls, business at first and then personal, quickly developed into meeting for lunches and dinners. A strong friendship catapulted into a powerful love bond, and before they knew it, they were sharing a living space. Then, recently, the pair had combined their individual strengths to form the successful firm of Caswell

& Lombard, Private Investigation, on Collins Avenue in Miami Beach. Life had been good. And Claire did not want it to change. She needed Guy to feel better.

THE FOLLOWING morning, the investigators opened their office for the day. Within minutes, the phone rang.

"Caswell & Lombard, Private Investigation," Claire answered.

"Claire, it's Piper and Jay Cantrell. We're on speakerphone."

"What a nice surprise!"

It had been a while since Claire and Guy had talked to their good friends from Miami who had moved to Montana some years back, and she was thrilled to hear from them.

"Hold on while I put our phone on speaker so Guy can jump in." Claire motioned to Guy and hit the speaker function button. "Okay, we're both here."

"How's everything in Miami Beach?" Piper asked.

"Funny you should ask," Claire said. "Just yesterday we were reminiscing about a certain difficult case of ours and saying how happy we were to be safely back home in Florida and into our regular routine . . . that is, if you can call anything about our line of work regular or routine. We were thrown into a dangerous web of circumstances in that particular matter, and we are happy to still be alive and kicking, as the saying goes."

"Sounds ominous," Jay said. "You're both okay, right?"

"Yeah," Guy said. "We'll fill you in on all the specifics another time. For now, let's just say it was a formidable case."

"We have an offer," Piper said. "In fact, it's the reason for our call. We're inviting you to come visit us at our lodge—Mountain Lake Lodge—for a few days as our guests. We miss the two of you and would love to see you. Any chance that could happen?"

"Right about now, a few days in Montana sound idyllic," Guy said. He looked at Claire and started to flash his famous grin, but something held him back from letting it develop fully.

At once, her eyes sparkled with hope. The half grin was the only sign she needed to see. She whispered, "Let's do it. Let's go."

Guy thought about the prospect briefly and nodded a cautious assent.

"We'll have to get some things in order first, but yes, we accept your invitation," Claire said. "We'd love to come for a visit!"

"Excellent," Jay said. "The rest and relaxation will do you good."

"Then it's settled," Piper said. "Just let us know what day and time you'll arrive, and Jay will pick you up at the Kalispell airport. We'll have a nice room ready for you. Can't wait. It's been a few years since you were up our way. In fact, we haven't seen you since our wedding."

"Well, we look forward to it," Claire said. "I'll call you back as soon as we can make the travel arrangements and get things at the office ready to be placed on hold for a few days. Thanks again for the invite. It's really just what we need."

Claire hung up and threw her arms around Guy's neck. "We certainly could use a break from work," she said. She planted a sweet kiss on his lips. "It's been a long time since the two of us have had simple, unadulterated *fun*!"

"Yeah," Guy said, feigning enthusiasm. "Time to pull out the old cowboy boots and pack some blue jeans." Again he attempted his famous grin, but cut it short.

Today was the first time in months that Claire had seen even a flicker of a smile on his face. Whether his expression was sincere or not, her eyes lit up with promise. If she had any remaining qualms about putting the firm's investigations on hold for a few days and taking a much-needed vacation, they disappeared on the spot. It was the right thing to do.

Her mind drifted. When she was brutally honest with herself, she accepted the fact that Guy had never bounced back completely after the episode in Crete. That case had taken unexpected and perilous twists and turns. And Guy did not fool Claire for a minute, no matter how much he pretended that things were getting back to normal. She knew the physical scars on his face were not the only scars remaining. Deep inside, and not evident to the eye, Guy had been damaged—his inner spirit harmed in a great way. And she knew those invisible scars would be there for some time to come. She would press for him to seek professional help again, when the timing seemed right. He would resist, but she would persist. Yet at least for now, they could get away from it all for some much-anticipated days of pleasure and sightseeing. The change of scenery would do them good.

"Let's get our files in order," Claire said. "We have some work ahead of us before we can leave. And we'll need to figure out what clothes to pack for Montana. I'll check the weather forecast."

Ten days later . . .
Tuesday
Kalispell, Montana

AFTER MAKING two stops, the flight from Miami delivered Claire and Guy to Kalispell, Montana. It was just after 9:00 p.m. when the plane landed. The airport was both welcoming and clean, and people strolled through the facility, smiling, laughing, and wearing pleasant faces. Everyone appeared relaxed and carefree. What a difference from the always-hectic, ever-congested streets of Miami Beach, Claire thought, where stress was the constant flavor of the day. Within minutes, the two had retrieved their luggage from the carousel.

As promised, Jay was standing there waiting when they stepped from the Glacier Park International Airport terminal. He hadn't changed a bit. His hair was sandy, his skin tanned, and his expression warm and filled with laughter. It was good to see their longtime friend.

All at once, the two investigators were hit with the invigorating scent of fresh pine needles wafting through the crisp mountain air.

"Aah. Now *this* is a nice change!" Claire said. She greeted Jay with a huge smile.

Jay quickly kissed Claire on the cheek and briefly embraced Guy. "It's good to see you both," Jay said, donning a straw cowboy hat.

Claire looked around and assessed her surroundings. "It's the total antithesis of Miami Beach here. Clean. Clear. Cool. Fragrant. Not crowded. Slower paced. I like it!"

Jay laughed. "Jump in." He opened the rear door of his blue Chevy Suburban parked only feet away, and his friends slid in. Then he placed their luggage in the far back of the vehicle. "Yeah, Piper and I really like living here," he said, taking a seat behind the wheel. "Every day we see the mountains off in the distance, breathe in the pine-scented air, glance out at Flathead Lake, and take in the *big sky* of this magnificent state. And we never tire of any of it or second-guess ourselves for deciding to leave Florida and head up this way. This environment has always drawn us like a magnet."

"I can understand that," Guy said. "We haven't been back to Montana in the six years since your wedding, and we've never even seen the lodge you built. How long has it been open now? Five years? How have the years passed so quickly?"

"Got me. The years do seem to fly by," Jay said. "We can't wait to show you the lodge. It's technically located in Woods Bay—Lake

County—but its address is Bigfork. Actually, the town of Bigfork is five minutes away, and it sits in Flathead County." He paused as if in deep reflection. "Even though it's been a ton of work to operate, neither Piper nor I would want to do anything else. I think we found our niche."

Claire's mind strayed back to the first time she and Guy visited Montana. "Jay," she said, and then hesitated a moment. "I still remember you on that white horse at your wedding ceremony, and Piper on her white horse, as the two of you rode all along the sidelines of the crowds and joined together up front near the reverend to recite your vows. You stayed on your horses the entire ceremony, until you rode off together . . . into the sunset." She relived the entire scene in her mind as she spoke.

"It really was something, wasn't it?" Jay asked. "People around here still talk about it." He paused. "Maybe you guys should try marriage one day soon." He looked into his rearview mirror for an instant and caught sight of Claire's expression. He fidgeted in his seat, instantly regretting his words. "Sorry. Sore subject. I forgot. Won't mention it again. Promise."

"No worries," Claire said. She turned her head and looked out the window next to her.

A brief uncomfortable silence followed. Then as they traveled the roadway toward Bigfork, the three continued to recount earlier times the quartet had shared. The two couples had been so close before Piper and Jay had surprisingly pulled up stakes and made their move from Miami Beach to Big Sky Country—a relocation taking them three thousand miles away from the Million Dollar Sand Bar.

Leaving the fast-paced surroundings of the Beach behind for several days of blissful and carefree unwinding appealed to the sleuths in a significant way. Claire became instantly intrigued as she absorbed the landscape of the area. The spirit of the place tugged at her inner being. She closed her eyes. Ancient wisdom of tribal elders who had once occupied this very land whispered loudly inside of her. The place held high spiritual activity, there was no doubt about it. She opened her eyes to again observe those things visible.

Claire and Guy had agreed to forget about work and the densely populated streets of Miami Beach for these few days away. This was their time to visit with old friends. And hopefully, it was an opportunity for Guy to start to heal. Nothing was going to get in the way of enjoying every single, solitary moment.

"Piper's cooking dinner as we speak," Jay said. "I know it's late, and I'm sure you're starving. We'll stop by the house first to say a quick hello, if you don't mind, and we can gulp down a few appetizers Piper has prepared. Then I'll take you over to the lodge, help get you quickly checked in, and then drive you back to our house for the real meal. Our place is in Woods Bay—only about a mile from the lodge. Sound okay?"

"Sounds perfect," Claire said. "I can't wait to see Piper. It's been too long. And yes, I'm famished."

"She can't wait to see the two of you, either. And don't forget, while you're here, it's cherry season," Jay said. "You'll see all kinds of roadside farm stands offering a variety of locally grown Flathead cherries for sale. Buck a bag. Make sure you stop for some."

"I remember those sweet cherries from the last time we were here," Claire said. "Yum. We'll pick some up for sure."

"We have an old green Land Rover Discovery 4 x 4 you can use while you're here . . . so you won't feel stranded without transportation," Jay offered. "As I seem to recall, you both like to explore your surroundings, so please feel free to use it all the while you're here. And above all else, you must use this time to de-stress." He tilted his head. "We actually make our guests sign a contract when they check in, promising to relax and enjoy the beautiful surroundings of Glacier National Park and Big Sky Country. That way, if anyone is tempted to turn on a BlackBerry or iPhone and engage in business, at least they'll think twice about it." He chuckled.

"Thanks for the sage advice, Jay," Guy said. "The tension level is mighty constant back home with our seemingly never-ending stacks of files. Teetering on the brink of doing more than we can handle seems to be our norm . . . but you know how that goes."

"What else is new, right?" Jay said. He chortled again. "Well, promise me you'll take long walks, swim in the pool, go horseback riding a couple times, play golf at Eagle Bend Golf Course, eat some good food, and visit an Indian trading post or two while you're here. And also leave plenty of time to visit with us." He smiled broadly, revealing the slight separation between his two front teeth.

Reality was starting to sink in. Claire and Guy were on their own for ten glorious days to do whatever they wished and not be under the thumb of pressing investigations. It seemed too good to be true.

"How's the lodging industry doing these days?" Guy asked. "You've been at it for a few years now. Is it financially worth the effort?"

"I must say that overall we've done okay. Until the recent downturn in the economy, that is. Now some months are a bit touch-and-go, I'll admit, but no doubt things will pick up when the economy does a turnaround," Jay said. "It's bound to, right?"

"We're all hoping for that," Claire said.

"Between weddings, receptions, corporate meetings, retreats, special events, and vacationers, we're hanging in there," Jay added. "Always could be better, though."

"What was *that*?" Guy shouted out of the blue. He pointed his index finger toward the right-hand shoulder of the road. "I saw some kind of animal sitting in the ditch, in the shadow of the light pole we just passed. Near a sign that said Kehoe's Agate Shop. Looked like a huge baby something . . . could have been anything."

"Let's take a look," Jay said. The tires squealed as he made an abrupt U-turn on the road, traveled a short distance, and then made another sharp U-turn to head back in the direction they'd been traveling when Guy made the discovery.

Guy watched the shoulder carefully, and before long, he again spotted the creature. "There it is!" He pointed.

Jay eased the vehicle unto the paved strip along the roadway and came to an easy, full stop. His eyes searched the undergrowth until he, too, spotted it.

A rotund young bear sat by the side of the road, contently gorging itself on the plentiful wild red berries dotting the surrounding shrubbery. All three locked eyes on the large, round ball of fluff, only feet away from Jay's Chevy Suburban. As the trio gawked with curiosity at the amazingly heavy baby mammal, the youthful bear glanced upward briefly to sniff the air in their direction. But it looked away just as quickly, having no particular interest in the obvious attention being showered upon it by the onlookers. The animal continued to inhale the tasty morsels. Nothing was going to interrupt the plentiful feast that nature provided the growing cub.

"Its fur is a light *tan* color," Claire said. "I've never seen a tan bear before."

"Believe it or not, they are actually a subspecies of the American black bear," Jay said. "They're called *cinnamon* bears. Most have brown or reddish-brown fur; hence, the name cinnamon bears. They're native to this area."

Claire and Guy watched in quiet amazement.

"Not a common sight in Miami Beach," Guy said, chuckling softly, "as I'm sure you remember."

Jay laughed. "They live to be about thirty years old," he said. "They eat meat and insects, but mainly survive on fruit and vegetation. Oh, and of course, nuts and honey would be a real treat for them." He smiled as he studied the young bear. "I must admit, though, I've never seen one with light-tan fur like this before. It's really quite a beauty. In fact, people who live out here rarely, if ever, see a regular-colored cinnamon bear, let alone a tan one. Good spot, counselor."

"Let's take a photo," Claire said. As she reached to pull her camera from a tote bag, the cub turned in the opposite direction and started to waddle off toward some denser greenery nearby. Soon the bear would disappear completely into the concealed shelter.

"I'll jump out and call to him," Guy offered. "Maybe he'll turn around, and you can grab a quick shot." He reached for the door handle.

"*Stop!*" Jay shouted at Guy. "Don't even think about it. Don't do that unless you want the scare of your life! Stay inside this vehicle! Where there's a young bear, there's a mother bear. Count on it. Never forget that. And rest assured, she will not take kindly to you approaching her cub. That's an absolute no-no, always."

Taking Jay's warning to heart, Guy settled back into his seat, feeling a bit foolish he suggested such a bad idea. He should have known better, and he was embarrassed by Jay's admonition.

Jay pulled the Suburban back onto the road and set out toward his and Piper's home.

"I'll sleep well tonight," Guy announced, breaking the silence. "I know that."

"Yes, you will," Jay said. "This mountain air does the trick. Works better than any sleeping pill ever invented."

Before long, the three arrived at the Cantrell home, and Piper ran out to welcome her guests.

"At last you've come for a visit. I'm happy," Piper said. She threw her arms around Claire and gave her a momentary hug. Then Piper grabbed Guy's hand and shook it warmly. "Come in, please. Welcome to our humble abode."

Sipping aromatic, fresh-brewed huckleberry coffee and tasting an assortment of delicious, just-out-of-the-oven appetizers, the couples fell into easy conversation. There was much to catch up on, and minutes passed quickly.

"Let's take a walk around the property tomorrow morning," Piper suggested. "We want to show you all of it in the daylight. But now, you need to check into your room and then get right back here for dinner. Jay will help you."

"Sounds like a plan," Claire said. "Those appetizers were fabulous!"

In no time flat, the investigators had checked into their room and were returning to the Cantrell home with Jay. Once there, Claire and Guy inhaled the delicious aromas emanating from the kitchen.

"Something smells terrific," Guy said.

The delectable and healthful food more than sated the investigators, and it turned out to be the perfect time for Jay and Piper to tell their friends more about the lodge.

"We've put a lot of time and energy into it over the years, and we're really quite proud of it," Jay said. "Folks come here from all around to stay with us and seem to truly enjoy it. They hike through the pines, bask in the hot tub next to the outdoor swimming pool, eat great food, visit nearby Glacier National Park, and take in the amazing vistas of the valley by day and the glorious array of stars in the sky by night. They throw their cares to the wind. Literally. Relaxation is what they're seeking, and relaxation is just what they find here in Montana at Mountain Lake Lodge." He smiled. "We've met interesting people over the years, as I'm sure you can imagine. Many return every single year for a long week or two of total and absolute tranquility, away from their otherwise whirlwind lives back home. We offer an atmosphere of calm and respite from the frenzied world—a chance to step off the merry-go-round for a time. More and more, it seems to be what people crave."

"You'll get no argument from me on that statement," Guy said, reflecting on everything Jay had just said.

"Or me," Claire said.

"Well, while you're here, please slow your pace down and do nothing except take pleasure in your surroundings. You deserve some free time," Piper said. "It might seem strange at first, allowing your muscles to release the tension big-city dwellers carry around. But in a short while, I think you'll like how you feel. And don't forget to go into our little town of Bigfork, just two miles down the road. The shopping and restaurants are charming. And you'll also want to drive to nearby Whitefish one day to mull around. Again, lots of fun stores to browse through. It's like an old Western town." Piper smiled widely, exposing her full set of very white teeth. "This will be a vacation you'll always remember, my friends." She ran her fingers through her short red hair.

The couples sat down on the front stoop after eating, breathing in the refreshingly cool evening air and staring in awe at the magnificent streaks of color presenting in the inky nighttime sky. Spectacular pinks and succulent oranges melded together into stunning formations, heralding a beautiful day to come.

Upon agreeing to call it a night, Jay returned Claire and Guy to the lodge.

It was late, and an oh-so-comfortable bed awaited the pair, but the investigators took the time to step out onto the balcony of their third-floor room to observe the sky one final time before retiring. Flathead Lake sat directly in front of them, deep within Flathead Valley, and its waters glistened under the glow of the moon. Dark mountain ridges paraded directly behind the lake, nearly obscured by the blackness of the evening. Once their eyes adjusted to the lack of light, the two could make out the ever-so-tall ponderosa pines seemingly placed in great numbers all around. And then they looked up and noticed the stars. *The stars.* The luminous and incandescent heavenly bodies, sparkling and dazzling with phenomenal brightness in the darkness. Before long, the burden of case files piled high on both desks at Caswell & Lombard, Private Investigation began to evaporate, and they beheld the amazing beauty all around them without restriction. The stillness of the surroundings captured the sleuths in an intoxicating way, and they couldn't seem to get enough of it.

"This is what we've been missing," Claire said. "It's so . . . untroubled here." A cool breeze grabbed her, and she shivered.

Guy put his arm around her shoulder and pulled her close. "Yeah. Almost doesn't seem real."

2

EARLY THE FOLLOWING morning, Piper and Jay Cantrell showed Claire and Guy all around the grounds of Mountain Lake Lodge and then led their visitors toward the stately lodge itself, walking though the adjacent parking lot to get there. The custom-designed structure, built of golden pine logs, wooden beams, and stone, epitomized rustic elegance in the Rockies. The covered main entrance was welcoming. Massive clay pots, brimming with colorful summer flowers, adorned each side of the two steps leading up to its front double doors. Vines of vibrant petals trailed downward from hanging planters within the coved area. And lanterns were strategically positioned on a pair of front support posts anchored by bases comprised of assorted stones.

Perched high atop a hillside, the lodge afforded its guests a view showcasing the vast vistas of Flathead Lake and Valley.

Two restaurants were housed within the lodge, the Terra Restaurant and Riley's Pub, both offering indoor and outdoor seating.

Original framed pieces of art by local artists—oils, watercolors, pastels, and acrylics—decorated the walls of the main and upper level. And Jest Gallery occupied the lion's share of the lower level, displaying an even greater selection of the unique, fine paintings of famed Montana artists. All the pieces in the lodge were consigned by the artists who painted them and were available for purchase.

Standing in the lobby, Claire and Guy paused to take in the entire scene. A stone-hearth fireplace, ablaze with flames of orange and blue, took up the greater space on one main wall, and a sofa and two oversized chairs covered in a deep brick-red fabric sat facing it. Lamps with moss-colored shades and bases made of native rocks emitted soft lighting and added to the ambiance of the setting.

A green leather guest journal with a pen attached sat open on the primitive coffee table, accessible to anyone sitting in the comfy area and wishing to add an entry. Claire quickly paged through it and observed that many visitors to the lodge had written clever and witty remarks or comments about the accommodations and the vacation they experienced while staying at Mountain Lake Lodge. Each note concluded with the name, hometown, and state of the guest who penned it, and Claire observed that the lodgers appeared to come from all across the United States. Alongside the journal, Claire spotted a photo album bulging with photographs of the lodge, its employees, past guests, and the various guest rooms. She browsed through it, moving with speed, marveling at the quality of the images the amateur photographers had captured.

For guests to read and enjoy during their visit, a variety of novels crammed the shelves of a nearby wooden bookcase. There was even a thick spiral notebook entitled *Unnamed Mystery* sitting on top of the cabinet. Claire opened it, scanned several pages, and realized it was an ongoing tale being crafted by guests of the lodge. Those interested could add a paragraph, or a page or two, in the ongoing mystery under development. Claire thought it was a great concept and noticed it had already been a couple years in the making.

Two well-worn brown leather saddles and other Western-themed items shared available spaces within the lobby area and created a most appealing milieu.

The atmosphere of the lodge was casual and friendly, and guests milled around freely, visiting with one another, viewing and discussing the artwork, or simply sitting down to enjoy a cup of Montana coffee. Even the check-in desk, along part of the left-hand wall as one walked into the area, seemed inviting. A woman with an affable smile stood behind it, ready to check in all arriving guests and to assist those already registered.

Tantalizing breakfast aromas emanated from the main-floor kitchen that serviced both the Terra Restaurant and Riley's Pub. And a large poster sat on an easel not far into the entryway, enticing patrons to treat themselves to a tasty Blue Mesa Ranch steak for dinner at the Terra Restaurant, or to enjoy a savory brick-oven pizza at the more relaxed atmosphere of Riley's Pub.

Five outlying buildings housed six suites each for a total of thirty units. Each set of rooms had a gas fireplace—and a breathtaking view of Flathead Lake, the surrounding pine forests, and Flathead Valley.

At check-in the previous evening, Claire and Guy had been assigned an exceptional room on an upper floor in one of the guesthouses. All rooms were given the name of a variety of tree—presumably easier to remember than a room number. Their room was named "Rocky Mountain Juniper."

The foursome gazed from painting to painting on the main floor, took the easy flight of steps leading down to the lower floor, and admired each original piece of artwork displayed in Jest Gallery. Afterward, they returned to the main floor and wandered over toward the breakfast buffet, filled their plates with a tempting array of foods, and sat down to chat while they ate.

"Spend the day doing nothing . . . or anything your hearts desire," Piper said.

Afterward, Claire and Guy returned to their room, changed into swimwear, grabbed towels, walked to the pool situated in the courtyard, and jumped in. They swam laps, and then sat in the hot tub, where they observed their surroundings with awe and curiosity. The lodge's position—built at the highest point on a tract of land—afforded a simply breathtaking view of the crystal-clear glacial lake wedged so prominently into Flathead Valley. Scores of tall ponderosa pine trees stood proudly, seemingly everywhere in the vicinity of the lodge, filling the glorious mountain air with the omnipresent, appealing scent of pine needles. Wild rose bushes and a variety of other flowers and shrubs appeared attractively placed in and around the grounds, and water features added to the almost surreal lush setting of the area.

"This is the stuff I dream about," Guy said. "I mean it. This beats Miami, hands down. It's an odd feeling, though, having nothing pressing to do. Feels kind of strange. I think I should be doing something."

"I know," Claire said. "I'm having trouble unwinding, too. We're both geared to work, and sitting idle seems . . . unfamiliar. But once I relax, I think I could stay here a long time and be happy."

Guy stared at her. Her strawberry-blonde hair, still partially damp from swimming, was starting to dry under the heat of the sun, and her green eyes sparkled like dazzling emeralds. She smiled. Oh, how he loved that smile. And oh, how he loved this woman. How he wished he could feel joy again, as he used to.

"Really?" he asked. "I admit it's a nice idea. Sometimes the smells of the overcrowded streets of Miami really get to me, and I've given some real thought to the two of us one day moving to a place like this. But could we really be happy here? It's the polar opposite of everything we're surrounded by in Miami, everything we're used to." He paused. "Probably pie-in-the-sky thinking, huh?"

Claire looked off into the distance. A look of contentment appeared on her face as she soaked in the uncomplicated beauty of western Montana. "I'm not sure. Want to take a walk?"

THAT EVENING over dinner at Piper and Jay's, lively conversation again ensued. It was comfortable spending time with good friends, and the couples laughed, traded stories, and reminisced. Claire and Guy took turns filling their friends in on the challenging case that led them to Crete, and Guy pointed to the scars on his face as the permanent remnants of the horrific ordeal. Then, like old times, they played a game of dominoes combining two identical sets for the remainder of the evening. The battle—women against men—was hard fought, and in the end, the women were the victors.

It was late, and Jay drove the investigators back to their room.

"Sleep well tonight, my friends," Jay said. "I'm glad you're here. Actually, it's just what Piper and I needed, I think." He paused. "Things have been tough between the two of us lately."

"I'm sorry," Guy said, furrowing his brows. "I had no idea."

Claire looked surprised. "What can we do to help?"

"Nothing, really," Jay said. "We need to work through some issues, that's all. I probably shouldn't have mentioned it." Then he abruptly changed the subject. "Remember, brunch is served at the lodge between eight and eleven. And if you don't care for that much food, you can order off the menu." He smiled. "See you in the morning."

The evening air carried with it a bit of a chill, and Guy flipped on the switch to light the gas fireplace soon after they entered the room.

"Oh, the heat feels good," Claire said. She snuggled deeply into an oversized chair and lifted her feet onto the matching ottoman. "What do you make of Jay's comment?"

"Hard to say. Seemed to come out of left field."

"Yeah. And why would they want us to come visit if things are not good between them? I would think that might be uncomfortable."

"You have a point," he said. "Or maybe they figured being around old friends might be a good thing."

"Maybe."

"I'm tired. Let's go to bed," Guy said.

The next thing Claire felt were Guy's sweet lips pressing down on hers.

"I feel better here," he said.

IN THE middle of the night, Claire awoke suddenly.

"What was that noise?" she asked. "And that odor. What is it? Smells like . . . copper . . . like pennies."

Guy did not respond. Sleep had captured him completely.

"Strange," Claire said, more to herself than aloud. "Something's going on."

She glanced at the alarm clock. Then she got up, tiptoed to the window, pulled back the drapes, and peered outside. There was no movement anywhere. It seemed everyone and everything in that part of the world was sound asleep—except for her. She returned to bed, now wide-eyed, and remained that way until morning, disturbed by the interruption.

Thursday

GUY AWOKE refreshed and happier than he had felt in months. Claire felt exhausted, and her usual vitality was absent, but she didn't mention her restless night to Guy for fear it would put a damper on his renewed spirits. They shared a shower and slipped into distressed blue jeans, plaid Western snap-closure shirts, and Western boots.

"I'm ready for a relaxin' day, pardner," Guy drawled. "Whaddya say?" He combed his once salt-and-pepper—now quite salty on the sides—hair back into place. His eyes looked like dark, shiny marbles, and his face remained handsome, despite the several scars now present.

Claire chuckled. She hadn't seen the playful side of him in such a long time. She looked him over from head to toe. "All that's missing is your cowboy hat."

"Easily remedied," he said. He disappeared into the closet and came out wearing the hat he had toted along on the airplane.

"*Now* you look like the quintessential cowpoke," she said, grinning. "And I like what I see! I like you in the cowboy way."

"Flattery will get you everywhere," Guy said. "Hold the thought until later, will you?"

"Of course, counselor. I mean, *wrangler*," Claire said. She winked at him.

Arm in arm, the two strolled toward the lodge, ready to consume large quantities of sumptuous breakfast cuisine. The mountain air had a way of rousing an appetite to great proportions, and they were hungry. Cumulus clouds clustered in the big, blue morning sky, as if suspended by invisible wires, promising a beautiful sunny day.

But as they neared the lodge, they quickly realized the day had other plans. A Lake County sheriff's car, three marked patrol deputy squad cars, and one unmarked car sat parked near the front entrance, lights flashing. Guests and nearby locals stood propped against each other on the steps leading up to the front double doors, stretching their necks to get a closer look at what was going on inside the lobby. Like an audience viewing a play, the onlookers appeared to be waiting with baited breath to catch a glimpse of what the next act would bring.

"What is going on?" Claire asked. She threw a concerned look in Guy's direction and grabbed him by the hand. "Hang on to me!" She pushed her way through the milling crowd, up the steps, and into the lobby, pulling Guy closely behind her.

The investigators walked into a situation of sheer mayhem. People—mainly employees and lodge guests—had crammed into a good part of the lobby, wringing their hands and talking incessantly. As the tsunami of shared shock swept over their collective faces, the gravity of the situation started to take hold. The Lake County sheriff, together with three of his patrol deputies and a resident patrol deputy from the immediate area of Woods Bay, all spoke authoritatively and seemingly at the same time, questioning staff members and guests alike, one after another, and also Piper and Jay.

The resident patrol deputy had arrived first to the scene, and he had quickly cordoned off one entire section of the lobby with yellow "Sheriff's Line Do Not Cross" tape. He had also propped open the front doors and taped off that area. The Lake County sheriff and other patrol deputies had made the twenty-two-mile trip from Polson to the lodge in record time. The patrol deputies jotted down notes fast and furiously, trying desperately to make sense of the horrifying scene and to obtain preliminary information about the victim and the obvious homicide. Some of the individuals present darted around wildly, as if in fast motion, yet at the same time stunned. Others stood frozen in place. The murder of the lodge employee was a disturbing bombshell.

Claire's eyes moved in a rushed manner in all directions, taking in everything around her. She first noticed the feet of a body lying face down on the floor behind the check-in desk. She moved in as close as possible to observe the victim. A substantial amount of blood had seeped onto the white sheet covering the backside of the subject's upper torso. And a significant amount of the red fluid had also spattered over a large part of the check-in desk, as well as the entire surrounding area, including the wall directly behind it. No shell casings were present, but she observed three bullet holes present in the wall behind where the victim presumably stood. No murder weapon was visible.

The odor of copper or rusting metal permeated the air. Now Claire realized the origin of the smell that had haunted her in the night. It was *blood*. And lots of it. The stench made her gag. As investigators, she and Guy almost always got involved after a crime was committed—when answers needed to be found or witnesses or culprits located. But never were they called to an actual murder scene. This was something for the police and the crime scene investigators to handle. She was not prepared for this scene of violence.

The patrol deputies forced people back, away from the victim and clear of the check-in desk, to protect against any contamination of the area. Any minute now, the major case team from the Lake County Sheriff's Office was expected to arrive to process the crime scene and to collect and bag any evidence the perpetrator left behind.

The lobby was quickly rolling into a disorderly jumble. Desperately, Claire searched the crowd for her friends. She needed answers. She spotted Jay and Piper standing several feet away with two patrol deputies. Piper was sobbing, and Jay stood silently by her side, eyes dazed. Valuable artwork had been ripped from the walls and, as the investigators would later learn, also taken from the downstairs gallery. In fact, none of the artwork Claire had viewed the day before on the main level was anywhere visible. The serene setting of the sofa and chairs—placed so strategically in front of the cozy, blazing fireplace only one day earlier—had been utterly disrupted, as the deputies had moved all furniture against one wall to make space to do their work. Claire noticed that the sofa and chairs had been slashed.

She focused her attention on the female patrol deputy standing next to Piper, riddling the co-owner of the lodge with questions. Claire moved in closer and listened in on the conversation.

"How long had he been in your employ?" Patrol Deputy Becca MacFie asked.

"Several years. Actually, since our opening," Piper wailed.

"What was your relationship with him?" the patrol deputy asked.

"He was like family to us. We all loved him." She tried desperately to stop her tears, but to no avail. "Who could have done this to him? *Why?*"

"Victim's full name?" the patrol deputy continued.

"Blake Hel . . . ms," Piper stuttered.

"Blake *Helms*, did you say? H-E-L-M-S?" Patrol Deputy MacFie asked. "Do you have a photo of him?"

Piper nodded to acknowledge the spelling of the surname and then trotted off in the direction of the coffee table. Her eyes searched until she spotted the photo album sitting on a chair, only feet away from it. She retrieved a picture of Blake Helms from the book and dutifully delivered it to the patrol deputy.

"His age?" the female patrol deputy asked.

"You'll have to ask my husband, Jay, that question. I'm not positive. Fifty-eight, though, I believe."

Piper's eyes looked puffy and swollen. She pursed her lips between answers, and she wrapped her arms around her upper body to stop from trembling.

Claire interrupted the questioning.

"I'm Claire Caswell," she told Patrol Deputy MacFie, "private investigator from Miami Beach, Florida." She extended her right hand toward the deputy and shook her hand vigorously. "My investigative partner—Gaston Lombard, former Miami-Dade state attorney—and I are visiting our friends Piper and Jay Cantrell. Can't we go somewhere to continue this line of questioning out of the limelight?" Claire gave Piper a brief look and then glanced at the photo of Blake Helms in the deputy's other hand. The photo showed a husky man with an appealing, rugged face. He had wavy black hair and pale gray eyes. "My friend is obviously upset, and I'm concerned about her welfare. Could we please sit down in an office and continue this?"

"Suppose so," the patrol deputy muttered under her breath. She eyed Claire and then Piper. "But let's get on with it. I want no delays."

Claire located a room just off the lobby and led her friend and Patrol Deputy MacFie to the private space. Claire indicated she would be right back. The investigator dashed out and asked a server to bring some water and coffee to the room. She located Guy standing next to Jay as he was being questioned. "We're over there," she told him, pointing to the location. "I'm with Piper. Thanks for staying close to Jay."

"How is Piper holding up?" Jay asked.

"She's okay, Jay. I'll be with her."

A strained look appeared on his face. "Thanks, Claire," Jay said, appearing sincere.

Claire grabbed a pad of paper and a pen from the hostess stand at the entrance to the Terra Restaurant. She jogged back to the room and arrived just as the server delivered the requested beverages. Claire poured three glasses of water and three cups of steaming black coffee. "I think we could all use a strong cup of coffee to settle our nerves," she said.

Piper accepted the hot drink graciously and sipped it continuously as she addressed each subsequent question the patrol deputy threw her way. Both Claire and Patrol Deputy MacFie jotted notes throughout the questioning.

Upon completing the preliminary interview, the patrol deputy made an announcement. "I need to take a break, but I'll return shortly. Don't go anywhere." It was time for her to check in with the sheriff and let him know how the questioning was proceeding. She stepped from the room.

"*What the heck happened here, Piper?*" Claire asked. It was her first opportunity to talk with Piper alone all morning. "Tell me every detail. What do you know about Blake Helms's death? Talk fast."

"Oh, I'm so afraid that . . ."

"Afraid that *what*, Piper?"

Piper went silent.

Outside of the room, the Lake County sheriff made his way over to Gaston Lombard. "And just who might you be?" he asked the investigator.

"Name's Gaston Lombard, sir." He shook the sheriff's hand. "Claire Caswell and I are private investigators from Miami Beach, here on vacation, visiting Jay and Piper Cantrell—the owners of this establishment. I'd like to know what happened here. Who's the victim?"

The sheriff looked Guy squarely in the eyes. "First, let me introduce myself. I'm the Lake County sheriff, Felton Bell. I'm here with some of my patrol deputies doing initial questioning. The night desk clerk of this lodge, Blake Helms, was murdered sometime during the early-morning hours of his shift today. Shot head-on at close range. We presume whoever did this killed him first and then tore out with the valuable artwork. Look at the walls. All bare. The unidentified suspect grabbed the money from the till and the artwork from the walls—both upstairs and downstairs. And as of now, we're not exactly sure what else. It'll take some time to sort through all of this and come up with a complete list of stolen items."

"And we were told this is a *quiet, peaceful* place," Guy said. He raised his eyebrows.

"Usually is," Sheriff Bell replied. "But we've seen a number of recent burglaries in the Whitefish area, not far from here, so I guess I'm not all that surprised it found its way down to our doorstep. Lots of artwork has been stolen in the Whitefish cases . . . and this place was crawling with it."

"Tell us how we can be of assistance," Guy said. "I'm a former Miami-Dade state attorney, and Claire is a former enforcement investigator for the State of Florida. We own a private investigation firm in Miami Beach. Despite the fact the Cantrells are friends of ours, I assure you we are professionals through and through and that relationship will not cause a conflict of interest for us."

The sheriff turned his full attention to Guy.

"We investigate all types of cases," Guy said, "including murder. So, consider us at your service. Let us know how we can help."

"We'll keep that in mind, Mr. Lombard. Thanks for the offer, but I think we can handle it ourselves," the sheriff said. He thought for a long moment. "There is one thing that would help, however. You could ask the owners to contact Blake Helms's relatives to break the news to them, gently of course."

"I'll take care of that," Guy said. "And my offer still stands. We can conduct interviews, if you'd like, and report our findings back to you, if that would prove useful. Claire Caswell's an expert when it comes to interviewing. You'll find no one better."

"As I said, I'll let you know if we need your assistance," Sheriff Bell said.

The sheriff walked off to interview a guest who had just walked into the lobby, and Guy moved in closer to Jay. The patrol deputy questioning Jay seemed to be asking him the same questions more than once. And while Jay appeared on the surface to be holding up well under the pressure, Guy sensed his friend was feeling overwhelmed and even a bit infuriated.

Like an ice-cream cone on a sweltering day, all thoughts of enjoying a tranquil Montana getaway melted away before Guy's eyes. His mission at once became clear. Jay needed the guidance and expertise that Gaston Lombard could provide, and he was there to give it to him. He snapped to attention.

After more probing questions, Piper's interview ended, and Claire and Piper returned to the main lobby area. Claire spotted Guy with no trouble and walked over to join him.

"I need to talk to you," she said quietly. "Right away." Guy excused himself, and the two walked to a spot away from the others. "Guy, last night, in the middle of the night, something abruptly woke me up. A noise. I think it was in my subconscious. I didn't know what it was at the time, but it bothered me greatly. Kept me up for hours. It must have been when Blake was murdered."

"Shit, Claire, that extrasensory stuff you tote around scares the heck out of me at times." He looked intently at her. "It's a blessing and a curse. What time did this happen?"

"At exactly 2:10 a.m. I looked at the alarm clock and got up to peek outside. I didn't see anything unusual." She paused for a couple of seconds. "We'll have to let the sheriff know what happened and at what time."

Guy stared at her.

"I also smelled *copper.* When I awakened . . . I smelled copper."

Claire and Guy walked over to Sheriff Bell and filled him in, but he seemed to ignore the information. "ESP?" He shrugged. "Never give it any mind." He looked at both investigators closely, as if deciding whether to ask the next question. He took in a deep breath and exhaled. "I understand the two of you are *highly* respected investigators from the big crime-ridden city of Miami. At least that's what the owners of this lodge tell me. I hesitate to get just anyone involved in this matter, but based upon what you told me earlier and also upon the owners' accolades regarding your talents, maybe we can use your help, after all. We're stretched mighty thin at this time, helping out the Whitefish Police Department with the series of burglaries occurring in their area. The Flathead County Sheriff's Department is also helping out with that case. We're going it together. Townsfolk up that way are paralyzed with fear, and we need to get that matter resolved. Got the bulk of our manpower working 'round the clock to help bring the perp in. And now *this.* My deputies and detectives will talk to the lodge guests to see if anyone saw or heard anything unusual during the night." He stopped speaking for a brief moment. "So, if you two would interview the lodge employees and give me a summary of your findings, that would be of great help."

"Consider it done," Claire said.

The sheriff handed a business card to Claire and another to Guy, jotting his cell number on the back of each. "Give me a call when you've completed some of the interviews, will you? Obviously, the sooner the better. Let me know how it's going." He hesitated. "We don't have many homicides in Lake County. Average is about one a year." He shook Guy's hand and then Claire's. "We appreciate your help."

Piper and Jay remained in the center of the commotion. "This is awful," Piper whimpered. "He was a great employee." She seemed unable to stop shaking her head from side to side.

Jay glared at Piper with questioning eyes.

"Hold me," she said.

He turned and walked away.

3

ALL AT ONCE, the major case team of homicide detectives and an evidence technician from the Lake County Sheriff's Office arrived on the scene and swooped into the lobby. Moving with gloved hands and with the ease of great expertise, the team members had one thing and one thing only on their minds—to process the crime scene and to search for and recover evidence. Based upon what they found, they could analyze both palm prints and fingerprints in-house, and, if needed, request firearm testing and comparisons from the small crime lab in nearby Kalispell. The body would be driven to the Montana State Crime Lab's Forensic Science Division in Missoula for a complete autopsy. Any other crucial evidence requiring high-tech analysis and testing would also be delivered or shipped to the State Crime Lab—a laboratory providing quality forensic services to the criminal justice system statewide. It was one of only 110 labs in the world awarded accreditation under the International Testing requirements, the highest level attainable.

Sheriff Bell, who also served as the county coroner from Polson, had checked Blake Helms for signs of life upon his arrival to the scene. He determined the cause, manner, and time of Mr. Helms's unattended death on the spot. The Lake County Sheriff's Office had full jurisdiction over this matter. Since it was a crime against person, discretion to move quickly would be granted to secure unusually fast turnaround times for the lab results. The sheriff could also call upon the Flathead County Sheriff's Office in Kalispell and the Whitefish Police Department, if needed, to coordinate the investigative efforts on this case.

Now the sheriff's homicide detectives and evidence technician took over. Everyone present was asked to step back. Great pains would be taken not to disturb the body as evidence was gathered.

First the crime scene team stooped low and under the yellow tape. Two of the team members cautiously peeled away the bloody covering from the corpse. Numerous photographs of the victim and of the entire lobby area were taken from various vantage points, as was a comprehensive videotaping. The victim was fingerprinted and blood, tissue, and hair samples were obtained for DNA purposes. Scrupulous notes were penned all along the way, making certain to include even the smallest of details. Later, the writings would come in handy when compiling a precise written report setting forth all elements of the crime scene.

Utilizing an ultraviolet light, the evidence technician scanned the area for latent fingerprints and palm prints and noted the presence of both on an inside front doorknob and on top of the check-in desk. He dusted both locations using a fluorescent powder applied with a large fiberglass brush. Then with a smaller brush, he swept away most all of it, leaving behind fingerprints and palm prints remaining from perspiration residues and body oils belonging to the person or persons who touched the surfaces. This allowed the technician to strategically place the sticky clear sheets over the impressions, one sheet at a time, and retrieve the prints for later examination back at the lab.

The evidence tech then dug out the three bullets that had lodged in the wall behind where Blake had stood. He marked and bagged them as evidence and made notes as to the precise locations from which they were extracted.

Certain members of the major case team moved on to examine the body, and detectives searched for other clues in the immediate vicinity. Using swab sticks, the evidence tech obtained blood samples from the floor, the top of the check-in desk, the wall behind the desk, and other nearby points, and carefully placed each specimen into an individual plastic bag. He followed the same protocol as with the bullets.

The specialized unit was in charge of the care and custody of all evidence gathered, and they acted with methodical and extreme caution and professionalism.

The quick-thinking Lake County resident patrol deputy, first on the scene that morning, had placed a line of chairs—each one touching the next—across the front desk area, in addition to the yellow tape, to prevent access to the body in an attempt to preserve any evidence that might be present. And he had the brilliant thought to also cordon off the inside front doorknobs, to prevent anyone from touching them and to maintain the integrity of any potential palm prints or fingerprints left behind by the perpetrator or perpetrators fleeing the scene. The lab techs greatly appreciated the astute work of the resident patrol deputy.

Sheriff Bell had quickly determined that the desk clerk had been shot to death while he stood behind the desk. He deduced that the bullets entered the victim's chest from close range while he looked head-on at his attacker. Since no guests claimed to have heard the shots, the sheriff also reasoned that a silencer or something else might have been used to minimize the sound of the gunfire. He surmised that the victim died instantly after the series of bullets penetrated his body.

Claire inched her way toward the members of the major case team working their way through the scene.

"Did you notice the gravel on the floor?" she asked. "It's a miniscule amount, I'm sure you'll agree, but it could be a clue."

The detectives and evidence technician looked up in unison and eyeballed Claire. They had not noticed her observing their work until that moment.

"And you are?" Matthew Mallory, the evidence tech, asked.

"Claire Caswell. I'm an investigator from Miami Beach, here on vacation with Gaston Lombard. We own a private investigation firm in that city. We're good friends of the owners of the lodge. My eyes searched the scene when we arrived here to eat breakfast this morning, and I couldn't help but notice the faint traces of small, coarse stones between the front door and the lobby desk. It'd be easy to miss. Thought you should probably check it out."

"Most likely just dirt, madam. This is the *lobby* of a lodge," Matthew said. "People *do* bring dirt in on their shoes when they enter the building. Anyway, we haven't gotten to that area yet."

"It doesn't look like regular dirt to me," Claire said. "It's different. Take a closer look." She stood firm until Matthew moved nearer to the area she pointed to. With gloved hands, he picked up and bagged some of the gravel and marked it as evidence.

"Happy now, Miss Investigator?" he asked.

"I am," she said. "There seems to be one irregular line of it coming in and another going out. Did you check the bottom of the victim's shoes?"

Two of the detectives looked at each other and rolled their eyes.

"As a matter of fact, we did. They're clean," Matthew said. "Now if you don't mind, we should get on with our—"

"Oh, and one more thing," Claire said. "I noticed a metal rivet way over there in the corner." She pointed to it. "That might have popped off a pair of blue jeans and rolled. Maybe even came from the killer's jeans."

Matthew Mallory and the other team members darted their eyes to the location Claire indicated.

Each one of them had missed it.

Without delay, Matthew bagged the rivet and marked it as evidence. "What *else* are we missing?" he asked.

"Nothing. You now have it all," Claire said. She smiled slightly. "We all know that two types of evidence in any case can connect an offender to a crime scene—the tangible physical evidence collected and the biological physical DNA evidence either visible or not visible to the naked eye. Usually it's the smallest of details that accumulate to eventually paint the big picture." She looked from one team member to the next. "And while witness statements can certainly be helpful, people can lie and often do. I'd place my bets on the hard physical and biological evidence any day." She smiled again. "By the way, do you have an extra pair or two of latex gloves you could leave with me? We didn't pack any for our *vacation*."

Matthew Mallory gave a quick look in the sheriff's direction and handed her two pairs of gloves. As the eyes of the experts stayed glued to the female investigator, she turned and walked away.

"She gets it," Matthew Mallory said aloud.

"I'd say so," one of the detectives said.

The major case team detectives and tech finished up processing the scene. The body of Blake Helms was covered with a heavy black tarp, lifted onto a stretcher, wheeled outside, and loaded into an awaiting coroner's van. The driver set out for Missoula.

CLAIRE REJOINED Guy, Piper, and Jay across the lobby. She handed Guy a pair of the gloves to keep in his pocket. Her gaze fell upon Piper, and Claire observed her friend's obviously distressed behavior. Piper was taking in short breaths, intermittently clenching and wringing her hands, looking in a downward direction, and kicking the floor. Her eyes appeared puffy from crying, and she seemed drained of energy. In short, the strain of the situation was rapidly taking its toll. Claire felt deeply concerned about her friend.

"Piper, let's take a walk. The fresh air will do us good," Claire said.

Piper looked up and gave Claire an almost undetectable nod.

Claire and Piper passed through the front propped-open doorway and stepped outside. The clean scent of pine, so predominant in the area, cleared Claire's head almost instantly. In silence, she walked alongside Piper on trails and roads around the lodge grounds, for what seemed like a very long time. In actuality, it was probably about an hour. Piper had withdrawn into a sullen state, and out of respect, Claire allowed Piper to be alone with her thoughts. Losing a long-term employee had to be much like losing a family member, Claire reasoned, and grief always presented itself in such a personal way. Sometimes not talking at all and just being present with someone in mourning seemed the strongest support of all.

It was Piper who finally broke the silence.

"He was wonderful, Claire." She stopped walking and looked Claire squarely in the eyes. "One of the few sensitive and caring men I've ever known." She paused. "He always made time for me . . . no matter how busy he was . . . asked how I was doing . . . wanted to know what I thought about things . . . seemed genuinely interested in my answers. I will miss him."

"I'm so sorry for your loss," Claire said. "Did Jay like him, too?"

Suddenly, tears flooded Piper's eyes, and she failed to respond.

Claire could have kicked herself. Probably way too early to ask Piper about Jay's liking or disliking Blake Helms. More questioning on this topic would just have to wait. But the sleuth couldn't help but wonder. Was there more to this story, or was she just imagining things? She couldn't be sure. When she had the opportunity, she'd ask Jay the question directly.

"Let's go back to the lodge and find Jay and Guy," Claire suggested.

Piper nodded.

When they arrived back at the scene of the crime, they found the men sitting at a table in the restaurant, drinking strong coffee.

"Come join us," Guy said. He stood and pulled out the two other chairs at the table for the women.

Once seated, Claire ordered a peppermint tea and another for Piper. "It will calm you. It always does the trick."

Again, Piper nodded.

Over the hot beverages, the foursome discussed the morning's event.

Claire took note that Jay's eyes hardly ever glanced over at Piper and that he seemed wholly unaware of her emotional state. Further, unlike Piper, Jay appeared cool and distant when talking about the murdered employee. "Things happen," he said. "Now I have to call the temp agency and find someone to replace Blake starting tonight for the all-night shifts, including weekends."

Claire thought it was an odd comment under the circumstances.

"Did Blake have any enemies?" Claire asked. "Did he ever have a run-in with anyone that either of you know about?"

"Enemies?" Jay asked. He shrugged his shoulders. "How would I know?"

Piper sat in silence, sipping her tea.

"What is the crime rate in this area?" Guy asked.

"Property crime is about average in Montana. Violent crime's a bit higher than average, I've read," Jay answered. "But not when it comes to murder in this county. Here, it's extremely rare."

"Tell us everything you know about Blake," Claire said. She took this opportunity to question the Cantrells and glean information.

"He came to work for us about five years ago, shortly after we opened the lodge," Jay said. "We had placed an ad in the paper for a nighttime desk clerk, he applied, and we gave him the job. It was as simple as that."

"Where did he come from?" Claire asked. "Was he from around here?"

"Said he was from Minnesota," Piper chimed in. "I believe the Twin Cities area—not far from the Mall of America. He had migrated this way to start over after a bad divorce. He had two grown children and wanted to make a fresh start." She held a tissue to her eyes.

"Did he have a girlfriend?" Claire asked.

"None that we know of," Jay said hurriedly.

"Close friends? People he hung out with after work?" Claire asked.

"Again, none that we know of. He seemed a bit of a loner. Not real social, but not antisocial, either," Jay said. "He performed his job well. He was reliable."

"Where did he live?" Guy asked.

"He rented an upper flat in a house in Bigfork, just a couple miles from here," Jay said.

"Did he always work the same shift?" Claire asked.

"He always did the 11:00 p.m. to 7:00 a.m. shift. No one else wanted it, and he never seemed to mind," Jay said.

"Did you keep cash in the register overnight?" Claire asked, attempting to zero in on a motive.

"No. We cleared out the cash every afternoon around 4:00 p.m. and rushed it over to our bank in town. Always got there just before the bank closed each day. So, the answer to your question is no, we did not keep cash in the register overnight. Except for a nominal amount . . . maybe fifty dollars or so," Jay said, "in case Blake needed to make change."

"So, if robbery was the motive, the robber or robbers would have been greatly disappointed as far as cash money is concerned," Claire said. "What about the missing paintings from the walls? What kind of value are we talking on those?"

"Retail value? I'm guessing between sixty and eighty thousand dollars. Maybe more. We need to figure that out," Jay said. "And we'll also need to contact our insurance company immediately. Those paintings were on consignment. They were in our custody, and we're responsible for them. We'll have to pay all the artists for their works if they're not recovered. What a mess!"

"Okay," Claire said. "Now *that* kind of money could equal motive." She hesitated. "What else was taken? Have either of you noticed *anything* else missing?"

"Not yet," Jay said. "The fifty dollars from the register and the artwork taken from the walls seem to be the only items missing at first glance."

"And the saddles," Piper said, restraining her sniffles. "Two worn-out saddles that we hung over a section of split-wood railing up in the wall cubby just above the check-in desk. I noticed they are missing, as well."

Jay looked at Piper. "You're right. I forgot all about those beaten-up saddles."

"Now that you mention it, I recall seeing them yesterday," Claire said. "Wonder what someone would want with a couple of distressed leather saddles. Not much value there, I'm going to assume. Would seem to me that hauling them away would be more trouble than they're worth."

"Yeah," Jay agreed. "We picked 'em up a couple years back at the French antique store just down the road. The owner has a very eclectic collection of items for sale, including some fine pieces of old French furniture. We found the saddles there. Can you believe it? And I think we paid around a hundred dollars each for them. I remember the owner even threw in the old blankets they were sitting on—a wool one and a deerskin one—probably 'cause I balked a little at the price. We threw the whole mixture up on our display. I thought those beaten-up saddles made for good Western décor."

"Well, Guy and I have offered to help the Lake County sheriff find Blake Helms's killer," Claire said. "We want to assist in getting this crime solved as quickly as possible and put the entire incident to rest, so you can carry on with the business of running the lodge."

"The bad publicity can only hurt us," Jay said. "And we don't need that right now."

"Not if we can wrap things up in a hurry," Guy said. "The longer the case stays open, however, the more opportunity there will be for conjecture, embellishment, and so on. You know how it goes."

"We'll do what we can," Claire said. "How many employees work here at the lodge?"

"Fifteen," Jay said. "Between the housekeepers, chefs, servers, restaurant supervisor, desk clerks, and handyman. And we have to meet payroll whether we're busy or not."

"We'll want to interview each one of them. Separately, of course," Claire said.

"We'll start with the ones who are working the day shift today and go from there. We want to start immediately, while this incident is fresh in their minds. Can you find an office for us to use, and then can you arrange to send them in, one at a time, every half hour? And will you please get us a list of the employees—full names, of course?"

"No problem," Jay said.

"I just realized you never ate breakfast this morning," Piper sniffled. "You should eat something before you start with all of this. In fact, I insist."

At that moment, Claire and Guy realized they were starving. It was close to noon.

The four ordered lunch and ate quickly. Jay excused himself halfway through to call the temp agency and find a replacement for Blake. He needed the person to start that very evening. He'd have to train the person in quickly when he arrived at 11:00 p.m.

"We invited you here for a nice visit, and now *this*," Piper said. "I'm so sorry. So very sorry."

"Don't give it another thought," Claire said. "We're your friends, and it's our privilege to help out with the investigation."

A SHORT time later Claire and Guy were seated in a private room at a table with chairs, and the first employee walked in. Because a tape recorder was not available, both investigators scribbled notes, each taking a turn at it whenever the other was the questioner. Claire scratched the first name off the list—a routine she would do with each subsequent interviewee as well.

"Please state your full name," Claire said.

"Ed Carter," the man replied. "Actually, Edward Carter is my full name."

Ed Carter had dark hair combed straight back and stunning cornflower-blue eyes. His short-sleeved shirt revealed a kanji tattoo of Chinese characters.

"Your age, sir?" she asked.

"Thirty-six."

"Position here at the lodge?" Claire asked.

"Daytime chef," Ed replied. "I cover breakfast and lunch, and brunch on weekends. Cook for both restaurants."

"How long have you worked here?" Claire asked.

"Three years."

"Where did you work prior to this job?" Claire questioned.

"I've been a chef since high school. Started as a short-order cook and worked my way up to this. Always worked in Montana, too. I grew up here in this great state, and they'd have to pull me by my heels, kicking and screaming, to get me to leave."

"How well did you know Blake Helms?" Claire asked.

"Good enough. Wasn't really much to know. He was a mellow, decent sort of fellow. I usually only saw him early in the mornings. I'd be arriving to prepare for the breakfast crowd, and he'd be leaving at the end of his shift. When I left after my workday, he wasn't on yet. So that was about it. And I saw him at staff meetings, of course—when he stayed around for them, that is."

Ed glanced at his watch. "I'm busy. Can we wrap this up?"

"We're busy, too," Claire said. "But we're all going to sit right here until we're through with the questioning."

"Now, where were you during, say, midnight and 7:00 a.m. this morning?" Guy asked.

"At home in my apartment, in my bed, sleeping, until I had to get up for work," Ed replied.

"Were you alone?" Guy asked.

Ed chuckled. "Yeah, I was alone."

"So, there is no one to verify that you were home sleeping at that time, I assume," Guy said.

"Guess not."

"Do you know anyone who held a grudge against Blake? Who didn't like the man?" Claire asked.

"Jay Cantrell, that's who. Talk to him."

"We're talking to you right now," Claire said.

Ed Carter stiffened in his seat and a solemn look appeared in his eyes. He rubbed his nose. Then his voice lowered as if someone had turned down his volume switch. "Again, if I were you, I'd ask Jay Cantrell some questions. Saw the two of them going at it in a heated argument outside a couple days ago." His eyes closed to slits. "Yeah. Don't waste your time on me or the other employees. If you really want answers, ask Jay Cantrell the tough questions. But don't tell him I ratted him out. I need my job."

4

THE NEXT EMPLOYEE appeared in the interview room. She sat down and set her purse in front of her on the table.

Guy started the questioning. "Please state your name."

"Hazel Schroeder."

"Age?" Guy asked.

"Fifty-two."

"And Ms. Schroeder, how long have you been employed by Mountain Lake Lodge?"

"Five years now," she replied. "Since its opening."

"In what capacity are you employed?"

"I am the supervisor for both restaurants here at the lodge. The meals are prepared in the same kitchen. Except for the pizzas in Riley's Pub, that is. Those are baked in a brick oven right there in the pub." She cleared her throat. "I work a variety of different hours, basically whenever I'm needed. Varies by the day. I make sure the food is correctly prepared and presented. I come up with the weekly specials. I plan the menus, train the wait staff, and generally make sure everything runs smoothly in the food area. I'm also the events coordinator. I plan weddings, receptions, and other special occasions." She stopped to again clear her throat. "I guess I'm kind of like the general contractor around here. Without me, the restaurants would not survive, and the special events would not take place." She chuckled softly and shifted anxiously in her seat. Sweat moistened her forehead. "The Cantrells are extremely picky people to work for, as you might guess. If one little thing is not exactly to their liking . . ." She stopped midsentence.

"If one little thing is not exactly to their liking . . . *what*?" Claire asked. "Please finish your answer."

"Well, let's just say I hear about it." She repeatedly touched her chin. "I get reamed out."

"By whom? Who reams you out?" Claire asked.

"It's always Jay. He has a side to him that's not nice."

Hazel Schroeder moved uncomfortably in her seat.

"Are you nervous about something, Ms. Schroeder?" Claire asked.

Hazel shifted her eyes to Claire. "No. Why do you ask?" She blinked her eyes in rapid succession.

"Because you're acting extremely uneasy," Claire said. "Is there something you'd like to tell us? Do you know something about the murder?"

Hazel swallowed with difficulty. "Mind if I get a drink of water? It's hot in here."

"No problem," Guy said. "We'll take a short break so you can do just that."

Hazel pushed her chair back from the table and exited the room in a hurry.

"She may know something," Claire said. "Let's push her."

"Be my guest," Guy said. "It's always a pleasure to watch you in action."

Hazel Schroeder was a pleasantly plump woman who needed to wear a size larger in her clothing than she did. Her deep auburn hair perfectly matched her reddish-brown almond eyes. Edginess poured from her being, as if she were handing it out for free.

Within a short time, the anxious woman returned to the room and took her seat across from the questioning duo.

"Better?" Claire asked.

"Better," Hazel said.

"Okay then, let's continue," Claire said. "Are you aware of something that may help us in this investigation?"

"Like, what?"

"You tell us, Hazel. What do you know that will be of help to us?" Claire asked.

"Well . . ." A long hesitation followed.

"Yes?" Claire asked.

"I don't want to tell tales out of school, if you know what I mean," the supervisor said.

"We're all ears, Hazel," Claire whispered, leaning forward. "Tell us something that will surprise us. Tell us a *secret*."

"Does it stay within this room?" Hazel asked. She tugged at an ear.

"Can't promise you that, exactly," Claire said. "But I will promise whatever you tell us will be used with extreme caution. How's that?"

"Okay then," Hazel said. She moved back and forth in her seat, much like a three-year-old playing on a rocking horse, seemingly unaware that she was doing so. "I'm not pointing the finger at anyone, mind you, but you might want to watch that friend of yours, Piper, a little more closely. She and that nighttime desk clerk seemed overly chummy, if you ask me. Always talking with each other kind of quietly, you know, like they didn't want others to hear their conversations. We were all curious about what the two of them were up to. And Blake would stay on sometimes after his shift ended to have breakfast and *accidentally on purpose* run into Piper, if you get my drift."

"Did the other staffers here at the lodge question their relationship, too?" Claire asked.

"Yep, there was never a shortage of gossip floating around about the two of them."

"And what do *you* think was going on between them?" Claire asked.

Hazel chuckled lewdly. "Probably a little nooky in the cookie." As she talked, she covered her mouth and feigned embarrassment.

"*Nooky in the cookie?*" Claire asked.

Hazel's face turned as red as a ripe summer radish. "Fun in the sun, bunk in the trunk," she said in a lowered voice. "You get what I'm saying?"

"Yes, I believe we do," Claire said. "Thank you for clarifying. But you have no proof that this was going on, do you, Ms. Schroeder?"

"Proof?" Hazel asked. "Not really. It's just that people know these things."

"Or think they do," Claire said. "Okay then. Let's move on. Did Blake have any enemies? People he did not get along with?"

"None that I know of. But if you ask me, I don't think Jay, the boss man, liked him much. I have nothing specific to tell you. It's just how I saw him look at the man from time to time."

"And how was that? I mean, how did Jay *look* at him?" Claire asked the obvious next question.

Hazel hesitated. "Like he wanted to kill him, that's how." She again covered her mouth with her hand as she spoke. "Probably because Blake was too friendly with Jay's wife."

"Ms. Schroeder, I have one final question for you at this time," Claire said. "Where were you between the hours of midnight and

7:00 a.m. today?"

"What an odd question," she said. "Duh. I was in bed, asleep, like most normal people. Then I got up around six to get ready for work."

"At your home?" Claire asked.

"Yeah."

THE QUESTIONING continued. Another employee appeared in the room. She looked pleasant and had a childlike face. Her flaxen hair was naturally curly, and freckles dotted her face.

"Please state your name," Guy said.

"I'm Heidi . . . Heidi Flynn."

"And Heidi, how long have you worked at the lodge?" Guy asked.

"Only three months," she said.

"What do you do here at the lodge?" Guy continued.

"I'm a housekeeper. I clean guest rooms."

"Where did you work previously, Heidi?" Claire broke in.

"Um, I worked in another state."

"What state is that, Heidi?" Claire persisted.

"Iowa."

"Where were you employed in Iowa?" Claire asked.

"Well . . . I cleaned and painted for my father. He owns rental properties, and I worked for him."

"What is your father's name?" Claire asked.

Heidi hesitated. "Orvis . . . Orvis Flynn."

"Heidi, what is your age?" Claire asked.

"Just turned twenty-one," she replied.

"What made you move to Montana? And when was that?" Claire asked the young housekeeper.

Heidi thought for a moment before responding. "I guess I wanted to spread my wings . . . to get away from family. You know . . . to make it on my own. It was about two years ago."

"So you just picked up and moved from Iowa to Montana when you were nineteen?" Claire asked. "Just like that?"

"Yep," Heidi said. "I did. Lots of folks migrate this way from the Midwest. It's a pretty place, and people are mighty nice out here. I saved up money to live on till I got a job."

"Do you have any siblings, Heidi?" Claire asked.

"No. I'm an only child."

Claire looked at Guy, signaling that he could resume the questioning if he had anything further.

"Heidi, is there anything you know about the violent murder of Blake Helms—the nighttime desk clerk—that may be of help to us?" Guy asked.

"Not a thing," she said. "I'm as surprised as everyone."

"Did he have any enemies you may be aware of?" Guy asked.

"Not that I know of. I work days, and he worked the night shift. I really only saw him at the lodge staff meetings every couple of weeks or so," Heidi said. "Didn't know him all that well."

"I have nothing further at this time," Guy said. "Claire?"

"One more thing. I have an additional question," Claire said. "Heidi, what city in Iowa do you come from?"

Heidi coughed. Swiftly, the coughing led to gag coughing that lasted a couple of long minutes.

"Do you need a glass of water?" Guy asked.

Claire observed the young lady tugging at her jeans.

"No, I'm all right," Heidi said. "Don't know what brought that on. Probably my allergies." She looked at Claire. "What was your question?"

"I asked you where you lived in Iowa, Heidi. Where do your parents live?"

"Well, my mother died when I was young. My dad raised

me." She pushed her chair back as if preparing to leave the room. "Anything else?"

"Yes," Claire said. "You never answered my question. Where in Iowa do you come from?"

She hesitated. "Burlington."

Claire jotted down the city name.

"Can I go now?" Heidi asked. "I have a lot of work to get done on my shift."

"One final question, Heidi," Claire said. "Where were you between midnight and 7:00 a.m. today?"

"Asleep. In my trailer home. Then I got up for work."

"Was anyone with you?" Claire said.

"Wow. Now that's personal."

"And the answer to that personal question *is* . . . ?" Claire asked.

"I was asleep. Alone. Just me. Solo. Alone. Anything else?"

"No, that's it for now. If we have any other questions, we'll track you down," Guy said.

Heidi left the room.

Guy glanced over at Claire. "She seems like a nice young gal to me."

"Could be," Claire said. "But she faked that coughing spell to buy time before she answered my question about where she lived in Iowa. I'd like to know why. And she was lying about being home alone during the time in question."

Claire jotted down more notes.

ANOTHER EMPLOYEE entered the room.

"Please have a seat," Guy said.

"Your name, please?" Claire asked.

"Charlotte Rodriguez."

"Where are you from originally, Ms. Rodriguez?" Guy asked.

"I am from Cuba. Came to this country as a child."

Charlotte was well groomed, had a petite frame, and wore a serious demeanor. She had shiny hair the color of a raven and black eyes.

"How long have you worked at the lodge, Ms. Rodriguez?" Guy asked.

"Since the beginning. Since it opened," she said. "Five years now."

"What is your age?" Guy asked.

"Forty-four, sir."

"Your position here?" Guy asked.

"I'm one of the two daytime desk clerks. June Howard is the other. We trade off with each other. One month I work the 7:00 a.m. to 3:00 p.m. shift, and then the next month I work the 3:00 p.m. to 11:00 p.m. shift. It alternates back and forth each month. Keeps it more interesting that way. June works the opposite shifts that I work."

"What shift are you working this month, Ms. Rodriguez?" Guy asked.

"Well, this month I'm on from 7:00 a.m. to 3:00 p.m.," the clerk said.

"What time did you arrive this morning for your shift?" Guy asked.

"I always arrive early. I hate to rush, so I'm always here a good half an hour before my shift actually starts. So, I would say close to 6:30 a.m."

"What happened when you arrived this morning?" Guy asked. "Please tell us what you observed."

Charlotte's face froze, and her eyes welled with tears. "I found him dead, that's what. Lying behind the desk on his stomach, blood all around him." She started sobbing. "He'd been shot several times."

"Charlotte," Claire said. "We are so sorry that you found your coworker in that state. That must have been very difficult for you."

"It was. I'll never get over it. Never seen someone who'd been murdered before. In person, that is."

Claire reached into her handbag and pulled out a tissue. She handed it to Ms. Rodriguez, who accepted it gratefully.

"Did you touch him when you saw him?" Claire asked.

"No, I know better than to do that. It was clear to me that he was dead."

"What did you do next?" Claire asked.

"I picked up the desk phone and called the sheriff. When I hung up, I dialed the Cantrells at home to let them know. When Jay Cantrell answered, I told him what had happened, and he rushed right over."

"What did Jay say when you told him about Blake Helms?" Claire asked.

"Nothing. Other than he'd be right over. He jumped into his car and was standing next to me in the lobby several minutes later. He warned me not to touch anything, as the sheriff would want to examine the room for clues. I already knew not to do that."

"How did Jay react to the murder when he saw the body? Did he seem surprised? Horrified? Upset? What?" Claire asked.

"Naturally, he was horrified, just like I was. But did he seem surprised? I guess not. He acted more appalled at the sight of all that blood." She stopped talking, as if deep in thought. "Now that I think about it, his reaction seemed somewhat odd. His voice sounded very matter-of-fact to me."

"Okay. Okay. Did Jay stay until the sheriff arrived?" Guy asked.

"No. He again warned me not to touch anything, and he instructed me not to allow anyone else reporting for work to touch anything. He drove home to pick up Piper and bring her back with him to the lodge. He was gone for only about ten minutes, I'd say. When he came back, the resident patrol deputy from the sheriff's office had just arrived. I guess he lives nearby."

"Thank you, Ms. Rodriguez. You have been most helpful," Guy said. He looked over at Claire and raised his eyebrows.

"Just a couple more questions, Ms. Rodriguez. What was your relationship with Blake Helms?" Claire asked.

"We were coworkers," she said, "that's it." She looked at the female investigator with a shocked expression on her face. "He was always pleasant, respectful, and a good worker. Surely you don't think there is anything more to it than that?"

"I'm not suggesting that there was, Ms. Rodriguez. But I did need to ask you the question," Claire said. "Did he ever talk to you about his private life?"

"Never. We didn't have that kind of relationship."

"Was he married? Dating anyone?" Claire asked.

"He was not married. He was divorced. That much I know. Whether he was seeing anyone special, I guess I'm not sure. There was the waitress at the diner just across the road here—a lady he sometimes had coffee with—but as far as I know, they were merely friends."

"Do you know the name of the waitress?" Claire asked.

"She goes by LoLo. That's her nickname. I think her actual name may be Lois."

"Did he have any other friends—female or male?" Claire asked.

"None that I know of. He was an extremely private individual."

"How about enemies? Are you aware of anyone he did not get along with?" Claire asked.

"I saw him arguing with Hazel Schroeder—the supervisor of the restaurants here at the lodge—on a couple of occasions when I came into work. Don't exactly know what the arguments were about. Each time, they both stopped talking when they realized I had walked into the lobby. Both being hard-headed, they were bound to disagree on certain things."

"Thank you, Ms. Rodriguez. You have been quite helpful," Claire said. "Oh, and two final questions for today. First, how did Blake Helms get along with the Cantrells? With Jay? And with Piper?"

The desk clerk hesitated for a full minute before she spoke. "Ah, now that's the question of the hour. Blake really seemed to have a soft spot for Piper Cantrell. Several times he commented about what a lucky man Jay was to be married to a woman like her. On the other hand, Blake didn't seem overly fond of Jay. Never did know the reason why, and I didn't ask. I'm not the nosy type."

"And lastly, where were you between the hours of midnight and 7:00 a.m. today?" Claire asked.

"Sleeping at home with my husband. And then up early to get ready to come in to work. That's where I was." She hesitated. "I'm not a suspect, am I?"

5

CLAIRE SCRATCHED A few notes as her mind raced. Was it possible that Jay was involved in the death of Blake Helms? Was her friend Piper, Jay's wife, having an affair with Blake Helms? Did Jay find out and end the private trysts permanently? She dropped those thoughts from her mind as soon as they entered. Things often appear to be other than what they really are, she reminded herself. She knew Piper and Jay Cantrell well. They would not involve themselves in this type of drama. Would they? But then, Jay had alluded to her and Guy that there were some problems on the home front. As an investigator, she couldn't rule out the possibility completely . . . until she had all the answers.

With extreme anxiousness, the sleuths awaited the results from the labs. The hard evidence, as always, would help paint the true picture. In the meantime, she and Guy would continue interviewing witnesses to extract information and possible clues to the murder.

THE NEXT witness was led to the interview room, and Guy crossed his name from the list. The man took a seat.

"Let's start with your full name, sir," Claire said.

"I'm Harv . . . Harvey Powell, that is."

Harvey Powell was a jumbo-sized man. He was bald and wore a friendly face.

"Your position here, Mr. Powell?" Claire asked.

"Full-time handyman and pool man for the lodge. I make repairs, keep the pool clean, and do just about anything else that needs to be done around here. And believe me, I stay busy. Every day, many things require work."

"I'm sure that's true," Claire said. "Your age, please?"

"Just turned sixty-five."

"*Sixty-five?*" Claire asked, unable to contain her surprise. "You look much younger, if you don't mind me saying so. I would have guessed you in your mid-forties."

"Don't mind at all, ma'am. Hear it all the time."

"How long have you worked here as the handyman and pool man?" Claire asked, continuing with her line of questioning.

"Let me think. Well, it's been almost four years. I retired from my job as a junior-high art teacher four years ago, but couldn't see myself sitting home, doing nothing, for the rest of my life. So I applied to work here at the lodge and got hired on the spot. It keeps me out of trouble, and I like to work with my hands, so it fits the bill. Gives me something to do with myself, and I feel valued around here. Plus, it gives my wife and me a little extra spending money. It's a win-win."

"What can you tell us about Blake Helms, Mr. Powell?" Claire asked. "Or would you prefer I call you Harv?"

"Harv is fine," he said. "I'd like that. Everybody calls me Harv." He took a breath before continuing. "Now, about Blake. He was a regular kind of person, I guess. Polite, well mannered, reserved . . . the kind of coworker who makes you feel better just knowing he's around. The place won't be the same without him."

"You're the first person to tell us that," Claire said. She paused. "Why do you think that is?"

"Can't say for sure. I can get along with just about anyone. I guess others can't. People make life overly complicated sometimes, when often there's no need. I let go of a lot of things that could make me fester. I forget about them, and that works for me."

"Are you aware of any specific individual or individuals who did not particularly like Blake . . . who maybe had something against him? A grudge, perhaps? Anything like that?" Claire asked.

Harv thought for a minute. "Not really. I guess I assumed this was not a personal kind of killing. I assumed it was a robbery, pure and simple. A robbery with a real bad ending. Now you're making me question my thinking. Do you think it was someone here who did it? One of us who killed the man? Is that what you're saying?" He shuddered.

"I am *not* saying that," Claire responded. "At this point, we're merely gathering information. Looking at all the possibilities. That's it. Now, back to your answer. You said 'Not really' when I asked if anyone had a grudge against him. Can you expand on that, please?"

"Well, I meant that I occasionally saw him disagree with other employees, but to a certain extent, that's normal in a workplace. There are lots of different personalities around the lodge. Nothing more than that."

"Which employees did you see Blake *disagree* with?" Claire asked.

"That young housekeeper, Heidi Flynn, for one. And both Charlotte Rodriguez and June Howard, the two daytime desk clerks. They argued with him on different occasions, too. I always noticed it from afar, so I can't tell you what the arguments . . . or discussions . . . were about. Blake was a bit of a perfectionist, I guess. Always wanting work to be done just so—a certain way, Blake's way. Always expected 100 percent from every other employee, too, just like he gave, and sometimes I think he was disappointed in performances. Maybe he just knocked heads with employees over the quality of their work, especially if a complaint came in to the front desk on one or the other. Not sure."

"What about the owners, the Cantrells?" Claire asked. "Did Blake get along with both of them?"

"Well, the missus for sure. He liked her a lot." Harvey smiled. "Now Mr. Cantrell, I'm not so sure. They seemed to be too similar in many ways, and who knows if that triggered their disagreements. Maybe Blake stepped on Jay's toes now and then."

"Did Blake have any close friends?" Claire asked.

"Don't think so. He seemed happy just coming to work each day and living his life as a single man. Unattached. That nice lady at the roadside café next door—LoLo—they were acquaintances, but nothing more. We all know her. Her name is Lois Whiting, I believe, but we all just call her LoLo. She'd stop over to the lodge once in a while to say hello to Blake, and sometimes they'd have a cup of coffee together before her 7:00 a.m. shift began. No big deal. Just two people shooting the breeze for a few minutes. Likewise, he'd often stop by the café after his shift ended at 7:00 a.m. to grab a quick cup of java or breakfast. It went both ways."

"You don't think it was more than a friendship?" Claire asked.

"No, I do not. LoLo's a married lady."

"Who do you think killed Blake Helms, Harv?" Claire asked. The question was direct, penetrating, and unexpected.

"Probably the same criminal who has been committing the rash of nighttime burglaries up in Whitefish. There have been numerous articles in the local papers about the crimes. You should read them all.

The police and sheriffs' forces in this entire area are working day and night to get these cases solved. My guess is the burglar probably just moved south a few miles to a new neighborhood. Everyone around here knew about the gallery of original pieces of art here at the lodge. It was no secret. And the paintings were stolen. That's the only thing that makes sense to me. Maybe Blake tried to stop the thief and . . ."

"Harv, you have been most helpful to us," Claire said. "Thank you. And one last question before you leave. Where were you between the hours of midnight and 7:00 a.m. today?"

"That's nighttime for me. I was asleep in my bed, next to my wife. Then I got up around six-ish to get ready for work."

"Her name?" Claire asked.

"Susan. If you need anything else, please let me know," Harv said.

Claire said, "Before you leave, can you tell us exactly where the café is—the one where LoLo works?"

AFTER HARV walked from the room, Claire looked over at Guy. "I think we should take a break from this questioning and walk over to find LoLo. We need to talk to her," Claire said.

"I agree."

The two found Jay in the lobby and asked that he hold off on sending in more staff for a short time. Guy indicated they would be back shortly.

"How's the questioning going?" Jay asked. "I'm curious to see where this is all heading."

"Right now, we're merely gathering pieces of the puzzle," Claire said.

"Does anyone have an idea so far who might have done this?" Jay asked.

His demeanor was that of an edgy man. It was clear that the

weight of the murder had started to sink in. Once over his preliminary shock, the gravity of the situation had taken a hold of Jay.

"I mean, has anyone pointed a finger at someone here?" Jay persisted.

"Someone at the lodge, Jay?" Guy asked. "Why would you presume someone at the lodge committed the dastardly deed? Wouldn't you assume it was a stranger? A person from the outside? A robber? The Whitefish burglar?"

"Of course," Jay said. "Of course. I've considered the possibility that it was the Whitefish burglar from the start. I don't know why I asked that question. It was foolish. I guess I'm not thinking straight."

JUST A short distance away, across the road and approximately half a block from Mountain Lake Lodge, stood the roadside café—Woods Bay Grill. Claire and Guy walked over to it, entered, and took a seat at the counter. The place resembled an old-time diner. It was a locals' hangout with friendly people, great food, and good prices. One that had been there for generations. But on this day, it smelled so strongly of burned food that Claire's eyes immediately started to water.

A middle-aged woman approached, wearing a vintage red-and-white-checkered half apron over a white uniform dress. She toted menus. Claire's tearing eyes darted to the woman's nametag. It read "LoLo."

"I apologize for the odor in here. I burned an entire double batch of cookies in the oven today, one pan after another. Kept forgetting they were in there. It's been that kind of day," the waitress said. "Mind's on other things." She stopped talking for a brief moment and dabbed her dark eyes with a tissue to blot the tears about to flow down her cheeks. "Now, what can I get you folks?"

LoLo's red eyes and the trail of mascara streaming down her cheeks signaled it may have been more than a day of burned cookies, but perhaps a day of mourning.

Claire scanned the menu in a hurry. Her eyes fell upon items such as homemade jams, huckleberry pancakes, banana-and-huckleberry bread, and Cream of the West oatmeal.

"Black coffee for both of us," Guy said.

"Want a couple slices of fresh-baked apple pie to go along with those coffees?" the waitress asked robotically.

"Sure," Claire said. "Why not. Pie sounds good. Bring us one piece to share, please. Can you warm it and add a scoop of vanilla ice cream?"

"Is there any other way?" LoLo asked. She trotted off and returned with two cups of steaming coffee. She turned on her heels and before long reappeared with a large portion of pie à la mode and two forks. "I cut an extra-large slice, seeing you're sharin'."

Claire smiled a kind smile. "Thanks, LoLo."

This was a slow time in the café, long after the noon lunch crowd had disbursed. Claire introduced herself and Guy to LoLo and informed her they were investigators from the Miami area, here in Montana on vacation to visit their friends at the lodge next door, and that they were helping the local sheriff's office look into the homicide of Blake Helms.

"You actual name is Lois Whiting, correct?" Claire asked.

"That is my legal name. Lois Whiting. But everyone calls me LoLo." She sighed a deep sigh, wiped her cheeks, and pushed her naturally platinum Dutch-boy-cut hair behind her ears.

"LoLo, we understand that you knew the deceased, Blake Helms . . . maybe better than most," Claire said.

"I did. I've been crying all morning since I heard the news. *Why?* Why would anyone do this to him? I can't understand it."

"We plan to find out," Claire said. "Mind if we ask you a few questions?"

"Sure. I'll help in any way I can."

"How long did you know Blake Helms?"

"Since he first started working at the lodge across the way. Sometimes he'd come over here to the restaurant after he got off work at seven to eat breakfast. We'd talk. Other times, I'd go over to the lodge before I started, and we'd have a cup of coffee together. He was a friend."

"We're so sorry for your loss," Claire said. "No one realizes how important friends are . . . until we lose them."

LoLo began to weep. She reached into an apron pocket and pulled out a wad of tissues. She held them to her eyes for some time.

"Was your relationship with Mr. Helms more than a friendship?" Claire asked in a quiet voice.

LoLo looked Claire squarely in the eyes. "I'm a married woman. Of course not."

"I apologize for the question, but it had to be asked," Claire said. "We're in the early stages of the investigation, and right now our goal is to try to collect every bit of information about Blake Helms that we possibly can. So I apologize for the personal and awkward question."

"LoLo, are you aware of anyone who might have wanted him dead? Anyone he had ongoing problems with, perhaps?" Guy asked.

"No," she said, appearing not completely sure of her answer.

"So he never mentioned any person, anyone at all, who bothered him or whom he argued with, fought with, disagreed with, maybe didn't like so much?" Claire asked.

LoLo hesitated, and her answer came slowly. "I know he had a battle with his ex-wife during the divorce. He mentioned that on several occasions. But that's not abnormal."

"What about staffers at the lodge?" Claire asked.

"Well, let me think," LoLo said. "He didn't particularly like the owner, Jay Cantrell. Said he could be a control freak. Made him do things a certain way, even when another way was more efficient. That bothered Blake a great deal, but he lived with it. The two argued from time to time, I understand, but in the end, the owner would always get his way. Course, that kind of thing happens all the time at places of employment. Even happens here. Lots of different types of folks from different backgrounds are thrown together, and it's not always easy for everyone to get along. But that's no big deal. People adjust."

"Anyone else?" Claire asked. "Think hard. It's important."

"Well, there's a housekeeper at the lodge named Heidi. Afraid I don't know her last name. Blake told me on more than one occasion that the young lady could be excessively rude . . . uncivil, actually. He said she showed no respect for her elders. Claimed he often lectured her about that." She nodded as if remembering. "Yeah, that kind of thing bothered him greatly. You see, Blake was a real gentleman . . . from the *old school*."

"Did Heidi's behavior ever lead to a violent confrontation between the two of them?" Guy asked.

"Oh, heavens no. He actually liked the young lady . . . just wanted her to learn to be polite. Told me he informed her she'd never get ahead in the business world with that attitude of hers. He tried to help her. Kind of like a father figure, I guess. He'd talk to her when guests complained about the way their rooms had been made up. She'd argued that she'd done a good job." LoLo stopped talking and looked into their cups. "Excuse me for a minute, please." She left to retrieve the coffeepot, returned, and refilled their cups.

"Like the pie?" she asked. "Made it myself."

"It's the best apple pie I've ever tasted," Guy said.

"I agree. It's the best," Claire said.

LoLo blushed at the compliments, and with the black streams of mascara hardened onto her cheeks, she was quite a sight to behold.

"Can you think of anything else that may help us in the investigation, LoLo?" Claire asked. "Anything you think we should be aware of? Anything at all? Whether you think it might be significant or not?"

LoLo snuffled. "I don't get why you're asking me about workers at the lodge. Certainly this was a stranger attack, wasn't it? It was a robbery, correct? I heard all the paintings were taken. Whole town is talking about it. Why do you think it was anything other than that?"

"We're not saying that we do," Guy said. "Just covering our bases. We gather up the facts, and then we analyze them. Don't want to leave a single stone unturned."

At that moment, a foursome walked in and sat down at a table near the grill's front windows.

"Sorry. Have to cut this short. I need to wait on those people," LoLo said, nodding her head in the direction of the customers. "The coffee and pie are on me. Let me know what you find out, will you? Keep me posted."

"Yes, of course. Thank you for the coffee, the pie, and the information," Claire said. "Oh, and by the way, where were you between midnight and 7:00 a.m. this morning?"

All color drained from LoLo's face. "Surely you don't think that I . . ."

"We're asking everyone that question, LoLo," Claire said. "No exceptions."

"Asleep. I was asleep in my bed, in my home. My husband was asleep in the other room. Then I got up for work around six." She tilted her head. "Find out who did this to Blake." Tear-filled eyes locked on Claire and then on Guy. "Find out who did this!"

AS CLAIRE and Guy walked back in the direction of the lodge, Guy turned his gaze to Claire. "Your impression of LoLo?"

"Gut feeling? She's a woman crushed by the loss of someone she cared for deeply," Claire said. "She was in love with Blake Helms, if you want my opinion. Still is. The emotion on her face is way too intense for a passing friendship. She's broken by his death. And if I were a betting woman, I'd wager the two were much closer than mere friends."

"If Blake was having an affair with LoLo, then what about Piper? Was he also having an affair with Piper? He'd have been one busy man." Guy paused. "We need to question LoLo further."

"We do," Claire said. "But let's give her a little time."

"It's amazing how much we've learned in a relatively short period," Guy said. "They make up an interesting lot, don't you agree?"

"Yes, I do." She kicked a stone. And then another. "We still have to interview the rest of the employees and see what they know, and I can't wait for those crime lab findings. The thrust of our investigation might change at any point. I'm very curious to find out about the weapon used, whether they got a match on the prints, and what the heck that strange-looking gravel was leading back and forth between the front door and the check-in desk. And the blue jean rivet," Claire said. "Can't wait to hear about that, either."

"Claire, what are your thoughts on Jay's possible involvement?"

"I've been dreading that question."

CLAIRE DAYDREAMED. Sometimes investigations paved the way to a stranger. But many times, the perpetrator was close by . . . even a familiar face, she reminded herself.

6

THE INVESTIGATORS TOOK a break from interviewing and sat down with Piper and Jay in Riley's Pub, located on the top level of the tri-level lodge. The lobby and the Terra Restaurant comprised the main level, and a coffee bar and large boardroom shared the lower level with Jest Gallery. Because the structure had been built into a hillside, the architect had allowed for a separate entrance to Riley's Pub from the property's lakeside as well.

It was late afternoon, and Jay requested his kitchen staff to toss a flat-crust Margherita pizza into the wood-burning brick oven. He also ordered a pitcher of iced tea for the table.

"How goes the battle?" Piper asked. "Making any progress?" Her eyes remained swollen and bloated.

"I would say, yes," Claire said. "But most of all, we're waiting for the crime lab results. If the lifted fingerprints and palm prints, as well as the other physical evidence collected, can lead us directly to the killer, then the person will be located, arrested, prosecuted, and hopefully convicted."

"And if not?" Jay asked.

"Then it becomes a whole lot more complicated, real quick," Guy said. "That's why we're interviewing the lodge staff right now, to see what they know that might help us pinpoint the murderer."

Jay appeared overly antsy, and the muscles tensed in his neck.

"Something wrong, Jay?" Claire asked.

"We need to talk," he said, looking from Claire to Guy. "I've wanted to broach the subject all day, but you know how busy it's been. I'm sure you're hearing from some of the employees that Blake and I didn't get along that well, and I need to clarify this. You need to know the truth. We liked each other just fine . . . only we disagreed on how to do certain things here at the lodge. Blake was a stubborn man, and so am I. Sure, we had our differences, and we argued from time to time, and we even got into some pretty heated situations on occasion. But that's where it started and ended. We respected each other's viewpoints. We talked . . . or sometimes *yelled* at each other . . . but the two of us always walked away on a civil note. No matter what you're hearing, or may be thinking, that's how it was."

Piper appeared keyed up, as though she wanted to add something to the conversation. Suddenly she blurted out, "But what about . . ."

The look Jay shot her way stopped her midsentence. And at once, the atmosphere at the table became so thick that all conversation came to a grinding halt. Several minutes passed.

"Thanks for telling us that, Jay," Guy said, breaking the lull. "It's helpful to know as much information as possible. More knowledge is always better. You know the saying, *knowledge is power.*"

The four drank the cold tea, but hardly touched the pizza.

Despite everyone's attempt at normality, the circumstances dictated otherwise.

What was Piper about to say, the sleuths wondered. What was really going on between Jay and Piper? Maybe Piper would tell her more when Jay was not around, Claire thought.

"We notified Blake's two grown children in Minnesota," Jay said. "They both told us they had been estranged from their dad since the divorce and wanted nothing to do with his funeral or burial. Nice, huh?"

"It happens," Guy said.

"Hope they don't regret that decision later in life," Claire said. "You can't turn back time. At least no one has figured out how to do it yet."

"If he had assets, you know they'd show up to claim those," Piper said. "But he was a simple man who didn't store up treasures on earth. He owned nothing of value. Material possessions never appealed to him. He was more interested in learning, in expanding his ever-growing knowledge. That's what was important to him."

Claire looked at Piper intently, listening carefully to her every word. Piper definitely seemed to have some confidential insights into the man Blake Helms. There was no question about it.

Piper explained that they were planning a memorial service for Blake on the lodge grounds. The date and time would be announced as soon as the State Crime Lab in Missoula gave the word that it planned to release the body and deliver it back to Bigfork. He would be laid to rest at a nearby cemetery.

"I'm sure everyone who works for us, and his friend, LoLo, will attend," Piper said. "And of course, the four of us will be there."

Nearby Whitefish, Montana

THE STRING of burglaries continued to stump the Whitefish police. The culprit had struck again. Two nights earlier. Using his usual mode of operation, the perpetrator had entered another house at Iron Horse—yet again under the dark cover of the night—and absconded with numerous valuable pieces of artwork. But something was different about this break-in. The owners had locked up their home tightly and caught a late flight out of Kalispell only hours before the thief entered the premises. An unlocked front door met the couple's regular housekeeper the following morning when she arrived to do a final cleaning. She ran to her car and skidded out of the driveway before calling the police, fearing the intruder might still be inside. It was the first time the culprit had entered a house so near the time the owners had been in residence, and that worried the police to no end. Perhaps the intruder was getting more desperate, and that was definitely something of great concern. Or maybe, as the Whitefish police chief thought for the first time, it meant the culprit was getting insider information about when owners would and would not be occupying their homes. Perhaps the homeowners had changed plans and departed later than originally planned, when all the while the intruder had expected the home to be vacated for some time. The police hoped this was the case, but there was no way to know for certain.

The police chief took two of his patrol officers and drove out to the manager's office at Iron Horse. Once there, the law enforcement team questioned the on-duty manager at length regarding who would be privy to this type of sensitive information regarding the owners' schedules.

"We're all one big family here," the manager said. "*Everyone* knows *everyone else's* business." He smiled. "It's always been like that. The homes are isolated and private, but the people are connected in a friendly and caring sort of way. They see each another—on the golf course or in the clubhouse, at the swimming pool or on the tennis courts, or in our restaurant—when they're in residence. They know each other's children and grandchildren. They participate in a gift exchange at the holidays. I said they're like family, but I need to correct myself. The homeowners are actually *closer* than most families." He laughed, but cut it short when he realized the chief and his officers did not see the humor. "Certainly you're not thinking that someone who works here at Iron Horse is behind the burglaries? That is not the case, I can assure you."

"Nevertheless, we'd like a complete listing of all full-and part-time employees working at Iron Horse—at the golf club and for the community at large," Chief Soderberg said. "And please include any independent contractors who do work of any kind within the development."

"When do you need this?" the manager asked.

"Yesterday," the chief said. "Scan and email it to me as fast as you can." He proffered his business card with his email address.

Bigfork

CLAIRE AND Guy returned to the interview room. The next staffer was led in.

"State your name, please," Claire said.

"I'm June Howard," the woman said.

"Your position here at the lodge?" Guy asked.

"I am one of the two daytime desk clerks. Between us—Charlotte Rodriguez and I—we cover the desk from 7:00 a.m. to 11:00 p.m., at which point Blake Helms takes over . . . or rather, he *used* to take over. I guess that won't happen again." A sorrowful look engaged her face. "What a horrible thing it is that happened to him. This world has become so violent. It's different than when I was young. Seems to be all around us now."

"It does," Guy said. "How old are you, Ms. Howard?"

"I'm fifty-nine. Turning sixty next month."

"How long have you worked at the lodge?" Guy asked.

"Two years."

"Did you have a job before this one?" Guy asked.

"I've had a variety of part-time jobs throughout my life. My husband works full-time. Prior to this, I worked in Bigfork at a real estate company. Answered phones."

"Shall I call you June, Ms. Howard?" Claire asked.

"I'd like that," the interviewee said.

"Okay then, June," Claire began. "How well did you know Blake Helms?"

"I knew him because we both worked at the same place. Between the three of us, Charlotte, Blake, and I manned the front desk all week. We'd register the guests, make sure the accommodations were to their liking, and answer any questions the visitors had. On the weekends, the owners sit at the front desk during the days to register and greet guests. Then, Blake would come back in to do the nightshifts on Saturdays and Sundays, too. He didn't mind working, and it made life easier for the Cantrells, too. That way, they didn't have to hire someone else just for the weekend nightshifts."

"So Blake worked seven nights a week?" Claire asked. "Is that correct?"

"He did. But again, he didn't mind doing it. He liked working, and he enjoyed working the all-nighters. Always had a book or two under an arm when he arrived for his shift, he did, so I guess he got a lot of reading done during those slow hours. Again, it was at his suggestion that he work seven nights a week, you understand. It gave him some extra money, probably to buy more books, and he enjoyed it."

"June, where were you between midnight and 7:00 a.m. today?" Claire asked.

"That's when Blake was killed, right? I was sleeping next to my better half, Joe, until I got up for work. I'm sure you have to ask us that question, but alibis are going to be tough. I'm going to guess everyone will say they were at home sleeping during that time, but without a mate to back the story up, how can anyone prove it? Even with a mate, how reliable is that kind of alibi going to be? You've got your work cut out for you, you do."

The sleuths did not respond to her remarks. They were well aware that alibis in a case of this nature would be difficult to substantiate.

"June, did Blake have any enemies? Was there anyone who didn't particularly like him?" Claire asked.

June did not answer immediately. Instead, she considered the question. As she did, a pensive look sprawled across her face. "Well, I guess you'd say that Blake and Heidi Flynn probably didn't care much for each other. He would sometimes get complaints from the guests early in the morning—when he'd hang around after his shift—that their rooms were not being made up properly. He'd ask Heidi about it, and she'd argue with him. She'd say she had made up the rooms flawlessly. She'd use an insolent tone with him—say she didn't appreciate being 'falsely accused'—and he had problems dealing with her attitude. He'd put her in her place. Nothing bothered him more than Heidi's rude remarks about 'impossible-to-please guests,' as she would call them." June paused to catch her breath.

"Laziness bothered Blake," she went on. "He thought each person should carry his or her own weight and provide an enjoyable atmosphere for the lodge guests, no matter how difficult they may be. The guests were always his main concern. 'Make them happy, whatever they want' was his mantra. 'We are here to serve,' he often said."

"Did he have arguments with anyone else?" Claire asked.

"Let me think," June said. "Hazel Schroeder—the restaurant supervisor and events coordinator—she quarreled with Blake about noise levels at certain events that were held here. See, the lodge rents out its grounds for weddings, graduations, birthdays, and other types of parties in a tent set up outside on the grounds. Oftentimes the parties would go on late into the night or early-morning hours, and Blake feared the hullabaloo would disturb the sleeping guests. Hazel was concerned that the event should occur without a hitch, and that those attending the special event should have a good time. Blake, on the other hand, was concerned that the checked-in guests were trying to get a good night's sleep. It was a push-and-pull between the two of them whenever a special occasion was held here. I'm sure you can imagine."

"Did these quarrels ever take on a violent tone?" Claire asked.

"They got pretty nasty sometimes, all right, but *violent*?" June asked. "Not really *violent*. Except for the one time. One time it was close. I heard Hazel screaming at Blake. It was obvious that emotions ran high. He shouted back at her to get a hold of herself. They went at it for a time. She looked like she was about to strike him, but she didn't." She paused as if thinking more about it. "Yeah, the tension between the two seemed palpable much of the time. At staff meetings, they always made a point to sit at opposite ends of the table, as far away from each other as possible. I guess we all knew they hated each other."

"Does any staff member at the lodge own a gun, June?" Claire asked.

"It's *Montana*, so that's a funny question," she said. "The great majority of folks in this state own a firearm . . . or several, for that matter. Some own as many as twenty or thirty. It's a state of fishing and hunting." She hesitated. "But that's not what you're asking me, is it?" She paused again and lowered her voice. "I shouldn't know this, but I saw one once in an employee's purse—here at work. I wasn't snooping, mind you, but it was sticking out of her purse. We're prohibited from bringing a firearm to work, you know, so it disturbed me quite a bit."

"Whose purse was it, June?" Claire asked.

"Can I have a piece of paper and a pen, please? I'd rather not say it out loud."

Claire ripped a sheet of paper from her notebook and passed it over to June, together with a pen.

June scribbled something down, held her index finger to her closed lips, and handed the note to Claire. "You didn't get this from me. Don't want any trouble."

Claire read it and passed it to Guy.

"Are you absolutely sure about this, June?" Claire asked.

PIPER AND Jay insisted that Claire and Guy join them for dinner at the lodge that evening. The day had been emotionally draining. The couples sat outside on the veranda in the brisk evening Montana air and under the light of a nearly full moon. Conversation came from random directions, each of the four trying desperately to avoid any discussion about the murder.

"Glad I brought a sweater along," Claire said. "It's actually a bit chilly out here."

Piper nodded.

"I would recommend you try the prime beef," Jay said. "It's our specialty."

"And the lemon mousse for dessert," Piper added. "It's one of our best."

At that moment, a group of lodge guests got up from their tables and walked over to speak to Piper and Jay and to meet the Miami investigators.

"Are we safe staying here tonight?" one man asked. "I'm terrified to stay here."

"Yes," Jay said. "As a precaution, we hired a security guard to walk the grounds all night. And the patrol deputies will be here throughout the night, as well. You have nothing to worry about."

"But the desk clerk was *murdered* during the night," another guest said. "How do we know the murderer is not still hanging around? Looking for another victim? Or worse yet, walking among us?"

"We're monitoring the situation closely," Guy intercepted. "With full protection from the Lake County Sheriff's Office, you have nothing to worry about."

"Are you certain?" a female guest asked. "Can you *guarantee* our safety? What if there *is* another murder?"

"There won't be another murder," Jay said. "Enjoy your evening and your days at the lodge. We apologize that this terrible incident occurred, and we're doing everything possible to find and arrest the perpetrator. An incident like this has never happened before, and it will not happen again. You can rest well knowing that fact."

Claire thought quickly. "Perhaps you can all become junior investigators and help us out. If you notice anything out of the ordinary, see something that doesn't quite fit, notice anyone lurking around—I'd like you to tell us immediately. Many eyes are better than a few. And stay together. Exercise good common sense. Don't go out alone, especially at night. Always walk with someone else . . . or in a group. That's even better." She smiled. "If you're strolling around the grounds and find an item of interest, something that seems out of place, don't touch it, but rather come find one of us and take us to it. If you touch it, you will ruin our chances of lifting any prints off of it. Remember that."

Suddenly the mood of the crowd seemed to swing, and its members appeared exuberant at the prospect of assisting the real-life sleuths. Many started whispering with each other, and their cheeks flushed with excitement.

"Like *CSI*?" a thin woman asked.

"Yes. Just like *CSI*," Claire said. "Just think of it as *CSI: Bigfork*." She smiled slightly.

Guy thought it was brilliant. Claire had subdued the contagious fear element igniting within the lodge guests and actually put them to work on the case to help solve the crime.

"Get a good night's rest after you finish your dinners tonight, and then you'll start out fresh in the morning," Claire said.

The guests hurried back to their tables and to the savory food being served. They ate, drank, and entered into lively conversation. Being deputized as *CSI: Bigfork* agents seemed to be more than they could handle. Exhilaration pumped through their collective veins, and they couldn't wait to begin the group assignment the following day.

"Thank you, Claire," Jay said. "You certainly know how to calm a crowd. I was concerned everyone would check out early and demand a refund of the money they paid up front. That would have been a double disaster for the lodge."

"Glad to do it, Jay. I don't really expect one of them to come up with a clue, but it will keep them occupied so we can do our job."

"Tomorrow, as soon as the sheriff gives us clearance and removes the yellow tape, I need to have the front desk area cleaned up and sterilized," Jay said. "And the lobby needs to be straightened up, as well. What a mess!"

"Guy and I would like to take a closer look at that area ourselves first thing in the morning, in the light of day, before anything is moved or cleaned," Claire said. "We want to make certain no clues were overlooked."

"I'm sure the major case team found anything worth finding, Claire," Jay said. "What's the point?" Suddenly Jay seemed irritated.

"Jay, I'm afraid we're going to have to insist," Claire said. "The smallest things can sometimes be missed. Just want to be thorough. Certainly you understand. And Jay, by the way, do you think you can round up about fifty whistles by morning?"

7

Friday

MORNING ARRIVED IN resplendent glory. A new day. A fresh start. *Tabula rasa*—a clean tablet. The opportunity to begin again. The clear, sunny blue of the big sky brought with it the promise of something better than the day before.

Claire and Guy woke up early. Claire seemed eager to get a closer look at the crime scene and also to continue interviewing the lodge employees. Sleep had been restless. As the interesting pastiche of already-interviewed staff members—most of whom subtly or not so subtly had pointed a finger at one or another of their coworkers as a suspect—paraded continually through her dreams, certain faces came to the forefront: *Jay Cantrell*, *Heidi Flynn*, and *Hazel Schroeder*. The arrival of morning brought with it welcomed relief.

Today would provide the opportunity to view the crime scene firsthand. Something had been nagging at her to take another look, to inspect the scene once again, and she didn't understand why. Certainly the major case team experts had not missed anything else. Or had they? Then there were the other staff members. After interviewing six staffers yesterday, there were still nine to go. And then there was LoLo—Lois Whiting. They had talked with her, too. Was she holding something back? Did she know a fact or two that would aid them in identifying Blake's murderer? Were they wasting valuable time by interviewing the lodge employees in the first place, when an outsider may have committed the murder and may still be on the loose, maybe even planning another murder? Was the killer the same person committing the series of burglaries in Whitefish? She thought for several minutes, staring straight ahead. No. Her inherent inclination, her investigator instincts, told her to continue with the lodge employee interviews—that the answer may well reside with one or another of the staff members. Besides, they had promised the sheriff a full report on the interviews. She was anxious to get back to the questioning.

Claire refused to accept the theory that an outsider, pretending to be checking into the lodge in the early-morning hours, had pulled a gun equipped with an unidentified silencer on Blake, shooting the unsuspecting desk clerk repeatedly face-on at close range. "Looks like robbery was the motive, pure and simple," one patrol deputy at the scene had commented. A detective at the scene thought for sure it had to be the continued work of the Whitefish burglar, who had merely changed neighborhoods.

But she did not agree with either of them. Blake's killing was personal, her sixth sense informed her. The killer knew Blake, the little voice inside her kept screaming out. This special instinct had been a part of her for as long as she could remember, and it had never let her down. In fact, during her prior fifteen-year career as a government fraud investigator, she had gained the reputation of seeing things others did not. That unusual perception ability had come in handy when working up investigations, and she had solved the most complicated cases thrown her way.

But then again, was it personal? she pondered as she always did, debating with herself. Expensive artwork had been taken . . . and a couple of old saddles, as well. The modus operandi appeared to be similar to the rash of burglaries occurring in the Whitefish area—less than forty miles away. There was no question about it. Yet, in a significant way, this crime was also very different. Unlike this situation, a *murder* had never been committed in the case of the Whitefish burglaries. And that was a detail most worthy of attention.

At Mountain Lake Lodge, the crime had turned violent, her pondering thoughts continued. Was it simply a robbery of expensive artwork that had ended in murder? Or was it private? Intimate? Secret? Personal? Did someone hate Blake Helms and intentionally end his life? If so, who? Or perhaps did Blake instantly realize something was amiss when the man entered the lobby during those early-morning hours, and when Blake reached for the phone to call the sheriff, that action triggered his demise? These questions and more circulated 'round and 'round in her head.

The truth would come out. She was sure of it. Claire would suggest to the sheriff that his office send out alerts to art galleries, art buyers, private collectors, brokers, and others who might be contacted to purchase the stolen pieces of art. She wondered how and where the thief would try to fence the original creations.

As she and Guy approached the lodge for a quick breakfast, Claire's sense of anxiety heightened. The tables in the dining room were filled with lodgers, all chattering excitedly at the prospect of spending the day as *CSI: Bigfork* agents. It was more fun than could have been imagined when they planned their trips.

The sleuths spotted Jay and Piper sitting at a table, drinking coffee, and walked toward them.

"Please sit down with us," Piper said.

"Morning," Claire said. "I won't ask how you slept because I'm sure I know the answer."

"It was a rough night," Piper said. "I didn't sleep."

Claire and Guy ordered scrambled eggs, toast, juice, and coffee.

"Jay, were you able to track down those whistles?" Claire asked.

"Yeah. I have them right here." He lifted a plastic bag from the floor and handed it across the table to Claire. "I asked my friend at the hardware store down the road to open early and sell me all the whistles he had. We were in luck. He had a full box of fifty in the back, and I took them all."

"Nice work, Jay," Claire said.

She stood to make an announcement to the guests. "Good morning, crime scene investigators. We hope you are all ready to help us out today. I want each of you to grab a whistle from this bag when you finish breakfast." She set the sack down on a table located in the center of the room. "While you are out and about today, walking the grounds, if you see anything suspicious, as we talked about yesterday, I want you to blow your whistle loudly three short times in a row. One of us will find you immediately. Again, *do not touch* any evidence you may come across. Just whistle." She paused and looked around at the crowd. "Thank you in advance for your anticipated help and cooperation."

As Claire walked back to her seat, the lodgers scrambled en masse to the central table—cheeks flushed with eagerness and mouths stuffed with food—to grab a whistle. Not one could wait until after they had finished eating. Soon the bag sat empty. The guests whispered and talked among themselves as they returned to their tables to consume many forkfuls of the delicious breakfast buffet feast, all the while deciding who would be paired with whom for the day's adventure.

"They're taking the mission seriously," Claire said. "Good."

"Yeah. And it'll keep them out of our hair as we try to get the lobby put back together later this morning," Jay said. "That is, as soon as the sheriff gives us the go-ahead." He smiled at Claire. "Thanks again for the quick thinking. You turned a potentially chaotic situation into something positive."

Claire ate a few bites and excused herself. She desperately wanted to take her own look at the crime scene. "Guy, join me as soon as you finish," she said. "I'm going to get started."

She walked to the check-in desk and stood in front of it. As she pulled on the pair of latex gloves Matthew Mallory had given her, she closed her eyes. Soon she felt the presence of the murderer. She opened her eyes and carefully ducked under the yellow sheriff line tape. Then she moved slightly to the left, until she felt certain she stood precisely where the killer had stood as he pulled the trigger. She opened her eyes, dropped her glance to the long, flat check-in desk countertop, and studied it. Reaching into her shoulder bag, she pulled out a small magnifying glass she always carried with her and examined the surface at close range. Although the magnifier aided her inch-by-inch inspection of the polished wooden surface, she found nothing.

Guy walked over to join Claire in her examination. He stood still, watching her in action. Morning sunshine poured in through the windows near the check-in desk, lighting up its countertop and the entire lobby area in a brilliant manner. He watched Claire drop to her hands and knees to take a better look at the floor where the killer had likely stood.

No sound emanated from Claire as she worked. Her head moved from side to side as she mechanically and thoroughly searched the floorboards for a clue. After minutes had passed, she shrieked, "Ah-ha. Here's something!" She looked up and turned her head around to face Guy. "Grab me a small plastic storage bag from the kitchen, will you, please? Preferably one that zips closed."

"I'll be right back," Guy said. He tore off in the direction of the kitchen.

Two minutes later, Claire oh-so carefully picked something up with the thumb and forefinger of her gloved right hand. She dropped it into the bag and zipped it shut.

"What is it?" Guy asked. "What'd you find?"

Claire stood up. "An eyelash. A single, solitary eyelash. It might have dropped from the killer's clothing or directly off the murderer's eyelid. It needs to go to the crime lab at once to be processed for DNA."

"Good work, Claire. Leave it to you . . ." Guy said. He shook his head in utter astonishment.

Claire pulled her cell phone and the business card the sheriff had given her the day before from her bag. She dialed his number.

"Sheriff Bell? Claire Caswell. I want to update you on the interviews we've conducted so far. And also, I found another piece of evidence here at the lodge near the check-in counter. I bagged it—wearing gloves, of course. Thought you should get it to the lab as soon as possible."

"What is it, Ms. Caswell? What did you find? I'd like to know now," Sheriff Bell said.

"An eyelash," she said. "One eyelash. And I almost missed it."

"I'll be there as soon as I can," the sheriff said. "You can fill me in then on the interviews you've conducted."

Claire and Guy continued to comb the scene for evidence, but found no other clues.

Guy pondered how forensic science had forever changed the components of the art of investigation. He knew what would happen in this case. The major case team at the Lake County Sheriff's Office would electronically transmit the forensic *impression* evidence collected—the fingerprints and palm or partial palm prints recovered from the crime scene—to the Integrated Automated Fingerprint Identification System (IAFIS), the national computer storage system managed by the FBI. It was an index containing all fingerprints entered throughout the country.

Additionally, he had recently learned that Montana was one of eight states comprising the Western Identification Network (WIN). It was the first multi-state automated fingerprint identification system (AFIS). This high-speed computer network specifically digitized, stored, and compared fingerprint data and images within the western US states and Alaska.

If any fingerprint or palm print lifted from the scene matched an impression of a criminal profile entered into either one of these systems, they'd get an identification match.

As far as DNA comparison, profiles identified from the *biological* evidence collected at the crime scene—such as blood, hair, and saliva—would be electronically entered into the FBI-funded Combined DNA Index System (CODIS), a computer-software index of local, state, and national DNA profiles. Guy had recently heard the index contained about fifty million profiles, and close to sixteen thousand of those offender profiles had been entered into the system from the state of Montana alone. And now *touch DNA* could be entered into the equation. Even the slightest bit of genetic material left behind at a crime scene could now be profiled. Yes, knowledge in the world of investigation was multiplying tenfold, he thought.

The *forensic DNA* blood analysis would determine if blood other than that of the victim was found at the murder scene, scientific methods and techniques would be used to analyze the gravel lifted from the lobby floor to determine its composition and origin, and hopefully enough DNA would be present on the eyelash to build a profile. *Ballistics* evidence would help determine the type of firearm used; the caliber of the bullets; and the trajectory, or flight path, of the projectiles that killed Blake Helms. And even the blue jean rivet would be examined to determine the type of jeans it came from and whether it held partial prints.

The ever-progressing science of investigating a crime scene never ceased to amaze the former criminal prosecutor. He had seen things change so much in that regard over his two-decade career as the lead Miami-Dade state attorney in charge of prosecution of the major felony-level cases throughout the county. *We've come a long way over the years*, he said to himself.

SHERIFF BELL arrived to collect the eyelash and to learn about the employee interviews the sleuths had conducted the day prior.

"Rest assured, I'll send this lash to the State Crime Lab right away, Ms. Caswell," the sheriff said. "Can we review your interview findings now?"

"Yes. Let's go to our interview room," Claire said.

Claire led the way as Guy and the sheriff shadowed behind her. Together, Claire and Guy paged through their respective notebooks and took turns summarizing the information obtained from each witness interviewed the day before.

"Most interesting, isn't it?" Sheriff Bell asked, looking at the Miami Beach investigators and trying to sum up his opinion of the duo. "What do you make of it all?"

"As always," Claire said, "our best evidence is yet to come—the crime lab findings. Physical evidence leaves no room for speculation. However, the interviews of the staff members may prove useful, too. Certain patterns are developing. For example, we now know there was ongoing tension between Blake Helms and certain other employees. I think by the end of today, after we talk to most or all of the remaining staffers, we'll have a pretty good idea which ones may require closer examination."

"When do you expect to receive the various lab and autopsy results, sheriff?" Guy asked.

"Well, since this is Friday, we won't hear a thing until early next week," the sheriff said. "There's always a delay when a weekend is involved. But I did request both the Kalispell and the Missoula labs to give this matter top priority. And my lab will, as well. I told them we need the results ASAP, as a killer is still on the loose. We're doing all the fingerprint comparisons in-house, so that information will come back rather soon. Otherwise, for now, we're playing the waiting game. By the way, call me on my cell if anything urgent comes up in today's interviews. If nothing requires my immediate attention, however, let's reconnect first thing Monday morning, and you can fill me in on the remainder of your witness statements then."

"We'll do it," Guy Lombard said.

"Oh, and by the way, so far I'm impressed." The sheriff nodded his head at both investigators.

"Is there any reason the crime scene area cannot be cleaned up now?" Guy asked.

"No. Go ahead. I got the all-clear from a member of the major case team on my way over here," Sheriff Bell said. "I'll collect the yellow sheriff tape on my way out. Oh, and have your friends—the owners—compile a full list of the artwork and any other items stolen. I'd like to have the title and the artist's name for each piece of art before we alert the art world and other potential buyers to the theft. As soon as they get that done, scan and email it to my office, will you, please? Email address is on my card. Once we have that, we'll get the alert out without delay."

CLAIRE AND Guy caught up with Jay and Piper outside, near the pool and hot tub area.

"You won't believe it," Jay said. "These lodgers are driving me and Piper literally crazy, tooting on their high-pitched whistles. It's constant. If they spot litter of any kind, a remnant of dog or bear excrement, an empty root beer can, a Styrofoam cup, a bird feather, a broken pine bough, a deceased hornet . . . you name it, they blow on the blasted whistles. We've been running from three clear, shrill sounds to the next three ever since we got out here. And the day is young. They're wearing us down."

Claire muffled a chuckle. "Me thinks me created some monsters. Sorry about that."

"Well, you never know," Piper said. "Maybe one of them will actually find a clue worth following yet."

"I wouldn't count on it," Guy said. "In the meantime, it's keeping your guests occupied." He shot a half grin toward the Cantrells.

"What are your plans for the rest of the day?" Jay asked. "How can we help you?"

"We'd like to resume the interviewing of your staff," Guy said. "If you would, please send the employees into the interview room that we did not talk to yesterday. One at a time, every half hour, just as before."

"No problem. How many are left?" Piper asked.

"By my calculations, nine," Claire said.

"Okay. We'll send in the employees working the day shift first.

Then, at 3:00 p.m., the others report in for the evening shift. We'll send those staffers in when they arrive, too," Jay said.

"Sounds good," Guy said. "Thanks."

"Oh, can the two of you put together a list of the art stolen from the lodge? The sheriff wants it as soon as possible. Both title and artist on each piece," Claire said. "Scan and email it when you're done, will you, please?" She jotted down the email address for the Lake County Sheriff's Office and handed the note to Piper. "And Jay, go ahead and have the crime scene cleaned up. The major case team got everything it needed and just gave the okay."

"Thank goodness," Jay said. "The lobby's a real mess. I'll ask Harv, the handyman, to get it done. Personally, I think I'd have trouble cleaning up Blake Helms's blood." He grimaced. The thought of it was clearly repugnant to him. "We'll have to replace some of the furniture, too."

"After today, we face the weekend. Nothing is going to happen at the labs for a couple of days, at least," Claire said. "I thought Guy and I would take a drive up to Whitefish tomorrow and see what all the commotion is about . . . you know, with the series of burglaries. We'd like to be able to rule out the possibility that the Whitefish burglar came to Bigfork and committed the murder."

"You just missed the annual Bigfork Festival of the Arts by a weekend, but there's an art fair in Polson on Sunday, at the south end of Flathead Lake," Piper said. "It's a nice drive down there, and you'd enjoy the day. Besides, it would give you both some time away from this case." Her eyes misted as she spoke, and it was readily apparent that she continued to mourn the death of Blake in a significant way. "Jay and I will be manning the check-in desk during the days this weekend, or we'd join you."

"Good suggestion, Piper," Claire said. "We'll do it."

THE INTERVIEWING resumed. A housekeeper appeared in the doorway and walked into the room.

"Your full name, please?" Claire asked.

"Dahlia Young," the woman said.

"Age?" Guy asked.

"Twenty-four," she said politely. Straight dishwater bangs hung long across the top of her eyes. She was tall and thin, and her hair reeked of cigarette smoke. She appeared frail and fatigued.

"Your voice is shaking," Claire said. "In fact, your entire body seems to be shaking. Are you okay?"

"Yes," Dahlia said. "Never done nothing like this before. Guess I'm nervous."

"Well, please try to relax, Ms. Young," Claire said. "We're only trying to see what everyone here at the lodge knows about the murder of Blake Helms. Just pretend you're talking with us over a friendly cup of coffee. Will that help?"

Dahlia took a deep breath. "Yes, I think so."

"By the way, would you like a cup of coffee, Ms. Young, or a glass of water?" Guy asked.

"No, I'm good. Thanks anyway," she said.

"How long have you been employed by Mountain Lake Lodge?" Guy asked.

"Nearly three years."

"What do you do at the lodge? What is your position here?" he asked.

"I'm a housekeeper. I usually work the seven-to-three shift, unless they need me to come in later for some reason. Late checkouts or whatever. And alternate weekends."

Dahlia motioned with her hands the entire time she spoke.

"Did you know Blake Helms?" Claire asked.

"To say hi to."

"What did you think of him?" Claire asked.

"He seemed okay . . . far as I could tell." Her voice went to a higher pitch and she clenched her hands.

"Where were you yesterday between midnight and 7:00 a.m.?" Guy asked.

"At home. Asleep. Until I got up to get ready for work."

"Do you know of anyone who might have wanted Blake dead?" Guy asked.

"What a strange question," the housekeeper said. "Do I know of anyone who might have wanted Blake dead? I've never known anyone who wished another person dead. Not ever."

JAY DELIVERED A server from the Terra Restaurant for the next interview.

"Hello, sir," Claire said. "Have a seat, and please state your full name for us."

"Carlton Warner. I go by Chaz."

"Age, Chaz?" Guy asked.

"Twenty-two."

"Position at the lodge?" Guy asked.

"I'm a server. In the main dining room."

"How long have you worked here, Chaz?" Claire asked.

"A little over two years. I work breakfast through lunch, then come back and work the dinner crowd, too."

"Are you from Montana originally?" Claire asked.

"Yep."

"How well did you know Blake Helms?" she continued.

"Good as anybody, I reckon."

"What does that mean, Chaz?" she asked.

"I don't know. I saw him leaving when I came to work in the morning. That was about it. Never really talked to him much. Except . . ."

"*Except* . . .?" Claire asked.

"Well, the man read me the riot act a couple mornings for being late. I mean, what the hell business was it of his? He was an employee, just like me. I mean, what gave *him* the right to chew *me* out? Who did he think he was, anyway?"

"Okay, Chaz," Claire said. "Calm down. What exactly did Blake Helms say to you?"

"He told me people in the workplace notice these things. People being late, and all. And if I wanted to make something of myself . . . to get ahead in this world . . . to be respected by others . . . I should not show up late to work. He embarrassed the hell out of me. I mean, he yelled at me in front of my coworkers for being fifteen freaking minutes late! The fucking nerve of that man." Chaz looked at Claire. "Excuse me, ma'am. Pardon my language."

"Okay, Chaz," Claire said. "Let's get on with this. How did it make you feel when Blake chewed you out?"

"Like punching the breath out of the old sucker, that's how," Chaz said.

"Where were you yesterday between midnight and 7:00 a.m.?" Guy asked.

"Keeping my mattress company, that's where. Till morning, when I got up for work."

ANOTHER STAFFER appeared for an interview. Claire crossed her name from the list.

"Please have a seat," Claire said. "We'll start by asking you to state your full name for us."

"Katie Kyle. Well, actually, my first name is Katherine, but everyone has always called me Katie. No one even knows that Katherine is my real name."

"Okay, Katie," Claire said. "Please tell us your age and how long you've worked at Mountain Lake Lodge."

"I'm twenty-five. I've worked here three years as a waitress . . . a *server* . . . in the main dining room—Terra Restaurant. I work the breakfast, lunch, and dinner shift and take a several-hour break between the lunch and dinner service every day. Once in a while, I fill in at the pub, too, when they're short-staffed. All the staff here kind of float around as needed."

"Where were you born, Katie?" Claire asked.

"In Missoula. That's south of here."

"Have you always lived in Montana?"

"Yes."

"Did you know Blake Helms, the murdered desk clerk?"

"I knew who he was. I'd say hi to him when I came into work." She stopped to gather her thoughts. "Oh, and I'd see him at our staff meetings. Never really talked to him for any length of time, though."

"Katie, did you ever hear anyone verbalize bad feelings about Blake? Did you ever see anyone confront him?" Claire asked.

"Well, my coworker hated the man. One day, I even heard him say the man should be dead—that he should be put out of his misery."

"Really?" Claire said. She glanced at her notes. "And that would be Chaz Warner, the other server?"

"Yeah. Kind of scared me at the time, but you know how people say things they don't really mean. Talk is cheap. I never thought he was serious. Not really. He was embarrassed 'cause Blake criticized his service that day. Said he was slow and that he would disappear for long periods of time without checking on his tables. See, Blake had come in for breakfast that day, something he did from time to time, but I think he had a meeting with someone later on, and he'd ordered a full breakfast off the menu. He waited a long time for it, and when he got the meal, it was cold. He stormed into the kitchen and found Chaz standing in a corner, texting on his cell phone. Blake rebuked Chaz about his service and about the fact that the pancakes and eggs were cold when he finally got them." She paused to take a deep breath. "Chaz takes great pride in his server abilities, and I think Blake's comments hurt his pride and damaged his enormous ego. It was the second or third time that Blake had reamed Chaz out for something. Chaz got extremely angry with the man. Ordered him out of the kitchen that day. After that, Chaz refused to talk to him."

"Did Blake ever chew Chaz out for being late? Or was it always about the service?" Guy asked.

"There are two kinds of people in this world: those who are always early and those who are always late. Chaz clearly fits into the first category. He is always early or right on time for work. So to answer your question, Mr. Lombard, it was *always* about the service and Chaz's attitude, *never* about his tardiness."

"When did Chaz have this last argument with Blake, Katie? Do you remember?" Claire asked.

"I'd say about a week or a week and a half ago," Katie said. "Hey, please don't mention that I told you this. I'd be scared about what Chaz might do to me. He's got a bad temper. Real bad. And he refuses to discuss the fact that Blake criticized his service. It would embarrass him. It's a sensitive issue."

"A final question. Where were you between midnight and

7:00 a.m. yesterday?"

"Getting my beauty sleep." She smiled. "Never can get enough of that." She fluttered her eyelashes and made a funny face. "Then, up for work."

WITH EVERY subsequent interview, the list of suspects with a motive for the murder of Blake Helms seemed to be growing. The obvious ones were just that . . . obvious. It was those who might have hidden incentives that worried Claire. What, if anything, were they *not* seeing? And the alibi issue was of growing concern. Without the ability to check the alibis of the suspects—all of them purportedly *sleeping* at the time of the murder—they would have to rely almost exclusively on the evidence the labs came up with. The test results would make or break the case.

ANOTHER WITNESS approached the investigators and took a seat across the table. He was the tenth staffer to be interviewed.

"Please tell us your name and tell us your position at the lodge," Guy said.

"My name is Phil. Philip Kagan. I'm one of the two daytime chefs. I work alone on quiet days and with Ed Carter—the other daytime chef—on busier days. Between us, we cover breakfast, brunch, and lunch during the week for the Terra Restaurant and Riley's Pub, and then we always work together on weekends to cook up the grand brunch." He paused and then raised his right hand. "And I swear to tell the truth . . . the whole truth and nothing but the truth, so help me God." He chuckled.

Phil was a large man, tall and big boned. An irregularly shaped purple birthmark dotted a portion of his upper lip.

"How old are you, Phil?" Guy asked, ignoring the interviewee's attempt to inject humor into a serious situation.

"Twenty-one." He looked at the investigators. "Just kidding! I'm really fifty-one."

"Are you from Montana, sir?" Guy asked.

Phil broke into the song "Born in the U.S.A." by Bruce Springsteen.

"I will ask my question again," Guy said loudly, breaking into the inappropriate deflection. "Are you from Montana?"

"Yes, I am. Indee-dee."

"Married?" Guy asked.

"Me? Married? Not in this lifetime. Might share a place, though, if I found the right lady, but that handcuffed-together stuff ain't for me." He immediately broke into the beginning of the song "Just the Two of Us" by Bill Withers, slithering his body from side to side and snapping his fingers to the rhythm.

His flippant attitude was wearing thin on the investigators, but they ignored it and continued with the questioning.

"How long have you worked at the lodge?" Guy asked.

"Coming up on five years now. One, two, three, four . . . *five* big ones!"

Claire was nearing the end of her patience with this employee. It was time to get down to business. "How well did you know the nighttime desk clerk, Blake Helms?"

"Me? I liked the man. Can't believe he was murdered." He sighed. "We were about the same age. Used to shoot the breeze most every day when I'd come in for my morning shift."

"How well did you know the man?" Claire asked again. "Please answer the question."

"On a scale of one to ten, ten meaning I knew the man really well, I'd give it a . . . five, maybe."

"What did the two of you talk about?" Claire asked. "Did he have any problems?"

"Not that I knew of. We'd talk about anything that was on our minds, I guess."

"Such as . . ." Claire pursued the question.

"Well, now, that's rather *personal*, isn't it?" He raised his eyebrows and tilted his head toward Claire. His expression was quite dour, until he burst into outrageous laughter. "Just kidding, again!"

"Sir, I'm going to have to ask you to put aside all of this silliness and singing and simply answer the questions," Claire said. "This is a grim matter, and we'd appreciate it if you would treat it that way. Do you understand?" Her eyes locked in on Phil's, and she stared at him without blinking.

"Yes, ma'am. I do." He saluted her.

She ignored the gesture.

"Now, I asked you earlier what you and Blake would talk about. You told us, 'Anything that was on our minds.' I'm asking you to expand on that for us. Was there anything in particular that you and Mr. Helms would talk about?" Claire asked.

Her voice tone had lowered one entire level, and Phil got the distinct message that he should stop wasting time and answer the questions directly.

"Well, Blake was an American Indian history buff. He read all the books on the tribes from this area of Montana, and he used to fill me in on lots of interesting stuff he learned. He'd become a real *expert* on the Blackfoot and Flathead tribes, in particular. Got me real interested in it, too, he did."

"That's the first time we've heard of this from a lodge employee," Claire said. "Thank you for sharing."

"Well, I was probably the only one he talked to about those things," Phil said.

"What was one interesting thing he told you about either of those tribes?" Claire asked.

"Well, let me think," Phil said. He paused. "One day Blake told me the reason the Blackfoot people have the name they do is because the Blackfoot always wore dark-colored moccasins. I found that interesting." He shifted in his seat. "Also, he told me that the Canadians refer to the Blackfoot as the *Blackfeet*; in the US, we refer to the tribe as the *Blackfoot*. Oops. I apologize. Please forgive me. I gave you two examples, and you asked for only one. I'm so sorry. So very sorry." As soon as he stopped talking, he muffled laughter.

"Do you find this funny, Phil?" Claire asked.

"No, of course not. Please forgive me. Next question?" He held back a smirk.

"Did Mr. Helms have any enemies?" Claire asked.

"What do you mean by the term *enemies*?"

"What do you think I mean?" Claire asked. "I mean anyone openly or secretly hostile toward the man."

"He had this way about him, Blake did. He'd scold workers who didn't measure up to his standards. Belittle them, really. Even took on the owner, Jay Cantrell, many times, and the two would lock horns. Blake demanded things be done to a particular standard . . . *his* standard, which was perfection. Anything less fell short. He didn't care who he took on, and he did so liberally. So when you ask me if he had any enemies, I'm sure he had many. Or at least many people who didn't care two hoots for his style—the victims of his public humiliation, to name a few. But I personally did not happen to be one of his enemies. I was his fan! I was in awe of his smarts! As I said before, I liked the man." He broke into a huge staged smile and held the expression for a full minute.

"Phil, where were you during the early-morning hours of Blake's murder—yesterday between midnight and 7:00 a.m.?" Claire asked.

"Where was *I* when Blake was murdered—between midnight

and 7:00 a.m. yesterday?"

"That is the question," Claire said. She stared at the man without blinking.

"I was busy."

She asked, "Busy doing *what*?"

"I was busy . . . relaxing my body. Sleeping. At home. By myself. Without a spouse. Unmarried." He faked a yawn. "Then up and at 'em for work."

"We get the picture, Phil," Claire said. "Thank you."

Claire jotted notes.

CLAIRE AND Guy needed a break after the interview with Phil Kagan and decided to eat a late lunch. They walked out to the lobby and spotted Piper and Jay.

"Do you have time to sit down for a quick bite?" Claire asked.

"Sure," Piper said. Her tone was not overly enthusiastic.

The foursome found a table near the windows in the dining room and sat down. Each ordered either a sandwich or salad, along with iced tea.

"How's it going in there?" Piper asked. "Any clues jumping out at you yet?"

"I would say we're talking to a bevy of *colorful* employees," Claire said. "Each one with a story to tell."

"I can only imagine," Jay said. "Making any progress?" He eyed them with seemingly excessive interest.

"Right now, we have more questions than answers," Guy said. "Let's leave it at that."

"Our focus will surely narrow once we receive all the lab reports," Claire said. "Cases always start out this way."

"Well, the whistlers are still at it, in case you're interested," Jay said.

"Keeping us busy. If they come up with anything of real interest, I'll be surprised. Thankfully, most or all of them are checking out tomorrow morning."

"Hooray," Guy said.

The meal was a pleasant diversion from the interviewing process.

"We have only five more employees to talk to," Claire said, glancing at her wristwatch. "It's almost midafternoon. I assume the three-to-eleven-shift staffers will arrive shortly."

"They will," Piper said. "We'll send the last five in so you can wrap up the questioning yet this afternoon. Then, you can actually spend some time seeing Montana this weekend. Your vacation will not be a total loss." She attempted to turn the corners of her mouth upward, but her face muscles refused to cooperate.

"Well, we're looking forward to walking around Whitefish tomorrow. And then on Sunday, we plan to drive down to Polson, as you suggested . . . to the local art show you told us about," Claire said.

MINUTES LATER, the next staffer appeared in the interview room and sat down across from Claire and Guy.

"Please state your name and age, sir," Guy said, crossing the young man's name from the list.

"Erik—with a *k*—Johannson." He spelled his last name. "I'm twenty-seven. I'm one of the two dinner chefs. Darlene Nichols is the other. Together, we prepare the food for the two restaurants. I've worked here just over two years."

"Thank you," Guy said. "You just answered the next two questions I planned to ask you, as well."

Erik chortled. "Sorry. Is this supposed to go in some order? I've never been questioned before. When I came in to work a few minutes ago, the others told me what questions you'd be asking."

"No problem, Erik. You feel free to share with us anything you think we should know during the interview. Deal?" Claire asked.

"Deal," he said.

Erik was a dramatically good-looking, fair-haired young man, graced with deep dimples on his baby face.

"Erik, please tell us how well you knew the murder victim, Blake Helms," Claire said.

"Not very well. He started work as I was leaving at eleven, so I'd pass him on my way out. That's all."

"Did you see him at staff meetings, too?" Claire asked.

"Oh, sure, but never to talk to."

"Did you ever hear that anyone disliked him? Had a bone to pick with him?" she asked.

He paused. "I don't want to get anyone in trouble . . . especially a coworker. I mean, that could make things really tough around here."

"We can only do our job if people tell us the truth," Claire said. "Right now, we're trying to gather facts in order to somehow connect all the dots. We need to find out who murdered Mr. Helms in cold blood."

"Okay," Erik said. "Okay. But you didn't hear it from me." He paused and looked at the investigators for a long minute. "Darlene Nichols told me not long ago that she overheard Heidi Flynn whispering on her cell phone in a stall in the women's bathroom. Heidi didn't know Darlene had walked in. She heard Heidi talking about needing ammunition for her pistol. Maybe that is something you should know."

"Did Darlene tell you she heard any more of Heidi's conversation?" Guy asked.

"No," he said. "I believe that was all."

"Last question for you today," Guy said. "Where were you when

Blake Helms was murdered—between midnight and 7:00 a.m. yesterday?"

"I was asleep at home. Believe me, we all knew you'd be asking us this question."

THE NEXT employee took a seat across from the interviewers.

"Please state your name, age, and position at the lodge," Guy said.

"Nora Sanders. Age thirty-one. Server in Riley's Pub. I work the lunch and dinner shifts. Riley's doesn't serve breakfast."

"And how long have you been employed by the lodge?" Guy asked.

"Five years. Since it opened." She fiddled with her brunette ponytail and then picked at her fingernails.

"What was your relationship with the murder victim, Blake Helms?" Claire asked.

"We were coworkers at the lodge. Didn't know him all that well," Nora said.

"Did you ever talk with him?" Claire asked.

"Not really. Nothing other than saying hello when I saw him and maybe commenting on the weather."

"Where were you yesterday—between twelve o'clock midnight and seven in the morning?" Claire asked.

"Sleeping, like I always am at that time of day."

"Did Mr. Helms have any enemies?" Claire asked.

"I've heard that some people didn't like him. Something about his superior attitude, I guess."

"Did you ever hear anyone threaten him, either to his face or behind his back?" Guy asked.

"Well, my immediate supervisor, Hazel Schroeder, didn't care for the man. The two were always arguing about something or another. One time, after a terrible argument, I heard her say, 'The man needs to exit stage left.' I never gave her comment much thought . . . until he wound up dead."

THREE INTERVIEWS to go. A young man walked in. His hair resembled corkscrew pasta, and he had a spring in his step.

"Have a seat please," Claire said. "Let's start with your name, age, and position here at the lodge."

"No problem. My name is Mitchell Green. Mitch. I'm twenty-five, and I'm a server at Riley's Pub. Actually, I'm the bartender *and* a server. I wear two hats. Cover both lunch and dinner. Usually take a few hours' break between them." His right eye twitched.

"How long have you worked at the lodge, Mitch?" Claire asked.

"'Bout three years."

"So you and Nora Sanders are the servers at the pub, and you also act as the bartender?" Claire asked.

"Exactly." The tick under his eye returned. "Nora starts at noon when the pub opens, works lunch, and then returns to work the dinner rush. I come in around three. We both stay until 11:00 p.m.—closing time," Mitch said.

"Did you know Blake Helms?" Guy asked.

"Yeah. I mean, I knew who he was. He had a bad ending, didn't he?"

"He did," Guy said. "What do you know about that?"

"Only what I've heard. That he was shot several times at the check-in counter during his shift on Thursday—early in the morning. Heard it was a robbery. That he probably should have let the thief steal the paintings and not tried to stop him. Stolen art wasn't worth his life. Heard he probably went for the phone to call for help, and that's when he got it." His eye went into spasms.

"There was no evidence of that," Guy said. "That he went for the phone. Who told you that?"

He thought for a few seconds. "Must have been Hazel Schroeder. Yeah. It was Hazel, all right. Anyway, that's what everyone is probably thinking. He wasn't the kind of man to stand by and watch something bad happen without trying to stop it. More than likely, he'd have tried to control the situation."

Claire wrote down a few notes.

"Mitch, did you ever have a run-in with Blake Helms?" Claire asked.

"Me, personally? Certainly not! Did someone tell you that I did? Because if they did, they're fibbing."

"No, no one told us that. I was just asking the question," Claire responded. "A simple question."

"Oh." The eye tremor returned. This time, Mitch applied pressure just under his eye with the index finger of his right hand.

"Did you ever witness a run-in, argument, or fight between Mr. Helms and anyone else?" she asked.

"Okay. I've seen the owner, Jay Cantrell, wrangle with Blake. Don't think they cared much for each other. He's the only one."

"How often did you see the two of them arguing?" Claire asked.

Mitch chuckled under his breath. "Least once a week, I'd say." His right eye acted up again. "It happened a lot."

"Was it just words? Angry words? Or did you ever see either one throw a punch?" she asked.

"Well, mostly words, but one time I saw Blake pointing his finger in Jay's face. It was outside on the grounds. Jay raised his fist to Blake, but didn't strike him. Seemed like quite an argument, though, between the two of them."

"How long ago did this happen?" Guy asked.

"Several days ago, I'd say. Staff started to gossip about it. They didn't know if it was work related or . . ." His eye spasm seemed uncontrollable now. He grabbed the skin under his eye with his right hand and pinched it, desperately trying to stop the tic.

"Or *what*, Mitch?" Claire asked.

Mitch sat in silence. "I don't know if I should even bring this up."

"Please do," Guy said. "We need to hear it."

"Well, there has been talk among the staffers that Piper Cantrell and Blake Helms were a little too friendly with each other, if you get my drift. So, workers thought maybe Jay threatened Blake that day . . . told him to stay away from his wife or lose his job . . . something like that." He covered his eye completely with his right hand.

"What do you think about that rumor?" Claire asked. "About Piper Cantrell and Mr. Helms?"

"Beats me. Stranger things have happened. Jay is always so busy with things that he never seems to pay attention to his wife. So, who knows? Maybe Blake paid attention to her." He shrugged his shoulders.

"Mitch, where were you at the time of the murder? Between midnight and 7:00 a.m. yesterday?" Guy asked.

"Well, probably watching a little late-night TV, and then sleeping."

THE SEEMINGLY endless insinuation that Piper Cantrell was having an affair with Blake Helms had to be addressed. After all, it provided motive for the murder. Soon, Claire thought, they would have to broach the subject with their friends. They could put it off no longer. The prospect did not appeal to them.

9

TWO LODGE EMPLOYEES remained to be interviewed. The next witness appeared before the investigators.

"Have a seat, please," Claire said. "Tell us your name, age, and position at the lodge."

"I'm Rosie Flores. I'm twenty, and I'm one of the housekeepers. I clean guest rooms."

A heavy-set young lady, her dark, curly hair framed a face riddled with severe acne.

"Okay, Rosie, how long have you worked at the lodge?" Guy asked.

"A year and a half now," the housekeeper said.

Claire checked her notes. "Then you work alongside Heidi Flynn and Dahlia Young? To clean the guest rooms?"

"Exactly. The three of us split up the rooms," Rosie said. "I came in late today because I wasn't feeling well this morning, so I'm here till five. Usually, my workday is over at three, unless they ask me to work later. If folks have late checkouts, sometimes I don't leave until six or so. Depends on the day."

"Where were you born, Rosie?" Claire asked.

"Mexico. My family moved to the States when I was a baby. We lived in Texas for five years before coming to Montana."

"How well did you know Blake Helms?" Guy asked.

"Only by face and name. We never talked."

"Did you ever hear that someone didn't like him? Had a grudge against him? Anything like that?" Claire asked.

"Not really. I know Heidi Flynn didn't like him. She called him an—can I say the word?"

Guy nodded.

"An asshole. She said he reamed her out a few times for nothing. He told her to start cleaning the rooms more thoroughly or she'd be in big trouble with the boss, Jay Cantrell. Blake didn't want to get any more complaints on her work. She didn't like how he talked to her. She didn't like his 'tude."

"As in, *attitude*?" Claire asked.

Guy held back a smile.

"Exactly," Rosie said.

"Are you friendly with Heidi Flynn and Dahlia Young?" Claire asked.

"Dahlia and I are friends, I guess." She smiled. "At work, anyway. Dahlia's a nice girl."

"And how about Heidi Flynn?" Claire asked.

"I'd rather not talk about her, if you don't mind," the housekeeper said.

"Why is that?" Claire asked.

"I'd rather not say," Rosie responded.

"Well, Rosie, now you've piqued our curiosity. I'm afraid we need an answer to that question, so I'll ask you again," Claire said. "Are you friendly with Heidi Flynn? If not, why not?"

Rosie sat stiffly and looked downward. She bit her lip and refused to answer.

Claire studied the employee intently. "What is it?"

Rosie slowly raised her head until her eyes met Claire's. "I fear her. That girl makes me pee my pants."

Claire continued to observe the witness with keen interest.

"So, you're afraid of her? Has she ever threatened you?" Guy asked.

Again Rosie dropped her head and refused to answer the question.

"Rosie," Claire said. "We're trying to identify a murderer. Anything you know that may be helpful to our case, please tell us. It will stay right here in this room."

"She won't know what I tell you?" Rosie asked. "Promise? No one will?"

"We give you our word," Claire said.

Guy nodded.

"Heidi got real mad at me one time. Thought she had to clean an extra room . . . thought that I hadn't done my share. But I had. She had counted wrong. She picked a fight with me and threatened to sock me in the stomach. Then she pulled a pistol from her purse and aimed it at me. I thought she was going to kill me."

"Then what happened?" Claire asked.

"Heidi started to laugh. She opened the chamber to show me the gun wasn't loaded. Said she kept the bullets separate from the gun, in a box in her purse. She laughed herself silly when she realized I had wet my pants. Called me a whiny wimp."

"Did you tell anyone about this, Rosie?" Claire asked. "Report the incident to the sheriff? Or to Jay or Piper Cantrell?"

"No. Heidi warned me not to, or she said the next time the gun would be loaded. I kept silent, and from then on, I've kept my distance from her. She's no good, that one. She's not right in the head. Plumb *loco*, if you ask me. But somehow, she has a boyfriend."

"A boyfriend?" Claire asked. "Heidi has a boyfriend? What's his name?"

"Don't know. Never seen him. Neither has Dahlia. But we've both heard Heidi talking to him on her cell phone. Never calls him by name, though."

"Getting back to the incident with Heidi—did anyone witness her pointing a gun at you?" Guy asked.

"No. It was just the two of us. She made sure of that."

"Rosie, where were you at the time Mr. Helms was murdered? Yesterday, between midnight and 7:00 a.m.?" Guy asked.

"In bed. Sound asleep. I live by myself." She looked down. "Then up early, getting ready to come back into the lodge."

THE FINAL staff member came into the office and took a seat. She was a sturdy woman with a serious demeanor. Claire scratched a line through the last name on the employee list.

"Please state your name, age, and position here at the lodge," Guy said.

"Darlene Nichols. I'm forty. I'm a dinner chef at the Terra Restaurant and Riley's Pub. You've probably heard that the same kitchen prepares food for both restaurants. I have the same position as Erik Johannson. He told me the questions you'd be asking me after his meeting with you earlier. So, let's begin and get this over with."

"Okay then, Darlene, how long have you been a chef at the lodge?" Guy asked.

Claire eyed the witness.

"Two years. Erik and I were hired at the same time. There's lots of turnover at a job like this. People come and go fairly often."

"Tell us about Blake Helms. What was your relationship with

him?" Claire asked.

"*Relationship?* I wouldn't refer to it as a relationship," Darlene said. "I think I spoke to the man fewer than a dozen times, ever. And each time it was the same two words, *good evening.* I would leave the lodge at eleven, and he would arrive at the same time to start his all-nighter."

Claire referred to her notes. "Do you know Heidi Flynn?"

"Yes, she's a housekeeper here."

"Does Heidi own a gun?" Claire asked.

Darlene shot Claire a dumbstruck look. "How would *I* know *that*?"

Claire had to be careful. She did not want to betray the trust and testimony of Erik Johannson.

"There have been some statements made to us indicating that she may own a gun, and I'm interested in learning if you know anything about that," Claire said.

"No, I certainly do not." Darlene avoided eye contact with the investigators, and her body tensed. Her hands touched her throat.

Claire observed the glaring nervousness surrounding this employee. She knew the look, the movements. This interviewee wanted to get up from her chair, walk briskly from the room, and never look back. But that option was not on the table. Now was the time for her to make a decision, and Claire realized Darlene was struggling fiercely with it. Should she continue to lie? Or tell the truth? Which choice should she make? Claire had seen this before. People who did not want to get involved in a criminal matter. Individuals who feared having to testify in court. Witnesses who had *convenient* memory losses. But it was now or never. Tell the truth, or lie about the situation from this moment onward. The decision fell squarely on Darlene's shoulders.

Claire sensed Darlene's straddling with how much to reveal, so she tried to coax the chef to come clean. "If you do know anything about this, now would be a great time to tell us. The truth always has a way of coming to the surface."

Darlene looked at Claire. The employee tucked her heavily highlighted, shoulder-length hair behind her ears. Their eyes locked. Claire did not blink nor look away. Darlene held her own for a long minute or two. Then her eyes darted off to the side. She turned ashen.

Claire continued to sense Darlene's internal struggle and could almost hear her inner debate. Darlene felt trapped. Certainly, she did not want Heidi on her bad side by thrusting the interrogators in her direction. But on the other hand, she did not want to lie to the investigators and get nailed for that down the road, either. She knew Heidi owned a gun. If she continued to lie, she could face perjury charges, should testifying in this matter on the witness stand ever become a reality. What should she do? *What?* Claire knew that a myriad of these types of thoughts raced through the interviewee's head. It was decision time. And it was apparent the witness felt great pressure bearing down on her from the eyes of the investigators. It was time to face the music and decide what to do. There was no time left for Darlene to stall.

Silence owned the room. Neither Claire nor Guy said a word. The powerful absence of speaking became wholly uncomfortable for the employee, and she squirmed in her seat like a worm being eyed by a large bird. A full five minutes passed. Sweat poured from Darlene's brow, and she looked alarmed. Her face flushed, and she shivered with apparent chills.

"Want to try your answer again, Darlene?" Claire asked, at last breaking the silence.

"Do I have a choice?" the chef asked.

"Well, we all have choices," Claire said. "But in this case, your best choice is to level with us. To tell the truth. The whole truth."

"Okay. Okay. Okay." Darlene exhaled deeply. "I walked into the ladies' room one day, on the upper level, and I heard Heidi whispering in a closed stall. She didn't know I had walked in, and I want it to stay that way. She was talking to someone about getting ammunition for her pistol. I snuck out, and she never knew I was in there. But before I left, I peeked into her purse. She had left it sitting wide open on the countertop—by the sink. That's when I saw it." She paused. "The handle of the gun sticking out." She inhaled deeply. "You realize bringing a gun into the lodge is grounds for automatic and immediate dismissal from employment. I didn't want Heidi on my case for getting her fired if I said anything, so I remained quiet about seeing it. I've been around guns my whole life, but seeing this one scared me to death. I'm not sure why."

Claire picked up her pen and furiously scratched notes.

"Where were you between midnight and 7:00 a.m. yesterday?" Guy asked.

"Where was *I*?" She rubbed her nose with her right hand. "Well, I get home a little after eleven, watch some TV, have something to eat, and then hit the hay. That's what I always do, so that's my answer."

"Are you married, Ms. Nichols?" Guy asked.

"I am not."

THE INITIAL interviewing of the employees had concluded earlier than expected. Claire grabbed the landline phone in the room and dialed Sheriff Bell's number. When she gave him the good news, he said, "I'm on my way. I'll be there soon. Please wait."

When he arrived, the two sleuths filled the sheriff in on each of the day's interviews, one by one.

"Most interesting," he said. "You've done yeoman's work. As I told you before, I'm impressed, and it takes a lot to impress me. Looks like we need to do some follow-up work on several of the employees

ASAP. I've made up a list of names based upon what you've reported to me." He placed his hand under his chin, as if holding up his face. "And if you wouldn't mind, we'd like to keep the two of you on this case for a short while longer. After we get the lab and autopsy reports back, perhaps we can kick this investigation into high gear and get an arrest made."

"Say no more. You've got our help," Claire said.

"It'd be a good idea for you two to meet with the Whitefish police chief and his team, working the burglary cases in Whitefish. Take a look through their files. See what you can find. As you know, my department has been called upon to assist on those break-ins in the Iron Horse community. We're all wondering if this murder and robbery in Bigfork is related. Maybe the two of you can review the evidence collected so far in those cases and see if anything jumps out at you? You could look for similarities between the two matters—and differences, as well. Are you willing to do this?" the sheriff asked.

"We had already planned to drive to Whitefish tomorrow, so that'll work out just fine," Guy said. "Please let the Whitefish Police Department know we're coming and arrange to have the files available for us to look at. Perhaps you can also request that an officer working the burglary cases be available to sit down with us to review the facts surrounding the invasions. That, of course, would be helpful."

"Consider it done, Mr. Lombard," Sheriff Bell said. "What time do you plan on being there tomorrow?"

"By 10:00 a.m.," Claire said.

"The files will be waiting for you at ten o'clock sharp. And I'll ask the lead detective to make sure he's there to fill you in on everything. The rash of crimes occurring in Whitefish has us at a loss. Most all of the homes in that expensive Iron Horse community have sophisticated security systems. Yet in each case, the burglar has been able to get past the front-door lock and somehow bypass each and every system. Alarms never activate. By the time we become aware of the burglary, the thief is long gone. The townsfolk are emotional wrecks. They're afraid to go to sleep at night. It's been ongoing for weeks now." The sheriff sighed. "Maybe two fresh sets of eyes are just what we need to bring this string of disasters to a conclusion."

"We'll do our best," Guy said.

"See if there's any connection between what's happening in Whitefish and what happened here in Bigfork," Sheriff Bell said. "Are we looking at the same perpetrator who simply moved into a different territory? Are we looking at a copycat criminal hoping to make off with valuable pieces of art in Bigfork and then walk away scot-free, seeing the Whitefish culprit eventually take the blame? Did Blake end up murdered because he refused to cooperate during a robbery? Or was the Bigfork murder different from the others? Was it personal? Was Blake the target? Check it out, and give us your professional opinion, will you? Lots of questions, I know. We need the answers."

"We've considered the possibility from the start that the target may not have been the artwork at all in the Bigfork case," Claire said. "The killing of Blake Helms may well have been the motive for the crime, pure and simple. And the murderer then lifted the artwork and slashed the furniture only and solely to throw us off the track, to mimic the Whitefish cases. We just don't know yet."

Sheriff Bell stared at Claire. "You think that's what it is, don't you? I can see it on your face. You believe someone walked into the lodge with the premeditated intent to murder Mr. Helms."

"Right now, I only have my hunches," she said. "And I never verbalize hunches. I will say I think there's a lot more to the story than we know at this point. Once the lab results are back, we'll have some hard facts to go on, and it can't be soon enough."

"Very well, then. Contact me over the weekend if you need me," the sheriff said. "And I'll catch up with you as soon as the results from the crime labs come in," the sheriff said. "Remember, you've got my cell number on the back of my card."

"Got it," Guy said.

"We owe the two of you a big thanks for pitching in," Sheriff Bell said. "We usually don't see this much serious criminal activity in our little part of the world. It's most unusual."

"Don't thank us yet," Claire said. "The murder and the burglaries are still not solved."

"A final issue. Are you planning to interview the Cantrells?" the sheriff asked. "I realize this cannot be an easy situation for the two of you—viewing your friends as potential suspects and considering the possibility that Piper may be having an affair. But knowing you both the short time I have, I'm convinced you will act in a professional manner and do what you have to do. I have no doubts about that."

"Of course," Claire said. "We've been talking to them every chance we get to learn additional information. But we do need to ask them both where they were at the time of the murder and also attempt to confirm whether Piper and Blake were involved."

"Well, good luck with that, and keep me posted. I want answers to those questions," Sheriff Bell said. "Because right about now, it looks like Jay Cantrell had a powerful motive to commit the murder."

THAT EVENING, the investigators and the Cantrells ate dinner at the Terra Restaurant. They supped outside on the veranda, under the dark, star-filled Montana sky. Since the time Claire and Guy had arrived in Big Sky Country, they had been almost exclusively consumed by the murder investigation—the lunches and dinners with their friends providing the only real respites for the pair.

That evening, the women ordered the coconut-crusted grouper served with kaffir lime sauce, and the men ordered the Blue Mesa Ranch tenderloin steaks with cracked peppercorn topping. Fry bread, salads, savory vegetables, and rice pilaf accompanied the entrées. Jay ordered a bottle of wine for the table, and for dessert, the foursome shared a huckleberry mud pie. Afterward, Katie Kyle cleared the table, and the foursome sipped on freshly brewed coffee while enjoying the crisp Montana air.

Claire was the one to raise the difficult subjects with Piper and Jay.

"It's difficult for me to broach this subject with you, my friends, but I'm afraid I have to," Claire said, keeping her voice low. "We need to ask you both where you were at the time of Blake's killing. We're asking everyone."

"We were both at home sleeping," Jay said. "Where the hell do you think we were?" He glared at the sleuths.

"Back off, Jay," Guy said. "It's a fair question."

"Piper?" Claire asked.

"Yeah, we were asleep in our bed."

"There is one other question," Claire said. "And this is more difficult to ask than the first. Several of the employees we interviewed have implied that the two of you may be having some marital problems." She paused. "In fact, many believe that you, Piper, might even have been involved in an *affair* with Blake Helms. And while this would be none of our business under normal circumstances, these are not normal circumstances. A cold-blooded murder has been committed at your lodge."

Piper dropped her gaze to her lap, and Jay looked off in another direction.

"So, I must ask the question. Is there any truth whatsoever to these rumors?" Claire asked.

Piper did not respond. Jay's face reddened, and a disgusted demeanor owned him.

"Now that's a *very* personal question," Jay said. "*Especially* coming from a friend."

"I realize that it is," Claire said, "and believe me, I dreaded asking it. But we must know the truth. The sheriff's office is demanding to know. As soon as we are able, we'd love to remove you both from the list of possible suspects."

"I'm . . . *we're* actually on a *suspect* list? Are you kidding?" Jay asked. He inhaled and exhaled in rapid succession, beside himself with sudden fury.

Piper stared at Jay, then bolted from the table in tears.

Jay got up and walked away.

"So much for asking the horribly sensitive questions," Guy said. "That just blew up in our faces. More coffee?"

Saturday morning
Whitefish, Montana

THE CLOCK IN the green Discovery 4 x 4 displayed 9:00 a.m. when the investigators started out on the drive to Whitefish. Guy manned the wheel as Claire watched the map. They traveled north on Montana Highway 35, headed west on Montana Highway 82, and then turned onto US Highway 93 to drive north again all the way up to Whitefish. It was a twenty-seven-mile trip.

The mainly rural drive offered the sleuths a firsthand view of much of the landscape of Flathead Valley, or the Flathead, as local Montanans called it; the natural beauty of the untroubled plains that went on for miles and miles; the seemingly endless mountain ranges of the Rockies; and the thick western forests of ponderosa pines. The enormous, clear blue sky hung precisely just above it all, as if cranked closely to the ground by a stagehand. Neither Guy nor Claire had ever seen *so much sky.* Veils of white clouds hung innocently within the overhead mass of baby blue that morning, appearing to be pasted in place. Deer—alone, in a pair, or in a grouping—stood quietly in many of the open areas. And large flat fields bordered either side of the roadways for much of the trek. Under the radiance of the sun's summer light, sections of yellow, purple, gold, and green grasses emerged within the fields, as if illuminated from beneath the surface.

The investigators passed occasional logging trucks that morning. Each carried a shipment of logs to a specific site, where contractors would construct the home or cabin by matching the numbers on a building plan to the numbers on the logs. The two also observed farms along the way, many with sun-weathered, dilapidated red barns and silver-capped silos. And pastures, dotted with large tubular-shaped hay bales, drew their attention. Several older-model broken-down trucks sat just off the roadway, never to be driven again.

Claire rolled down the front passenger window and inhaled the miscellany of pleasant outside aromas, enjoying the delightful drive with Guy.

"I can't get over the dramatic contrast between this area and Florida," she said. She inhaled deeply again. "It's hard to believe we're even in the same country."

"It's nice, I must admit," Guy said. "But you'd get bored if you lived here full-time, Claire. I know you. What would you do to stay busy up here in northwestern Montana? How would you handle all those pent-up investigator instincts with so few cases to work on? Keep them bottled up inside until they screamed to come out?

No, Claire, you would not be happy unless you were investigating some case or another all the time. It's in your blood. You were born a sleuth, and that is what you must be." He looked over and started grinning, but cut it short.

"You wanted to grin your famous grin, didn't you?" Claire asked. "I saw the beginning of it. I did. The grin I've missed so much. The real Gaston Lombard thought about returning for a quick second there, but you held back." She stared at him with a fixed gaze. "No one else notices the change, but I do. I want the old Guy back."

He looked at her and said nothing.

"You're considering returning, aren't you?" Claire persisted. "With all of your heart and all of your soul, you want to. You're thinking long and hard about letting go of the past and coming back to the present. You can't fool me. Just let it happen. Don't fight it." She slid a hand over to his upper thigh and left it there. He liked to drive that way. "And you might be right about what you just said about me having to be an investigator. I could no more turn it off than I could stop breathing . . . at least for the time being. But who knows about the future? Retirement in Montana doesn't sound half-bad, does it? That's years away, though."

They passed a sign indicating a turnoff for Glacier National Park and another indicating the remaining travel miles to the well-known Big Mountain ski area in Whitefish. Then before they knew it, a white sign with black lettering appeared, announcing their arrival in the town of Whitefish. Their first stop was the Whitefish Police Department at 275 Flathead Avenue, and they needed to get there fast. It was only minutes before ten, and they wanted to be on time. Claire reached into her purse and pulled out the directions Sheriff Bell had jotted down. She read them aloud to Guy as they traveled down the streets of Whitefish, and minutes later they pulled up to their destination.

The investigators walked into the police station and up to the dispatcher's desk.

"You would be Claire Caswell and Gaston Lombard, I assume?" the woman sitting behind the desk asked.

"Correct," Guy said.

Both Guy and Claire handed the woman a business card.

"We've been expecting you," the dispatcher said. She greeted them both with a hearty handshake. "It's not often we see investigators from Miami in this neck of the woods. In fact, I think I'm safe in saying it's *never* happened before." She chuckled and smiled at the two. "Detective Lieutenant Keller and Detective Briggs are waiting for you in the conference room. Chief Soderberg also came in for the meeting, and it takes a lot to get him to come in on a Saturday. That alone speaks volumes for your reputation." She got up from her chair. "Follow me, please."

She led the sleuths to a good-sized conference room and closed the door behind her on her way out. Inside the room, a massive golden pine table and fourteen matching chairs took up the space. When the investigators walked in, the three men quickly stood and rushed over to make formal introductions.

"I'm chief of the Whitefish Police Department, Stan Soderberg," the milky-haired man said.

"And I'm Detective Lieutenant Herb Keller," the tallest man said.

"Detective Curtis Briggs," the youngest of the three men said.

Claire Caswell and Gaston Lombard introduced themselves, and business cards were exchanged all around. Everyone took a seat. The table was littered with files and other paperwork from end to end.

A knock was heard at the door, followed by a reserve officer delivering a tray of coffee and cookies to the group.

"First, let me say that it is our utmost pleasure to discuss this matter with the two of you," Chief Soderberg said. "In fact, when I heard you were here in Montana and learned the full extent of your reputation as investigators, I felt a flicker of hope for the first time in weeks." He sighed deeply. "Whitefish is a low-key, tightly knit community. We're known as a resort and retirement area. People come here to enjoy winter sports—especially downhill skiing and boarding—and also summer sports like golf, fishing, hiking, canoeing, and horseback riding. We live an uncomplicated life here in Whitefish, far away from the whirlwind of a big city. And we like it that way."

"That is, until recent weeks," Detective Lieutenant Keller jumped in, "when all hell broke loose here in our quiet little town. The good folks of Whitefish are now afraid to close their eyes and go to sleep at night . . . in fear of what is going on. They're simply scared silly." He paused and furrowed his brow.

"We're idling in neutral," Detective Briggs said. "We've put in a lot of time and manpower on this case, yet we've hit nothing but roadblocks at each and every turn. Whoever this person is, he's a pro. He's in and out of the houses before the police are ever notified. And the homes are strategically positioned among the trails and pines of the eight-hundred-and-twenty-acre Iron Horse property—just far enough away from each other so that neighbors never hear or see a thing at the time a burglary is underway. It's usually a housekeeper, or a neighbor checking in on a house for another owner, who discovers the crime."

"Please tell us everything you know," Claire said. "Consider no detail too small. Let's start with how many of these burglaries have occurred. And over what period of time."

"There have been nine now," Chief Soderberg said, "over the past two months. About one each week since they started, plus another recent one."

"He always hits when the owners are away," Detective Briggs said. "Some live in the homes permanently, but many use these residences as vacation homes, making only short, irregular visits throughout the year. We figure the intruder must stake out each property he intends to enter, surveilling it for some time prior to make certain the owners are not at home. It's always the same mode of operation."

"He's in and out quickly," Detective Lieutenant Keller added. "He's able to gain entry and then disarm any security system within thirty seconds—before the alarm sounds and before the monitoring company is alerted. There appears to be no system he cannot disable. In every case, he moves with the speed of lightning, clearing the properties of the valuable art and other items in a flash."

Claire and Guy listened wide-eyed.

"In no time at all, the intruder empties the safe contents of money, jewelry, and other valuables, and he lifts specific pieces of original artwork from the walls," the detective lieutenant continued. "He seems to have a knack for knowing which pieces of art are the most valuable. He never takes anything other than original oils, acrylics, and watercolors. Never wastes his time on a mere print. He enters, does his thing, and is gone in a flash."

"He works not only quickly, but with great precision," Chief Soderberg said. "We've never seen *anything* like it before. He is daring and fearless, but not reckless. He knows exactly what he's doing. The man has nerves of steel."

"What evidence or clues to the burglar's identity have you found at any of the entered homes?" Claire asked.

"Almost nothing," Detective Briggs said. "That's the most difficult part." A look of utter frustration took over his face, and he scratched his brow. "We've searched each house, inside and out, with a fine-tooth comb. The robber leaves behind no evidence of his being there. No fingerprints or palm prints or other DNA, and no tire marks, almost as if the tires on his getaway vehicle are bald. And no shoeprints, except for a single imprint found at one location. It almost looks as if he has swept away his print path with a large pine bough afterward."

"You've had the shoeprint analyzed, I assume?" Guy asked.

"We have," Chief Soderberg said. "It belongs to a man with a size 9 foot. The print was made by a tennis shoe, a common sneaker. We figure the thief missed one print in his hurry to leave the scene in that particular case. Maybe he heard us or a neighbor's car approaching."

"Did you ever consider the print might have been made by a *woman*?" Claire asked.

All eyes in the room darted to her.

"We did," Chief Soderberg said. "Ruled it out, however. Due to the depth of the imprint and of the walking pattern, the lab determined it was definitely made by a male. Great question, though." He thought further. "And we're of the assumption he acts alone."

"But you have no proof of that, do you?" Claire asked.

"We do not," the chief said, "but it's the angle we've been working from."

Claire closed her eyes. "The thief is nimble, probably not carrying too much weight on his frame. He's adept with intricate detail work. And he's absolutely desperate," she said.

The chief, detective lieutenant, and detective eyed her carefully.

"This is exactly what the profilers we consulted with told us," the detective lieutenant said, "except for the 'absolutely desperate' part. That's something new."

"He's living on the edge," Claire continued, her eyes remaining closed. "We all know the saying, *desperate people do desperate things*. This thief is in a dire financial situation. Identify a man with *enormous* money problems, and you may find your perp." She opened her eyes.

"Have any of the stolen paintings or jewelry turned up anywhere?" Guy asked.

"Not yet," the detective said. "We keep waiting for that to happen. We've notified all the big buyers and galleries around this area and throughout the US." He paused to reflect. "We're in a foggy blur on this case. We have almost nothing to go on, and the townspeople are demanding action on our part. They want the perp picked up *yesterday*."

"I'm thinking . . ." Claire started. She stared straight ahead, and Guy knew the wheels inside her head were turning at a rapid rate. "Do you have an aerial photograph of the Iron Horse property?"

"We do," the detective said. "Right here in this folder." He lifted a yellow file from the table, sorted through it, and handed Claire two aerial photographs of the area—one pristine, the other marked with encircled *X*s made with a black felt-tip marker. "The *X*s indicate where each of the burglaries has occurred to date."

Claire studied the photos for a few long minutes without saying a word. She then passed them to Guy for his perusal.

"I have a question," she said. "How do you know the thief actually leaves with the stolen property in his vehicle at the time of each heist?"

The three members of the Whitefish Police Department looked stunned. "Meaning exactly *what*, Ms. Caswell?" Detective Lieutenant Keller asked.

"Yes, what is the implication, Ms. Caswell?" Chief Soderberg asked.

"Well, what if he simply lugs the stolen items outside and hides them in a covert spot among the pines, not far from the house, to be picked up later? This is a heavily wooded area from the looks of it," she said. "That way, he could run away on foot to his vehicle that he left parked on a side road away from the residence. He could even stay in his vehicle, hiding in plain sight, so to speak, if the police are somehow alerted and arrive quickly to the property, that way avoiding any possible confrontation with a squad car rushing to the scene."

All eyes in the room were glued to Claire Caswell.

"He could come back the following night to retrieve his booty," she continued, "after everyone presumes he's long gone. Or he could even wait a few days. Then he could roll up, or even back up, in the dead of night to a position near the house with his vehicle lights turned off. He'd be able to collect the stolen property he secreted away with no one being the wiser."

The occupants of the room sat still.

"I guess we never even considered that possibility, Ms. Caswell," the detective lieutenant said. "It would make for a clever plan, though, wouldn't it? And it might explain how he does it. We could never understand how he gained access, lugged everything out, loaded it up, and made off without ever being seen by a security guard making rounds throughout the area during the nighttime hours. It seemed impossible."

"For now, it's just a theory," Claire said. "You might want to have your patrol officers look closely around the densely wooded perimeters of each of those houses. See if they can spot any evidence of items being stowed in a particular place. Framed artwork is heavy and would most probably leave an imprint."

"We'll do it immediately," the chief said. "Could I interest the two of you in driving out there with us to take a look around?"

"I thought you'd never ask," Claire said. She smiled.

"Before we leave," Guy said, "let's discuss the recent murder at Mountain Lake Lodge in Bigfork. Are you assuming it was committed by the same unidentified perpetrator of these crimes?"

"It seems the logical conclusion," Detective Briggs said. "The murder and theft of artwork happened in the dead of night, a relatively short driving distance from here. Seems to be a similar modus operandi. Yes, I guess it's the same intruder in all probability. Odds of having two art thieves operating within this area at the same time would be extremely remote."

The chief and detective lieutenant nodded in agreement.

"Or the murderer is someone who wants us all to think just that," Claire said. "The Bigfork killer could be someone taking advantage of the Whitefish situation. Think about it. The burglar in the Whitefish cases has never committed murder. He seems to be a burglar through and through. Bigfork, although admittedly only a forty-or forty-five-mile drive from here, is a wholly different geographical area. And consider this: the culprit in the Whitefish cases never leaves behind a clue that he's been in the houses. He is meticulous to a fault in covering his tracks, with the exception of the one missed shoe impression you told us about. In the Bigfork incident, we have found several clues left behind. In fact, we're waiting to hear back from the various crime labs on their findings in the coming week." She hesitated for a moment. "No. My gut instinct tells me we're looking at two different criminals."

Again, silence dominated the room.

"I've learned to listen to Claire's instincts over the years, gentlemen," Guy said. "They're usually right on the mark."

All three men exhaled in unison, each nodding his head, seemingly dazed by the revelations.

"Ready to take a drive over to Iron Horse?" Chief Soderberg asked the investigators.

"We are," Guy said.

"Great. We'll take my SUV."

THE DRIVE into the Iron Horse development was absolutely breathtaking. Spectacular residences, each an ingenious blend of rustic and elegant construction, were sporadically scattered on either side of the roads throughout the hilly, private golf enclave. A dense old-growth forest of pine trees and other vegetation provided the backdrop. Claire noted that the magnificent, mostly custom homes were distanced far enough apart from each other to offer the homeowners the feeling of ultimate privacy. The residences oozed luxury, comfort, and extravagant living, each with an obvious price tag of several million dollars. The neighborhood smelled of wealth and prosperity. Prime temptation for a burglar, she thought.

The chief eventually slowed his vehicle and pulled into a specific driveway, steering the SUV toward a masterpiece home.

"We're here. This is the first home hit by the burglar," he announced. He stopped near the front entrance. "Before we get started, I want to let the homeowners know what we're doing here. That is, if they're in residence." He walked to the front door, rang the doorbell, and waited a couple minutes. There was no answer. "Nobody here," he yelled out. He waved his hand high in the air, signaling it was okay to get started.

All four men walked off in different directions to start searching.

Claire walked to a location thirty feet from the front entrance and stopped to face the house's facade. She assessed the layout of the property with her eyes. *If I were a burglar, carrying property from this house, where would I store it?* she asked herself. She thought for a moment and walked in a direction the others had not.

Two minutes later, she called out loudly.

"Over here! You'll want to see this!"

11

EVIDENCE IN THE form of a bed of broken twigs, crushed leaves, and matted pine boughs confirmed Claire's suspicion, at least at this location. The burglar had lifted things from the house and stowed and concealed the items in a particular spot in the surrounding brush—to be picked up at a later time. Once Claire identified and pointed out what she had discovered, it became plainly visible to the chief, detective lieutenant, detective, and Guy.

"You'll have to check out each burglarized location," Claire said. "Look for a similar pattern at each property, not too far from the house."

"I'm on it," Chief Soderberg said. "Men, gather near." He motioned for his staff members to come closer. "Check out each one of the crime locations, and see if we can confirm this theory. If it pans out, this breaks the case wide open. It propels our investigation forward and into an entirely new direction. If we can establish this as the culprit's repeated and regular method of operation, we'll know how to conduct a proper stakeout to catch this guy." He stopped and cleared his throat. "Keep this knowledge quiet. We'll tell no one of our findings. We'll nab the intruder the next time he returns to retrieve the stolen goods. With a bit of luck on our side, we'll arrest this felon at last."

"Sounds like a sterling plan. Please keep us posted," Guy said. "If there's anything more we can do, let us know."

"You have our cell numbers on our business cards," Claire added. "Don't hesitate to call anytime. We plan to stay in the area until the Bigfork murder is solved, so we'll be around for the foreseeable future."

The chief delivered Claire, Guy, Detective Lieutenant Keller, and Detective Briggs back to the Whitefish Police Department. The three men thanked the investigators for their assistance and promised to keep them appraised on any developments in the Whitefish burglaries case.

Claire and Guy hopped into their vehicle.

"Let's find food," Guy said. "I'm famished."

"You read my mind," Claire said. "I'll look for a restaurant."

As Guy drove in and around the quaint downtown section of Whitefish, Claire searched for a place to eat.

"Let's stop there." She pointed to the Buffalo Café.

Over hamburgers topped with fried onions on dark rye buns, sweet potato fries, and sodas, the two discussed the situations in both Whitefish and Bigfork.

"The more I think about it," Guy said, "the more I, too, am convinced we're looking at two different perps. It's the most logical conclusion."

"We are," Claire said, not hesitating for a moment before blurting out her answer. "And you know what I'm thinking at this very minute? I'm thinking the burglar in the Whitefish cases may be a resident living within that very prestigious Iron Horse community—one of the homeowners themselves. Or someone who did or does work in the development. If I were a betting person, though, I'd put my money on a *homeowner*."

"Explain," Guy said.

"Well, the person knows the area far too well to *not* be an insider. The road system within that development is curvy and would be very confusing to an outsider unfamiliar with its layout—particularly in the dark of night." Claire thought for a moment. "And any stranger milling around to stake out the area would surely eventually . . . at least in *some* of the cases . . . be noticed by a homeowner, groundskeeper, clubhouse employee, or repair or service person driving by. One would think the culprit observing these homes would stick out like a sore thumb. Yeah. The more I mull it over, that's what I think. My guess is that the burglar is a homeowner in the Iron Horse community. Someone privy to the comings and goings of the other homeowners. That's what I'd check out first."

"Better call the chief and share your thoughts," Guy said. "I'd do it now."

Claire pulled out her cell phone and dialed the chief's number.

"Chief Soderberg? It's Claire Caswell. Sorry to bother you so soon after we left, but I have another theory on the Whitefish burglaries." She quickly conveyed her thoughts. "Look for an *owner* who has recently been confronted with grave financial problems."

CLAIRE AND Guy spent the remainder of the day strolling through the town of Whitefish. They visited the shops on both sides of Main Street—those offering pottery, clothing, premium Western and leather wear, antiques, original art, and gifts. And they couldn't help but notice the abundance of bars in the small community—bars that seemingly were pulled right out of an old Western movie. The sense of going back in time had a strong emotional effect on the sleuths, and they were immediately drawn into the experience.

"How is it possible Whitefish and Miami are only hours apart by plane? They're the antitheses of each other," Guy remarked.

Claire chuckled briefly. "Refreshing, isn't it?"

But as hard as they tried to enjoy themselves, to relish their time in Montana, neither could stop thinking or talking about the pressing case. It hovered over them like a covering of thick, gray clouds on a rainy day.

The investigators walked into a local coffeehouse and ordered caffè mochas. They sipped on the delightful whipped cream-topped lattes with added chocolate as they meandered arm in arm down the streets of the town. The remainder of the afternoon passed, but the case continued to take front stage in their thoughts.

Unexpectedly, Guy stopped and pulled Claire close to him. He touched her cheek in a slow motion with the back of his hand and leaned down to press his forehead on hers.

"I love you," he said. He kissed her tenderly on the lips. "Just wanted you to know that."

"Me, too—you, too," she said softly. "Love you back." She smiled sweetly.

"Whatever did I do to deserve you?" he asked.

"Whatever did *I* do to deserve *you*?" she parroted. Her face broke into a warm expression, and her eyes twinkled.

At that moment, Guy wanted in the worst way to ask Claire to marry him. Right then. Right there. *Marry me! Marry me!* he shouted the simple words silently. But something held him back from asking. Despite everything that was happening, he wanted so badly to pose the question and hear her say *yes*. But what *if*? What if she put off answering him yet again? It would be the third time, and he wouldn't allow himself the potential humiliation, the possible sense of appearing too desperate. After all, he had his pride. He was Gaston Lombard, former Miami-Dade state attorney. Fearless. Formidable. Uncompromising. He was a man causing anyone and everyone who came in contact with him in the professional realm to cower. Then why did this woman intimidate him so? Quickly thinking better of it, he decided against posing the question. At least for now.

"I'm telling you," Claire said. "I think I could actually live in a place like this with you. We could leave fast-paced Miami Beach behind and enjoy the tranquility of this laid-back setting. I could really do it . . . one of these days. Down the road."

"No. You couldn't," Guy said. "You'd be happy here for a short time, but then you'd miss the energy, the vitality, of the Beach. I know you would. I stand by my earlier assessment. You could never leave Miami Beach on a permanent basis. Never."

"I'm not so sure. Glad you are," she said. She looked directly at him and pondered the thought. "And what about you, Mr. Counselor? Could *you* leave our life on the Beach behind and move to a place like this one day? Could *you* be happy here?"

Back in Bigfork

CLAIRE PHONED Piper to let her know they'd returned.

"I hope you'll have dinner with us this evening," Piper said.

"Love to. Our treat. We noticed a sign just before arriving back in Bigfork for Moroldo's Ristorante Italiano, Italian fine dining. How does that sound?"

"Sounds rather perfect to me. And Jay loves Italian. Is seven good for you two?"

"Seven it is. That'll give us a chance to take a short nap and shower," Claire said.

"Good. You both have been working too hard. I feel guilty about the whole thing—inviting you here for a vacation and then seeing you dropped into the middle of *all of this*." She sighed. "Well, we'll pick you up then around a quarter to seven. Looking forward to it."

"Great. We'll be waiting in the parking lot by the lobby entrance," Claire said.

The investigators settled into the comfortable rustic bed, snuggled closely together, and in no time fell into a hard sleep. Rest was always the ticket for the exhausted. They woke, showered, dressed for dinner, and walked the short distance across the parking lot to the lodge entrance. The Cantrells had not yet arrived, so Claire and Guy walked up the steps and took a seat in the lobby to wait.

Claire picked up the book of lodge photos sitting on the coffee table, set it on her lap, and started turning pages. She glanced from image to image and let her mind drift. The photos of the lobby taken prior to the murder grabbed her interest. Her mind darted to her memory of the way the area had been torn apart by the person or persons who had committed the crime.

All evidence of the murder scene had now been wiped down and washed completely away. In fact, other than the empty wall spaces where framed artwork had previously hung, the lobby looked mostly as it did when Claire and Guy had first arrived. The former sofa and chairs had been quickly replaced with nearly identical pieces from Ciao Interiors in Kalispell, undamaged items had been set back in their original spots, and suitable substitutions had been found for those things unsalvageable. The holes in the wall caused by the bullets had been filled and repainted. Claire's thoughts meandered. In addition to the original paintings taken on the night of the murder, two saddles had also been heisted. This fact puzzled her. It seemed incongruous. What was she missing? Why would the murderous thief lug the old leather-worn saddles away with him? For what possible purpose? They had next-to-no value compared to the original works of art. It didn't make sense. Why bother with the saddles? She stared at the photos of the two saddles that had been placed so predominately over a section of split-wood railing in the wall display cubby above the check-in desk. The killer had to go up to the next level to gain access to them. Most burglars acted quickly, spending three minutes going in and out of a place. Why take the time to go upstairs to retrieve two distressed saddles of little value? *Why?*

She noticed a few photos of Blake Helms—some when he was standing behind the desk in the lobby and others of him standing amid certain staff members. The man would never again return to Mountain Lake Lodge to work the nightshift behind the check-in counter. He would never again read books on the Native American tribes of the area. He would never again have coffee with LoLo or talks with Piper. His life had ended. She took in a deep breath and exhaled slowly. His murderer needed to be apprehended and sent to prison. It wouldn't bring Mr. Helms back, but it would allow for justice and some form of closure to the hideous crime. She and Guy could not slow their efforts until that happened.

Just then, the honk of a car horn roused Claire from her thoughts. She returned the album to the table and together with Guy bolted down the stairs to the Cantrells' car.

The evening provided amazing authentic Italian cuisine—and strained conversation as all four tried desperately to avoid discussing the case. Piper seemed unusually quiet, obviously remaining stunned and saddened by Blake Helms's death. Jay, on the other hand, appeared unhappy and testy.

"Did you learn anything of interest on your trip to Whitefish today?" Jay asked, taking a break from eating the homemade tiramisu he ordered for dessert—and unable to avoid the subject of the investigation any longer.

"Well, we believe the man responsible for the murder of Blake Helms may not be the same man responsible for the string of crimes in Whitefish," Guy said.

"*What?*" Jay asked. "How can it *not* be the same man? In every single instance, the motive was clearly to steal valuable art. This makes no sense." He emitted a long, audible breath of downright frustration. "I've read every article about the Whitefish crook that's been posted in the newspapers. Each crime took place in the wee morning hours. Just like the lodge incident. Whitefish and Bigfork are less than an hour apart drive time." He shook his head. "I know you're the so-called *experts*, but your conclusion seems preposterous and almost laughable in my humble opinion. Ha! Ha! Ha!"

"Jay! Don't talk to our friends like that," Piper said. "I'm serious. Apologize."

Jay did not apologize nor did he relent.

"I mean, really, a kindergartner could figure this one out. It's simple two-plus-two-equals-four kind of thinking. Obviously, the same man who is stealing from people in Whitefish is the man who murdered Blake Helms to steal from us!" Jay's voice became louder and louder with each word he uttered. "How could any worthwhile investigators think differently? Shit! Maybe the two of you should consider relinquishing your private investigator licenses and instead get into another line of work!" He was shouting now, and all other patrons were watching him.

Neither Claire nor Guy had ever seen Jay act out in this type of manner. His behavior seemed strangely out of character for the man they had known so many years. He was rude and clearly out of line.

"That's enough, Jay! I mean it!" Piper said firmly. "We're leaving now. You're embarrassing yourself . . . and me, not to mention our friends." She flagged down the waiter and asked for the check. It appeared on the table within seconds of her request.

"It's on us tonight," Guy said. He grabbed the bill and quickly paid.

Jay didn't say another word. The two couples rode back to the lodge in difficult silence. Goodbyes were awkward.

Claire and Guy walked to their room and settled in for the remainder of the evening.

"What was *that* about?" Guy asked.

"I have *no* idea," Claire said, "but something's definitely wrong with Jay. Maybe pressure of some kind has been building up in him for a long time, and tonight it simply spewed out onto us. We were in his path, so we got it. I wouldn't take it personally. I think he's a man in pain."

"Well, whatever the cause, I don't like him taking it out on us. We're friends, after all," Guy said. "Or at least, I thought we were. And we're spending *our* precious vacation trying to help the authorities solve a murder that occurred at *his* lodge so *his* business will not suffer. His attitude makes me want to pack up our things and leave tomorrow."

"We can't do that," Claire said. "I think the real target of his anger is Piper, but he's unwilling to verbalize it."

Guy looked over at Claire and pondered her words. "Do you think Piper was having an affair with Blake Helms? Yes or no?" Guy asked.

"Not sure," Claire said. "Obviously, the employees of the lodge believe that to be the case, but I'm not convinced. Whether it happened or not, though, I think Jay suspects it did."

"That might explain his ill temper."

"It might."

"I hate to agree with Sheriff Bell, but it also gives Jay a gigantic motive for murder," Guy said. "The murder of Blake Helms."

"Believe me, the thought has crossed my mind more than once," Claire said. "Love . . . *passion* . . . can make a person do unpredictable things." She looked at Guy intently. "And Jay would want to see the murder pinned on someone else, if he did do it."

"Like the Whitefish burglar."

"Yeah," Claire said. "Like the Whitefish burglar." She stared straight ahead.

"What's your take?" Guy asked. "I mean, what do you believe is really going on here?"

"From the start, I've thought the killer wanted us all to think he was the same person as the one committing the burglaries in Whitefish. The timing of those incidents seemed just too convenient. The newspaper articles even stated that in addition to the thief stealing original works of art from the walls of those luxury residences, he had overturned, cut, or ripped up furniture in a couple of instances—presumably in his search for stashed valuables. So the instructions were all there for someone else to copy."

Claire paused before continuing. "But my instinct from day one has been that the killing of Blake Helms was personal, and that the stolen art and lobby scene was simply staged to mimic the Whitefish incidents after Mr. Helms was shot in a premeditated act."

"Okay, now for the tough question, Miss Crack Investigator. Is Jay Cantrell the murderer? Did he murder Blake Helms because the man was having an affair with his wife?"

"I don't think so," Claire said. "But I do think the killer is close by. My guess? Someone who works at the lodge."

"Well, *that* certainly narrows our list of suspects," he said with a half smirk.

"I know," Claire said. "The list is long."

"Can't rule Jay out, though," Guy said. "Not yet. He remains on the list until we determine the identity of the killer."

"Of course he does," Claire said. "And we never did get an answer from Piper about the alleged affair."

"Right," Guy said. "Now, for a change of subject. What time should we be on the road tomorrow to drive to Polson?"

"I'd like to leave early, since tomorrow's a 'vacation day' for us. Once Monday morning breaks, we're back on the case full-time. So, let's leave around eight." She thought for a moment. "On further thought, I think we should probably bring along our notes of the employee interviews. We can review them on the drive."

"Sounds like a plan," Guy said. "So much for a full day of vacation . . . but I know we need to review those notes."

He got up and walked over to Claire.

"It's not too late, my love," he said, glancing at his watch. He scooped her up from the chair. "Let's sit out on the balcony for a while and look at the stars. There's so little pollution here, they light up the sky."

"Hmm. Sounds romantic."

"Could be," Guy said, flashing a half grin.

He was trying hard to act like the former Guy—the person he was before the horrible incident in Crete. And that effort made Claire happy.

They walked out onto the balcony and sat down on chairs. The indigo sky squeezed a multiplicity of stars in its arms, each celestial body twinkling as if it had been newly washed and polished. The Montana mountain air was brisk and, like always, exuded the aroma of fresh pine needles. Looking straight forward, the nighttime view of Flathead Valley portrayed a still and unconditionally peaceful mountain lake landscape.

"If only this moment could last forever," Claire said.

"It doesn't get any better than this," Guy said.

The two sat in silent wonderment, enjoying Montana and each other.

It was almost impossible to believe that a brutal murder had taken place only yards from where they sat. The thought seemed incomprehensible.

After a while, Guy stood up and grabbed Claire by the hand. He pulled her up from her chair and cupped her face in his hands, kissing her tenderly under the light of the Montana moon. He whispered "*I love you*" into her ear and swept her up into his strong arms. He carried her back inside and placed her gently on the bed. Climbing in beside her, he embraced her with tenderness and kissed her passionately. Lovemaking was gentle—and intense. Afterward, the two fell into heavy sleep.

CLAIRE'S DREAMS that night were extremely graphic and lucid, and she tossed and turned relentlessly.

In the morning, Guy kissed her gently on the cheek. "How'd you sleep last night, my beauty?" he asked.

"Not well," she said, looking at him fixedly. "We're looking at homicide, Guy. Premeditated first-degree murder. I have no remaining doubts."

12

Sunday morning

CLAIRE AND GUY walked to the lodge for an early breakfast. Jay walked in just as the two were finishing coffee and approached them shamefaced.

"I owe you both an apology. I'm real sorry about last evening," he said. He looked at the investigators briefly before looking downward. "I haven't been myself lately." He scratched his head. "Nothing seems right."

"No need to apologize," Guy said.

"Already forgotten," Claire said.

MINUTES LATER, Claire and Guy were seated in the green Land Rover Discovery on their way to Polson. Hugging closely to the east perimeter of Flathead Lake, the eleven-mile trip took the investigators along a curvy and picturesque road traveling south and eventually west into the Flathead Valley. The drive was unhurried. And the route offered the pair a magnificent view of Flathead Lake—the largest natural freshwater lake in the western continental United States—on their right-hand side and the impressive vertical walls of pine forests on their left. Adding the endless blue sky to the mix, the scenic journey was jaw dropping. The day was clear, and the sun bright and hot.

Guy had picked up a map of the Flathead area and a handful of other brochures at the check-in desk after breakfast, and as he gazed at the diagrammatic representation of the area, Claire guided the 4 x 4 toward their destination.

"There's a notation here that Flathead Lake is slightly larger than Lake Tahoe," he said. "It's about thirty miles long and fifteen miles across, and for its size, it's one of the cleanest lakes in the world. Says here it was created by Ice Age glaciers."

"And where does all that clean water come from now?" Claire asked. "Does it show?"

Guy studied the map further. "Looks to me like both the Flathead and Swan Rivers supply water to Flathead Lake." He looked on. "It covers about two hundred square miles of Montana. That's huge."

"*Big* sky . . . *big* lake," Claire said, shooting Guy a passing glance and smiling. "Certainly is *big*, beautiful country."

"Yeah, you can say that again," Guy agreed.

Claire snuck another quick peek at the man she loved and realized that he, too, was smiling. It was a slight, almost undetectable smile, but a smile nevertheless. Despite being tied up in a murder investigation, she continued to have great expectations that being far away from the Beach was doing him good. It represented a change of scenery and a real chance to leave that ugly part of his recent past behind.

"Look at the art fair brochure, will you?" Claire asked. "I'm excited to hear everything it says."

Guy pulled the Polson pamphlet from among the others on his lap and scanned it.

"It's called the Sandpiper Outdoor Art Festival. Apparently, the festivities are set up on the Polson Courthouse lawn. There are a hundred booths of crafts and original art. That's a lot of art."

"Sounds like fun, doesn't it?" Claire asked. "I can't wait. Maybe we can find a small oil painting of Montana to take home with us as a memento. I'd like that."

"That's a great idea," Guy said, continuing to study the handout. "Hey, they have food and live entertainment, too. As long as there's food, I'm interested."

"As much as I hate to bring it up, I suppose we should use this driving time to review the lodge employee interviews. Maybe we can zero in on which staffers we need to take a closer look at," Claire said.

"I think most all of them could be considered suspects at this point."

"I have to agree, but we'll need to narrow the list. At least for now, we should figure out which ones stand out from the group as the most likely candidates. We can work our way down the list from there."

Guy pulled a spiral notebook from the backseat, flipped it open, and began reviewing his interview jottings.

"Where should we start?" he asked. "We interviewed fifteen employees, plus Lois 'LoLo' Whiting."

"Let's take the witnesses in order. My mind works better that way, especially when I'm driving," she said. "Can you star the names of the ones we agree warrant further investigation? One star if they warrant *some* extra scrutiny, and two stars if we consider them major suspects needing *intense* scrutiny?"

"Yeah, that will work. Let's begin with Ed Carter—one of the two daytime chefs in the Terra Restaurant," Guy said, scanning his notes. "He's thirty-six and has worked at the lodge for three years."

"He's the Montana man through and through, and he's been a chef since high school, if I remember correctly. He pointed the finger at Jay Cantrell," Claire said.

"Exactly. And he described Blake Helms as a mellow, decent sort of fellow."

"Funny thing is," Claire said, "many or most subsequent interviewees told us that Blake confronted and argued with other staff members on a regular basis. I'd hardly consider that a *mellow*, decent sort of fellow. It's odd that Ed would characterize him with those words. But then again, people see things differently."

"Good point, Claire. Star or no star?"

"For now, I vote no star."

"Me, too. That's two no-star votes from us. Next is Hazel Schroeder, restaurant supervisor, age fifty-two. She's been employed by the lodge for five years," Guy said.

"Let me think," Claire said. "She supervises both restaurants. That's a demanding job. She also plans special events for the lodge—weddings, parties, etc. Her plate must be overflowing much of the time. Works odd shifts throughout the day, depending on when she's most needed."

"Right. She called the Cantrells extremely picky people to work for," Guy said. "Told us Jay would ream her out if something wasn't done to his liking. She said Jay Cantrell has a not-so-nice side to him."

"She exuded an extremely on-edge demeanor," Claire said. "And she seemed highly defensive about it when I asked her if she was nervous about something."

"Yeah," he said, scanning his notes. "I wrote down that she left the interview partway through to get a drink of water."

"I remember that. She claimed it was hot in the room. But it wasn't," Claire said. She thought further about the interview as she drove. "And she implied that Piper Cantrell and Blake Helms were having an affair."

"Yes," Guy said. "She also told us that Jay Cantrell looked at Blake like he wanted to kill him."

"Her behavior raised red flags for me—the rocking back and forth in the chair; shifting uncomfortably; leaving for water; setting her purse in front of her on the table, almost like a barrier between her and us. I say we give her two stars. Yes, *double* stars for Hazel Schroeder. Her actions were one of a liar."

"I agree one hundred percent," Guy said. "Something seemed not quite right with her. And she obviously wanted to set us on the trail of Jay Cantrell."

"Uh-huh. Exactly."

Guy referred back to his notes. He turned a page. "We interviewed Heidi Flynn next. She's a housekeeper at the lodge, has worked there only three months, and is twenty-one years old."

"She's the one from Iowa," Claire said. "The one whose mother died young and whose father raised her, according to what she told us." As she gripped the wheel, it appeared obvious to Guy that the cogs in Claire's mind were turning rapidly. "It would be interesting to know why she *really* moved to Montana. Away from the only family she has? And at twenty-one years of age? Bet there's more to that story."

"And we were told she owns a gun," Guy said. "It was seen in her purse, if we can believe the people who informed us. Also, Rosie

Flores—one of the other housekeepers—told us about the time Heidi pulled a gun on her, a gun that wasn't loaded. Scared Rosie to death, according to her. Again, if we believe the account."

"Well, three witnesses directly associated Heidi with a gun—June Howard, Darlene Nichols, and Rosie Flores, all of who claimed to have actually seen it. And then there is Erik Johannson, who told us that Darlene had mentioned overhearing Heidi on her cell phone saying she needed more ammunition for her pistol. We'll need to do some checking on that gun," Claire said. "If three or four employees knew about it, I'll bet more did, too."

"Good point. We'll need to verify that a twenty-one-year-old can own a gun in Montana; see if Montana is a carry permit state; determine if Heidi Flynn *has* a carry permit; confirm whether she owns a gun; and if she has one, determine the caliber. We'll also need to determine that her gun, assuming she has one, is properly registered," Guy said. "I just made notations next to her name. I'll check these things out."

"Other witnesses told us that Heidi and Blake Helms did not get along . . . that he chastised her for not doing her work properly," Claire recalled aloud. "Although, strangely, Heidi never mentioned that to us."

"No, she did not." He looked down at his notes. "She told us she hardly knew the man, that she really only saw him at staff meetings. She certainly made no mention whatsoever about him confronting her at any time."

"Makes me wonder why," Claire said. "And the fake coughing spell. We can't forget about that, either. Heidi deflected her answer when I asked her what city in Iowa she came from—to buy time before she answered that question. And I noticed she played with her jewelry in a jittery manner as she pretended to cough before she answered that simple question. I'd say Heidi Flynn earned two stars from me. Wouldn't you agree? We need to check out her background thoroughly."

"Without question. Double stars." Guy jotted notations. "I thought initially she was a nice young lady, but once we review all the statements and implications here, she may not be what she appears."

"Who was next?" Claire asked.

"Charlotte Rodriguez, the forty-four-year-old front desk clerk. She's worked at Mountain Lake Lodge five years."

"Let me think," Claire said. "She and June Howard are the two daytime desk clerks, correct? They alternate the seven-to-three and three-to-eleven shifts, and then Blake would come in at eleven to start his all-nighter and relieve one or the other of them. Charlotte was the one to find Blake Helms's body the morning of his murder."

"Precisely." He referred to his notebook.

"What else did Charlotte Rodriguez have to say, Guy?"

"I wrote down she informed us she had seen Hazel Schroeder arguing with Blake Helms on occasion. Also that Blake seemed very fond of Piper and not so fond of Jay. And she's the one who first mentioned the name LoLo—Lois Whiting."

"My gut tells me she told us everything she knows and that she was being honest. I say we hold off on placing a star by her name, at least for the time being."

"I agree." Guy turned another page.

"Did we walk over to the grill and talk to Lois Whiting after that last interview?" Claire asked.

"Hang on. Not yet. We interviewed Harvey Powell first, before visiting LoLo."

"Oh, yes."

"Harv," Guy said, "age sixty . . . the handyman and pool man. He's worked at the lodge for four years. Former schoolteacher."

"A likable man," Claire said, "as I recall. Had a high regard for Blake Helms. He was the only employee to verbalize that he will miss the victim, at least up until that point in our interviewing."

"Right. He also told us he had witnessed Heidi Flynn arguing with Blake. And he said he witnessed both daytime desk clerks—Charlotte Rodriguez and June Howard—having words with the man, too, on different occasions. Harv claimed he never knew what any of the quarrels were about, however," Guy said, paraphrasing his notes.

"Let's move on. I say no star by Harvey Powell's name at this time. But we need to add one star to both Charlotte Rodriguez and June Howard."

"So noted," Guy said. "Next we interviewed Lois Whiting—LoLo." He quickly reviewed his several scribbled pages concerning the server at Woods Bay Grill. "She told us Blake had some run-ins with Heidi Flynn over her insolent attitude. Also, LoLo said Blake often didn't agree with Jay Cantrell about how to handle things at the lodge. And she mentioned that Blake and his ex-wife argued over the divorce."

"Yet another witness setting up Heidi Flynn with a motive. And unfortunately, our friend Jay again." Claire thought for a moment. "Let's make a note to check out Blake's divorce. See how it was finalized. If the settlement was acrimonious, we might have ourselves another person with a motive. And the children. We need to check them out, too. See if there's any motive there."

"Do we star LoLo's name?" Guy asked. "I say no."

"I say no, also. Not as a suspect. But we should make a notation to talk with her again real soon. Maybe she'll remember something of importance . . . after she's had some time to digest it all."

"When we returned to the lodge, we interviewed June Howard," Guy said. "She's fifty-nine and has worked at the lodge for two years. Covers, alternately, the day and evening front check-in desk shifts."

"She's the one who told us Heidi Flynn and Blake Helms argued over the quality of her cleaning whenever he received complaints about her work, correct? And she's the one who informed us—by writing Heidi Flynn's name on a note and passing it to us—about seeing a gun in Heidi's purse on the counter in the ladies' room one day."

"Yes. And yes." He referred to his writings. "She told us Heidi acted arrogantly or rudely toward Blake Helms when he confronted her, something he would not tolerate."

"June was also the one who told us about the arguments between Hazel Schroeder and Blake Helms," Claire said, "over the noise issues—loud noise that went on late into the night or early-morning hours—in connection with the events Hazel had arranged. According to June, Hazel and Blake really had it out one day over the issue. Sounded mighty serious."

"Correct. June Howard is a font of information, but I see nothing to warrant a star by her name," Guy said. "Not at this time."

"Ditto," Claire said.

Claire noticed a sign indicating the remaining miles to Polson and realized they would soon be arriving in the city. She was looking forward to enjoying several hours of the festival and taking a break from the case. The day was quickly turning into a scorcher, with a temperature reaching close to ninety degrees. Thankfully, the air-conditioning in the vehicle was working, but in a short time, the two would be walking around outside in the midst of the pounding heat.

"The next day, Friday, Dahlia Young was the first employee we interviewed," Guy continued. "She's twenty-four, employed as a lodge housekeeper, and has worked there for three years."

"Dahlia Young," Claire repeated her name. "She's the immature, almost-childlike young woman. Seemed fragile in a way. Acted terribly innocent and naïve. Her body shook the whole time, she was so nervous about being interviewed. Really didn't tell us much, though, did she?"

"No, she didn't. Other than to say she thought Blake Helms seemed like a nice man, as far as she could tell."

"Nothing helpful. Let's not star her name."

"I'm with you." Claire nodded, glancing at a road sign. "Now that we're almost to Polson, we might have time to review a couple more interviews, but then we'll have to wait and consider the others on our drive back to the lodge," Claire said.

"Okay. Next interviewee was Carlton 'Chaz' Warner, twenty-two, a server in the Terra Restaurant. Has been with the lodge for two years," Guy said.

"An angry young man," Claire said. "Seemed irate that Blake had embarrassed him in front of his coworkers."

"That's him. According to my notations, and I quote, he felt 'like punching the hell out of the old sucker.' He could be a prime suspect. He's definitely got motive."

"Yes, he does, but think about this: Blake embarrassed Chaz, and that made the young man angry—really angry. And granted, Chaz said he felt like hitting Blake Helms. But he didn't say he felt like *killing* the man. He was trying to sound macho to us. That's all, in my opinion. His pride was hurt." Claire thought for a long minute. "My investigator instincts tell me he's not a killer. I think he's filled with hot air, but that's it. I say no star."

"I strongly disagree," Guy said. "I say we give him a star. Actually, two stars. Chaz Warner felt anger, or rage, toward our victim, and that's often the impetus for murder!"

"Okay. Okay. Star his name. Either one or two. You decide. Reasonable people can disagree, and we do on this one." She looked at Guy and raised her eyebrows. "We'll look at him further."

"Good."

"Who came next?" Claire asked. She noticed they had just entered the small community of Polson. She decided to follow the crowds and drive around to find a parking spot.

"Okay, we talked with Katie Kyle after we finished with Chaz Warner. Katie is twenty-five and also a server in the Terra Restaurant. She's been at the lodge for three years."

As luck would have it, Claire spotted a space just as another car was backing out, so she pulled the Land Rover in close to the curb. The city looked as if it were pulled right out of a *Bonanza* episode—except that it was brimming with modern-day vehicles. Sidewalks were jammed with people all out to enjoy the sizzling day and art festivities, and the merriment was well underway.

"What do your notes say about Katie Kyle?" Claire asked. "Let's finish up with her."

"I wrote down a direct quote she gave us when talking about Chaz Warner. She said, 'My coworker hated the man,' meaning Blake. She said, 'One day, I even heard him say the man should be dead—that he should be put out of his misery.' He made that statement, according to Katie Kyle, two weeks before Blake was found murdered." He paused. "She also told us Chaz Warner has a bad anger problem. Now what say ye to the stars I placed by his name?"

"I forgot about that statement. Two stars are warranted next to Chaz Warner's name. I stand corrected. I agree we need to take a closer look. He's young, and he has a bad temper, granted, but we need to determine if that hostility pushed him over the edge. I still think he's not the killer."

"No stars for Katie Kyle, though, correct?" Guy asked.

"Yeah. That's my take, too," Claire said.

Guy tossed his notebook onto the backseat. "Let's enjoy the day, my dear." He jumped from the car. "How does an ice-cold lemonade sound?"

13

Sandpiper Outdoor Art Festival
Polson, Montana

HUNDREDS OF BODIES crammed the small downtown area of Polson. The sun's heat sizzled everyone and everything beneath it that day, but it did not deter or slow down the festive event. People everywhere competed to stand in the few areas of available shade interspersed along the quaint streets of the town, seeking a minute or two of relief.

Vendors offering sodas, iced teas, lemonades, and bottled waters were having a heyday. In front of each stand, streams of people wiping sweat from their brows formed lines doublewide and a half a block long. They were hot and thirsty.

"I'm parched," Guy said, observing the others.

"Pick a stand," Claire said.

He looked around and spotted a kiosk selling ice-cold lemonade and limeade and took a place in the very long line leading up to it. Claire joined him.

"Okay now," Guy said. "It's *really* steamy standing out here in this blazing sun. Even for me. I can hardly stand it."

Just then, a young girl and her sister walked past the line, pointing to an adorable makeshift lemonade stand they had set up across the street. It was a simple card table, covered with a blue-and-white paisley-print tablecloth, and the children were trying to compete with the grown-up vendors for customers. A huge, hand-painted sign taped to the front of the table said, "Lenomade for sale." The girls had made a noble effort to spell *lemonade* correctly. It was simply too cute to pass up the young entrepreneurs.

"Let's make a dash for it," Claire said, "before the rest of the crowd catches on."

Claire and Guy sprinted over to the stand and ordered two lemonades.

A third young girl, working with the sisters, reached into a giant cooler and filled two clear plastic glasses with ice cubes. Then she poured the sweet beverage to the very rims. She dropped a maraschino cherry, a thin slice of lemon, and a straw into each.

"That will be fifty cents apiece," the little girl said, smiling broadly and revealing a missing tooth.

Claire handed the girl ten dollars. "Keep the change. It looks delicious!" She took a sip. "It *is* delicious! You saved us from waiting in those long lines. Thank you!"

The child's eyes lit up. "Thank you, too, lady."

GUY REFERRED to the brochure regarding the delightful lakeside community of Polson. He read aloud, "Sitting proudly on the Flathead Indian Reservation, on the south end of Flathead Lake, Polson is blessed with perfect soil for farming. Countless cherry orchards dot the area and produce its famous sweet dark-red cherries. City parks are strewn here and there along its lakeside, and museum signs welcome visitors. Whitewater rafting is available for sightseeing, and tourists can view the Kerr Dam or play golf on a nearby course. Visitors are urged to hold their cameras in a ready position in case they have the fortune to spot the Flathead Monster—a huge, prehistoric eel-like lake creature supposedly seen raising its repellent head in Flathead Lake on rare occasions over the past one hundred years."

He read on. "The immense and far-reaching Mission Valley, south of Polson, borders the craggy snowcapped Mission Mountains; the Flathead River flows from the region; and the nearby National Bison Range contains herds of bison, deer, antelope, and elk."

The investigators took in the almost surreal setting of the picturesque area that looked like a mammoth bowl with mountains surrounding its rim. The topography of the area was so different from everything they knew and grew up with. The tranquility of the setting mesmerized Claire.

"Excuse me," Guy said, calling her back to reality. "Let's make our way to the art show. It's a couple blocks from here."

"Love to," she said. She grabbed his hand, and they strolled off in the direction of the art and craft show.

Along the way, they passed restored classic, custom, and hotrod cars lined up diagonally on certain of the town's streets. Hundreds of them. Guy was in his glory that the outdoor festival included the Cruisin' by the Bay car show. He enjoyed seeing the autos up close, and his eyes sparkled as he tried to identify every model for Claire.

She cherished this time with Guy. He seemed almost back to his former self. If only it would last. If only Guy could forget about his beating and let go of it forever. She had noticed that he suffered the bouts of melancholy and depression less frequently, and he had told her repeatedly that it was something he had to deal with in his own way and in his own time. How she hoped this trip to Montana would trigger a permanent change in him, urging him back to his former self now and for the future. Today, she witnessed steps in a positive direction and saw a glimmer of light at the end of the tunnel. Guy was being *Guy*, and she was tickled.

They spent the next two hours walking slowly along the sidewalks of the town—sipping on waters and lemonades and observing the amazing and eye-catching reconditioned automobiles. Then they meandered the two blocks south of the downtown traffic light to the festival on the courthouse lawn. Lines of covered booths stood neatly arranged on the green grass in every direction the investigators looked. Each table within every station displayed a different variety of fine paintings, stunning photography, or original sculpture. Quality crafts made from ceramics, leather, wood, pine needles, glass, textiles, and basically anything else one could think of called passersby to come and take a closer look. Handmade jewelry and quilts also commanded attention.

Live music added to the festiveness of the event, and merrymaking poured out over that small corner of the world. Children frolicked as parents enjoyed the show, an occasional dog jumped and spun around in the air, and even the elderly felt like kids again. It was good to take time to simply have fun.

Numerous food booths—emanating delightful and distinctive aromas and offering a miscellany of edible temptations—enticed shoppers and visitors alike to taste their unique fare.

"I'm hungry," Guy announced.

Claire said, "I'm starving."

"What do you feel like eating?" Guy asked.

"We passed a booth selling grilled barbequed chicken a short time ago. It smelled heavenly. That's what I'd like. And a slice of huckleberry pie for dessert." Her face lit up.

"Sounds great. And I'll pick up some of the wok-fried noodles and vegetables. We can share it all."

The two purchased their selections and found a spot on the lawn under a tree to sit down and eat. Claire ran off and returned with two fresh raspberry limeades. The shade provided a much-needed interlude from the sun's blazing rays, and the choices sated their hunger pangs.

Guy stretched his body out flat on the soft grass and lay his head down on Claire's lap. She stroked his hair with her fingers and gently touched the scars on his face. She kissed his forehead. It had been ages since the two of them had had any real alone time away from everyone and everything that consumed their waking moments. It felt good to breathe in the pure Montana air, look out onto the sweeping vista of the beautiful land, and do absolutely nothing but enjoy the day and each other. *Why does life become so busy that timeouts like this become so rare?* Claire asked herself. She savored the moment, so afraid it would disappear all too quickly.

To her great surprise, Guy fell fast asleep in his reclining position. Maybe a nap was just what both of them needed, she reasoned. Remaining in a sitting position, she closed her eyes and fell into easy slumber. Soon a kaleidoscope of images whirled through her dreamworld in an entertaining yet peaceful sort of way. As always, the afternoon siesta sated her better than a full night's sleep.

Both investigators awoke a short time later, feeling refreshed, cooler, and ready to continue enjoying the show.

"Will you help me find a small painting of Montana to take home with us?" Claire asked.

The two walked leisurely down additional paths of tents and kiosks and peered into many. Making a decision on a painting was going to be difficult. Claire had never seen more beautiful oils and watercolors in her life.

Guy walked into a covered booth selling handmade, lathe-turned wooden bowls in a variety of unique shapes and sizes. Claire followed him in. The woodturner himself—Charlie Fudge, otherwise known as the "Woodsman of the Rockies"—manned the space.

"Feel the surface of one of my bowls," he said. "Go ahead."

Claire and Guy each touched a bowl and were astounded at the smooth and silky finish of the crafter's extraordinary works of art.

"They get that way after lots of sanding and then finishing with oils and wax," the artist explained. "Bowls hold no emptiness."

"No *emptiness*?" Guy asked, puzzled by the remark.

"The space in the middle of a bowl is actually part of its shape," Charlie explained. "It's part of the form of each bowl. You need put nothing in them. They are beautiful as they are. Folks around here collect my works. Most just set them on a coffee table to look at. "

Charlie Fudge was an instantly likable man—friendly, knowledgeable about his trade, and a lover of life. His eyes danced. Guy decided on the spot that he wanted to purchase one of the unique wooden bowls.

"I'm from Polson. More of my pieces are on display at the Sandpiper Art Gallery and Gift Shop, a couple of blocks over on Main Street," Charlie said. "That is, if you don't find anything here that suits you."

"Actually, I'm deciding between these two," Guy said, pointing them out.

"Tough choice," Charlie said. "The grain of the wood in both is outstanding. You'd most likely be happy with either one of them. Or both." He smiled.

"Okay, you twisted my arm," Guy said. "I'll take the two."

After settling up on the transaction, the investigators shook hands with Charlie. Something told Claire that he would be a friend of theirs for a long time to come.

"We'll look for you the next time we're in town," Claire said. "Pleasure to meet you."

The investigators continued to stroll the grounds.

A young boy playing near a booth yelled out, "Come see my mom's things," as they walked past. "They're the best!" With his hand, he gestured to his mother's booth.

Claire chuckled. How could she resist this animated, adorable child?

She grabbed Guy by the hand and led him into the lady's booth. The table inside was filled with framed oil paintings, mostly of native Montana landscapes. The artist's style immediately attracted Claire and Guy, and they studied the pieces carefully.

"I like this one," Claire said. She pointed to a wintery scene of ponderosa pines covered with the whitest of snow. The work was breathtaking and seemed to glisten with wonder. And it was small enough to pack in her suitcase.

"Very nice," Guy said. "I think you found a winner."

Guy looked at the boy's mother sitting behind the table.

"How much for this one?" He indicated the painting Claire had selected.

The artist looked at the two investigators with interest in her eyes. "For you?" she asked. "For you, the price is ninety dollars. It's an original oil."

"I'll take it," Claire said. She reached into her purse and pulled out four twenties and a ten. "This should do it." She handed the money to the lady.

Graciously, the artist accepted the payment and wrapped the painting in bubble wrap before placing it in a plastic bag with handles. "Thank you."

Just as Claire was turning to leave the booth, the young lad tugged on her sleeve. "Lady," he said. "My mom has new art, too, in her shop. You'll like it."

Claire looked at the woman behind the table.

"My son. He is always trying to help his mother," the artist said.

"Please come look," the boy said. "Please." His eyes pleaded with Claire. "It's special."

Claire chuckled. "Your little boy is mighty persuasive. Can we take a peek at this art he's talking about?"

The woman said, "My son is talking about some art I newly acquired. The pieces are over at my shop, but I can't leave to show them to you until we close up here this afternoon at five o'clock. But if you can wait around, I'll show you then."

Guy looked at his wristwatch. "It'll be three soon. I'm sure we'll be here for another couple of hours. Where exactly is your shop?"

"I own the custom framing shop on Main Street. You can't miss it. My studio is in the back." She handed Guy her business card and pointed out the address. "I'll see you both there just after five."

"We'll be there," he said.

As the sleuths stepped from the booth, Claire thought she glimpsed the face of Heidi Flynn staring directly at her from about half a block away. She glanced at Guy and asked him to take a look, but when she turned her head back around to point the young lady out, she was nowhere to be seen.

"I'm sure it was her, Guy," she said. "And she was with a man about her same age. Wonder who he is. Her boyfriend?"

"Maybe they came to take in the art show, just like we did. It seems to be a big deal around these parts."

"Yeah. But why do you suppose she ran off when our eyes met? I know she recognized me."

"Hard to tell," he said.

Claire's mind drifted. Was there a reason Heidi didn't want her to see whom she was with? What was the big secret?

Suddenly, she heard the young boy's voice. From just outside his mother's tent, the lad yelled goodbye to the investigators with a smile on his face that could brighten up a sunless day. "See you soon," he said.

"Are you sure you want to do this?" Guy asked. "Wait around and go to the frame shop?"

"How can we *not*? I could never disappoint that child," Claire said. "We don't have to buy anything. I think just the fact that we show up to look will mean everything to him."

"I guess so. I can't fault the youngster for helping steer business his mother's way. And I have to say, her paintings were the nicest I've seen today."

"I agree," she said. "How should we spend the next two hours?"

"Well, I noticed lots of shops in town. We could look through them and maybe sit and have an iced coffee somewhere—that is, if we can find an air-conditioned place."

"Sounds good."

After an hour of browsing around the local shops and another hour spent drinking the cold coffee, the two were more than ready for the rendezvous. They walked to the frame shop, found it locked up tight, and waited by the front door for the woman and the boy to appear. It was exactly five.

Ten minutes later, the sleuths spotted the owner and her son walking toward them speedily. When they arrived, the lady unlocked the door without delay. She flipped on the light switch and welcomed Claire and Guy into her store.

"I apologize for being late," she said. "I tried my best to shut down on time, but a couple stopped in just as I was closing up and started asking me questions. They wouldn't leave." She looked at the investigators. "Strangely, the woman wanted to know all about the two of you. What you purchased . . . if you asked me questions about the art I sell . . . and so on and so on. I finally told her it was none of her business, and I rudely asked them to exit my booth. Can't imagine why they were so interested in you."

"I have no idea," Claire said. "But we appreciate you telling us about this. How old were these people?" An image of Heidi and her companion instantly popped into Claire's mind.

"I'm not good at guessing ages. But if pressed, I'd probably say middle aged."

"*Middle aged?* Not young?" Claire asked.

"Yeah. Middle aged. Definitely not young. They both wore caps and sunglasses, though, so I didn't get a real good look at either of them."

Claire found it quite interesting. The lady just ruled out Heidi Flynn and the unidentified male with her, if her assessment was accurate. So, who were these two asking questions?

Claire looked around the shop. "Now, what do you have to show us? Where is this *special* art?" she asked.

The lady suggested they look around while she went to the back room. The boy stayed close to Claire, and every time she looked at him, he broke into a broad smile. It was obvious that he liked her.

The frame shop not only displayed a wide variety of framing options—both wood and metallic in a host of different colors—but also offered for sale a prominent exhibition of framed original works of art by various Montana artists. These pieces took up one entire wall.

"My mom does nice framing," the young lad said. "She promised to teach me some day." He beamed.

Claire smiled back at the child. "What's your name?"

"J. B."

"And what does J. B. stand for?" Claire asked.

"Jacob Bailey. That's my first and middle name."

Just then, J. B.'s mother re-entered the storefront, toting a covered package under each arm. "This is the framed art my son told you about. Just took them in. Haven't even cleaned or marked the works yet." She set the pieces down on a worktable.

Claire and Guy were eager to see the artwork.

The woman unwrapped the first one, set it down on the floor, and propped it against a table leg so the back of the painting faced outward. Then she removed the wrap from the second. She grabbed a work in each hand and whirled them around to show off the stunning pieces at the same time. "Voilà," she said.

Guy stared at the original art the woman unveiled.

Claire gasped at the pieces without blinking her eyes. "*Where* did you get these? And *when*?"

The woman sensed the urgency in Claire's voice. "Is something wrong?"

"Where did you get these and when?" Claire repeated.

The boy's mother turned pale. "What's wrong? Did I do something bad?"

"Please answer my questions, madam. It's very important," the female sleuth said.

J. B. grabbed onto his mother's leg and held on tightly. "You're scaring my mommy. Please don't scare her," he begged. As large tears filled his eyes and streamed down his cheeks, he caught them in his hands.

14

THE BOY'S MOTHER fumbled for words.

"Am . . . I . . . in trouble? Did I do something . . . wrong?" she stuttered. "If I did, it was not . . . intentional. I didn't . . . know."

Claire looked at the woman. "Please tell us who sold you these paintings."

"A local teenager came into my shop late in the day last Thursday. Three days ago." The lady trembled as she spoke. "He offered me the two pieces at a price I couldn't turn down. Two famous artists from these parts painted these, and I knew I could easily sell them for triple what he wanted for them. So I bought them both."

"Did the teenager tell you where he got the paintings?" Claire asked.

"Yeah. Said his aunt had died recently and his parents needed to sell the pieces quickly to raise some cash for the burial."

"How much did you pay this teenager for the two paintings?"

Claire asked.

"Is my mommy in trouble?" the little boy blurted out. "Is she?"

"No, honey. Your mommy's not in trouble," Claire said. She gave the lad a reassuring pat on his head.

"Do you recall how much you paid for the two pieces?" Claire repeated. "It's terribly important."

"He would only take cash," the woman said. "I went to my safe in the back room to retrieve hundred-dollar bills. I gave him twelve hundred dollars in hundred-dollar bills. Six hundred for each piece. It was a *great* deal for me, and he seemed happy as well."

"What did the teenager do when you handed him the money?" Claire asked.

The lady thought about Claire's question. "He stuffed two hundred-dollar bills into his pocket and walked out with the rest in his hand."

"Did you see where he went after he left your store?" Claire asked.

"No, I didn't watch him," the woman responded. "Guess I should have."

"I did," the young child interrupted eagerly. "He went to the corner and gave the money to two people."

"What did these two people look like? Do you remember, J. B.?" Claire asked.

The child looked at his mommy and then at Claire. His eyes evinced innocence. "It was a man and a lady."

"How old do you think they were?" Claire asked.

"I dunno," he said.

Claire smiled at the child and then looked at his mother.

"I'm afraid we'll have to take these paintings with us for the sheriff to hold temporarily—as evidence," Claire said. "We're investigators from Miami, assisting the Lake County Sheriff's Office on a murder and robbery case that occurred in the early-morning hours last Thursday at Mountain Lake Lodge, up in the Bigfork area." She proffered her identification to the owner and handed her a business card. Guy did the same. "The night desk clerk was shot in cold blood, and original artwork was stolen off the walls. These are collection pieces from the lodge's Jest Gallery. I recognized both of them instantly. They're two of the pieces stolen from the lodge. So, again, I'm afraid we have to take the artwork with us. It will be returned to the lodge once the case is solved."

"Murder? Robbery? How awful," the lady said. "I'm sorry for the man's family." She trembled convulsively. "Does this mean I'm out the twelve hundred dollars? I can't afford this kind of loss. It will take me months to make it up."

"I would suggest you contact your insurance carrier at once," Guy said. "I'm going to guess you're insured against this kind of loss. After all, you were acting in good faith when you made the purchase. You had no way to know the art was stolen property. Ask your insurance agent to contact one of us if more information is required."

Claire pulled her cell phone from her purse and called Sheriff Bell to fill him in on the new development. Carefully, she and Guy each grasped a painting to tote to the 4 x 4.

"Call us if you have any questions or if you recall anything else about the transaction, will you, please?" Claire asked the artist. "I'm sorry about this. Really."

The woman nodded slightly.

With sad eyes, the young boy waved goodbye to the investigators.

THE PERVADING mood turned pensive on the drive back to the lodge. Finding two of the paintings stolen from the murder scene was a major breakthrough. It answered some questions, but raised others. They now realized the culprit may still be in the area, fencing the ill-gotten property, or at least some of the pieces. And they now knew that a couple—a male and female—stood in the background of the illegal sale to the woman at the frame shop. But the identity of the couple remained a mystery. Was it Heidi and her male friend? Was it the two middle-aged people riddling the frame shop owner with questions about the investigators that afternoon? Or perhaps two totally different individuals were involved in this. Questions flooded the sleuths' minds.

It seemed obvious that the unidentified duo setting up the sale of the artwork had flagged down a local Polson teenage boy and unwittingly lured him into their scheme with the promise of a two-hundred-dollar reward for moving the art. It appeared doubtful that the teenager even realized the paintings were stolen property. Two hundred dollars for carrying out a simple request must have seemed like a fairy tale come true for the adolescent.

Guy drove as Claire held her notebook in hand.

"Getting back to the interview notes . . . I think Phil Kagan was the next interviewee," Guy said. "Not counting LoLo."

"Let me find him here," Claire said. She thumbed through her notes until she found his name. She quickly scanned her jottings. "Ah, yes, how can we forget Phil Kagan?" She grimaced. "He was the tenth employee we questioned—the real comedian."

"I remember him well. He was a real pain in the arse, especially for his age," Guy recalled.

Claire muffled a snicker.

"Phil Kagan is fifty-one, the other daytime chef for the Terra Restaurant. He's worked at the lodge for five years. When he finally settled down, he gave us some substantial information that no one else did," she said. "He informed us that Blake Helms was an American Indian history buff and a real expert on the Blackfoot and Flathead Indian tribes of this region. He's the only interviewee who mentioned this."

"And that helps us . . . *how*?" Guy asked.

"Not sure," she said. "But no one else talked about it, and I find it interesting that he did. That's all. It may be nothing. We'll have to wait and see."

"Did he tell us if Blake had problems with anyone? I don't recall."

"Yes. He said Blake and Jay Cantrell often quarreled. He also said Blake was a perfectionist, and that he'd scold and belittle employees who didn't measure up to his standards. Something at that point we'd heard many times."

"Back to Jay, yet again," Guy said. "As much as I hate to admit it, many roads seem to be leading directly to Jay Cantrell."

"Hold that thought," Claire said. "Once the crime lab results come in, we may find ourselves on a totally different road leading directly to someone else. We might have the information early this week."

"Well, let's hope so, because right about now, it's not looking particularly good for our friend."

"We need to keep an open mind at all times. As you know all too well, nothing is a 'for sure' until it can be proven. My gut tells me Jay is not involved, but I'm waiting for the hard evidence to come in before drawing any conclusions," Claire said.

"Of course."

IN BETWEEN reading her notes, and with Guy behind the wheel, Claire had more opportunities to take longer looks at the surrounding scenery on their return trip to Bigfork. She noticed occasional log homes and cabins, but mainly just mile upon mile of tall, elegant pine trees and other thick shrubbery—dazzling in more shades of green than Claire even realized existed. The setting seemed dreamlike in appearance—pristine and unspoiled. The picturesque, still waters of Flathead Lake vied for her attention, too.

Guy glanced over at Claire. She looked and seemed content absorbing the splendor of Big Sky Country. "You like it here more and more, don't you?" he asked. "I think it's growing on you."

"It's nature at its finest." The outside air had cooled off with evening approaching, and she lowered the passenger window. She inhaled a gulp of the mountain air and exhaled it slowly. "Look what we've been missing."

"Now, where were we?" Guy asked. "Who came next after Phil Kagan?"

Claire returned her concentration to the spiral notebook. "Wait a minute. Do we give Phil one star? Two? No star?"

"I think we should find out more about him," Guy said. "My vote? One star."

"Yeah, especially since Phil and Blake had some kind of talking relationship," Claire said. "Phil may know more than he's letting on. Also, his buffoonish behavior bothered me greatly. Why did he act so clownish during an interview about a man he worked with, presumably a friend, who was found murdered? Doesn't make sense. I say one star, too."

"Unless he's just the extremely nervous type. Some people use humor to deflect and defuse their real feelings."

"Could be," she said. "We need to give him a thorough second look, though. His name is starred."

"Who was next?" Guy asked.

"Erik Johannson," she said. "Twenty-seven, dinner chef in the Terra Restaurant, an employee of the lodge for just over two years." She scrolled through her scribbles. "Claims he didn't know Blake Helms very well. Told us that Darlene Nichols—the other dinner chef—had mentioned walking into the ladies' room and overhearing Heidi Flynn telling someone on her cell phone that she needed more ammunition for her pistol."

"Back to Heidi Flynn again," Guy said.

"Nothing remarkable or suspect about Erik Johannson. Let's not star Erik's name at this time. Agree?"

"Agree."

"Next we interviewed Nora Sanders, a server in Riley's Pub. Age thirty-one. Employed by the lodge for five years. She told us that people didn't like Blake Helms, that he had a superior attitude. Nora also informed us that her supervisor, Hazel Schroeder, did not care for Blake Helms. She said the two were always at each other's throats, and that one time following a bad argument, she heard Hazel Schroeder say, and I quote, 'The man needs to be put out of his misery.' Nora told us she never thought more about the threat until Blake wound up dead."

"Another finger pointed Hazel Schroeder's way," Guy said. "I say no star for Nora Sanders." He thought for a minute. "So far, it seems that Jay Cantrell, Heidi Flynn, Hazel Schroeder, and Chaz Warner seem to be jumping out from the crowd as the strongest suspects."

"Yeah. And we can't forget one witness told us that Charlotte Rodriguez and June Howard also argued with Blake on a regular basis. And then there's Phil Kagan—Mr. Funny Man. They all deserve a closer look, as well."

"Right," Guy said. "At least we're narrowing the list. Three witnesses to go?"

"Correct. Mitch Green was our next." Claire rapidly skimmed her notes. "Twenty-five, Riley's Pub server and bartender, with the lodge for three years."

"He had that constant eye tic, didn't he?" Guy asked.

"He's the one," Claire said. "Maybe he was overly tired or simply feeling stressed. Who knows? The fact of being interviewed alone might have brought it on."

"Yeah. Tics are pretty common, actually," Guy said. "What did he tell us?"

"Mitch told us that Blake Helms 'wrangled'—that was his word—with Jay Cantrell at least weekly. Mitch said one time, out on the grounds, he witnessed Blake pointing a finger in Jay's face. Jay raised his fist to Blake, but didn't throw a punch."

"Did he say when this happened?" Guy asked. "I can't recall."

"He told us that incident happened several days before Blake's death."

"Did he tell us anything else of interest?" Guy asked.

"Yeah. He said there's a rumor among the staff members that Piper Cantrell and Blake Helms were very friendly. Told us that workers questioned whether Jay had threatened Blake that day of the altercation—maybe told him to stay away from Piper or lose his job."

"Back to Jay Cantrell yet again, aren't we?" Guy asked.

"We are," Claire said. "There's no question there was friction between Jay and Blake. But that doesn't mean Jay killed the man. Why on earth would Jay murder an employee after inviting us to Montana to spend time at the lodge? That's not logical. He would have known that the two of us would get to the bottom of it. Doesn't add up to me."

"Shall I play devil's advocate?" Guy asked. "Jay would never expect us to finger *him* for the murder—under any circumstances. Also, in the heat of the moment, who knows what might have happened? Sudden rage or heartbreak often leads to a crime of passion. You know that. So you have to admit that at this point, Jay's a prime suspect. Friend or not, he's a prime suspect. As much as I hate to think about the possibility, it does exist, and right now, it seems a *strong* possibility."

Claire shrugged her shoulders, refusing to agree verbally with

Guy's assessment. "I'm not convinced," she murmured. She returned to the discussion about Mitch Green. "Mitch informed us that Jay always seemed busy and never appeared to have time for Piper. Maybe Jay's had his mind on the business? This economy must have impacted the number of guests staying at the lodge. Financial worries can be a horrendous burden to lug around."

"True," Guy said. "Maybe he's not even conscious of the fact that he's been ignoring his wife."

"That could be. Any way you look at it, the truth about that issue needs to surface. I'd like to clear Jay as a suspect as soon as possible, if we can."

"And Piper, too. I'm with you."

"No star for Mitch?" Claire asked.

"No star."

Claire returned to her notes. "Our next interviewee was Rosie Flores. Housekeeper, twenty years old, employed at Mountain Lake Lodge for a year and a half."

"She was born in Mexico, correct?"

"Yes. Her family moved to the States when she was a baby. First they lived in Texas and then made their way to Montana," Claire said. "Rosie confirmed that her coworker Heidi Flynn did not like Blake Helms one little bit. Said he reamed Heidi out on occasion for not doing her work properly. Rosie told us that Heidi referred to Blake as an asshole."

"Rosie's the young lady who claims that Heidi Flynn picked a fight with her and pointed a gun her way," Guy said. "Rosie told us she thought Heidi was going to kill her. I remember Rosie's account clearly. It was chilling. And then Rosie told us that Heidi started to laugh hysterically before showing Rosie that the gun was not loaded. Pretty sick behavior."

"Yes, *if* it's true," Claire said.

"*If* it's true? Do you have reason to doubt Rosie's statement?"

Claire remained silent for a time, recalling Rosie's demeanor. "Something makes me question Rosie's story. Girls that age can be brutal with each other. There might be some jealousy there—on Rosie's part, toward Heidi—and perhaps even a desire to see Heidi get into a heap of trouble. Rosie may have heard that Heidi had a gun or may have even seen it in her purse, so maybe now Rosie is concocting this story. I can't understand why Rosie didn't report the incident to anyone at the time it happened, if it actually did. That would have been a very scary thing to go through, and a reasonable person would have reported it immediately, but Rosie did not. Makes me doubt her word. We need to ask Heidi about it. Get her side of the story, too."

"Okay. Fair enough. But if it is true, it's a criminal act," Guy said. "With no witnesses, however, it would be Rosie's word against Heidi's in a court of law, making for a difficult case to prosecute. We need to find out whether Heidi has a permit to carry in Montana, as we've discussed. If she doesn't, she's in deep trouble, whether or not she admits to the incident with Rosie. And if she does admit to exhibiting the behavior Rosie told us about, she'll end up in prison. Something would be seriously wrong with Heidi."

"I underlined a note by Heidi's name to make it a priority to check on the gun permit."

"Moving along," Guy said. "We must be close to wrapping this up."

"We are," Claire said. "Next we interviewed Darlene Nichols, the other dinner chef at Terra Restaurant, forty years old, employed by the lodge for two years."

"She acted extremely ill at ease, didn't she?"

"Unbelievably so," Claire said. "She exhibited many of the signs of a liar, really—hands over her mouth while speaking, her voice tone dropping several octaves, eyes darting to the ceiling, tugging at her ear lobe and clothing, and squirming in her seat. I noted them all. Similar to the behavior exhibited by Hazel Schroeder in her interview, if you'll recall."

"Yeah. After quite a delay, Darlene confirmed seeing a gun in Heidi's purse and hearing Heidi tell someone on her cell phone that she needed ammunition for her pistol, correct?"

"Yeah."

"Star or no star by Darlene's name?" Guy asked.

"I say star, simply due to her behavior," Claire said. "I don't want to rule Darlene Nichols in or out as a suspect right now. There's no doubt her behavior raised a red flag, but other than that, we have nothing specific on her. On the other hand, it was difficult to extract important information from her, and that makes me question whether she may know more than she finally told us."

"Or whether she's just a seriously on-edge, neurotic individual?" Guy asked. "One who totally melted down during the interview because she didn't want to get involved?"

"Exactly." Claire closed her notebook. "Good work. It helped to discuss those interviews. We've cut our list of lodge suspects considerably."

THE REMAINDER of the ride home was consumed with questioning minds. Where would the investigation end? Who would the sleuths determine to be responsible for the heinous murder of Blake Helms? Would it be Heidi Flynn? Hazel Schroeder? Chaz Warner? Another lodge employee not yet an obvious suspect? Jay Cantrell, their longtime friend? An unknown outsider? The same perpetrator who committed the Whitefish burglaries? The sleuths allowed all possibilities to swim around in the aquariums of their minds. Claire reminded herself again of a belief she held dear: *The killer is usually close by. Always look close.*

At this time, fingers pointed in several different directions. Blake Helms was a man with enemies. Many. But the question remained: Who hated him enough to take his life? Tomorrow would be the start of another workweek, and perhaps the results from the crime labs would silence some of the baffling questions. Claire knew all too well that the findings based upon the evidence lifted from the crime scene could easily put a new spin on the investigation.

15

Monday morning

THE BEGINNING OF the new workweek brought with it fertile ground for great possibilities. Endless big blue sky capped the day, and the stately pines stood most everywhere the eye could see. Flathead Lake rested tranquilly off in the distance, appearing to be placed with purposeful confidence, as if waiting to be captured by a famous photojournalist. As the investigators had now come to expect, the tantalizing, ever-present smell of pine needles permeated the surroundings, as if the refreshingly natural scent was sprayed divinely over Montana on a daily basis.

Claire and Guy showered, dressed in casual clothing, and walked with a quick gait toward the lodge for their first meal of the day. Along the way, they inhaled as much of the fresh mountain air as their lungs could possibly hold. They stepped into the lobby and immediately spotted Jay and Piper.

"Mind if we join you for breakfast?" Piper asked. "I want to hear all about your weekend." Piper's spirits seemed higher.

"Please do. We'd love it," Claire said.

The foursome devoured scrambled eggs, chicken-apple sausages, sourdough toast, juice, and fresh-brewed huckleberry coffee while they talked. Claire and Guy filled their friends in on their meeting with the Whitefish Police Department regarding the burglaries in that vicinity, and they also discussed the happenings at the Sandpiper Outdoor Art Festival.

Jay and Piper were thrilled to hear that some of their art had been recovered. They said it was good news after a rather slow weekend. The lodgers attempting to practice the art of *CSI*-type investigating had thankfully checked out and finally given the owners a rest. Despite all attempts to locate a *smoking gun* clue, the group of newbie crime scene investigators had found nothing of value. As they checked out, though, they all commented that they had experienced the most fun ever on a vacation and that they could not wait to return the following year.

Claire laughed. "I guess there's a bit of investigator in all of us. It's the puzzle-solving aspect that appears to be the draw. Sorry the lodgers didn't find anything helpful, but at least the mission kept them busy."

"And hopefully overshadowed the dark side of their visit to Mountain Lake Lodge," Guy said. "Based upon their parting comments, I'd say you're assured repeat business next year."

"Yeah," Jay said. "We'll need it. This economy is taking its toll, although I must say that a number of new guests checked in this morning. So that's good."

"Let's hope the economy picks up for all our sakes," Piper said. She smiled a weak smile. "I'm simply fascinated you located a couple of the stolen paintings. What an incredible break! Now, if you can only find the others."

"Hopefully, we will, before too long," Claire said. She paused. "We don't know who sold the pieces to the owner of the frame shop. Not yet, anyway. But we intend to find out."

Just then her cell phone rang.

"Please excuse me," she said. "I should take this." She got up, walked to a corner of the lobby, and pulled her notebook and pen from her purse.

"Give me everything you have, Sheriff Bell," Claire said. "I'm curious to hear it all."

"Unbelievably, my lab in Polson, the Kalispell lab, and the State Crime Lab each worked all weekend on this for us. I had relayed the urgency of the matter, and they took me seriously. We have some interesting information already, Ms. Caswell," he began. "Blake Helms took five shots from a .38 Special revolver. The bullets were fired straight into his chest at close range. No shell casings remained at the crime scene because a revolver was used. As you know, you get no shells using a revolver, because they remain in the gun. The three bullets that passed through his body and wedged into the wall behind him have been analyzed. Once we find the murder weapon, we'll be able to have the lab confirm that those bullets came from that gun. The other two projectiles ricocheted through Helms's rib cage and stayed lodged in his body. Those were extracted during the autopsy. Time of death was set between 1:00 a.m. and 4:00 a.m."

"I'm taking all of this down, sheriff," Claire said. She paused briefly. "Go ahead."

"Our crime lab was able to get some darn good prints off an inside front doorknob and from the check-in desktop. I understand from talking to the owners that the entire lobby had been thoroughly cleaned immediately prior to Blake Helms beginning his shift at 11:00 p.m. The cleaning crew wiped down and polished the check-in counter and even the front doorknobs. Apparently, Jay Cantrell instructed them at the time of hire to keep the lobby really clean and the doorknobs shiny. Not only so that the lobby looks appealing to guests, but also to avoid the spread of germs. We talked to the crew this weekend to verify all of this. So I'd say the prints we lifted may well be some solid evidence."

"Excellent! Did any of the prints produce a match in the national fingerprint identification system?" Claire held her breath.

"Unfortunately, no, they did not. But the crime lab asked us to obtain fingerprints and palm prints from each employee at the lodge ASAP—even the owners—and deliver the prints for comparison purposes. We're prepared to head over in a few minutes to get started. The lab will then attempt to identify just who left the last prints on the doorknob. That is, if a person connected to the lodge left them there."

"Sounds good, sheriff," Claire said. "And make sure you return around 3:00 p.m. as well to catch the afternoon crew." She cleared her throat. "What else did the crime labs find?"

"The eyelash you found is from a female. The lab was able to pull a smidgen of DNA from it, and they're working up a profile as we speak. The lab also requested we obtain a saliva sample from each of the female employees and the female owner of the lodge. We'll do that at the same time we conduct the fingerprinting and palm printing."

"Okay. Good. Anything else? What about the rivet?" Claire asked.

"The rivet is from a pair of Levi's blue jeans. Because of its size, they believe it to be from a pair of women's jeans. But this is not definitive. Could be from a pair of men's Levi's jeans, as well. Not terribly helpful."

"And last but not least, did the lab determine the source of the gravel on the floor leading back and forth between the front door and the check-in counter?"

"Yeah. They say it's sapphire gravel," the sheriff said.

"*Sapphire* gravel?" Claire asked.

"Yep," the sheriff said. "Likely from the pits of one of Montana's sapphire mines. People go to the mines and sift through bulk sapphire gravel in search of Montana sapphires in the rough. The stones can then be heat-treated and faceted, and, presto, a brilliant sapphire appears."

"Fascinating."

"Yeah. Some mines even send out sapphire gravel concentrate in the mail so purchasers can sift through it in their own homes, looking to find a nice-sized, quality gem. If they can't travel to the mine, the mine will send gravel to the buyer's front doorstep—for a fee, of course."

"So, sapphire gravel mysteriously appears on the lobby floor at or about the time of the murder. Intriguing, wouldn't you say?" Claire asked. "*Most* intriguing." She thought for a moment. "Are there many sapphire mines in this vicinity that are operating at this time?"

"Actually, many have closed down in recent years," the sheriff said. "But there are some that are still operational."

"Can you tell me where the three closest sapphire mines are located?" Claire asked.

"I'll have to check on that, Ms. Caswell, and get back to you."

"Thanks, Sheriff Bell."

CLAIRE RETURNED to the breakfast table and slid into her chair.

"Who was it?" Guy asked.

"Sheriff Bell," Claire said. "He's on his way over with his major case team to fingerprint and palm print all the employees and get DNA samples from the female employees." Claire looked at her friends. "Jay, Piper, they'll want to obtain prints from you two, as well. And Piper, they'll want a swab of your saliva for DNA purposes."

"What?" Piper shrieked. "Now *I'm* a suspect? *Me?* And Jay, too? What on earth is going on here? How can you allow this? I thought we were your friends!" Piper looked at Claire with glaring disbelief pouring from her eyes.

"Piper, calm down. Please. It's routine," Claire said. She looked her friend directly in the eyes. "This happens in every investigation. Everyone is a possible suspect until he or she can be eliminated from the list. The sooner you both can be cleared, the better. I'm sure you understand this."

"What about the guests who were here at the time? Are they all suspects, as well? They've all gone home now. What about them?" Piper asked.

"The patrol deputies took statements from all of them initially to see what they knew. If we cannot find a successful fingerprint or palm print match among the people who work here at the lodge, of course the lodge guests will be considered next," Claire said. "But I believe the killing was personal, Piper. Committed by someone who knew Blake Helms well. Someone with a motive. And chances are great that none of the guests had a motive to kill Blake."

Piper darted an icy glare toward Claire. It was an angry stare that pierced to the core of the investigator's heart. Then Piper pushed her chair away from the table and walked off in the direction of the front door. Without uttering a word, Jay got up and trailed behind his wife.

Claire and Guy locked eyes. A long minute passed before either of them could speak.

"This is real tough," Guy said. "And we still need to get to the bottom of the affair allegation, too."

"Tell me about it," Claire said. She exhaled deeply. "I want to go over the lab results with you."

"Let's take a walk and talk outside," he suggested.

As the two sleuths ambled around the grounds of the lodge, Claire filled Guy in on everything Sheriff Bell had shared with her.

"Now what?" he asked. "I say we'd better find out what caliber gun Heidi Flynn owns—and fast."

"My thoughts exactly. And I want to learn more about sapphire gravel."

They jogged back to the lodge and asked if Heidi Flynn was working that morning. Upon learning that she was cleaning the "Balsam" room, they went to find her. When they knocked on the door, Heidi pulled it open.

"Yeah? What is it this time? More questions?" she asked.

"Just a few, Heidi," Claire said.

The investigators pushed past the housekeeper and entered the room.

"Heidi, please shut the door and come over and talk to us," Claire said. "It's important."

Heidi Flynn pushed the door closed and reluctantly approached the investigators. She sat down on the edge of the bed.

"Heidi, we know that you own a gun," Claire said. "We'd like to see it."

"I can't show it to you," Heidi said.

"And why is that?" Claire asked.

"Because it's missing," the trembling housekeeper said. "It's gone from my purse. Along with the box of ammunition I also kept there."

"How long have they been missing?" Guy asked.

"Several days ago—they both disappeared."

"Did you report them missing?" Guy asked.

"No," Heidi said. "Should I have?"

"Do you have a permit to carry a gun, Ms. Flynn?" Guy asked.

"I do," the young lady replied.

"Why do you carry a gun?" Claire asked.

"For protection. My boyfriend makes me."

"What is your boyfriend's name?" Claire asked.

"Sam."

"Does Sam have a last name?" Claire asked.

"Yes."

"And that is?" Claire persisted.

"Why? Are you going to call him?" Heidi asked.

"Probably," Claire said. "His last name?"

"Barlone," Heidi replied. "His name is Sam Barlone."

"Does Sam also carry a gun?" Guy asked.

"He does. We go target shooting together. Is that a crime?"

"What type of gun do you own, Ms. Flynn?" Guy asked.

"A .38 Special," the housekeeper replied. Her hands shook violently.

"That fires five rounds, doesn't it?" Claire asked.

The frightened girl looked up at Claire. "Yes. Why?"

"Because Blake Helms was shot five times in the chest with a .38 Special," Claire said. "That's why."

Heidi Flynn fainted.

GUY LOMBARD and Claire Caswell walked into the lodge conference room and found it empty. Stepping inside, Guy closed the door behind them. He picked up the phone and began making the appropriate calls to inquire as to whether Heidi Flynn was properly registered to carry a firearm in the state of Montana.

The room had a desktop Apple iMac computer sitting on one end of the table for lodge business use, and while Guy made calls, Claire logged on to begin her online search to find out more about Heidi's Iowa connections.

Minutes later, Guy looked up at Claire. His expression told the story.

"Heidi Flynn is okay to carry a gun in Montana," he said. "She's properly licensed, and the gun is registered to her. She obtained her carry permit in Iowa, and Montana recognizes that permit. So, she's perfectly legal."

"Okay. Good information," Claire said. Her attention strayed.

"Now, using the gun to threaten a coworker, that of course is not legal—even though the revolver was not loaded. But as I said earlier, without a witness, the case will go nowhere. It would simply be Heidi's word against Rosie's."

Guy realized that Claire was not paying attention to what he was saying.

"I'd like to talk to Heidi's boyfriend," she said. "Let's track him down."

Claire hammered away on the keyboard, seeking an address for Sam Barlone, and in no time flat, she found it.

The investigators had walked Heidi to a room in the lodge next to the kitchen to rest after she had revived from her fainting spell. The room had a cot, blanket, and pillow, and Heidi gladly agreed to lie down and take a break until she felt better. Claire delivered a glass of water to her and said they'd be back to check on her. Now was the time.

They walked to the room and found Heidi fast asleep.

"Let's go find Sam," Claire said. "She'll be fine here."

They drove to the address only miles from the lodge and pulled up to a white trailer home. A young man, looking to be only slightly older than Heidi Flynn, was on his knees, peering into the flowerbed in front of the dwelling. He stood up when Guy and Claire exited the Land Rover Discovery, and he walked over to meet them.

The knees of the young man's blue jeans were covered with dirt, and he held a spade in one of his gloved hands.

"Are you looking for someone?" he asked.

"Yes. We're looking for Sam Barlone," Claire said.

"What do you want with him?" the young man asked.

"We're investigators assisting the Lake County Sheriff's Office. We're looking into the murder of Blake Helms at Mountain Lake Lodge," Guy said. "Are you Sam?"

Sam's face turned grim. "Why are you here? Has something happened to Heidi?"

"No, Heidi is fine," Claire said. "I'm presuming you are Sam Barlone."

"Yeah," he uttered slowly.

"I hate to tell you this and don't want you to worry," Claire said, "but Heidi fainted not long ago when we were asking her some questions. She's perfectly okay now, though."

"Where is she?" Sam asked, a sincere look of concern on his youthful face. "I need to call her." He pulled his cell phone from a shirt pocket.

"I'd wait awhile, Sam," Claire said. "Heidi is resting now. At the lodge. We left her sleeping. I'd give her a few more minutes."

"Oh, thank goodness," he said. "So, why exactly are you here?"

"We wanted to tell you about Heidi, and we'd also like to talk with you about some other things," Claire said. "Is there a place where we can sit down and visit for a few minutes?"

"Sure. Come on in," Sam said.

The investigators followed Sam up a couple steps and into the trailer home, where he offered them each a seat at the kitchen table. "I just baked some chocolate-chip cookies. Would you like some?

And a cup of coffee?"

"Sure," Guy said. "Never pass either of those up." He raised his eyebrows and smiled.

Sam set a full plate of still-warm cookies on the table and poured two cups of hot coffee.

"Now, what is it you'd like to talk with me about?" Sam asked.

"We'd like to talk to you about your girlfriend, Heidi Flynn," Claire said.

Sam laughed a silly laugh. "My *girlfriend*? Is that what she told you?"

16

THE SEEMING NORMALITY of the situation surprised the sleuths. They hadn't expected it. Sam Barlone appeared to be a rather well-adjusted and respectful young man.

"I chuckled because you called Heidi my *girlfriend*," Sam said. "Actually, she's my *wife*. Kept her own last name, though, so I can understand the confusion."

"We didn't know the two of you were married," Claire said, trying to hide her surprise.

"Yep. Heidi is the love of my life. We met right after she moved out here, and we hit it off. Got married after dating just a few months. She's my girl." He grinned widely.

Claire eyed the band he wore on his left ring finger and studied Sam as if trying to ascertain his truthfulness. All signs indicated that he was being honest.

"I try to provide Heidi with a stable family life—something she's never had before," Sam said.

"Tell us about her gun," Claire said.

"Well, I insist she carries it wherever she goes. Most everybody's armed around here, and I want her to have the same kind of protection they all have, just in case she ever needs it."

"Is she a good shot?" Claire asked.

"I'd say so," Sam said. "We practice at the shooting range whenever we can. She's a regular Annie Oakley." He grinned. "A natural."

"Are you a good shot, too?" Claire asked.

"I guess so. They call me a sharpshooter at the range," Sam said, chuckling. "My father taught me to shoot when I was old enough to hold a gun in my hands. And he always stressed gun safety. The more familiar you are with firearms and how they operate, the more you can safely use them, he used to tell me. I always emphasize that fact with Heidi, too."

"Is your father alive?" Claire asked.

Sam's eyes instantly moistened.

"No, he passed away a couple years back. Never had the chance to meet Heidi, and I've always felt bad about it." He sniffled. "He would have liked her. And my mom, she passed shortly after my dad. It was a tough time for me . . . and then along came Heidi, like she was dropped from heaven, just for me."

"Do you know if Heidi has ever used her gun to threaten anyone?" Guy asked.

The color drained from Sam's face. "She would *never* do that. Not under *any* circumstances. Not possible."

"So if a coworker of hers said that Heidi threatened her with a gun, what would you say to that?" Claire asked.

"What I'd say is, hogwash. I'd say the coworker has a gift for creating fairy tales."

"Did you ever meet Blake Helms?" Claire asked.

"The murdered employee at the lodge?" Sam asked.

"Yes, that's the man," Claire said.

"No, I never met him. My wife told me that he was found murdered at the lodge, though."

"Yeah," Guy said. "Mr. Helms was shot five times with a .38 Special."

Sam stared at the investigators.

"Heidi told us her gun is missing," Guy said.

Sam looked away. It was clear to Claire that the cogs in his brain were quickly putting two and two together.

"Did Heidi ever talk to you about Blake Helms?" Claire asked.

"Oh, sure. He used to ball her out about the quality of her cleaning. She said he reminded her of her own father, in that nothing she did ever seemed to be good enough for him. It was a bit of a sore spot for her."

"How so?" Claire asked.

"Well, Heidi's father always criticized everything she did, whatever it was. She could never seem to do anything right. He was a tyrant. A bully. She finally moved away from Iowa just to escape him. Actually, she hasn't talked to the man since she moved out here. He doesn't know about us," Sam said, staring off. "But then Heidi had to deal with Blake Helms here in Montana. He wasn't much different than her own father in certain respects."

"How much did she dislike Blake?" Claire asked.

"As strange as it might seem," Sam said, "I think she hated Mr. Helms and liked him at the same time. She told me she loathed how he spoke to her, and she said she always fought back—just like she did with her father when he criticized her work. But despite it all, I think his presence was strangely calming to her . . . maybe because it was familiar. I guess it reminded her a bit of her home life, and oddly, that brought a level of comfort to her." He shrugged his shoulders. "Go figure."

Just then, the sound of a crying baby could be heard from the adjoining room.

"Excuse me," Sam said. He left the room and returned coddling an infant in his arms. "Meet Ethan. He's our nine-month-old son. And the pride and joy of our life."

The baby cooed and gurgled with spirited eyes, obviously feeling quite secure in his father's arms.

"We had no idea the two of you had a child," Claire said. "He's beautiful."

"Thank you," Sam said. He paused and kissed Ethan on the top of his head. "For now, I'm the house hubby. I take care of little Ethan when Heidi's at work. I inherited a nice sum of money and some land when my parents died, so we don't have to work." He looked at his son lovingly. "Heidi, on the other hand, *wants* to work. She insists on it, in fact. I tell her it's not necessary, but she says it does her good to get out of the house every day and to bring some money into the household. As hard as I've tried, I can't talk her out of it. She has a strong work ethic, pounded into her by her father." He gently caressed one of his son's tiny hands. "She found a job six months after little Ethan was born." He paused. "Heidi told me she never mentions us at work. Apparently, no one even knows she's married or that she has a child. She likes to keep her private life private. It's a form of self-protection, I think. The less people know about her, the less her chances are of being hurt, I suppose. Not sure I understand her thinking fully."

"Well, we won't keep you any longer, Sam," Guy said. "Thank you for talking with us." The former Miami-Dade state attorney had seen and heard enough.

"You're sure Heidi is okay?" Sam asked. He looked at Claire for an answer.

"She's fine. Why don't you give her a call now," Claire said. "I'm sure she'd love to hear from you."

Sam grinned and showed the investigators to the door. "Thanks for stopping by. You're welcome back anytime." He pulled out his cell phone.

"NOW *THAT* was an overwhelming surprise!" Claire said. "Very unexpected."

On the drive back to the lodge, the sleuths discussed the interview with Sam.

"I have a different impression of Heidi than I did before," Guy said. "However, one thing we'll never know for sure is whether she threatened Rosie with a gun. I wonder why Rosie might have lied about that. And, if so, why did Rosie want to disparage Heidi to such a great degree? Why did she point us directly at Heidi? Did Rosie do that so we wouldn't look more closely at *her*?"

"Now you're thinking like me," Claire said. She smiled a sweet smile. "It's astonishing how a few facts thrown into a situation can sometimes change the picture so quickly and without notice. Supposedly reliable testimony often evaporates instantaneously when factual information trickles in. We'll have to wait and see if anything more comes out on Rosie. Stay tuned."

As Guy pulled the 4 x 4 into the parking lot near the lodge, the sleuths noticed two squad cars parked in front of the building's entrance.

"They're here doing the fingerprinting and palm printing and obtaining DNA samples from the women," Claire said.

"What do you suppose they'll find?" Guy asked.

"We should know soon. They'll expedite processing the DNA comparisons in a case like this, where the murderer is still at large and could strike again at any time. It will be interesting to see if they'll find a match."

Whitefish Police Department

THE ASSISTANT chief, Detective Lieutenant Herb Keller, Detective Curtis Briggs, the patrol lieutenant, the patrol sergeant, and the patrol officers each took a seat in the conference room. Chief Stan Soderberg had called an emergency meeting. The mood was somber. No one knew what to expect, and the entire force sat in trepidation, fearing what was about to unfold. A pot of hot coffee sat in the middle of the table, along with cups. Today no sweets were brought in.

"Listen up and listen good," Chief Soderberg said. His tone was low, his facial expression austere. "As you all know by now, another house in the Iron Horse community was struck over the weekend, and this one is the most troubling invasion to date. The terrorized homeowners are still in a state of shock. I just got off the phone with them. The burglar surprised them in their sleep, in the dead of night. Each of them awoke from a sound sleep to the horror of being bound, gagged, and blindfolded. Then the intruder pressed a cold metal object—presumably a gun—into the victims' foreheads to terrorize them. He instructed them that one move by either would result in death to both. He made his way around the lavish home, grabbing prized oil paintings from the walls—artwork the couple had collected throughout the years, artwork with sentimental value. He managed to open and clean out their safe and made off with its contents, too. Cash, jewelry, and watches. The couple seems to think they might have forgotten to activate their alarm system before going to bed, saying they fell asleep watching TV." He reached for his cup and gulped his coffee.

"This is the first time the burglar has hit with the owners at home. Whether they surprised him by being there, or whether he's simply getting more desperate, we can't be sure. Whatever the reason, this kicks our investigation up to a whole new level. As you are also aware, two of our patrol officers rushed to the scene immediately after learning of the situation." He lifted an arm and pointed to the officers. "They looked for the stashed items somewhere on the grounds near the house, in hopes of picking the perp up on his return trip to claim the stolen goods, but they found nothing. This time, the culprit took everything away with him at the time of the invasion. I'm guessing he changed his pattern, in case we were closing in on the way he operates. Certainly not uncommon for a serial burglar."

Detective Lieutenant Keller and Detective Briggs shook their heads.

"This is chilling," Detective Lieutenant Keller said.

"It's the tenth invasion at Iron Horse, and the worst one of all." Chief Soderberg let out a sigh of exasperation. "I want this criminal stopped." A grim expression possessed him. "Ms. Caswell suggests we take a look at the Iron Horse homeowners. She thinks we need to determine if any of them are in dire financial straits. Funny, I never gave as much as a fleeting thought about looking at the homeowners themselves. I thought about the Iron Horse employees, but never the owners. I merely viewed the owners as the victims . . . or potential victims." He looked around the room and settled his eyes on Detective Briggs. "This is your assignment, detective. Find out what you can about each and every homeowner at Iron Horse, and do it fast. I want you to check bank accounts. Understand? Let's find out who we're dealing with."

"Roger that, commander," Detective Briggs said.

"And once Briggs determines which of the owners may be in desperate situations, I'll want you to help arrange stakeouts at each of their houses. Work out the logistics with my patrol lieutenant and my patrol sergeant," Chief Soderberg stared directly into the eyes of Detective Lieutenant Keller.

"Got it," Detective Lieutenant Keller said.

"This cannot go on," Chief Soderberg boomed. "We must stop this perpetrator in his tracks. *Whatever* it takes! We need to get the job done. The people of Whitefish deserve peace of mind, and they expect us to restore it. And, dammit, we're going to."

"Where is the burglar fencing the stolen property?" Detective Briggs asked. "So far, nothing has turned up anywhere. I've been checking that on a continual basis."

Chief Soderberg looked at the detective for a time without speaking. Good judgment, years of experience, and vast knowledge of criminal minds afforded the chief wisdom that could not be ignored.

"Let's search outside of this area. Try New York, Los Angeles, Santa Fe . . . the big art hubs." The chief reflected upon what he'd just said. "Yes, try the major art communities throughout the US. Send out the word. Call it out from the hilltops. Tell them all what we're looking for. Give them the names of the pieces and the artists." His gaze continued to zero in on the detective. "Send urgent alerts to all the large jewelry-buying centers across the country, as well. We need to figure out where this guy is dealing the goods."

"I'll get that done today, too," Detective Briggs said. "Count on it. Obviously, the criminal needs cash, so he's got to be dumping the stolen property somewhere. If we find the property, perhaps we find the thief."

"He's a lot more than a *thief*," Chief Soderberg thundered. His face contorted into an ugly expression. "This man's now committed aggravated assault and battery and made terroristic threats. He's rained crazed chaos and violence onto our otherwise quiet community." The chief slammed his fist down hard on the table. "This man goes away for a long time when we find him. And, dammit, it had better be soon. Bring him in, boys. Bring him in."

Back in Bigfork

CLAIRE AND Guy hurried into the lodge. Two small tables had been carried into the lobby area, equipment had been set in place, and the scientific undertaking was well underway. Four members of the sheriff's major case team, operating in pairs, were in the process of obtaining prints from the lined-up employees. Claire and Guy watched in amazement at the state-of-the-art manner in which the team performed its duties.

"Things have certainly changed," Guy said. "I remember when *rolled* fingerprints were the thing . . . when an individual's fingers were first cleaned with alcohol and then dried, and then one by one, the person's entire fingerprint area on each finger was rolled from side to side in ink and then rolled onto prepared cards. And, of course, back then a flat set of inked impressions was taken, as well, to establish the accuracy of the rolled impressions. Guess I'm dating myself, huh?"

"Now it's all digital," Claire said. "No more need for ink and cards." She looked on at the very efficient procedures taking place. "Today, the individual places each finger on an optical or silicon reader surface and keeps it there for just a few seconds. The reader amazingly converts the information taken from the scan into digital data patterns. The computer maps the points on the fingerprints and utilizes them to search its database for a similar pattern—a match."

She paused and considered the speed of the system. "Police officers and crime scene processors can now analyze fingerprints on the spot to see if there's a national match. A waiting period is no longer required to make comparisons. It's mindboggling."

"It still astounds me," Guy said. "Knowledge and technology seem to be increasing tenfold—almost faster than we can keep up with it. Oh well, one thing is certain: we live in interesting times."

"I think I've read there's a one-in-sixty-four-billion chance, or something like that, that of anyone's fingerprints actually match another person's. Pretty darn good odds, I'd say," Claire said.

"Yeah. I'd bet on those probabilities all day long," Guy said.

"Of course. And just think, we get to be a part of it all." She smiled. "Crime investigation is a whole new ballgame nowadays—since forensic science came onto the playing field."

One at a time, each employee moved up in the line until it was his or her turn for fingerprinting and palm printing. From the expressions on the many faces, most everyone seemed anxious to get the whole thing over with and hopefully put the entire ordeal behind them.

The team members used a whole-saliva collection device to obtain a saliva sample from each female employee. This involved collecting a vial of saliva from each person tested, as opposed to using the older, popular method of swabbing inside an individual's mouth. This newer technology produced a superior DNA yield.

All the women appeared to be cooperating fully. Heidi Flynn was up next. She walked over to one of the tables, and the fingerprinting commenced. Claire thought Heidi looked flushed and either excited or nervous. It was impossible to tell. She darted a look at Claire just before the detective started collecting a saliva sampling. The housekeeper's expression struck Claire as peculiar, but again, she could not read it. What was it in Heidi's eyes that bothered the sleuth? Was

Heidi simply tense about being tested? Or did she have something to hide? Was she afraid that the law was closing in on her with every approaching moment? Did she worry about her young son, should this evidence very quickly turn the investigation directly onto her?

The team detective completed both procedures on Heidi and told her she was free to return to her work duties. The housekeeper quickly wandered off, looking downward as she walked.

The lines were drawing to a close.

It was Piper Cantrell's turn. Without words, Piper's face told Claire what she thought about the procedures she was voluntarily subjecting herself to. She was not happy. Not one little bit. Her expression appeared stiff and her lips pursed. Throwing her nose high in the air, she hurried to the table.

"Let's get this done," she said. "I don't enjoy being treated like a suspect in this matter." She gave a disgusted look to the detective assisting with the fingerprinting. "Just what do you think you'll find? I'm an owner of this lodge. My fingerprints are all over the place. Why wouldn't they be?"

"Yes, ma'am," the detective said. "At this time, it's simply procedure. In a homicide case, we can't exclude anyone from the testing until we can rule them out as a suspect. Does that make sense?"

"Not really," Piper said. Her tone echoed hostility. "As if *I* would kill Blake Helms!"

CLAIRE'S CELL phone rang.

"Claire Caswell," she answered.

"Ms. Caswell, it's Chief Soderberg, Whitefish Police Department." He could not hide the exuberance in his voice.

"Chief Soderberg, what is it?" Claire asked.

"The burglar. We figured out who he is!"

"Good job, chief. Who is he?"

"A homeowner right here in the Iron Horse community. Just as you suspected. We checked out all of the owners and found one in *big* financial trouble—an owner sinking in debt, way over his head. He was laid off from his job several months earlier. Bills are piling up and drowning him. We just picked him up for questioning."

"Did he admit to committing the crimes?" she asked.

"Hell, no," the chief said. "He vehemently denies it. And now he's refusing to talk. Won't say another word, as a matter of fact. He's lawyering up."

"How long can you detain him without charging him?" Claire asked.

"We'll hold him forty-eight hours and see if he finds his voice. We plan to search his house during that time. If we don't find any evidence, we'll have to let him go."

Claire nodded pensively and ended the call.

Sheriff Bell looked at Claire and Guy and saw the duo observing the collection of evidence techniques. He immediately walked over to them. "It's going faster than expected," he told the investigators. "No glitches whatsoever. My team will complete the procedures on the afternoon employees when they arrive today for their shift, and before we know it, we'll either have ourselves a real suspect or we'll know we need to look elsewhere."

17

AT ONE-THIRTY THAT afternoon, a short memorial service took place on the lodge grounds for Blake Helms. The State Crime Lab had performed the forensic autopsy and returned the body to Bigfork late that morning. Jay, Piper, Claire, Guy, Sheriff Bell, and all the employees from the morning shift were in attendance. As well, the afternoon shift staff members came to the lodge early to pay respects to a fellow employee who had met with an untimely and violent death. LoLo from the Woods Bay Grill attended, as well as several folks from the Bigfork area who had known Mr. Helms in one capacity or another. Neither of Blake Helms's children, nor his ex-wife, flew in for the service.

The overall tone of the crowd was glum. A slight breeze relieved the heat of the day and circulated the smell of pine needles throughout the air. Comments could be heard amid the gathering, such as, "He was here one minute, gone the next," "*Who* would have killed that poor man?" and "It could have been any one of us."

Claire eyed the crowd without being obvious, taking in the expressions, gestures, and movements of everyone present, looking for anything that seemed out of the ordinary. Suddenly, she hesitated. She grabbed Guy gently by the arm and whispered, "The murderer is here."

Guy's eyes looked quickly but not thoroughly over the lineup of guests. He did not sense what Claire did, but he also respected her rather abnormal powers of perception. The thought that the killer may be standing only feet away sent a chill down his spine. He looked over the entire assemblage a second time, but again, no one and nothing jumped out at him.

A local man of the cloth started the service with two spirited questions: "*What is life?*" he said. "*What is death?*" He paused an uncomfortable minute or two to let his questions sink in. Men and women alike started to squirm in place. "Do we ever really ask ourselves these simple questions?" he continued. "Or perhaps these are not simple questions at all."

Another interlude occurred as his full attention fell upon the gathering. "Each of us lives as if we have endless years ahead of us. But in reality, as witnessed here today, we can never know for certain just how long we have." Attendees listened attentively to the words of the sermon. "The sting of death visited our dear friend Blake Helms in a most unexpected and untimely manner. The process of life that he so enjoyed was violently brought to an end."

The message continued, filled to the brim with powerful, poignant, and particularly moving words, all along calling for deep reflection on the purpose of life. It ended with a directive to show kindness, consideration, and generosity to neighbors, friends, and coworkers. Even to strangers.

A fleeting hush fell over the crowd at the conclusion of the message, and Claire observed many wiping tears from their eyes. For those few moments, it was safe to say that all present—with the probable exception of the murderer, assuming he or she was there—felt a tidal wave of goodwill, compassion, and tenderheartedness toward their fellow man pass through their beings.

All joined in the singing of a hymn, "Amazing Grace," and the ceremony ended. Attendees scattered in various directions.

SHERIFF BELL rounded up the afternoon crew, and the finger-printing, palm printing, and DNA-saliva-collecting procedures started up again. He stood next to Claire and Guy, observing his major case team at work.

"The murderer was here today. At the service," Claire said to the sheriff.

He looked at her, startled by the revelation. "*What?* How could you possibly know this?" He eyed her with great skepticism. "Please explain."

"I have no doubt." She looked determined.

The sheriff raised his eyebrows and shifted his gaze to Gaston Lombard, without words, demanding an explanation.

"Don't question her," Guy said. "She's got . . . a gift."

Sheriff Bell returned his eyes to Claire, and he continued to consider her with keen interest. He scratched his chin and squinted his eyes. Claire lifted the corners of her mouth slightly, knowing exactly what was going through his head. He didn't believe in an inherent mental ability to perceive things by means other than the known senses. He thought it all a lot of mumbo jumbo.

"I see," he said, "*that* again." But he didn't see at all.

"We plan to go over to Blake Helms's apartment tomorrow and take a look around," the sheriff said, "to see if we can find any clues to lead us to his murderer. Care to tag along? We could no doubt use the help."

"Of course," Guy said. "Plan on it."

"Good. We'll finish up here with what we have to do, and then we'll let our lab start the comparison process with the information collected here today," Sheriff Bell said. "Tomorrow morning, let's meet here at the lodge—say, 9:00 a.m.? We'll drive you over to the flat where Blake lived. There's nothing more to do on the case till then."

Jay Cantrell had sauntered over to the conversation and caught the last of it. He looked at Claire and Guy. "Sounds like you two can take a break this afternoon. Piper and I thought we might go horseback riding for a couple of hours. Care to join us?"

Claire and Guy looked at each other and then nodded to Jay.

"Sounds great!" Claire said.

"I'll need to get my cowboy hat," Guy said. "Where's my horse, pardner?"

"Oh boy," Jay said, rolling his eyes at Claire.

Things had remained somewhat tense between the quartet, and Claire thought riding as a couples' activity might remind them all of the friendship they shared apart from the murder investigation.

"I want to grab my boots," she said. "Can we meet you and Piper back here in fifteen minutes?"

"Make it a half hour. I'll go pick Piper up," Jay said. "There are some trails I want to show you."

Claire and Guy walked to their room and changed into casual Western wear. Claire pulled on her red cowboy boots, and Guy donned his favorite bolo tie with a turquoise stone.

"I can't remember when I last rode a horse," Guy said. "Hope it's not difficult."

"It's been a few years for me, too," Claire said. "We should probably take it easy. Being saddle sore is not a pretty picture."

THE FOURSOME met back at the lodge, ready to jump into the saddle and enjoy Big Sky Country the Western way. The day's sky looked like an enormous artist's canvas of bright, clear blue stretched across the heavens and splashed with a handful of fleecy white clouds. The temperature was in the low eighties, and the sun was radiant—a perfect day for riding.

"Come on," Jay said. "The day's a-wastin'."

Jay looked dapper in his jeans, boots, cowboy hat, and elk antler bolo.

"We're ready," Claire said.

"Jump in the Suburban. We'll drive over to the stable," Jay said. "It's on a piece of property I own not far from here. I have a man who takes care of that land, and I gave him a heads-up. He agreed to have four of our best quarter horses saddled up and ready to go. You're in for a treat."

Claire and Guy looked at each other and smiled. "Can't wait," they said in unison.

Piper was quiet, and Claire realized she still harbored anger about being included in the testing procedures.

After driving a few minutes, Jay turned the vehicle into a commercial-development area that housed a gas station, convenience store, office building, and yarn shop. The fine antique stagecoach on display near the convenience store garnered Guy's attention as they passed by. The foursome made their way through the area and onto and up a bumpy, winding dirt road—Stage Ridge Road. At the top, Jay pulled up near an old farmhouse. A rustic barn greatly in need of a coat of white paint stood on the property, as did a corral brimming with quarter horses.

"They're beautiful!" Claire announced. She looked from horse to horse as she spoke.

Jay pointed to an area just outside the enclosure. "These are the horses we're riding today, a little more on the spirited side than the rest of 'em. They're all saddled up—Western style, I might add—so you'll have a pommel on the saddle in front of where you sit, to hang on to."

"I might need that," Guy said under his breath. "It's been a while since . . ."

Jay chuckled.

"You'll be fine, Guy," Piper said. "Both you and Claire have ridden before, and actually, it's a lot like riding a bike . . . You'll see."

The foursome alit from the vehicle and walked toward the readied horses. They stopped a few feet away to observe the animals at closer range.

Claire felt immediately drawn to the champagne-colored horse with white markings on his body, a white mane and tail, and greenish eyes. "I like this buff-colored one," she said. As she spoke, the horse nudged its way closer to her and rubbed its nose gently on her shoulder. She stroked his face over and over. "Aren't you a big baby," she said.

"I've never seen anything like it," Jay said. "He's usually standoffish around strangers." As he watched the interaction between Claire and the palomino paint, an amused expression took over his face. "Looks like you'll be riding Whispering Spirit today, Claire. No question about it."

"Guy, I'm putting you with Giddy Up, the grullo." He pointed him out. "He's the rarest color of quarter horse, and he's got a great disposition. You two will get along fine."

"What did you call the horse? *Grew—what?*" Guy asked, not sure he had heard the word correctly.

Jay laughed. "Grullo," he repeated, pronouncing the word as *grew-yo*.

Guy thought he heard Piper emit a muffled chuckle, but he

couldn't be sure. The creature Jay indicated had a smoky—almost silvery—color, with a black mane and tail and black lower legs. He was a startlingly stunning animal with kind eyes.

"I'll be riding Hawk of the Wind, the black horse, and Piper will ride Danny Boy, the light chestnut," Jay continued.

"Use their names when you give them a command," Piper said. "They like that."

Claire smiled at her.

Jay looked at his friends. "Each of you spend a few minutes getting to know your horse," he said. "Pet his nose, talk to him using a soothing voice, and allow him to smell you. Be calm and confident around your animal. A horse can tell if his rider is scared or nervous, and your attitude will have an effect on your horse. Oh, and another thing, don't forget these are big animals. Always exercise caution and good common sense."

Claire and Guy took the assignment seriously and did exactly what Jay had recommended. Ten minutes passed.

Jay mounted his horse and demonstrated to Claire and Guy how to sit—pulling his spine and lower back slightly in, holding the reins just so, and cueing the horse using his legs. "Always mount your ride from the left, and once you're in the saddle, keep your center of gravity over the horse's. That way, you'll never fall off," Jay said. "Let your legs relax, and position your knees flat against the saddle. And remember not to put too much of your boot in the stirrup. Best to keep your toes pointing a bit upwards and only have the balls of your feet resting on the stirrups. That way, should anything necessitate it, you can kick your feet out quickly."

"The reins are held how?" Guy asked. "One more time."

"Down and over the front of the saddle," Jay said. "Don't pull tightly on them, or the horse will think you want to stop. Instead, give the horse room to move. Kick your horse gently in the side and make a clucking sound with your tongue to get him to move." He demonstrated. "Pressure from your left leg will signal your ride to move to his right; pressure from your right leg will signal your horse to move to his left. Also, our horses have learned to neck rein. So, holding the reins in one hand and simply moving the reins to the right—so that the left rein lies across the left side of the horse's neck—will turn your horse to the right. The reverse is also true."

"It sounds more complicated than it actually is," Piper said. "You'll see that it all comes quite naturally."

"To stop, we pull the reins firmly back toward us, correct?" Claire asked.

"Yes. And say, 'whoa,'" Piper explained.

"One last thing," Jay said. "When you're traveling uphill, lean forward in your saddle; when you are traveling downhill, lean back in the seat. This helps the horse keep its balance. Now, if we're all ready . . ."

One by one, Piper, Claire, and Guy mounted their horses from the left, each placing their left foot in the stirrup and hoisting their right leg up and over the top of a magnificent gelding. At once, they settled into their saddles and grabbed the reins as instructed. Claire and Guy were a bit tense, but eager to see more of the Montana countryside. After all, the day was utopian. *What could go wrong?* Claire asked herself.

"All set?" Jay asked.

"Ready," Claire said.

"Ready," Guy said.

"Give your horse a soft kick into the sides with your heels to get going. Just as I showed you," Jay said.

Claire gently kicked Whispering Spirit in the sides. He whinnied loudly and bolted off, like the wind, quickly moving from a trot to a canter to a full gallop within no time at all, his feet leaving the ground with each stride. Holding the reins in her right hand, she grabbed the pommel with both hands, thankful it was there. She desperately tried to keep her center balanced, as Jay had told them, but she found it was no easy task. It was as if Whispering Spirit had a mind of his own.

Guy was alarmed at what he saw. Piper, an obvious expert rider in full control of Danny Boy, rode off after Claire. In no time at all, Piper pulled ahead of Claire and took the lead. "Come on, follow me," she yelled back, turning in her saddle to look behind. "Whispering Spirit is unusually frisky today. Hang on tightly."

Guy gave Giddy Up a kick with his heels, and the horse walked off slowly in the direction Claire and Piper headed.

"Give him a stronger kick, Guy," Jay instructed. "Sometimes he needs a little extra encouragement to get going."

Guy followed instructions, and his horse at once picked up speed, trotting toward the others. Jay rode alongside Guy, sensing his apprehension with the situation.

"In a few minutes, you'll have the feel of it, counselor," Jay said, giving Guy a reassuring thumbs-up. "Claire will be just fine with Piper. Don't worry."

"No problem," Guy said. He felt anxious, and he worried whether Claire was really okay. "It's already coming back to me, Jay. Really." Sensing that Jay was looking at him in a questioning manner, Guy said, "Let's go, Giddy Up. Show me what you've got."

Jay choked back laughter, seeing how stiff Guy was sitting in his saddle. It was easy to imagine Gaston Lombard dressed in a double-breasted suit, standing before a jury, but in Western garb, sitting on a horse—now, that was a different story.

Guy could now see Piper on Danny Boy and Claire on Whispering Spirit in the far-ahead distance. In the worst way, he wanted to be riding alongside Claire.

A half hour passed, and Piper and Claire slowed their horses to a trot and rode up to a clump of noble pines. They got off to wait for the others to catch up.

"This is exhilarating!" Claire said. "I can't believe how much I've missed riding. I was terrified at first, but within a few minutes, I couldn't get enough of it." She stroked Whispering Spirit's velvety nose. "You are a good horse, yes, you are." The horse turned his large olive eyes toward Claire, and they stared at each other. She kissed him gently on the nose. "You have fierce courage. I like that."

Whispering Spirit whinnied softly and threw his head back into the air.

"It's addicting . . . this riding," Piper said. "Follow me. There's a mountain stream a few feet from here. Let's walk our horses to it and let them drink.

Claire pulled the reins over her horse's head and led him toward the water, following only steps behind Piper and Danny Boy. While the horses drank the cool spring refreshment, the women talked.

"You can never be too careful around horses, Claire. While they would never hurt you intentionally, something outside of their control can spook them and cause them to act irrationally. Always have an escape route—a way off the animal in your mind's eye. A plan. Just in case something goes wrong."

Claire listened intently to the warning from her friend. Then she changed the subject. "I'm sorry about the fingerprinting and other testing, Piper. I know you're upset about it and furious with me. But that's the drill in a murder investigation. There's no way around it." Piper did not respond. Claire paused to collect her thoughts. "How are you doing, Piper? I mean, how are you *really* doing? It's been only a short time since Blake's murder. How are you handling it?"

Piper's silence continued for a time.

"If you don't want to talk, I understand," Claire said.

"Death is so final, Claire. I never had a chance to say . . . goodbye. I never got to thank him for being . . . my friend." She looked at Claire with sad eyes.

"I'm sorry, Piper. I'm sorry that you lost your friend."

In the worst way, Claire wanted to ask Piper if it were more than friendship, but the timing did not seem right. Just then, they heard the sound of approaching hoof beats. They turned their heads to see Guy and Jay riding up. Both men dismounted and led their horses to the water, a treat the creatures clearly welcomed.

Guy walked over to Claire and hugged her. "Are you all right?"

"I'm great. Couldn't be better," she said. "How about you?"

"Well, Giddy Up needs a little more *oomph*, if you know what I mean. He's not the fastest horse in the world, but he's also not the slowest. All in all, he's a good ride. I'm enjoying myself, too. But your horse took off like a bat out of hell, Claire. I was worried."

"It was a little touch-and-go at first, but it didn't take me long to get into the swing of it."

Jay pulled four small apples from his saddlebag. He handed one each to Claire, Guy, and Piper and kept the last for himself. "As soon as they stop drinking, we can give the horses a real delicacy. Hold the apple flat on the palm of your hand, like this, and let your horse take it from you." He showed them the proper way. "You'll have a friend for life."

The horses sated themselves with water, and the riders presented each one with a sweet red treat.

After consuming his apple, out of the blue Whispering Spirit jerked his head high into the air, as if sensing something was amiss. He began to move his legs nervously in place, and he turned his head from side to side over and over again. A low whinny emanated from the jumpy creature.

"It's okay, Whispering Spirit," Claire said, using a soothing voice.

"It's okay." She gently stroked his nose over and over.

"Wish I knew what's spooking him," Piper said. "He seems kind of wild today."

"Maybe he smells a bear or deer in the area," Jay suggested. "That will do it. Or he might have seen something unfamiliar that scares him."

"I don't know," Claire said. "This came on fast."

"Well, whatever it is, he seems to be quieting down now. Are we ready to ride again?" Jay asked. "We still have some time."

18

THE RIDERS MOUNTED their horses and in four-abreast formation trotted down the pathway. Whispering Spirit continued to twitch, and Claire could do nothing to quiet him down. What was getting to him? She wished she knew.

Forty minutes passed as the two couples rode and delighted in the day, taking in the sights and sounds of Big Sky Country. The investigators could not seem to get enough of it all.

"I like Montana," Guy declared. "How beautiful is it here?"

Claire smiled.

Piper smiled, too. "It's working, Jay. They're getting hooked."

"Happens to the best of them." Jay chuckled. "This is God's country, and it never takes long for visitors to realize it."

Claire had been noticing more and more that the change in scenery was working its magic on Guy. And of course, being thrown into another intriguing case, that alone helped keep his mind off the haunting time in Crete, at least for now. She found herself smiling when she realized Guy was having fun again. And she admired him greatly for being able to put aside the low spirits that had been weighing him down.

Out of the blue, Whispering Spirit reared his head and took off in a full gallop. Despite noble efforts, Claire was unable to stop the gelding or even slow him down. She clutched the pommel in lonely desperation as he ran unrestrained and out of control. A bee sting, rattlesnake bite, or wild animal nearby could have explained the unpredictable behavior, had the onset been sudden, but that wasn't the case. Something had been bothering the creature all afternoon. *What was it?* Piper and Jay took off after Claire, but were unable to catch her. Soon both Claire and Whispering Spirit were totally out of sight.

"Something's wrong with that horse today," Piper yelled to Jay. "I've never seen him like this."

"Like the wind," Jay hollered back. "Just like the wind. We'll never catch him." He slowed his horse to a trot, and Piper followed suit.

"Let's hope she stays on," Piper said. "It'll be the ride of her life."

"The gelding will stop when he's good and tired," Jay said. "Let's ride back, collect Guy, and then we'll all go after Claire together. Poor man must be frantic by now."

Guy was more than frantic when they found him. He was agitated. "What the hell's going on? Where is she? *Where is she?*" he bellowed. "We've got to find her."

"We lost her for the time being," Jay said. "When a horse takes to frightened flight like that, there's no stopping him until he chooses to stop. No one can catch him."

"Great. So there's nothing we can do to help her?" Guy asked. "What did you do today, Jay? Give her the horse that spooks and takes to *frightened flight*? And put me on the slowpoke of the herd? Is this funny to you? Your idea of a joke? Your concept of getting back at us for the tests the detectives put you through? Is it because I said you're a suspect? Is that it? Well, I've had it!" Guy had reached—and gone over—his breaking point, and his temper now controlled him. "I've *fuck-ing* had it!"

"We'll ride in her direction," Jay said. "Eventually we'll find her." He made a conscious decision to ignore his friend's rant.

"Comforting," Guy fumed. "*Real* comforting."

Silence followed as the three rode off in the direction Whispering Spirit had taken Claire.

CLAIRE FELT numb as she clung to the reins and pommel and dug her knees into the saddle. She leaned forward, desperately trying to stay balanced as Whispering Spirit flew through the air. Her eyes watered as the wind cut into her face, and her hands seemed to be inching down the pommel. She held on with all her strength, but she didn't know how long she could last. *Don't let go!* she yelled to herself. *Hang on!* The leather on the saddle seemed slick, and she found herself sliding to the left and to the right. *Stay centered!* she screamed silently. *Stay centered!* She repeated these words in her head and tried to remember everything Jay had told them before the ride. Time jolted into slow motion as she self-anesthetized to get through the sensation of losing all control.

At once, in her mind's eye, she started to relive the drive up the treacherous road to Omalos in Crete. The memory, so deeply embedded within her subconscious, played out as if she were living it for the first time, and there was no way to stop it. She saw herself behind the wheel. The road was dark and too narrow, barely wide enough for her to pass an oncoming car on a curve. It was steep and had no shoulder. The drop was straight down and deadly. Her hands were slipping from the wheel, and she felt lightheaded and out of control—totally and completely incapable of getting out of the potentially deadly situation. She was going to be sick. She needed to throw up.

Then, in a flash, she jolted back to reality. Instead of gripping the steering wheel with all her might, she was again grasping the saddle pommel with impressive strength. She desperately tried to slow Whispering Spirit by pulling back hard on the reins with her other hand, but the creature failed to respond to her attempts to maneuver him and continued on in his unrestrained wild flight. It was as if he were running in the Kentucky Derby with blinders on. She whimpered and tried to scream, but no sound came out. She thought she would black out at any moment and be thrown into the wind.

Then inexplicably, just as suddenly as Whispering Spirit had become unnerved and taken to frenzied flight, he started to slow his gait. He turned sharply to the left and loped for some time, until they came upon a thick grove of trees. At that point, he turned to the right and trotted down a weathered dirt path. High pines lined the way on both sides. The horse progressed as if following a map. Claire watched with misgivings as Whispering Spirit led her to an unexpected clearing at the end of the trail and then stopped dead cold.

She looked around. Why had the horse delivered her to this spot? She slid from the saddle, holding onto the pommel until she stood solidly on terra firma. Whispering Spirit turned his head and looked at her. He was overheated, his hide wet from sweat. She returned his gaze. "What happened to you? You nearly killed me." He acted strangely serene, as if nothing unusual had occurred. He batted the eyelashes on his huge olive eyes.

Claire heard the snap of a twig, and she darted her head around to take a look. "Who is it?" she demanded. "Who's there?"

No reply came.

Her eyes were suddenly drawn upward to a soaring eagle, circling directly above.

She sensed the presence of someone approaching.

"Who's there?" she asked again. The sleuth felt vulnerable and filled with fear.

All at once, a figure appeared. He crossed him arms and stood stoically only feet from her. The man was dressed in a fringed garment made of antelope and deer hide and decorated with colorful beads and hand painting. Long leggings up to his hips, a loincloth, and a belt completed the attire. And he wore leather moccasins on his feet with the bottoms dyed coal-black—the color matching his long, straight hair. A single braid showed prominently near the left side of his face and supported a solitary eagle feather. And a necklace of grizzly bear claws hung loosely around his neck.

"I am Running Cloud, descendant of a great Blackfoot chief," he said. He placed his hand on Whispering Spirit's face and stroked it gently. "Rest, splendid one."

Seeming to enjoy the attention immensely, Whispering Spirit bobbed his head repeatedly and moved in closer to Running Cloud. For a horse usually not at ease around strangers, the two seemed to bond instantly—just as the creature had done with Claire.

"I'm Claire Caswell," she said boldly, uncertain where the encounter would lead. She tried desperately to appear calm.

"Why do you seek me?" Running Cloud demanded.

"Why do *I* seek *you*?" she asked. "My horse literally brought me here, to this very spot. I had nothing to say about the matter, believe me. I just held on for dear life." She eyed the man curiously. "Perhaps you can tell me why I'm here."

"I've been expecting you, white woman. Come with me. We will walk and talk." He grabbed the horse's reins, pulled them over its head, and led Whispering Spirit behind him as they strolled. "This is beautiful country. My ancestors dwelled here for many suns. I come back every summer to visit the senior leaders who remain. Many live in Canada now, but a portion still live here under the big sky. Each time, I learn more about the history of my heritage. Those remaining in the council of village elders teach me about the role of animals and about the traditions of the Blackfoot—their songs, ceremonial rites, culture. They relay to me what they've learned, what they know from vast experience and lore. It's different than what you read in books. I put on these clothes once each year and become one with nature, one with the unspoiled countryside, and one with my people. Does my soul good." He stopped, turned, and faced her. "The Blackfoot call themselves *Niitsitapi*—the real people."

Claire felt uncomfortable. "I think you've made a mistake. You see, my horse galloped to this spot. I have no idea why I'm here. My friends are looking for me as we speak."

"You sought me out!" he boomed. "To seek my wisdom!" He looked deeply into her eyes. "Now, what is it you need, white woman?" He started walking again, and this time, Claire moved briskly beside him to keep up.

She was dumbfounded. But she believed all things happen for a reason. She convinced herself to go with the flow, to talk to the stranger, and to not show uneasiness with the unplanned meeting.

"I'm . . . not sure. I'm an investigator from Florida—Miami Beach, to be exact—here on vacation with my partner, visiting friends."

"What troubles you, woman of pale skin?"

A stunned expression grabbed her face. "What troubles me? I'm not sure I understand . . ."

"Something is puzzling you. What is it?"

She looked at this man in disbelief. What was happening here? What really prompted this unexpected experience? Thoughts of grabbing the reins from his hand and jumping on Whispering Spirit's back to make a rapid getaway flashed through her mind. But as quickly as those notions appeared, they left. For some unknown reason, she felt compelled to stay and talk with him. "We're working on a murder investigation," she said. "A desk clerk was killed . . . shot to death . . . while working the nightshift at a lodge in nearby Bigfork, and the Lake County sheriff asked my partner, Gaston Lombard, and me to help solve the case."

"And?"

"And . . . we have very few clues to follow."

"Who do you suspect did the killing?" Running Cloud asked.

"The sheriff believes it happened during a robbery, due to the fact that valuable paintings and some other items were stolen at the same time. And since many burglaries have occurred recently in the Whitefish area, he also feels the crime was most probably committed by the same perpetrator."

"I asked you, who do *you* believe committed this crime? I am not interested in what law enforcement is inclined to believe."

Walking had lessened to a slower pace and once again stopped altogether. Running Cloud turned and narrowed his eyes as he observed Claire.

"Now answer my question, white-faced woman."

"I don't know," Claire replied. "There are many suspects. It's too early to—"

"Silence!" he thundered. "I don't want excuses. I will ask you again. Who do *you* believe the killer to be?"

Claire was rattled. She didn't have the answer. Did she? The faces of the suspects flashed before her. "I'm not sure . . . I have more work to do."

"You look in all the wrong places, investigator woman. Close your eyes and see the *big* picture. Like gazing across the big sky in this vast territory, you must concentrate on the big picture first. Details will follow. You do not always see with your eyes wide open, so close your eyes to see. Do it now!"

Afraid she'd ignite his ire to a greater degree if she refused, Claire shut her eyes.

His voiced dropped to a whisper as he cued her. "Now let yourself envision the murder scene. Stand in the background and watch it unfold before your eyes. Think carefully. Take it in piece by piece. Touch it. Hear it. Smell it. Taste it. See it. Judge with all of your senses. What are you missing in your investigation? The answer lies in the big picture."

Claire started to speak.

"Silence!" he said authoritatively. "Let your mind do the work, not your voice."

For the next several minutes, Claire let her thoughts return to the time she had entered the lodge lobby on that fateful morning. Before long, she entered a dreamlike state. In her mind, she soared through the air, like a raptor, looking down upon the crime in progress. It was as though the lodge's rooftop had opened up and allowed her a secret look inside. She saw the night desk clerk, and she saw a shadowy figure standing in front of him on the other side of the check-in desk. Close. Too close. The figure pulled a gun from beneath his jacket and aimed it at Blake Helms. Her eyes darted to Blake's face, and she saw his horrifying look of utter disbelief. He didn't try to defend himself. It happened all too quickly. In an instant, Mr. Helms reeled and fell to the floor, dead. Claire's eyes remained firmly closed. What did she see surrounding the shadowy figure? She couldn't focus in on it. She lost all track of time.

Unexpectedly, Whispering Spirit let out a high-pitched whinny and gently nudged her back with his nose. The illusion playing in her mind came to an abrupt halt. She opened her eyes. Running Cloud was gone. He had left without making a sound. How much time had passed? Minutes? An hour? She wasn't wearing her watch, so she couldn't be sure. She looked at Whispering Spirit, grabbed the reins, threw them over his head, and pulled herself up and into the saddle. "Let's go find the others," she said. She clicked her heels into his sides and turned him around. "But please just trot this time."

She regretted that Running Cloud had left without telling her. The encounter had been strange, surreal. She wanted so badly to ask him more about the murder and what they may be overlooking in the investigation. And for some reason, she wanted to ask his opinion about Guy, too. She needed to know if he'd fully recover from the trauma he'd been through, and she sensed Running Cloud may have some insight into that situation, as well. But now the opportunity was gone. Maybe forever. Then, all at once, she knew the answer: Guy would heal completely and return to how he had been prior to the tribulation in his life. Like a bolt from the blue, she no longer had any doubts about it.

Whispering Spirit took the lead, retracing his steps to get back out of the secret area. When he reached the open land, Claire took full control of the reins and said to the gelding, "Find my friends. They'll be searching for us." Dutifully, the horse trotted along in the direction they came from earlier, as if the two had never taken the detour. After riding quite a distance, she spotted Guy, Jay, and Piper riding toward her. She felt great relief.

"Claire!" they screamed in unison. Each waved a hand in the air.

"Hey!" she hollered back.

In no time, the group reunited. Everyone started talking at once, and a sense of joyous relief filled the air. Jay and Piper took immediate notice that Whispering Spirit was no longer skittish and seemed back to his old self. They also observed that a peaceful expression replaced the one of deep concern and anger on Guy's face.

Riding side by side, the couples began the journey back to Jay's farm. The day had been challenging. Right now, what they wanted more than anything else was to end the adventure with an uneventful ride back to the place where it had all started with a simple climb into the saddle.

When they arrived at the property, Jay said, "I don't know about the rest of you, but I've worked up a gargantuan appetite. Let's grab a bite at the lodge, and Claire, you can tell us exactly what happened to you today. We're all curious to hear about it."

Once seated in Riley's Pub, and after ordering food and drinks, all attention turned to the female sleuth.

"It was the strangest thing," Claire started. But when she tried to recall the details of the encounter, it all blurred. It was as if the private meeting had been for her eyes and ears only. At least for the time being.

19

Tuesday
Bigfork

CLAIRE SIPPED STEAMING peppermint tea as she settled into the chair in front of the lobby computer. As always, the fragrant hot beverage calmed her. She began her online search for any new information she might find on the recent spate of Whitefish burglaries. Guy sat next to her on a comfortable, chocolate-hued leather chair reading the *Flathead Beacon*, a weekly print newspaper. He was on his second cup of strong black coffee. The sheriff was due within minutes to lead the way to Blake Helms's flat.

"There's a front-page story in the online *Whitefish Pilot* today setting forth the entire history of the ongoing Whitefish burglaries,"

Claire said, "including the latest—where a couple was at home during the time of the invasion. It talks about the arrest of a suspect, a homeowner, and states the police had to release him based upon a lack of evidence."

"That doesn't sound good for the police department," Guy said, looking up. "That last invasion is a new twist to the burglaries. Entering when the owners were at home makes this a whole lot more dangerous than before. What else does the article say?"

"Well, for the story, the reporter interviewed Iron Horse management, the homeowners victimized by the criminal, Detective Briggs, and several patrol officers working the case. Each gives his or her opinion of the 'plague' besetting Whitefish—that's how the reporter refers to it—and the unsuccessful efforts of law enforcement to date to stamp it out. Apparently, the Whitefish Police Department is now calling for help from the community to identify the perpetrator."

Claire continued, "Detective Curtis Briggs is quoted as saying, 'The person committing this series of home burglaries has insider knowledge. We have no doubt about it. He knows when folks are away, and he knows when folks are at home. That said, this last time the owners surprised him by being asleep in their bed when he entered the property, as they had altered their travel schedule. And while the owners were not harmed, they remain highly traumatized. We believe the intruder is someone we may all be familiar with. He could be a neighbor, friend, coworker, home repairperson, or anyone else. He has in-depth knowledge of security systems and how they work, and we think he has a keen eye for art. Keep your eyes peeled and your ears open. The person committing these acts is clever—skilled at lockpicking and an ace at disarming home security systems. So far, he has eluded law enforcement in a masterful way; in some cases, narrowly escaping our clutches, but escaping them nonetheless. He wipes all fingerprints from surfaces he touches, or he wears gloves from the point of entry to the point of exit. He leaves no clues behind of his being at a property.'"

Guy listened intently as Claire read on. "He ended with a serious plea, 'If you hear, see, or know *anything* that may be of help to us, please call our station or stop in and see us. We need the help of the community on this one. Help us solve these crimes!'"

Claire scanned the remainder of the article and then paraphrased it for Guy.

"The citizens of Whitefish are becoming increasingly irritable and full of anger. Their displeasure is growing day by day. They're asking how long this criminal will be allowed to ravage their peaceful little area of the world without being stopped; they're questioning why the police department cannot catch this culprit; and they want to know how the villain is always able to outsmart law enforcement." Claire tapped her heel on the floor. "Reasonable questions certainly, but I'm thinking the tone of the article is egging on the citizens, instead of quieting them."

Guy nodded. "The people have every right to be upset, but the war drums are beating. This situation could easily spiral out of control real soon."

Claire continued relaying the article contents to Guy. "Listen to this. It sounds like a small group of picketers started to gather outside the Whitefish Police Department days ago, protesting about the thief causing such great havoc on their doorstep—a criminal threatening their peaceful existence and seemingly outwitting the police at every turn. Men, women, and even children joined the cause. Each day, the crowd is getting larger and more hostile. 'Get the job done!' people are yelling at the patrol officers and other members of the force as they pass the group to enter or exit the department building. 'Do your damn job! Catch the good-for-nothing sonofabitch! Nab the sucker!' Ire is mounting with each passing day, and the situation is rapidly escalating from rage to fury."

"There's no doubt about it," Guy said. "The situation is snowballing. Soon it will be impossible to manage, if something doesn't happen. The local police have egg on their collective faces for failing to bring the perpetrator in. Despite valiant efforts, the department looks inept and bungling. Wish we could help them."

"Perhaps we can," Claire said.

Whitefish Police Department

"WE LOOK like idiots!" Chief Soderberg hammered his force. "Freaking *hillbilly* idiots!"

The chief had called another urgent meeting, and his assistant chief, detective lieutenant, patrol lieutenant, patrol sergeant, detective, and patrol officers squirmed uncomfortably in their seats.

"This news coverage is causing me great embarrassment," the chief said, "and I don't like to feel great embarrassment." The glare in his eyes left no doubt that fury possessed him. All officers swallowed hard, as if signaled to perform the muscular movement on cue. "We have one lousy criminal to corral. *One*," he continued to bleat. "And there are *several* of us. Yet we cannot seem to find and arrest this *one* criminal." He paused and looked from officer to officer. "We know the home intruder usually stores his booty on site after he pulls a job and then returns to retrieve it, but this last time, we found none of the stolen items near the property when we searched for them. So he's outsmarted us again! I believe he intentionally altered his modus operandi, just in case we were close to catching him." The chief wiped perspiration from his brow. "I want this bastard found! Set a trap, throw a lasso around his bloody neck, and drag him in. I don't care how you do it, just do it!" He again looked from officer to officer and then stormed from the room.

The team members exchanged glances and raised their shoulders slightly and momentarily.

"How do we rope this guy?" a patrol officer asked. "Seems like he's Teflon coated."

"Well, we'd better figure out right quick how to nab him, if we want to keep our jobs. I've never seen the chief so dammed mad," the patrol sergeant said.

The others nodded.

"Then let's do it," Detective Briggs said. "The burglar's not smarter than we are, but I bet he's laughing his ass off all the way to the bank. Let's plan another stakeout after the next hit, and another, until we catch the contemptible weasel."

"That will take too long," Detective Lieutenant Herb Keller said. He shook his head. "We're out of time. And I'm plum out of any other bright ideas."

Blank faces stared at each other.

Clearly, strong feelings of exasperation and anger abounded both inside and outside of the police station.

Bigfork

CLAIRE FINISHED the article with great interest. She picked up her cell phone and dialed Chief Soderberg.

"We saw the article, chief. You've got a bad situation on your hands. Things just went from bad to worse. You can count your lucky stars the homeowners weren't harmed during this last heist," Claire said. "Did your men find a flattened patch outside the entered property, where the burglar temporarily stashed his loot?"

"For all the sites of his first burglaries, yes, but on the most recent burglary, he didn't follow his pattern. It's almost as if he were tipped off that we might be on to his mode of operation. We were hoping to take him this last time for sure, Ms. Caswell. Hoping he'd revert to his well-established regular sequence, but he fooled us. Toted off everything at the time of the invasion. And we were so optimistic . . ."

"Don't give up yet, chief. The last incident may not have broken his pattern for good. Try looking for a flattened area close to the house again if there's another burglary," she said. "It's possible he saw law enforcement milling around some of the properties and thinks you figured him out, so he's changed his method . . . for a time. Be strong. Stay with it. As you know, thieves often return to a method that's worked for them in the past." As they finished their conversation, she said, "Keep us posted."

The Whitefish police officials she and Guy had met with the past Saturday seemed both intelligent and competent. In fact, she had commented to Guy that she was highly impressed with them. So, what was the Whitefish Police Department missing on this case? How could this burglar continue to elude them? She thought for a moment. The burglar seemed to go unseen . . . to enter and exit any house of his choice on impulse, whenever he so desired, and then take whatever he wanted for his own purposes . . . almost as if he were invisible.

Claire continued to ponder the situation as she sipped the remainder of her tea. Then a word came to her as if a loud voice screamed it out. *Camouflage!* The capability of blending in with the surroundings. All at once, it seemed the only logical explanation. If the criminal was using some type of disguise technique to gain access to these high-end properties, then the police—and she and Guy, for that matter—could play the same game. One, two, or ten could employ trickery and subterfuge to manipulate the situation and change the odds. Perhaps the sleuths would be able to assist the

Whitefish Police Department after all.

She picked up her cell phone and called Chief Soderberg back. "Chief, Gaston Lombard and I would like to meet with you again. How about Friday?" she said. "I have an idea."

Guy looked carefully into Claire's eyes. "What's up? Care to explain your idea to me? That look of determination on your face is hard to miss. I'd recognize it anywhere. Now I'm curious."

She smiled. "Feel like catching a thief? It's going to take some thought and planning, but I think it can be done."

Guy raised his eyebrows. "You've got my attention."

"We need to be one step ahead," she said. She filled him in on her thoughts.

Even as they discussed her plan to catch the Whitefish predator, Claire was convinced the thief was different from the criminal who had murdered Blake Helms. It had been her opinion from the start, despite the fact law officials thought otherwise. The crimes and the methods of operation were wholly different. One was repeatedly after items of value convertible to lots of cash; the other had targeted a specific person. She was sure of it. The Whitefish thief had never committed murder. The items stolen in the early-morning hours of Blake Helms's murder were part of a ruse, done strategically to point the finger directly at the Whitefish burglar, to make it appear the motive was yet another burglary and the clerk merely got in the way. She was sure of it. Blake Helms had been shot at close range. He had looked his shooter in the eyes. Someone he knew had ambushed him.

IT WAS early, and Claire was energized to take a look around Blake Helms's apartment.

Sheriff Bell walked in, right on time, and said, "Ready?"

The investigators left with him and followed behind in their vehicle to the flat that had been home to Blake Helms. Upon arrival, they saw three detectives from the major case team standing beside a patrol van, waiting for them. The property's landlord was outside talking to the men. When Sheriff Bell and the sleuths approached, the landlord handed a key to the sheriff for the upper flat and explained that they needed to walk up the tall flight of stairs around back to access Blake's dwelling—as the place he rented had a separate entrance.

"Only charged him four hundred dollars a month to live here," the landlord said. "He was a quiet tenant. Ideal, really. Never gave me any problems. Paid his rent in full the first of every month. It's a tragedy, it is."

As Claire took each step upward, she pictured in her mind the number of times Blake had taken those very stairs. He had been a vigorous person until someone cut his life short. Who was his murderer? Who had the means? Who had a motive? Who had the opportunity? Blake must have known his assailant. It did not appear that he tried to run or phone for help, and no defensive wounds were found on his body. All instincts told the sleuth that Blake's assailant was someone he knew and no doubt trusted. Someone he did not expect to attack him. Of course, the killer could have been a stranger who pretended to need lodging and then unexpectedly pulled a gun on the night clerk. But for some reason, Claire didn't buy into that theory. There was no evidence whatsoever that Blake had been checking in a would-be guest at the time of his demise. No paperwork or room key had been sitting on the check-in desk, and the registry book had not been open.

When the group reached the platform at the top of the flight, the sheriff handed each of them a pair of latex gloves. Claire stretched them onto her hands and stepped inside. She was initially struck by the neatness and organization of the living space. The second thing she observed were the sheer number of hardcover books filling the six bookcases that lined the living room walls. The colorful works brightened the quarters and added a feeling of warmth to the setting.

Claire found the virtual library impressive. "We now know what Blake did in his spare time and with any spare money."

All eyes riveted to the collection of books, and as they walked around the place, they saw additional titles stacked on the kitchen countertop, sitting on the shelves of the open dining room hutch, and placed on the side tables in the man's bedroom.

Other than the plethora of hardback books, the apartment appeared unremarkable—tidy, sparsely furnished, and not particularly interesting or surprising.

Claire scanned the titles and authors of some of the books sitting on the living room shelves, and she noted that Blake appeared to enjoy both fiction and nonfiction books in a variety of genres. Then her eyes fell upon two full bookcases housing nothing but bound works on the history of Native American Indians in the western United States. Book after book, she observed titles concerning the Blackfoot or the Flathead tribes of Montana.

"Fascinating," Claire said, mostly to herself. "The man must have been a walking encyclopedia when it came to the Native American tribes of this area." Her thoughts reverted to the interview with Phil Kagan and how he had mentioned that Blake was an expert on the Blackfoot and Flathead Indians.

Guy looked up and for the first time took notice of the specific books that had cornered Claire's attention.

"Looks like they've all been read many times over, doesn't it?" he asked. As he talked, he pulled several from the case, one after the other, and opened each front cover. Handwritten notes, presumably penned by Blake himself, referenced page numbers and identified points of particular interest in each work.

"Read, or *studied*," Claire said. "The man must have been an aficionado when it came to the subject." She touched a few spines of the older books and paused as if taking in the history contained between their covers. She pulled a dark green one from the shelf, held it close to her nose, and inhaled. The aroma of the old tome filled her nostrils, and she could almost envision history in the making and hear the author reciting his words.

The detectives listened carefully to the Miami investigators and watched them in action.

"And just how does all *this* help us, Ms. Caswell and Mr. Lombard?" the sheriff asked.

"Not sure yet," Claire said. "But you must admit, it's all quite thought provoking. Tells us a lot about Blake Helms, really."

"Perhaps somewhere among all of this lies a hidden clue," Guy said.

The detectives opened and looked through cupboards, closets, and dresser and cabinet drawers, desperately searching for something that would point a finger in the direction of the murderer.

Claire walked to the kitchen phone and touched the button to retrieve messages. "No messages," she grimaced loudly. She spotted a memo pad and pencil on the nearby counter. Holding the pencil in hand, she drew from side to side, back and forth, with a light to medium touch—over and over again in rapid succession on the top sheet. Unfortunately, no impressions showed from whatever may have been written on the sheet once above it. It was a trick that sometimes worked, but not today. Next she walked to the side table adjacent to Blake's double bed and opened the single drawer. It contained two books, both on the subject of the Blackfoot Indian tribe. She looked around and spotted a laptop computer on a small desk in the corner of his bedroom.

"Mind if we take a look at his computer?" Claire asked.

"Go ahead," the sheriff said.

"Guy, will you take a look? You're good at this," she asked. "See what you can find."

"It's my favorite thing to do," he said. He sat down on an antique oak chair and pulled open the computer lid. Instantly, his eyes grew large as he examined the contents on the desktop. "There's even more Native American information here. Scads of folders."

Claire continued perusing the two books she found in the bedside table drawer. Both detailed the culture of the Blackfoot tribe, and both contained Blake's typical handwritten notations tucked inside the front cover.

"Any objection to my taking these books with me?" Claire asked the sheriff. "I'd like to spend some time looking through them later."

"No objection, Ms. Caswell," he said. "Not sure what you think you'll find, but go ahead. We'll make a note that they're in your possession."

She smiled. "Thank you, sir."

Claire walked back to the kitchen to take another look around. A pair of unwashed coffee mugs sat in the sink.

"Have your men bag these mugs as evidence, will you, sheriff?" she called out. "I'd like to see whose prints are on them. Looks like Blake may have had company recently."

She opened his refrigerator. It contained only a few items: one carton of eggs with three remaining, a partial loaf of white bread, a quart of orange juice, and a partial bag of ground coffee. The victim lived a simple and spare lifestyle by choice, she deduced. His rent was nominal, and his salary at the lodge was more than sufficient—especially with the amount of overtime he put in on a regular basis—to live in a more comfortable manner, if he had chosen to do so. But obviously he had not.

A delightfully strong scent suddenly drew her attention to the bunch of purple-blue lilacs sitting in a wide-mouthed Mason jar on the kitchen table. Would Blake have purchased these flowers? Or cut them from a shrub? Claire pondered the idea. Or was this the touch of a woman? Leaning over, she inhaled the fragrant, slightly withered blossoms.

"Sheriff Bell, I think we should bag this Mason jar and check it for prints, too," she said. She pointed to the container holding the arrangement. "Also, please make a note to obtain fingerprints and palm prints from Lois Whiting—LoLo—at the Woods Bay Grill, and collect her saliva sample, as well. I have a hunch about these flowers . . . and about the potential fingerprints you may find on the two mugs."

"No problem, on both counts," he said. He asked one of the detectives to accede to her requests, and he jotted a note to himself about Lois Whiting.

The team was coming up with nothing of interest, but continued searching.

Guy called Claire over to the computer.

"Look at this," he said. "I didn't know this much information even existed on Native American art, collectibles, and antiques. Blake must have been an expert in all of these areas. And what did he do with this knowledge? It had to be oozing from his being. Bursting at his seams. And to think he was a mere night desk clerk at the lodge, with no real outlet to discuss this with others. He could have taught his vast grasp of the subject to eager students. What a grand waste."

"We don't know that he didn't discuss his knowledge with others," Claire said.

"Pardon me?" Guy asked. "We know about only one person. Phil Kagan."

"Let's find out whom else he may have talked to," she suggested. "Maybe that will explain the second mug I found in his sink."

Claire checked Blake's closet and satisfied herself that he was the only one living in the flat. Shirts, slacks, and jackets hung neatly on the pole, all in various shades of brown or black, and shoes were displayed in systematic order by color. She examined the bottom of each shoe and found no gravel matching that found at the crime scene. She opened the dresser drawers. Sweaters were also colorized and folded to the highest standards of neatness. All underwear was black and neatly stacked, and socks were orderly and sorted by lights and darks. Nothing seemed out of place.

"Has your team dusted the inside of the front door knob for prints?" she asked the sheriff. "No one has touched it since we got here, and we should check it out."

"Already done, Ms. Caswell," Sheriff Bell said. "First thing we did."

Claire was extremely thorough in her search. Sheriff Bell appreciated her help and all, but he also didn't want to be upstaged in front of his men. Claire sensed this to be the case.

"I was sure you had," Claire said, blinking her eyes in unison. "Just wanted to make certain." She smiled kindly.

As he inhaled the history that filled the computer's gigabytes, Guy eyes remained glued to the screen.

Claire looked around again. She hoped they weren't missing anything important. She walked to the bathroom, opened the mirrored medicine cabinet above the sink, and peered inside. Nothing seemed unusual or out of the ordinary. But then she spotted a small container of perfume on the lowest shelf. She took a closer look. It was a woman's perfume. It had a name she didn't recognize, but when she pulled off the top to smell it, the odor was definitely sweet and flowery . . . like fresh lilacs.

On a whim, she raced to the bedroom and pulled down the duvet. She smelled the sheets on both sides. One side definitely smelled fragrant . . . like fresh lilacs. A woman had definitely been there . . . and recently. Who was it? LoLo? Piper? Another female they had interviewed? A stranger? The murderer? Someone who could shed light on who may have wanted Blake dead? They needed to identify the female as soon as possible and question her.

Claire dropped the perfume vial into a zipped evidence bag to preserve it for future fingerprinting, if warranted, then slipped it into her pocket. She had an idea. She returned to the group. Guy had closed the computer and was now filling in the others on his findings. She listened with interest to what Guy reported. After he finished, she told them of her findings and mentioned that she was keeping the perfume with her for the time being.

"Intriguing, Ms. Caswell," the sheriff said. He eyed her with rapt curiosity, as did the others from the major case team. "Any idea just who this mysterious woman might be?"

"Not yet," she said. "But I plan to find out."

The detectives promised to lock up and return the key to the landlord, and the sheriff and investigators departed.

"Are you thinking this unidentified female might be our perp?" the sheriff asked the sleuths on the way down the stairs.

"Too early to tell," Guy said. "But until we figure out who pulled the trigger, she's definitely a suspect—an *unidentified* suspect."

Claire sat quietly on the drive back to the lodge, deeply immersed in thought. She pulled the bag holding the perfume vial from her pocket, unzipped it, held it close to her nose, and inhaled its distinctive aroma.

20

CLAIRE AND GUY consumed a quick sandwich at the lodge and then decided to hole up for the remainder of the day in their room. Jay supplied them with two laptop computers from the lodge. It was time to conduct several background checks. But first, the sleuths reviewed their findings at Blake's flat: the fact that he was a zealous reader; his insatiable craving to inhale everything he could find relating to the Blackfoot and Flathead Indian tribes of the area; and that haunting, sweet aroma of fresh lilacs emanating from the arrangement in the Mason jar on his kitchen table, the perfume vial found in his bathroom medicine cabinet, and the sheets of his bed. There was also the discovery of the two coffee mugs in his sink.

Claire was convinced that if they could find the female who had spent time at his apartment—and between his sheets—the now-unidentified woman might shed crucial light on the investigation. The fingerprints lifted from the flat would prove to be very enlightening if they belonged to someone on their suspect list.

The sleuths also reviewed their notes to determine which lodge employees warranted a closer look.

"The sheriff should be getting back to us shortly regarding whether any of the staff fingerprints or palm prints matched those lifted from the lobby," Claire said. "Can't wait to hear what they come up with."

"Jay told me they do not complete background checks on the people they hire, so when we were at Mr. Helms's apartment, I asked Sheriff Bell to run a criminal background check on each of the employees. That could prove interesting, as well," Guy said.

"Good thinking, counselor. Did you include Jay in that request?" Claire asked.

"I did. And Piper and Lois Whiting, too. As we've said, everyone is a suspect until proven otherwise. "

Guy picked up his cell and called Sheriff Bell. There was no answer, so he left a message. "We're anxious to hear the test results today of the print comparisons involving the lodge personnel and owners and the prints lifted from Mr. Helms's flat. Also, whether anything interesting shows up on those criminal background checks. Please give us a call as soon as you have anything. Thanks."

"I'm holding my breath," Claire said. "It's very possible that things are about to break wide open."

"Yeah. If they can only find a match . . ."

Their eyes locked. No words were necessary.

THE TWO divided up the work to be done, and the investigators got busy. Claire had a strong sense that something in the case would soon help them zero in on the killer.

Hours passed as the sleuths sought background information on the lodge employees most in question. They made countless phone inquiries; conducted numerous Internet searches; checked Facebook, LinkedIn, and other social media outlets; called friends in high places to ask for favors; and checked court records with the clerks of court—all the while frantically scribbling notes. The two stayed in opposite corners of the room, as if an invisible line divided them, and worked without ceasing until Claire finally broke the silence.

"There's something funny about Heidi Flynn," she announced suddenly.

"What'd you find?" Guy asked, looking up from his computer.

"Well, I've found hints of a checkered past. She and some of her friends back in Iowa were arrested in connection with several home burglaries. It was many years ago, and I can't tell if it resulted in an indictment for her. She may have testified against them, actually. Not sure. Something happened. Records are sketchy. Maybe the sheriff will be able to enlighten us."

"Did you find anything on her father?" Guy asked.

"Still looking," Claire said.

"Are you ready for what I found?" Guy asked. "Jay was charged with an assault a couple years ago. He got into a brawl with someone at a gas station. Not a lot of details are public. Looks as if he may have beaten the charge. We'll have to see what the criminal background check shows."

"Okay. I'm surprised. But let's wait until we find out more about it before we pass judgment. We always say things are often not as they seem." Claire got up, stretched, and walked over to the sliding glass door. She pulled it open wider to let in more fresh air. "As I said, I get the picture loud and clear that Jay and Blake didn't get along. And it looks as if Piper may well fit into that whole scenario somehow. But as hard as I try, I cannot imagine Jay losing it to the point that he *murdered* Blake Helms. That I can't digest. If you want my humble opinion, he doesn't have it in him. And I'll bet the assault rap against him disappeared because there was nothing to it."

"We'll know soon," Guy said.

"Yeah. But I'll stake my reputation on my belief that Jay was not involved in the murder. There's some other connection here with these employees. I've felt it from the start. Something is rotten within the lodge staff, and we need to find out who and what it is." A pensive look owned her face. "Jay didn't do it," she repeated. "He did not."

"Hope you're right," Guy said. "I'm half-convinced."

"Many staffers acted strangely during the interviews. Nervously. Eyes were blinking, and some covered their mouths when they answered. Others pulled at their ears, rubbed their eyes, or stroked their chins. Some shifted in the chair, and several were nonresponsive in their answers. These are all signs that liars display," Claire said. "I think we need to concentrate on those with the clear motives, but I'm not ready to strike any names from the list quite yet—regardless of whether they earned a star or stars from us."

"We did observe a lot of curious behavior in that interview room," Guy said. "You'll get no argument from me on that one. In fact, as we said before, the lodge employees are a *colorful* cast."

"So until we find something definitive in our research or until Sheriff Bell gives us clear information to set us on a particular track, we need to keep open minds and not assume anything," Claire said. She looked over her notes. "One thing I'm quite sure about: the Whitefish burglar did not come to Bigfork and murder Blake Helms. It's rare that a burglar suddenly becomes a killer. And the Whitefish criminal has never killed during the Whitefish invasions—even in the one case when the homeowners were at home. And while the couple in that case said he placed something cold and metal to their foreheads, a gun was never actually seen. It could have been something else." Claire stopped and paused to collect her thoughts. "No, I'm quite certain that Blake knew his murderer. The night clerk stared his assailant in the face as the five shots were fired. Tough to imagine Blake's last seconds of shock as someone he knew and probably trusted pulled that trigger again and again." She paused briefly. "The murderer was at the funeral. It's someone here at the lodge. I have no doubts about it."

"You might be right on," Guy said. "But as you know, we need hard evidence to get a conviction."

The two continued with their work until dinnertime. They changed clothes and walked to the lodge.

Jay and Piper were milling around the lobby when the sleuths arrived, straightening things and turning on mood lighting.

"Care to have dinner with us?" Guy asked.

"Yeah," Jay said. "We didn't have lunch today, and we're both hungry."

The four found a quiet table and ordered entrées and a bottle of wine to share.

"How's the investigation coming?" Jay queried. "You're six days into it now."

"We're making headway," Claire said.

"How long do these things normally take to wrap up?" Piper asked.

"They take as long as they take," Claire said. "There are numerous possible suspects in this matter, many with motive, and most all with opportunity. No one has been cleared yet. Once we hear from the sheriff on the print comparisons, we may know more."

Jay swallowed hard. "It's difficult to believe that someone at the lodge may have committed this murder."

"Scares me to think about it," Piper said, "knowing that I may be walking around in the shadows of a killer. I'll rest a lot easier when he's nabbed."

"When he or she is nabbed," Claire said.

Piper looked puzzled. "Are you saying a woman might have done this? I guess I never . . ."

"Again, we don't know at this point who committed the murder, Piper," Claire said. "We assume nothing."

"Well, when you said 'he or *she*,' it sounded as if you may have a female suspect in mind," Piper persisted.

"Sounded that way to me, too," Jay broke in.

"Please don't read anything into those words," Claire said. "I'm only stressing that at this juncture, we don't know for sure."

"Everyone is a suspect until cleared," Guy repeated. "*Everyone*."

The dinners arrived, and the foursome ate in relative silence. In an unspoken kind of way, uneasiness seemed to be developing between the couples to a greater and greater degree.

Claire and Guy excused themselves and returned to their room.

"Don't discount Jay or Piper as suspects, Claire," he said.

Claire stared at Guy, but did not respond.

WEDNESDAY MORNING arrived.

"I want to solve this case," Claire announced, walking from the shower. "It's Wednesday already. Tomorrow it will be one week since the murder."

Guy stopped to look at his beautiful Claire as he stepped around her to take his turn under the welcoming hot spray.

The phone rang, and Claire ran to answer.

"It's Sheriff Bell, Ms. Caswell. We've come up with some interesting findings. Can you and Gaston meet me at the lodge in, say, half an hour to forty-five minutes?" "We'll be there," Claire said. She glanced at the alarm clock on the bedside table and checked the time.

"Good. Grab a table and order some coffee. I'll be there as close to that time as possible. I'm already on my way. We need to talk in person."

The two investigators hurriedly readied for the day and made it to the lodge in exactly thirty minutes. They selected a back corner table for privacy and ordered breakfast and a pot of black coffee. They ate the food quickly, and the table was cleared of everything except the coffee cups.

"We'll need one additional cup," Claire informed the server.

"No problem, Ms. Caswell. Who are you expecting?" Katie Kyle, the server, asked.

Claire and Guy were stunned by the intrusion. Neither responded to her question, and both acted as if they didn't hear it.

Katie delivered the extra cup and saucer to the table and then quickly left.

Claire pulled a notebook and pen from her tote and shot Guy a quizzical glance. She turned her head to look in the direction of the kitchen, and she caught the morning staffers huddled together—whispering and watching the two sleuths with seemingly great interest.

"Don't look now," she said to Guy. "But me thinks we're being observed."

"The plot thickens . . ." Guy murmured in a soft voice.

Just then, Sheriff Bell entered the restaurant and walked toward the two. He sat down at the table and poured himself a cup of the steaming java.

"The staff here seems mighty inquisitive about what we're up to," Claire said.

"Well, a murder is *big* news in these parts, Ms. Caswell, especially when they all knew the victim," the sheriff said. "Guess you can't blame them."

"Maybe that's all it is," Claire said. "But they're behaving as if they all share a secret."

The sheriff ignored the comment. "Wait till you hear what I have to tell you," he said.

For the next part of an hour, he filled the two investigators in on the discoveries from the fingerprint and palm print comparisons and from the criminal background checks on the employees and Lois Whiting. Toward the end of the conversation, he mentioned that Jay had an assault charge on his record, but he indicated the charge had been dropped for lack of evidence. He also informed them that both Lois Whiting and Blake Helms's prints were on the mugs taken from Blake's flat, and that Lois Whiting's prints were processed from those lifted off the Mason jar.

But he left the bombshell for last. He told them they had identified the partial and full palm prints and fingerprints lifted from the lodge lobby—both from the inside doorknob of the lodge's front double doors and from the top of the check-in desk. That, coupled with a sealed juvenile criminal record for abetting in a burglary, made one of the employees now the prime suspect.

"That's good information," Guy said. "Who are we talking about here?"

"Heidi Flynn," the sheriff said. "I picked up a warrant to arrest her. We got our killer."

"*What?*" Claire was shocked. "This all needs to be developed further, doesn't it?"

"With a background like that, and the matching palm prints and fingerprints, as well as the .38-caliber gun ownership, we've got ample grounds to take the employee into custody. Even found her DNA on the eyelash you discovered, Ms. Caswell. That result came in early this morning," the sheriff said. "Puts her at the crime scene at the time of the murder. And reasonable minds concur that an arrest is in order."

"With all due respect, sheriff—and I think I have a *reasonable* mind—not one of those findings, or even all of them combined, constitutes absolute proof that this employee killed Blake Helms," Claire said. "You'll never get a conviction with this kind of spotty evidence. Someone needs to question Lois Whiting about her involvement with Blake before jumping to any conclusions. And there are other employees here that warrant further scrutiny, too." A look of total frustration occupied Claire's face. "We need to develop the case further. Right, Guy?" She looked to her partner for support.

"I agree," he said. "While it may look bad for the young lady, there could be a logical explanation for all of it."

"Let me be more specific," the sheriff said. "Just today, early this morning, we received written confirmation from the State Crime Lab in Missoula that the bullets removed from Blake Helms's body most probably came from the identical type of gun registered to Heidi Flynn—a 642 Smith & Wesson .38-caliber Special Airweight J-frame revolver. The lab is fairly confident of the model identification." He took a deep breath. "Now, we do appreciate your help, we really do . . ." He looked at both of the investigators. "But it's our job to collar the killer, and that's exactly what we're going to do. For all we know, we might also be nabbing the Whitefish burglar at the same time. Could be a twofer."

"This seems premature," Claire argued. "Have you checked the bank accounts of the lodge staffers to see if any large deposits have been made since the murder? If the paintings are being sold, unusually large deposits may be showing up. This needs to be done before—"

"Want to tag along when we make the arrest?" the sheriff asked, cutting her off and looking her directly in the eyes.

"With all due respect, sir, I think you're making a huge mistake," she said. "Call it investigator intuition or whatever you'd like. You're arresting the wrong person. How could Heidi Flynn have hauled away all the artwork? Have you taken that into consideration?"

"I'll ask my question again. Do you wish to be part of this when we make the arrest or not?" the sheriff asked brashly. "Your choice."

"Yes, I think we should come along," Claire said. She continued to maintain eye contact with Sheriff Bell and neither blinked.

"I agree. We'd like to be present," Guy said.

Claire signed the tab as a lodge guest.

"Follow me," the sheriff said.

At that moment, as if scripted, two uniformed Lake County patrol deputies walked through the lodge's front double doors. They joined the sheriff and the sleuths, and together the group walked in unison to make the arrest.

As the sheriff and patrol deputies led the way to one of the guest quarters, Claire and Guy lagged behind. Once there, the two patrol deputies each drew a gun and barged into the door. Heidi Flynn was patting a pillow on the bed when they entered. She jumped back in fear, and when she realized what was happening, all color drained from her face.

Sheriff Bell pulled a white note sheet from his pocket and in a loud voice read the required Miranda Warning to Heidi Flynn.

"Ms. Heidi Flynn, you are under arrest for the murder of Blake Helms and for felony theft of property in connection with the murder. You have the right to remain silent. Anything you say or do will be held against you in a court of law. You have the right to contact an attorney and to have that attorney present during questioning. If you cannot afford one, an attorney will be provided at no cost to represent you. Do you understand the rights I've just read to you?"

She trembled. "Yes. Can I please call Sam? He'll want to know what's happening to me." She did her best to fight back tears.

"You can make a call from the stationhouse, Ms. Flynn. Now please put your hands behind your back," one officer said.

She obeyed his command, and handcuffs were placed and tightened around her thin wrists.

"I'll grab your purse, Heidi," Claire said. "We're coming with you."

Heidi looked at Claire. "I had *nothing* to do with his murder. Is it because I own a gun? I have that for self-protection."

"We'll get this all straightened out, Heidi," Claire said. "You can count on it."

At that moment, Heidi Flynn wore the face of a terrified little girl, and Claire felt an immense pang of pity for the young lady. Heidi dropped her head as a huge tear rolled down her cheek. Each officer grabbed one of her arms and took a step forward to lead her from the room.

"Heidi, we're right behind you," Claire said boldly.

The sheriff darted a look of profound disapproval in the direction of the female sleuth, as if to say without words, *Lay off, lady*, but she paid him no heed. This was an unfounded arrest in her opinion, and she was angry about it.

Heidi Flynn turned her head back toward Claire. "I didn't kill him, Ms. Caswell. My gun and ammunition are *missing*. Someone took them from my purse."

Claire gave her a slight nod.

Heidi was forced into one of the squad cars parked in front of the lodge. Eagle-eyed morning staffers crammed into the front doorway, watching the scene unfold and engaging in voracious gossip.

Claire looked into the crowd and noticed that certain of the lodge employees working that morning were missing from the scene.

21

THINGS WERE HEATING up. That was certain. Claire and Guy dutifully trailed behind the deputy patrol cars on the way to the Lake County Detention Center in Polson.

"They don't have their evidence in order," Guy said. "They're going to blow the prosecution of this case."

"Heidi's not the one," Claire said. "I'm convinced. They're so eager to put the murderer behind bars, they've made a grave mistake." She paused. "Granted, Blake was shot with the same type of gun that Heidi owns; and granted, we now know that Heidi has a sealed juvenile record for some alleged connection to a burglary . . . although we don't know the circumstances. And granted, Heidi's palm prints and fingerprints were found on the inside of a front door knob at the lodge and on the top of the check-in desk, as well as her eyelash was found next to the body. And granted, Heidi arguably had motive. All together, it allows for a case to be built against her. I understand that. But really, nothing here equals solid *evidence* that she killed Blake Helms. She told us someone stole her gun and ammunition, and I believe her. We need to talk with her husband and ask him more about the missing gun. And see if he'll provide an alibi for his wife for last Thursday during the early-morning hours. Finding her palm prints and fingerprints at the crime scene is a giant hurdle to overcome, I concur, especially since it was cleaned before Blake started the night shift. I'll give them that. But there still may be some other explanation for it. The eyelash? Could have dropped on the lobby floor anytime and may have easily been missed by the cleaning people."

"I agree there's no airtight proof that she committed the murder," Guy said. "But there is a whole lot of circumstantial evidence against her. Yes, we need to talk further to Sam about Heidi's gun and about her alibi. I presume he'll back up her story, but we need to ask him nevertheless—although you and I both know how solid an alibi is coming from a spouse."

ARRIVING AT the Lake County Detention Center at the Lake County Courthouse, the patrol deputies led Heidi inside to the intake counter. The sheriff and the sleuths followed behind. A female detention officer patted the young woman down and removed the handcuffs binding her wrists. Sheriff Bell stood nearby—a stern expression on his face and hands on his hips—observing the procedure. Claire and Guy paced on the sidelines, watching attentively.

"I'll inform you of what will happen from this point on, Ms. Flynn," the officer said. "You must appear before the court within forty-eight hours at an arraignment hearing. This will be your initial court appearance, where you will be advised of the nature of the charges being brought against you, any possible sentence you may be facing, and of certain rights afforded you under Montana law. When you are before the court, you can respond to the criminal charges of murder in the first degree and felony theft by either entering a plea of guilty or not guilty to each charge. If you plead *guilty*, the court will proceed to sentencing. If you plead *not guilty*, the case will be set on for trial. Do you understand what I have just told you?"

With body language evidencing deep concern, Heidi nodded slowly.

"Please give a verbal yes or no response to my question," the officer commanded.

"Yes," the young lady replied contemplatively.

An appearance was scheduled for 10:00 a.m. the following morning. The officer further informed Ms. Flynn that she had the right to post bail pursuant to the warrant language—either by producing cash or a bail bond. "If you can post bail, Ms. Flynn," the female officer said, "you will be released, but you must appear back here at the courthouse tomorrow morning at 10:00 a.m. sharp for your arraignment. It will take place on the third floor on this building. Do you understand everything I have just gone over with you?"

Heidi nodded, nearly frozen with fear.

"Ms. Flynn, again, I'll need a verbal response from you," the detention officer said.

"Yes, I do," Heidi forced the words from her mouth. "Can I make my call now?"

The officer pushed the counter phone closer to Heidi. "Go ahead. Make your call. One call. Make it short."

With trembling hands, Heidi dialed Sam's number.

When she heard his voice on the other end of the receiver, she broke down in tears. "I . . . I've . . . been arrested . . . for killing

Blake Helms," she wailed. "I'm at the . . . Lake County Detention Center, at the Lake County Courthouse in Polson."

After listening to Sam's words on the other end of the line, she hung up.

The detention officer made a copy of Heidi's driver's license and walked her to an area to photograph her. Since the Lake County Sheriff's Office had already obtained her full set of fingerprints and palm prints, that step was skipped.

"What is your plan, Ms. Flynn, regarding bail?" the female detention officer asked.

"My husband's on his way. He'll know what to do."

A surprised expression appeared on Sheriff Bell's face.

"Then have a seat over there," she pointed, "and wait until he gets here."

Heidi wobbled as she walked, her entire being unstable. With a look of desperation on her youthful face, she quietly hummed a lullaby to herself. Lullabies always seemed to calm little Ethan when he was upset, and right now, she was the one who needed calming. She took a seat on one end of the long wooden bench. "*Hush, little baby, don't say a word. Papa's gonna buy you a mockingbird. And if that mockingbird won't sing, Papa's gonna buy you a diamond ring . . .*"

A handful of detention officers paced the floor all around the young woman.

At this point, Claire and Guy made their way over and shared the hard seat with her.

"I didn't kill him," Heidi said with pleading eyes. "Please, believe me. I never could have done something like that."

"You'll need an attorney, Ms. Flynn," Guy said.

"You're an attorney, Mr. Lombard. Can you represent me?" she asked, sniffling.

"I'm not licensed to practice law in Montana," he said. "So the answer is no, I cannot. You'll need to hire a competent Montana criminal attorney. But if you can't afford to hire an attorney, the state must provide one for you at no charge. Either way, you should not answer any questions until you have an attorney present. Remember that. Do not answer any questions until a lawyer is present who represents you," he stressed again. "This is a serious offense."

Sheriff Bell shot a menacing glace toward Gaston Lombard. All questioning of the accused would be off limits if she requested an attorney, and it raised the sheriff's ire to new heights.

"Have you reached a decision on the attorney issue, Ms. Flynn?" Sheriff Bell asked. "Do you need the state to set you up with one?"

"Sam is on his way. He'll know what to do," Heidi said. "Until I speak with him, I have no answer."

The minutes until Sam's arrival seemed endless.

When he finally stepped into the detention center, Claire ran over and took Ethan from his arms. A detention officer immediately patted Sam down and requested he produce identification.

Claire walked closer to Heidi. The baby immediately spotted her and started to coo and squirm relentlessly.

"May I hold my son, please?" she pleaded.

Another expression of surprise appeared on the sheriff's face. Until she had asked to call Sam minutes ago, he had not even been aware of a husband. And now, there was a child in the mix, too. He nodded. Claire walked over to Heidi and placed Ethan in her arms. She cradled the baby protectively and lovingly, not knowing when she'd be able to hold him again. Then she leaned over and kissed Sam on the cheek when he approached.

"Get me out of here," she whispered in his ear.

"Heidi, may we talk to Sam alone for a few minutes?" Claire asked.

Heidi nodded her head.

"But before we do," Claire continued, "I'd like to ask you a question. Did you ever pull your gun on Rosie Flores and threaten her?"

Heidi's mouth went dry, and she wiped her teeth with her tongue. "Never. Why? Did she say I did?"

"Right now, I'm just asking a question," the female sleuth said. "So, your answer to me is no?"

"Yeah, it's *no*! I never did that. I wouldn't. Guns are serious weapons. I know better than to ever play around with one."

"So, if Rosie or someone else told us that happened, how would you respond?" Claire asked.

"I'd say the person is an out-and-out liar. If it was Rosie, she's always hated me, so maybe she's behind all of this . . . to do me in. Maybe *she* framed me."

Claire, Guy, and Sam walked to the other side of the room.

"What can you tell us about Heidi's gun, Sam?" Guy asked. "As we told you earlier when we spoke at your home, Blake Helms was shot five times with a .38 Special, and Heidi told us her .38 is missing. What more can you tell us?"

Sam did not hesitate. "Yes, she told me, too, it was missing from her purse, along with her ammunition."

"When did she tell you this?" Guy asked.

"Several days ago." He paused to think. "I'd say early last week."

"Are you positive it was *prior* to last Thursday?" Claire asked. "Think about your answer. This is important."

"Yeah. For sure," Sam said without hesitation.

"Did you report the gun missing?" Claire asked.

"Yeah. I called the Flathead County Sheriff's Office, since we live in Bigfork."

"Did you file a theft report?" Guy asked.

"No. They told me to wait a few days to see if it showed up. They thought maybe it was simply misplaced. I guess I never followed through with a callback." He hesitated. "Is the sheriff's office implying that Heidi's gun was used to kill the desk clerk?"

"That may well be the case," Guy said. "As we said, the bullets were from the same type of gun."

Sam hung his head. "Oh, *shit*," he said under his breath.

"Her gun hasn't been found yet," Claire said, "so ballistic tests have not been run." She looked closely at Heidi's distressed husband. "One more question, Sam. Can you tell us where Heidi was during the early-morning hours last Thursday?"

An expression of total despair riddled his eyes. "I was hoping you wouldn't ask me that," he said. "Ethan was restless during those hours. He wouldn't fall asleep, no matter what we tried. Heidi took him out driving for about an hour or so, because he always falls asleep when he's riding in the car. I remember this clearly because later that morning—Thursday around 10:00 a.m.—I took Ethan in for his doctor's appointment."

"Were you with her when she drove Ethan around?" Guy asked.

"No. Heidi does better with Ethan when he's really upset. She told me to get some sleep. That she'd take care of it."

"Do you know exactly when Heidi left and returned?" Claire asked.

"Yeah. I remember checking the clock both times. She left with Ethan at 2:30 a.m. and returned at 3:30 a.m. She wasn't gone that long."

Claire said, "Thank you for your honesty, Sam. We're going to try to help Heidi."

"You'll need to find a good criminal defense attorney who can investigate the charges brought against your wife," Guy said. "The criminal process is complicated. You'll need the best."

"I know one thing about this great country and this great state of Montana. Anyone accused of a crime is presumed innocent until proven guilty beyond a reasonable doubt."

Guy pursed his lip and nodded at the young man.

"I'll line up a good attorney," Sam said. "And thank you both. Now, about bail . . . I brought money."

Sam posted the high amount of bond set in the arrest warrant, and Heidi was allowed to go home for the night.

"Will you be at my arraignment tomorrow morning?" Heidi asked the investigators on their way out. "It's at 10:00 a.m., here, third floor."

"We'll be here," Guy said. "By the way, Ms. Flynn, I'm assuming you plan to plead *not guilty* tomorrow. Make sure you request a *jury* trial."

THE SLEUTHS returned to their room to continue the background checks on the other employees. Claire remained convinced of Heidi's innocence, but Guy had growing doubts after hearing she had no alibi for one key hour during the time range established for Blake Helms's death.

Guy wrestled in his mind with the facts. One crucial hour. Sixty minutes. Plenty of time for Heidi to drive to the lodge, commit the evil deed, and return home. His mind raced. Could she have shot Blake Helms, singlehandedly carted out the stolen artwork and the saddles, and slashed the furniture—all in such a limited amount of time? It seemed impossible. And if she did all this, how did she transport the items, and where did she store them? Little Ethan was presumably asleep in her car the entire time. None of this made any sense. But Heidi had previously told them she was at home asleep in her trailer during the time in question. And now Sam told them she had been out driving Ethan around. Things were not looking so good for Heidi right about now, Guy reasoned. She had also lied about being single. *Why the lies?* He thought long and hard. Logistically speaking alone, she could not have carried off the murder and theft without help. He continued to debate the facts with himself.

It was imperative to study the backgrounds of the other employees with motive. If Heidi wasn't the killer, they needed to figure out who was. And quickly.

Guy set about to contact Blake's ex-wife and his two grown children. He needed to get a feel from each of them as to whether they had means, motive, and opportunity. He also wanted to look into Chaz Warner's anger problem. Discovering more about Jay's background also topped Guy's list.

Claire looked up from her work. "I just realized that Sam Barlone also does not have an alibi."

"Good point. We'll keep him on the radar screen, too, in case we need to delve deeper," Guy said.

"I want to talk to Heidi's father. I'm still looking for a contact number. He's unlisted, so it makes it a bit more difficult to locate him. And I'll look further into Hazel Schroeder's background, as well. Let's see how much progress we can make today. Remember, we've got to do research on others, too: Darlene Nichols, Phil Kagan, June Howard, and Charlotte Rodriguez. And we must go over and talk to LoLo again. Maybe on a break."

They worked a few hours, until Guy announced he needed a break.

"Let's go have lunch at Woods Bay Grill," Claire suggested. "That way, we can accomplish two things at once. We can fill our tummies and talk to LoLo."

They locked the door to their room and walked over to the diner. Since it was a late lunch, only some stragglers from the noon crowd remained, and the investigators had the place virtually to themselves.

LoLo walked directly over to them. "Welcome back . . . *Claire*? And *Gaston*? Did I remember the names correctly?"

"Exactly right," Guy said. "Can we grab any table?"

"Yeah. Sit wherever you'd like." She followed the two to a table. "What can I get you to drink?"

"Diet Coke for me, please," Claire said.

"Iced tea sounds good," Guy said.

The waitress disappeared into the kitchen and reappeared with the beverages in record time. "What have you found out . . . about Blake's murder?" she asked.

Today there was no smell of burned cookies in the air, and LoLo looked remarkably well. Her hair was tidy, makeup was in place, and she smiled some.

"Heidi Flynn was arrested this morning," Guy said.

The sleuths watched for LoLo's reaction to the news.

The waitress folded her arms and stared into space. Then she fiddled with her hair. "I don't like this," she said loudly. "This is not right. I don't think the girl did it."

"I'm happy to hear you say that, LoLo, because I tend to agree with you," Claire said.

"Who do *you* think committed the crime?" Guy asked. "Seems to be many folks around here who had a bone to pick with Blake."

"I've been putting great effort into trying to figure this out," she said. "Blake had his own way of doing things, and he made no apologies for trying to impose his beliefs on others. His motivation was pure, mind you, but it did have a way of wearing thin on others sometimes." As she spoke of the man, her eyes filled with tears. "I mean, he was always telling me not to sag my shoulders or round my back, how important good posture is in making a good impression. If I ever let my chin drop when I walked, he'd say I was giving the impression of having no confidence or enthusiasm for life. I mean, *really*, that kind of thing can get to a person if they're around it all the time." She paused. "Now, I kinda miss it."

"LoLo, have you ever been to Blake's flat?" Claire asked. The question was direct and unexpected. Instead of confronting the waitress on the fingerprints match, she decided to proceed in a different way.

Instantly, LoLo's face flushed and her eyes blazed with emotion. "It's hot in here today," she said. She fanned herself with her hand. "Hang on while I run back and crank up the AC." She turned and walked quickly to the back of the restaurant.

When she appeared moments later, she acted as if she'd forgotten the question. "What would the two of you like to order today? I should get it in soon if you're on a tight schedule."

The sleuths ordered albacore tuna fish sandwiches on sourdough toast.

LoLo walked the order over to the chef and did not return to the table.

Ten minutes passed. The waitress reappeared with the food and set the plates down in front of the investigators, together with the check.

Claire cleared her throat. "LoLo, it's important. Did you ever go to Blake's apartment?"

"Of course not!" she replied. "As I told you, I'm married."

"I mean no judgment by my question," Claire said. "Just curious if you'd ever been over to his place . . . perhaps for a cup of coffee?"

LoLo did not respond. Her eyes teared.

Claire got up from her chair and hugged the waitress for a brief moment. "Really. I mean no affront to you, LoLo. I know you are going through a difficult time." The sleuth sat back down. "Do you grow lilac bushes in your yard?" Claire asked.

"I do. Why?" LoLo asked.

"I've been noticing the most beautiful late-blooming lilacs around this area, and I thought perhaps you would know the name of the variety," Claire said. "They're purple-blue in color."

"Lilacs have always been a favorite of mine. They have an extraordinary fragrance," the waitress said. "In fact . . ." She stopped short. "I shouldn't go on and on. Please, enjoy your lunch." She turned and walked out of sight.

"What was with that hug?" Guy whispered.

"I needed to get close enough to smell her perfume. Guess what? It's lilac scented."

"Add that fact to her prints being identified on the mug and Mason jar at Blake's flat," Guy said. "We should have pressed her for answers. Confronted her on the prints confirmation. Not let her get away with refusing to answer. She was involved with Blake, and she may well have information critical to this case."

"She's married. That's why she will not admit it. She's been there all right, and for more than coffee. We need to get her to talk," Claire said. "Maybe I'll come back a little later today. Alone. I want to question LoLo further using extreme caution, or she may clam up altogether."

They ate the sandwiches, paid the bill, and left the restaurant without seeing another trace of the waitress.

Back in the room, the sleuths once again dug into their investigative work.

Claire finally located a number for Orvis Flynn in Burlington, Iowa, and called him.

"Mr. Flynn," Claire said, "I'm Claire Caswell, a private investigator from Miami, assisting the Lake County Sheriff's Office in Montana on a murder investigation." She paused. "An employee of a lodge here was murdered."

"And you're calling me *why*?" he asked in a gruff voice. "How am *I* involved in this?"

"You're not, sir. I thought you could possibly answer a few questions for me. Heidi, your daughter . . ."

The dial tone resonated loudly in Claire's ear.

22

Thursday
One week after the murder

CLAIRE AND GUY turned on the television as they readied for the day. The morning news headlined yet another burglary at Iron Horse. It was number eleven. The period of time between incidents was decreasing, and anger among the townsfolk was increasing to an even greater degree. Live coverage of the scene showed the hostile crowd of protesters gathered on the street outside the Whitefish Police Department. They now carried obscene signs and launched vile barbs at the police department staff as they passed. This time, the uprising was disorderly and defiant. Overly ripe tomatoes were lobbed at members of the force as they tried to pass, and some ducked mixtures of water and maple syrup thrown in their direction. The reporter informed that Chief Soderberg had called for officer assistance from neighboring communities to help quell the unrest. Several arrests were made on the spot when enforcement teams swarmed the area, but those did little to calm the complaining crowd.

"We thought we had him," the chief said when interviewed by a reporter, "but our search warrant failed to uncover evidence to substantiate any of the crimes when we searched the suspect's home from top to bottom. Obviously, we brought in the wrong man." He hung his head low. "We had to let him go. And now another burglary has occurred." A deflated look overtook the chief's face. "I personally apologize to all of you in the community. Know that we're on this full-time. We'll find this slippery character. Don't give up hope." His voice was not convincing.

"This is bad," Claire said. "Real bad."

"The police appear ineffective," Guy said. "And they sound desperate."

"We have to help them," Claire said. "Obviously, they jumped too soon without doing their homework. We're returning to Whitefish tomorrow morning. I still want to talk to the chief about my idea and offer our assistance. It's the least we can do. But first, Heidi needs our help today."

GUY AND Claire arrived at the courthouse a few minutes before ten. They were the only ones in the hallway outside of the room assigned for arraignment hearings. Within minutes, a well-dressed man in a dark suit, white shirt, and thin-striped tie appeared.

Guy approached the man.

"Gaston Lombard," he said, extending his hand. "Are you

representing Heidi Flynn?"

"I am. My name's Jasper Wilkes." He shook Guy's hand vigorously.

"Small world," Guy said. "My full name is Gaston Jasper Lombard. But everyone calls me Guy."

Claire joined the men. "I'm Claire Caswell," she said, shaking Jasper Wilkes's hand.

"I know who the two of you are," Mr. Wilkes said. "Sam filled me in when he called to hire me. Please call me Jasper. I have a feeling we'll be talking a lot."

"There's really not much I can do being here today," Attorney Wilkes said, "but Sam insisted on it. My real work will start after the arraignment, as you're well aware."

"We'd like to quickly fill you in on everything we know about the matter before Heidi arrives," Guy said. "It may or may not be helpful to you in this morning's hearing. You never know. But you need to hear all of it."

The three sat down on a bench, and the investigators speedily communicated their findings to date.

Claire glanced at her wristwatch. It was one minute to ten.

At ten sharp, Sam rushed in carrying little Ethan. Claire knew instantly that something was terribly wrong.

"Heidi left," Sam announced. "Sometime during the middle of the night, she disappeared. I've been frantically searching for her all morning. Her purse is gone. Her car is gone. She's gone."

Ethan started to bawl.

"Where the hell would she go?" Attorney Wilkes asked, exasperation in his voice. "This does not bode well for her."

Ethan wailed.

"I have *no* idea. Maybe she's scared. And she's hiding," Sam said. "The life that she loves so much is being threatened. What do we do next?"

"We'll have to explain it somehow to the court," Attorney Wilkes said, "and hope for the best. Other than that, our hands are tied."

Attorney Wilkes and Sam walked into the arraignment hearing, but not before Sam passed the baby to Claire to hold. The door closed firmly behind the men, and for the next half an hour, the investigators waited patiently on the bench outside.

When the attorney and Sam walked out, agitation encompassed them.

"She forfeited bail. I just lost a truckload of money. But that's not the worst of it," Sam said. "A date has been set for her trial and a warrant issued for her arrest. Now she'll be locked up in the detention center until the court case—once she's located, that is. How am I going to manage with little Ethan?"

Claire passed the fidgety child back to his father.

"Heidi just made a bad situation dire," Attorney Wilkes said, looking at Sam. "Call me as soon as you hear from your wife. And let's hope it's sooner than later. Her future may depend on it."

CLAIRE CALLED Chief Soderberg the moment they got back into their car after the arraignment. "We caught the whole story on television this morning," she said.

"Bottom line, Ms. Caswell, the burglar has thwarted all our efforts to pick him up," the chief said. He emitted a deep, audible sigh. "We've failed miserably, and right now, I'm dealing with a wild and angry sea of people on the street outside of my office, chanting that everyone in the police department must resign."

"We understand that you released the man you picked up—the homeowner steeped in financial problems. Tell me about him, will you, please?" she asked.

"Well, we conducted background checks on all of the Iron Horse homeowners, looking for anyone struggling financially, just as you suggested. This man, Andrew Hoyt, age forty-seven, catapulted to the surface as if he were shot out of an underwater canon. His main residence is in San Francisco, like so many of the other owners at that development, and historically, he has used his Iron Horse home mostly on weekends. He owns a construction company in California that has taken a huge hit due to the current economic downturn. In fact, he went from being a top-notch, in-demand builder to laying off every one of his employees. He went from living a cushy life to eking out a living, almost overnight. His money flow stopped, but his financial obligations did not. He has a huge mortgage on his Iron Horse property, and the bank is threatening imminent foreclosure. He seemed like a prime suspect, one in critical financial straits."

"You searched his home, correct? And found no evidence that he's the man?" Claire asked.

"We did. We found nothing. I brought four patrol officers along, and the five of us went through the place with a fine-tooth comb. There was absolutely nothing in there to implicate him."

"And since you haven't mentioned it, I'm assuming you also found no matted patch of ground near the house in this burglary, either?" Claire asked.

"Correct. We searched and found nothing," Chief Soderberg said.

"Gaston and I still plan to drive to Whitefish and meet with you tomorrow, as we had previously arranged. Are you still agreeable to this?"

"Of course. We welcome it. But let's not waste time. How about eight in the morning?" the chief asked. "Right now, we feel as if our hands are tied, and if we don't come up with something quickly, our safety may be on the line."

"Okay. We'll be there. Oh, and please pull together everything you have on Andrew Hoyt. We'd like to take another look at him," Claire said.

GOING BACK and forth between the two major cases—which may or may not be connected in the end—was proving to be exhaustingly time consuming. There was much to do in both matters, and the investigators were feeling stretched. They returned to their room to continue conducting research on the staff members for the remainder of the afternoon.

Claire focused her energy on Hazel Schroeder, and Guy concentrated his efforts on Chaz Warner.

Just as they started to work, Claire's cell phone rang.

"Ms. Caswell, it's Sheriff Bell. Wanted to let you know my patrol deputies are all out searching for the missing Heidi Flynn. This latest development further solidifies our case against her."

"There may be a reason—" Claire started to say.

"On another note, Ms. Caswell, sorry it took so long, but I just received that information you requested on the sapphire mines in the area. I also did a bit of research to learn more about the mines myself before I called you. Don't know if this matters any longer, seeing as we've already arrested Heidi Flynn for the crime. But I promised to get you the information, and I'm a man of my word."

"Great. I've been waiting for it," Claire said. "Can you also give me some history on sapphire mining in Montana?"

"I can. Sapphire mining started here in the late 1800s. Sapphires are a variety of corundum—corundum being their mineral name—and Montana is the *crème de la crème*, so to speak, of the world when it comes to finding different colors of the precious corundum," he began. "Rubies are the same mineral, but red in color."

"Can I stop you for a moment, sir? I'm aware of the typical, brilliant, bright blues of sapphires, but what other colors are found here?"

"All colors, really," he said. "Trace mineral impurities cause the variation in the color, and like fingerprints, no two are alike. I know this because I'm looking at a brochure showing the range of sapphire colors right now. The *fancies* are in hues of yellow, orange, pink, green, teal, violet, brown, and gray. Some are even a combination of colors. The famous blues are the most common, of course."

"Fascinating. Go on, please," Claire said.

"Well, sapphires are heat-treated to remove any cloudiness, to make them transparent. This process also intensifies their color, and it occurs before the stones are cut for jewelry." He paused temporarily, and Claire heard papers rattling in the background. "Now, Ms. Caswell, you asked me for the three sapphire mines closest to Bigfork. The Yogo Gulch mine is probably the most famous in Montana. It produces a blue and violet sapphire that, due to its clarity and rarity, is one of the most expensive varieties of sapphires in the world. But I digress. This mine is located in central Montana and would not be included in the three closest to Bigfork."

The sheriff continued, "The three closest to this area would be the Spokane Bar Sapphire Mine, located in Helena; the Montana Sapphire Mine in Choteau; and the Gem Mountain Sapphire Mine in Philipsburg. All three mines are roughly equidistant from here, but the Gem Mountain mine is the largest and oldest in Montana. It produces nearly four times the number of sapphires as all of the other deposits combined."

"How far away is Philipsburg?" Claire asked.

"About an hour-and-twenty-minute drive from Missoula. So, from here, I'd say you're looking at between three and four hours, one way, depending on traffic. It's about a hundred and seventy-five miles, give or take a few, but parts of the drive will be slow."

"Okay," Claire said. "When is the mine open?"

"Seven days a week from ten to five. You should call the mine for detailed directions or look them up online before you venture there. You could easily get lost trying to find it. It's hidden in the Sapphire Mountains."

"Got it," Claire said, scratching notes.

"People go to these mines to search for sapphires. They make family outings out of it. They sift through the gravel straight from the mine, using wash screens, tweezers, water troughs, and sorting tables—all in the hopes of finding a rare, large corundum that will polish up into a magnificent sapphire. In reality, most people only find small pieces to keep as souvenirs. These mines use an on-site heat-treatment on the stones and even facet them, if the finder wishes," the sheriff said.

Claire thought for a moment before speaking. "The person who murdered Blake Helms left sapphire gravel in the lodge lobby early that morning—one trail going in and the other going out. *Sapphire trails.* Now, if we can only determine who has recently visited the sapphire mine, we may find our real perpetrator."

Silence ensued on the other end of the phone. Dead silence. Claire did not say a word and waited for the sheriff to respond.

Finally he spoke. "Good day, Ms. Caswell. I hope you'll enjoy visiting the sapphire mine."

Claire sat for several minutes, absorbing what she had just learned from the sheriff. She went on the computer and Googled Gem Mountain Sapphire Mine to learn both ownership and contact information and to obtain directions. She jotted notes and shared what she had just learned with Guy.

Guy's cell phone rang.

"Mr. Lombard, it's Sam Barlone. I still can't find Heidi anywhere. I'm panicking. What do I do? I'm afraid her world's about to explode. Even when she's proven innocent, she'll have this arrest on her record and no doubt lose her job. What a nightmare. Help me. Please help me!"

"Sam, you're doing everything right. Just keep looking for her," Guy said. "She can't be far away, can she? Call everyone she knows. Go to every place the two of you have frequented together. Visit your regular haunts. People tend to hide in places they're familiar with. Don't give up. You need to locate her." He hesitated. "And Sam, take good care of Ethan. He needs you now more than ever. Call Heidi's attorney when you find her. And notify us, too. If she calls you, tell her the best thing she can possibly do to help her cause is to turn herself in to the authorities at once."

Guy hung up and shared the call with Claire.

"She'll show up soon," Claire said. "She's got too much at stake to stay away."

"I hope you're right."

Claire picked up her phone and called the Gem Mountain Sapphire Mine. When a clerk in the gift store answered, she asked to speak to one of the owners. When she was connected, she explained who she was, the reason for her call, and that she was interested in obtaining information about someone who may have visited the mine recently. Claire learned that the mine management did not maintain a log of visitors. She also discovered that about two-dozen employees worked at the family-owned mine. The owner suggested she come in with photographs of the persons in question to see if any of the staff or the on-site manager would recognize the individuals. She also informed Claire that all employees would be present at the mine over the next two days, as inventory was being taken. Either day would be a good day to come.

"Guy, we head to Whitefish early tomorrow morning for our meeting with the police department. After that, we'll need to drive to Philipsburg to see if any employees at the Gem Mountain Sapphire

Mine recognize any of the lodge employees. It's a three-or four-hour drive from here, so tack on another forty-five minutes from Whitefish. The mine closes at 5:00 p.m., and we'll have to arrive in time to question all the staff and the owners."

"Okay. Shouldn't be a problem, but it will be a long day of driving. And then there's the return trip back to Bigfork."

"I'll let Jay know we need a photo of each employee from the personnel files he keeps," Claire said. "We can pick them up at dinner tonight." She called Jay's cell and made her request. "Throw in a photo of you and Piper, too, please. You know the routine by now. Just covering all the bases."

The investigators returned to their work.

One hour later, Claire looked up. "Guy, listen to this. I found several photos of Hazel Schroeder when I checked social networking sites. In each case, she has *blonde* hair and *blue* eyes. If you'll recall, she now has *auburn* hair and *reddish-brown* eyes. In fact, I made a mental note to myself during our interview with her—I found it interesting that her eyes and hair seem to be a perfect color match. These must be old photos she posted."

"It's easy and not unusual for a woman to change her hair color, but why her eye color?" Guy asked.

"Exactly. Seems odd. Hazel's either wearing color contacts now, or she was then," Claire said. "And I believe her hair is dyed in both cases. If she's trying to look different or keep a low profile for some reason, maybe it means she fears being recognized by someone. And she acted so edgy throughout her interview, that now I'm really questioning her. I plan to look further into her background."

"Interesting. And listen to this. Chaz Warner was charged and convicted of assault a little over two years ago," Guy said, sharing his findings. "Shortly before he started at the lodge. The court sentenced him to a year's probation, ordered him to complete an anger management course, and stipulated that any future such incidents would land him behind bars. He's a young man with a bad temper. Apparently, he got into a melee with some of his friends at a local bar after a heavy night of drinking, and those on the opposite side of the brawl ended up with serious injuries."

"Wonder why the sheriff never mentioned Chaz's conviction," Claire pondered. She checked her wristwatch. "I'm going to run over to Woods Bay Grill to see if LoLo will talk to me. Should be back shortly. Keep digging."

CLAIRE HURRIED the short distance to the nearby restaurant and sat down on a counter stool.

LoLo approached, and the investigator ordered a cup of coffee.

"Care for a slice of huckleberry pie? Fresh baked today."

"Sure. I'd love to try it," Claire said.

Claire intentionally arrived before the expected dinner crowd, so there would be time for asking more questions. LoLo delivered the pie and coffee and started to walk away.

"LoLo," Claire said, stopping the server in her tracks. "I'd like to ask you a couple more questions, and I hope you'll be honest with me. It's important that we know everything if we're going to put all the puzzle pieces together."

"I've been truthful with you and Mr. Lombard all along," the waitress said.

"Well, I think that's pretty much the case. But when we asked you if you'd ever been to Blake Helms's apartment, you clearly didn't want to talk about it."

LoLo hesitated.

"I believe that you have been there," Claire said. "In fact, let me have a go at it. I think you and Blake had a real special relationship.

You talked over coffee at his apartment from time to time. He was a good listener. He may have offered you advice on dealing with tough situations. He might have known that your marriage was . . . difficult, and he became a sympathetic shoulder to cry on. He may have even shared with you his incredible knowledge of the Native American tribes of this region. How am I doing so far?"

The waitress looked at her, but did not respond.

"Humor me. May I go on?" Claire asked. "After a time, your friendship with Blake grew stronger. Things at home worsened, and you looked forward more and more to seeing Blake walk into the restaurant to eat a meal, and you also looked forward to spending any limited free time with him alone at this apartment. One thing led to the next, and your relationship with Blake changed course. It became romantic. Am I still on track?"

LoLo looked around and then back to Claire. "What do you want from me?"

"The truth. It will stay with me, unless it becomes imperative to release it during the investigation. I give you my word, though, LoLo, that I will do everything within my power to protect what you tell me."

The waitress stared at Claire, struggling with how to answer. "Okay, you're right. I loved Blake," she said softly. "I think he was the love of my life. I just met him at the wrong time. Now he's gone, and I will always be sad."

"Thank you, LoLo. I know that was difficult. I'm glad you admitted it, as your prints were found in his apartment." She took another bite of pie and a swallow of coffee. "Now I want you to think hard. You had a private seat in Blake's life. What did he talk to you about in the days before his murder? This could be one of the most important questions you ever answer. Try to remember your last conversations with Blake. Whom did he talk about? Did he mention any names?"

"I've told you everything I know already," LoLo blurted out.

"I don't want your answer now," Claire said. "I want you to do some deep reflecting before you respond. But don't wait *too* long. Here's my cell number." She wrote it on a napkin and passed it to the waitress. "Call me when you have the answer. Call me anytime. Day or night."

LoLo grabbed the napkin and stuffed it into her apron pocket.

"And LoLo," Claire said. She reached into her purse and pulled out the bag containing the vial of lilac perfume. "I think this belongs to you."

23

WHEN CLAIRE RETURNED to the room, it was time to break for dinner, and both sleuths were more than ready. They changed clothes and walked to the lodge. Dusk was descending, and the approaching evening sky brought with it an enchanting, almost ominous, mix of smoky gray, peach, and lavender swirls.

Jay was sitting behind the lobby check-in desk when they arrived. He saw the two, picked up a large envelope, and walked over to greet them.

"Here are the photos of the employees you asked for," Jay said. "And I threw in one of Piper and me, as requested. Hope you're satisfied." His tone was cold.

"Thanks, Jay. Appreciate it," Guy said. "We'll get these back to you when we finish with them." He refused to acknowledge Jay's last remark.

"No rush," Jay said. "But I sure as hell would like to see this investigation come to an end."

Guests milled around the main floor of the lodge, reading, chatting, and drinking beverages. Soon the Terra Restaurant would be filled with diners.

Claire's cell phone rang.

"Ms. Caswell, it's Sheriff Bell. I know it's late in the day, but I wanted to catch you."

"What is it, sheriff?" she asked.

"Have you heard any word on the whereabouts of Heidi Flynn?"

"Sheriff, if we knew, you'd know."

OVER DINNER, Claire filled Guy in on her conversation with LoLo Whiting and with Sheriff Bell. And later that evening, comfortably settled back in their room, the two investigators reviewed the hard evidence collected to date in the murder investigation.

"We know Blake was shot five times with a .38-caliber revolver at up-close range, and we know Heidi Flynn owns the same type of gun that fired those bullets," Claire said. "And we know the eyelash found near the body showed a positive match for Heidi Flynn's DNA. The blue jeans rivet was from a pair of Levi's jeans and could have popped off a man's or woman's pair."

"We've also learned that the palm prints and fingerprints lifted from an inside doorknob of the lodge's front double doors and off the top of the check-in desk were left behind by Heidi Flynn," Guy added.

"And the killer or killers left behind sapphire trails," Claire said. "I can't help but believe that this might be a piece of indisputably incriminating evidence—that is, if we can figure out who unwittingly brought it in. I've got my fingers crossed that we'll learn more tomorrow when we go to the sapphire mine."

"We know several lodge employees had trouble getting along with Blake, many had verbal arguments with him, and some even made threatening remarks that others overheard about the man," Guy said. "That gives us plenty of *motive* to go around. And while many or most of the staff employees pointed the finger at either Jay Cantrell, Hazel Schroeder, Heidi Flynn, or Chaz Warner, there were some other possibilities mentioned, as well."

"Yeah. And most all of the lodge staffers had *opportunity*," Claire said, "considering the murder occurred during the early-morning hours. And because of the time of the shooting, alibis are fewer and farther between than pools of water in a desert. Most everyone was purportedly sleeping."

"Right. Everyone was asleep—except for Blake and his murderer. Oh, and Heidi Flynn. We know Heidi Flynn was out driving around. And while Heidi had the *means*, she told us her firearm and ammo went missing from her purse just days before the crime. But on the flip side, this is Montana, so we must also assume that others might either own the same firearm model or at least have easy access to obtaining one just like it. It's a very common revolver," Guy said. He stopped and collected his thoughts. "And we can't forget that the young boy in Polson—J. B.—told us he saw that teenager hand the money from the sale of the two paintings to a *couple*, a man and a woman. We still don't know who they are."

Claire seemed steeped in thought. "That day we went riding, Guy, when I disappeared for a time, Whispering Spirit whirled me to a hidden place among the ponderosa pines. Suddenly, the descendant of a Blackfoot chief appeared—seemingly from out of nowhere. His name is Running Cloud. He appeared out of the blue, we talked, and then he vanished in a flash. I just recalled something that Running Cloud told me. I haven't shared any of this with you, because I've had trouble remembering the specifics, but parts of it are filtering back to me. He told me to look at the *big picture* first. He had me close my eyes and envision the murder scene anew. *Big picture first. Details later.*" She stared straight ahead as she talked. "There's something we're not seeing, and I feel as if it's right in front of us."

"Sounds like a fascinating encounter," Guy said. "I can only imagine." He paused to think more about it. "But *what* can we be missing?"

"Wish I knew," Claire said.

"And then there is Blake's ex-wife and children, but so far, it appears they all have steel-clad alibis. All three of them separately told me they had washed their hands of the man long ago. And as far as LoLo Whiting, Darlene Nichols, June Howard, Charlotte Rodriguez, and Rosie Flores, I agree we'll need to do some additional checking on each of them, as well."

"Still can't rule out Sam Barlone, either," Claire reminded him. "He's an ace shooter, and he owns guns, which gives him means. He also had motive, seeing Blake reamed out his wife, Heidi, on a regular basis. And he had opportunity when Heidi was out driving little Ethan around in the early-morning hours on that fateful Thursday. He could have taken Heidi's gun."

"But why would he have used her .38 caliber when he knew that would point the authorities directly at his wife?" Guy asked.

"Point taken. I guess I don't consider him a strong suspect, but we can't rule him out, either."

"Okay," Guy said, "then we have to throw Piper on the list, too. If she were involved with Blake Helms in a romantic way and then discovered LoLo was as well, could jealousy have compelled Piper to murder Blake?"

"That one's a stretch for me," Claire said. "And that would also mean Piper carried out and toted away the artwork all by herself. I don't think so." She quickly scanned her interview notes.

Possibilities rolled around in Guy's head. What if Jay and Piper committed the crime *together* for some reason? What if they staged the incident to look like a robbery? What if the real motive was to collect insurance money for the "stolen" paintings? To pad the claim to help them through the slow economy? He decided to keep these thoughts to himself for the time being.

"What about Phil Kagan? The funny man," Claire asked. "The interview clown. We put a star by his name. We need to check him out further, too. If you recall, his behavior was bizarre, to say the least, and his body language screamed out that he was making intentionally false statements. I want to make sure we give him a thorough look. Could be just a harmless nutcake, but we need to find out."

"Agreed. Tomorrow's a busy day for us. Whitefish Police Department in the morning and the sapphire mine in the afternoon. Again, it will be a lot of driving," Guy said.

"We need a break in this case," Claire said. "And Heidi Flynn needs to turn herself in. She's looking mighty guilty right now, and I don't believe that she is. Facing this arrest head on is her best chance for exoneration." Deep in thought, Claire closed her notebook. "I can't believe Heidi will stay away from her baby for too much longer." She stood up. "Time for bed."

FRIDAY MORNING arrived earlier than Claire thought it should have. She had not slept well. Thoughts of Running Cloud filled her dreams. What had he been trying to tell her? What were they not seeing? She took a long, hot shower and then let cold water beat down on her lower back. It was the routine she always followed after a restless, fitful night. She had to be at her best today, and despite a lack of rest, the shower worked to get her juices flowing.

The two were ready in no time. As now had become their daily morning routine, they walked to the lodge for breakfast. Once seated, they ordered and began to enjoy the fresh-squeezed orange juice immediately delivered to their table.

Hazel Schroeder rushed by, calling out a hasty greeting to the investigators. "Top of the morning, you two," she said. "Busy day. I'm in a planning frenzy. No time to talk."

"Guy, did you see *that*?" Claire asked once Hazel was out of earshot.

"See what?" he asked.

"Her ring. Hazel was wearing a *huge* diamond ring on her right ring finger. She shoved her hand into her pocket when she saw me glancing at it."

"Okay. And?"

"That's an expensive ring," Claire said. "She couldn't possibly afford it on her present salary here at the lodge. And she wasn't wearing it during her interview."

"Are you sure?" Guy asked.

"Positive," Claire said. "There's something strange about that lady. I'm just not sure what it is."

Thirty minutes later, the investigators were in the green Land Rover Discovery, wheeling their way to Whitefish.

Whitefish

ARRIVING AT the police station, Claire and Guy bravely fought their way through the collection of protestors already on the street. "Give 'em hell!" one loud voice yelled to them. Once safely inside the front door of the department, the two were ushered into a room filled with the entire staff of the Whitefish Police Department.

"Welcome back," Chief Soderberg said. "Please sit down."

Claire looked from face to face at those gathered around the long table. She could see a slew of expressions—sullen, morose, ill tempered, dour, surly, glum, moody, broody, and irritable. Clearly, the fact that the Whitefish burglar remained on the loose had worn thin.

"We have the information you requested on Andrew Hoyt, Ms. Caswell. It's sitting in the folders in front of you. It's all there," the chief said. "We've done a lot of work on this."

"Mind if Gaston and I take a look through these records for a few minutes before we begin?" she asked.

"By all means. We're at your disposal. Take the time you need," Chief Soderberg said.

While she and Guy searched through the files, the police force members drank coffee, one cup after the other. None of them uttered a word.

"Can you please bring in a laptop for us?" Claire asked. "We need to look up a few things."

"Of course," Chief Soderberg said. He picked up the phone and made a call.

Within minutes, an Apple MacBook Pro was sitting on the table in front of the two sleuths, plugged in and ready.

Claire and Guy reviewed the information contained in the files and worked diligently on the computer, seeking additional information on Andrew Hoyt and on his financial dilemma. They searched to find other clues to perhaps point the way directly to this person of interest. Was there anything in his background—other than his financial crisis—that would also support the hunch that he was the perpetrator?

As the sleuths worked, the force members seemed antsy, because of the situation at hand as well as the overload of caffeine pulsating through their bodies. Fingers tapped on the tabletop, as if they were hammering away on a piano while waiting impatiently for some good news, for something that might break the case open and allow them to make the proper arrest, for anything that could put an end to the calamity that had beset Whitefish.

"Okay," Guy announced. "I believe we're ready."

"Ms. Caswell, on Tuesday, you mentioned you had another thought, something that may be of help to us," Chief Soderberg said. He nervously shuffled some papers sitting on the table in front of him. "We had followed your earlier line of thinking, and it led us to pick up a homeowner out at Iron Horse, one buried over his eyeballs in debt. We thought we finally had our man. But as you heard, a thorough search of his property turned up no concrete evidence of the burglaries. So, we had no choice but to release Andrew Hoyt. We're all anxious to hear what the two of you have to say today."

"We've given this matter a lot of thought," Claire said. "Now we've had the opportunity to look through all the information you've collected on Andrew Hoyt, and we've looked up some relevant information of our own on the computer. He still seems like a prime suspect to us, as well."

Claire paused to collect her thoughts. "I'll address Mr. Hoyt's San Francisco situation first. We found numerous lawsuits recently filed against him personally and also against the construction company he owns. The personal lawsuits are alleging *fraud*, which means he cannot hide under the corporation veil on those. Creditors are suing for money owed on building supplies, subcontractors are suing for nonpayment on work completed, and lien waivers have been filed on properties he was forced to stop building mid-construction—thereby guaranteeing payment to the lien holders should the properties ever be completed and sold down the road. These issues are in addition to his drowning on the mortgage attached to his personal residence in San Francisco," she said. "His phones and other utilities have been cut off for nonpayment. And to top it off, his wife has left him."

Guy jumped in. "Now, moving on to Whitefish. We can't forget to consider the imminent foreclosure on his Iron Horse property, either. Throw that into the equation, and toss in the fact that Mr. Hoyt is currently unemployed, and what do we have? An impending recipe for disaster. A powder keg. The man has to be in a frenzied state of mind. And something's got to give. "

"Bottom line?" Claire said. "We think he may well know something about the burglaries, and we'd like the chance to interview the man in person."

"Remember I told you he refused to talk to us?" Chief Soderberg asked. "Said he wanted a lawyer present. Never hired one, because we had to let him go."

"Yes, but we'd like to give it another try. I'm curious if he'll talk to *us*," Claire said.

"Okay. I know he's at his house in Iron Horse all this week. He's been spending most of his time in Montana since things went downhill for him in San Francisco. I'd be happy to drive you over there, and then our meeting can reconvene here afterward."

The three used the rear door and walked to the chief's car parked in a lot out back. They could hear the shouts of the protestors out front as they drove away. Fifteen minutes later, they pulled up in front of the Hoyt residence. The trio walked to the front door of the stately custom home, and Chief Soderberg rang the doorbell.

When Andrew Hoyt opened the door and saw the police chief standing there, he immediately attempted to slam it shut. But Guy inserted his foot into the door opening before that could happen.

"Mr. Hoyt, we'd like a few minutes of your time. I'm Gaston Lombard, and this is Claire Caswell. We're private investigators from Miami, assisting the Whitefish Police Department. We think you may have information on the recent rash of burglaries in this area, and we'd like to speak with you. Please."

"I would suggest you remove your foot at once, if you want to keep it," Hoyt growled. "Do it now!"

As Guy kept his foot in the doorway, refusing to move it an inch, Claire peered inside the house and noticed a young man and young woman standing in the shadows.

"Slam the door on them, poppy," the young man yelled. "You don't have to answer any questions. Not without a lawyer."

The father glowered as he stared at Guy Lombard. "Your foot. Move it!"

Guy pulled his foot from the space. It was clear the man was not going to cooperate.

As they turned to walk back to the vehicle, Claire said, "Thanks, chief. I got what I needed."

BACK IN the conference room, the chief turned the meeting over to the Miami investigators. The weary force members lifted their collective eyes and pricked their collective ears. A new discovery in the case had the potential to breathe life back into the force, and together they waited in suspense.

"Let's discuss this Andrew Hoyt situation a bit more, shall we?" Claire asked. "Gaston and I think you're on the right track. And we're going to suggest what you'll need to check up on next."

24

CLAIRE AND GUY stopped at a drive-through on their way out of Whitefish to grab an early lunch. Each ordered a hamburger, fries, and soft drink, and they ate in the car. The morning meeting had been productive. The Gem Mountain Sapphire Mine was next on the agenda, and they had a long drive ahead.

After a time, they passed by Bigfork and then made their way to US 93 S. After a good hour, they took ramp I-90 E/US 93 W to Missoula. A short distance later, they merged onto I-90E/US 93 S and continued to follow I-90 E for close to another hour. The exit toward Drummond/Philipsburg appeared at last, and they took it. Soon they turned right onto MT 1 S/US 10A. Half an hour later, they made another right turn onto Skalkaho Pass Road toward Hamilton. They traveled west for sixteen miles down a narrow, winding road. Just when they started to question whether they'd taken the wrong road, the destination abruptly appeared on the right.

Seemingly from out of nowhere, a large sign popped up for Gem Mountain Sapphire Mine and a driveway appeared. They drove in. The outside area bustled with excitement, and the parking lot was overflowing with all types of vehicles, including many RVs. Visitors—from children to seniors—who had invaded the rather well-hidden spot appeared to be from all over the world. They sported wide smiles of anticipation as they hurried in, eager to sift through the buckets of gravel guaranteed to contain sapphires; that is, if they were willing to work hard enough to find them.

The investigators scoped out the workings of the tourist attraction. They walked over to the sifting going on outside. Groups of young people on summer break watched the staff demonstrating the proper method of swirling and shaking the gravel in the troughs of cold water the mine provided, until the sapphires almost magically seemed to jump out in the middle of the heaps.

Staff members had been placed at various spots all around the area to assist in the process and to offer words of encouragement and perseverance to those who had not found sapphires yet. Upon a guest locating a stone, a gemologist in the adjacent gift shop sat ready, willing, and able to provide the carat weight of each find and to give an opinion on its quality and best use. The finder would then make arrangements for the mine to heat-treat and facet the stone, and the finished product—the glistening-clear sapphire of extraordinary color—would be sent to the guest's home address. The investigators were enthralled by how smoothly the process seemed to work.

Playing in the mud and gravel seemed almost addictive to the participants, and Claire heard several people say they had been to the mine many times before. Screams of "I found one!" or "I hit the jackpot!" could be heard throughout the area and seemed to trigger the others to keep jiggling and whirling their sifters. "I found a pink one," a lady yelled out. "*Pink!*"

The atmosphere reminded the sleuths of a casino in an odd sort of way, from the excitement in the air, to the paying-to-play concept, to the shrieks from the people fortunate to land a big win. One man bragged that he was on his twelfth three-gallon bucket of the day, although he failed to say how many sapphires he'd stumbled upon. Partakers were dirty, wet, and fabulously happy.

Guy glanced at his watch. "It's nearly four, and the place closes at five. We'd better get started."

The investigators entered the gift shop and talked to the manager on duty. She had been expecting the two and told them to feel free to walk around and talk to all of the staff, wherever they could find them. "They have all been told you are coming, so each one will be more than happy to discuss this with you. Do you have photos of the people you want us to look at?"

"We do," Claire said. "Want to be the first?" She lifted the stack from the folder she toted and handed them over to the woman.

The manager peered through the lot, narrowing her eyes. "No one stands out to me," she said. "But then, I don't spend quality time out there with the people, as do the rest of the staff. They may be more helpful to you, and they're all here right now. Good luck!"

Staff members were easy to distinguish from the crowd, as they each wore a distinctive royal blue T-shirt. Claire held the photos of the Mountain Lake Lodge staff members in her hand, and the investigators diligently sought out one employee after another. Each time, they explained their purpose and then asked the Gem Mountain Sapphire Mine employee to look carefully at the photos and say whether he or she recognized anyone as a visitor to the mine, particularly within the previous two-to three-week period. Each photograph had the employee's name printed across the bottom with a black marker pen.

All staffers took the assignment seriously, and the hour passed quickly. Not a single employee said he or she recognized any of the people in the photos, although several staffers seemed to take extra time to look at one photo or another. Claire handed business cards to the employees as the investigators made their rounds and asked that they call, day or night, if anything came to mind.

Back in the car, Guy said, "That seemed like a grandiose waste of our time."

"You never know what may come of it," Claire said. "We have to stay positive."

They drove in silence until Claire spoke. "I have an idea. Let's stop in Polson on the way back and see if the frame shop is still open. If it is, and if the owner's son, J. B., is around, we can ask him to look at the photos. Maybe he'll be able to recognize one or both of the people he saw accepting the money from the teenager who sold the stolen art pieces to his mother. It's certainly worth a try."

"That's a long shot," Guy said. "He's a little boy, and the couple was standing pretty far off in the distance."

"We need to give it a try," Claire said. "We're getting desperate."

The drive toward Polson was a time of reflection for both sleuths. There were so many pieces to this puzzle. So many potential suspects. So little good evidence. For the first time, the burden of the tasks seemed almost too heavy. Yet the two of them were committed to following it through to completion. Claire continued to be haunted by Running Cloud and his comments to her. Why had he made her close her eyes to view the murder scene from a fresh perspective? He had made her believe that she knew the truth. But what was it? *What?*

As Guy maneuvered the green 4 x 4 into a curbside spot just in front of the frame shop, the owner was standing outside, locking the front door. Her son was standing next to her. The sleuths were in time. They jumped from the car and approached the two. J. B.'s face glowed when he saw Claire and Guy. Quickly, they explained their mission and held the photos at the child's eye level so he could take a look.

"It's him," the young boy said. He pointed to the photos of Jay Cantrell.

"Are you sure?" Guy asked.

The child giggled.

"It's her," J. B. next said, indicating Rosie Flores. His eyes sparkled with joy. "This is fun!" he said. "It's her. It's him. It's him. It's her." He pointed to several of the photos in quick succession. "No. These two," he said, pointing to yet two others.

Claire and Guy realized that the child thought it was a game. Claire stooped down and got on one knee. She looked J. B. in the eyes. "Honey, this is very important. I want you to look slowly at each picture. Tell me if you've seen any of these people before. Remember, it's important."

"J. B., don't make up an answer," his mother said. "Tell this nice man and lady only if you do remember seeing any of these people."

All attention was on the child, and he went silent.

"Not sure," he said. "Not sure."

"Have you seen *any* of these people before?" Claire asked.

The child looked at the photos again and finally shook his head. He walked over to grab his mother's leg. Then he hid his face in her skirt.

"He doesn't recognize any of them," the owner said. "I'm convinced of it."

"Thanks, anyway," Guy said. "And by the way, how are things working out with your insurance company?"

"Sounds as if they're going to reimburse me what I paid for the artwork. Thanks for the suggestion," the owner said.

The investigators said goodbye and left.

"Talk about one dead end after another," Guy said.

They stopped and filled the 4 x 4 with gas. The trip back to the lodge seemed longer than the trip down. Anticipation had been the trigger to urge them forward earlier in the day, and now that had dissipated. Both felt extremely fatigued. Mile after mile they traveled, taking turns at the wheel and lamenting their apparent bad luck on making any significant headway on the case.

When they arrived back at the lodge, it was half-past nine, and they were famished. Riley's Pub was open until eleven, so they stopped in and ordered a pizza.

Jay was at the lodge, making his final walk-through for the night, and spotted the two. He sat down next to them and asked the big question. "Any closer to finding the murderer than when you started? Assuming it's not Heidi Flynn, that is."

"I would like to give you a definite yes on that one," Claire said. "But this type of case takes time. I'd say we're making incredible strides, though, and soon it will all come together." She forced a hopeful expression.

"I know you two are not convinced Heidi Flynn did it," Jay said. "Neither am I. Never thought she was the one when they arrested her. She's not the type."

"My thoughts exactly," Claire said.

Jay left when the pizza arrived. "Enjoy, you two."

BACK IN the room, Claire said, "We need to think like the murderer. The murderer thinks he or she is home free because Heidi Flynn has been arrested. Sometimes as time passes, a perp becomes sloppy and lets down his or her guard. I'm hoping for a slipup."

The exhausting day reached an end, and sleep came quickly.

Saturday

A DULL, gray day with light rain added to the melancholic mood of the morning. Thick clusters of clouds inhabited the normally blue big sky. In the worst way, Claire wished she could stay in bed for another hour or two, but she knew she could not. They showered, readied for the day, and walked to the lodge for breakfast.

When they stepped inside the lobby, Claire walked directly to the sofa, sat down, and reached for the scrapbook of photos. She placed it on her lap and slowly started flipping through the pages. "Give me a minute, will you, Guy?" she asked.

"I'll get a table and order the usual," he said. "I need coffee in a major way this morning."

Claire stopped when Blake Helms appeared in any of the shots and absorbed his expressions. In a few photos, Blake was standing next to Phil Kagan, the funny man, and she reminded herself that he needed further scrutiny. She noticed other photos featuring the lobby area prior to the murder, and she stared at each one with particular interest. All at once, her mind whirled back to the chance—or destined—encounter with Running Cloud. She closed her eyes. When she opened them, she again turned her attention to the lobby photos for a renewed look. Then she set the album down, stood, and observed the actual lobby scene again, with a fresh mindset. Then she shut her eyes one more time to think clearly.

"Claire, our breakfast is ready," Guy called out from a few feet away.

His announcement jolted her back to the moment.

"Come on," he said.

After Claire sat down at the table, he asked, "What did you find? Anything?"

"No. And yes. I need to process it some more."

Guy's cell phone rang. It was Sam Barlone.

"Morning, Sam. What's the good word?" Guy asked. "I hope you're calling to tell me Heidi has turned herself in."

"No, but I'm looking for her again today. I'm not giving up. She hasn't used our credit card, and she hasn't made a withdrawal from our bank, either. That means she left with only the money she had in her purse. Not sure how much that was, but probably only enough to last her a few days. And I know she's going crazy not seeing our little man, so let's keep our fingers crossed she'll show up soon."

"I'm with you, Sam. Keep me posted," Guy said.

Just as Claire put a forkful of scrambled eggs into her mouth, her cell phone rang. She swallowed quickly.

"Claire, it's LoLo. I've been doing a lot of thinking, just as you requested, and I came up with something. I don't know if it'll be helpful or not, but here it is. I saw Blake the day before he died. I mean . . . I spent some time with him at his place. We drank tea, and we talked. He was real excited about something he'd been reading. It had to do with the Blackfoot Indians, that's all I know. I'm not sure exactly what it was, because he wouldn't tell me. He said, 'I'll *show* it to you soon.' He wanted to show something to me. But he said he wanted to verify something first, before he showed me. It may be nothing at all, as I said."

"How interesting," Claire said. "Do you have any idea what it was?"

"Wish I did," LoLo said. "I didn't think of this before, because it never occurred to me that it might have something to do with his murder. But after you told me to think hard and tell you anything I could remember that may be of help in the investigation, this popped into my head. Do you think it's a clue?"

"I don't know yet, LoLo, but thanks for the information," Claire said. "We'll check it out. Oh, and one more question. Did Blake tell anyone else about this discovery he had made?"

"Not sure. But if he did tell anyone else, it would have been Phil Kagan from the lodge. The two discussed Native American history quite often. Phil was fascinated by what Blake would tell him. He couldn't get enough of it."

"Thanks again, LoLo, you've been most helpful. We picked up a couple of books from Blake's flat during our search—they were by his bed. We've got them in our room now, and we intend to take a look at them yet today, to see if anything jumps out. And LoLo . . . be careful."

"Why did you say that?" the waitress asked.

"I'm not sure. I just want you to be cautious until this matter is resolved. Don't take any chances. Someone may think you know more than you do."

Claire hung up the phone and filled Guy in on the conversation.

"We need to talk to Phil Kagan again," she said. "But before we do, I think we should take a long, hard look at the two books I pulled from Blake's bedside table during the search of his flat."

The sleuths hurriedly finished breakfast and walked back to their room. When they got there, Rosie Flores and Dahlia Young were cleaning it.

"We'll just be a few more minutes," Rosie said. "Then we'll be out of here."

"With Heidi gone, we're doing the rooms together and working as fast as we can," Dahlia explained.

"We'll take a short walk and be back," Claire said.

The two investigators took a walk around the lodge grounds to kill fifteen minutes. When they returned, the housekeepers were gone, and the room was tidy.

Claire pulled open the drawer of the bedside table to retrieve the books.

"*They're gone!*" she shrieked.

A look of shock appeared on Guy's face.

"Come with me. Quickly," Claire said.

She ran from the room, and Guy followed.

They raced around the perimeters of the guestroom buildings, searching frantically for the housekeepers' supply cart. Finally, they spotted it and ran into the unit of the nearby building, where the two young housekeepers were working.

"Rosie! Dahlia!" Claire said. "We need to ask you a question." She was out of breath from running.

"What is it, Ms. Caswell?" Rosie asked, looking alarmed.

"We had two books in our bedside table drawer in our room. They were there this morning. I know because I saw them. But after the two of you cleaned our room, they're no longer there."

"*That's* what you're so upset about?" Rosie asked.

Both Rosie and Dahlia roared with laughter.

"We thought it was something serious," Dahlia said.

"The books. Where are they?" Guy demanded.

"When we were cleaning, Phil Kagan stopped by on his morning break. He said you had told him he could borrow the books, so we gave them to him," Rosie said. "Is there a problem?"

"No problem," Claire said. She attempted to appear calm. "We'll take care of it. Thank you."

"Now we need to talk to Phil Kagan immediately," Claire whispered to Guy.

The investigators bolted back to the lodge. When they got there, Phil Kagan was nowhere to be seen.

Claire ran to the kitchen. "Where's Phil Kagan? Anyone know?"

"He just went home sick," Erik Johannson said. "You literally missed him by a few minutes. I was here at the lodge eating lunch—something I rarely do—and Hazel Schroeder abruptly interrupted my eating and asked me to cover for him. I'll make a little extra in overtime pay, so I said, sure, what the heck."

The sleuths turned and jogged to the lobby.

"We need to locate Jay or Piper right away and find an address for Phil Kagan," Claire said.

Guy pulled his cell phone from his pocket and dialed the Cantrells' home number.

"Jay," Guy said when his friend answered. "We're at the lodge. We need a home address for the daytime chef, Phil Kagan. Now."

"He's at work. Can't you talk to him there?" Jay asked.

"He's not here. He went home sick," Guy said. "This is crucial."

"Hold on. I can look it up for you. Give me a moment." A brief delay ensued. "This is strange," Jay said, returning. "I'm looking at a copy of his application right now. We require a street address from all applicants, or at least I thought we did, but all we show for him is a PO box. Must have missed that when we hired him."

25

"LET ME CHECK with Piper about Phil's address," Jay said. "She's upstairs. Can you hang on another minute?"

"Of course," Guy said. "Hurry, please."

"Piper, do you know where Phil Kagan lives?" Jay yelled. "His home address?"

"You know, I don't," she said, running down the stairs. "If it's not on his employment app . . . And he doesn't socialize with any of the other staff, that I know of, so there's no one else to ask." She double-checked the records sitting in front of Jay. "We always either hand him his paycheck or send it to his PO box. That's odd. Looks like we never got a street address for him."

"Did you hear all of that, Guy?" Jay asked.

"Yeah. But you told me you required a street address on the employment application," Guy said.

"Well, I guess we don't. It really makes no difference to us one way or the other where an employee lives," Jay said.

"Is Phil Kagan sick very often?" Guy asked.

"No, hardly ever," Jay said. "In fact, come to think of it, I don't recall a time he's ever called in sick before or gone home sick from his shift, for that matter."

"He's due in tomorrow on the day shift, correct?" Guy asked.

"Yeah, he is," Jay said. "What's this all about, anyway?"

"We have some questions he needs to answer," Guy said. "Leave the employee work applications in a folder at the front desk, will you, please? We'd like to take a look at them."

"They'll be there waiting for you."

Guy ended the call and locked eyes with Claire. Anger penetrated the investigators. The nerve and shameless audacity of the day chef to walk into *their* room and persuade the housekeepers to hand over the two books—it stuck in Claire's and Guy's craws like nothing else had in a long time.

"Kagan must have heard me talking to LoLo on my cell phone this morning at breakfast," Claire said. "He wanted to look at those books before we did."

"Seems that way," Guy said. "I'm curious why."

"He knows something. Phil Kagan knows something about the murder. We have to talk with him."

"Well, we'll need to find him first," Guy said. "Otherwise, we'll be forced to wait until tomorrow." He paused.

Claire look annoyed.

"I'm calling Jay back on another issue," Guy said. He dialed the number.

"Jay, Guy here. I've got another question for you. It's about your employee, Chaz Warner. Is he related to Sheriff Bell, by any chance?"

"He is. How'd you find that out?" Jay asked. "Chaz is his cousin's kid. Chaz never mentions it, though. Doesn't want the staff to find out I did the sheriff a favor by hiring him."

"I figured it was something like that," Guy said. "Thanks, Jay."

Guy told Claire what he'd just confirmed.

"No wonder the sheriff conveniently forgot to tell us about Chaz's past conviction. Makes sense now. He was trying to protect a family member. This is a small community, and that's how things work," Claire said.

"Let's ask the other employees if they know where Phil Kagan lives," Guy suggested. "We may get lucky."

They hurried to the kitchen and asked the staffers on duty if they knew where Phil lived. Everyone said no.

Hazel Schroeder, the supervisor of the restaurants, threw her arms up into the air. "And what is it you want with Phil Kagan, I must ask?"

"Just want to talk with him," Claire said. "No big deal."

"Well, the man's sick. Is that okay with the two of you?" Hazel asked. "Or is he not allowed to get ill? He left grabbing his stomach. Probably exposed us all to the flu."

For whatever reason, Hazel certainly had an attitude that morning. She stomped off, but just before she vanished from sight, Claire observed Hazel pull a cell phone from her pocket and dart a look back toward the investigators.

"I'd be interested to know what set her off," Claire whispered to Guy.

"Phil's going home sick probably caused more work for Hazel," Guy said. "By the way, was she wearing that ring on her finger today?"

"I saw her turn away from us when we entered the kitchen, and she thrust something into her apron pocket," Claire said. "My guess? It was the ring."

"Okay. Strange. Things are definitely becoming more complicated."

"Or more intriguing," Claire said. "Heidi's missing. And now

Phil Kagan cannot be located."

"Let's pay Sam Barlone another visit," Guy suggested.

Claire nodded.

The investigators drove to Sam and Heidi's trailer home. As with the first time, they found Sam working outside in the garden. He looked up when the 4 x 4 pulled into the driveway and walked toward them.

"I have to get these watered," Sam said, pointing to the flowers. "Then I'll be on my way to look for Heidi, although I have to tell you, I'm running out of places to search for her."

"Still no word?" Claire asked.

"Nothing," Sam said.

"Damn!" Guy said. "She needs to turn herself in before the patrol deputies find her and haul her in. It'll look much better for her, believe me."

"I realize that," Sam said. "Her attorney calls me five times a day, asking if I've heard anything."

"Think carefully, Sam," Claire said. "Did the two of you ever fight or have an argument before you got married? One where Heidi took off for a while? Or did the two of you ever escape somewhere for a special night away?"

Initially Sam was silent. Then he said, "You've given me an idea. We once stayed at an inn in Kalispell. It's a small place with only a few rooms, and it's out in the countryside. I suppose there's a chance she could be there. I'll find the number and call the inn."

"Don't make that call, Sam," Claire said. "That will tip her, and she'll leave. Why don't you go get little Ethan, and the four of us will drive to Kalispell and check it out. She won't be able to resist seeing her son."

"You don't mind?" Sam asked.

"Not at all," Claire said. "Go throw a bag together for Ethan. We'll wait in the car for the two of you."

Sam disappeared into the trailer. He reappeared minutes later, holding the baby secured in a car seat and carrying a tote bag over his shoulder. He climbed into the back of the Land Rover Discovery and secured the infant's seat. After clamping on his own seatbelt, he announced he was ready to go.

The trip to Kalispell was only fourteen miles, and they were there in no time.

With Sam's help, they located the inn and parked nearby. Together, they walked into the lobby.

"We're here looking for Heidi Flynn," Sam said.

"What an adorable child," the female proprietor said, looking at little Ethan. "Let me check our registry. You said the name is Heidi F-l-y-n-n?"

"That's correct," Sam said.

"No, no one here by that name," the woman said.

"Are you sure?" Sam asked.

"Positive."

"She's twenty-one, blonde, and has huge blue eyes," Sam said.

The woman hesitated. "You said she has *blonde* hair?"

Sam nodded.

"No. Nobody like that is staying here."

"Check under the last name of Barlone, B-a-r-l-o-n-e, will you, please," Sam asked.

"No one here by that name, either," the woman said.

The group returned to the green 4 x 4.

Out of the blue, Claire shouted, "I just saw someone peering at us from around the side of the inn. She tiptoed off. Over there." Claire pointed. "I'm sure of it. It was a young woman, and she pulled her head back when I saw her. Let's take a look. Sam, you stay here with the baby."

Claire and Guy bolted from the car and tore off toward the place Claire had indicated. No one was there. They ran around to the back of the building just in time to see the female ducking down into a thick wooded area.

"Come on," Claire said. "It could be her."

The investigators raced to the area and found a young woman, hunched down, crying. She turned her head toward them and looked up. Her hair was black, but her eyes were blue. And huge.

"Heidi?" Claire asked.

The young woman started to bawl. "It's me."

Guy helped her to her feet.

"You had us all worried," Claire said. "It never helps to run away from a problem."

"I was so afraid. I didn't know what to do." Heidi let out a cry of grief.

"Heidi, we have a surprise for you," Claire said.

Heidi looked at her questioningly.

"There are a couple people waiting for you in the car, and they'll be mighty happy to see you," the female sleuth said.

Heidi ran as fast as her legs could carry her to the 4 x 4, and Claire and Guy shadowed closely behind. Sam flung the car door wide open and jumped out to embrace Heidi. He kissed her several times and wiped away her tears. Then she jumped into the backseat and kissed little Ethan over and over. "I've missed my boys so much," she cried. "Thank you for finding me."

The reunion was heartwarming.

"Whatever lies ahead, we'll face it together," Sam said. "But first, you need to turn yourself in."

Heidi nodded.

"And even before that, we'd like you to collect your things from the room, Heidi, and have you check out. We'll help you," Claire said.

A shaking Heidi grabbed one of Claire's arms and one of Guy's.

"Let's go," Heidi said.

"I'll wait here with Ethan," Sam said. He pulled his cell phone from his pocket and called Attorney Wilkes to let him know Heidi had been found. "We're bringing her back to the detention center," the relieved husband informed the also-relieved attorney.

"I'll meet you there," Attorney Wilkes said.

As Heidi, Claire, and Guy walked toward the inn, Claire pulled her cell phone from her purse and called Sheriff Bell. She let him know Heidi had been located and that they were driving her in to the Lake County Detention Center in Polson so she could turn herself in.

Minutes later, Heidi was checked out and all five were settled in the Discovery and on their way.

Sam looked over at his wife several times, taking in her new look. "I hope that hair color's not permanent," he said. He grinned.

Through misty eyes, Heidi laughed.

THE DETENTION officers at the Lake County Detention Center in Polson were expecting the arrival of Heidi Flynn, as Sheriff Bell had called ahead with a heads-up on the situation. Both the sheriff and Attorney Wilkes were waiting in the lobby when the investigators walked in with Heidi, Sam, and Ethan.

Heidi was immediately cuffed and led to a holding cell.

Attorney Wilkes announced that he would like a few minutes alone with his client, and he was led to the small locked room.

Sheriff Bell, Claire, Guy, Sam, and Ethan waited in the lobby. At that moment, Ethan started to bawl. His face turned bright red, and he started to hold his breath. Sam tried his hardest to console his son, but the crying only got worse.

"He wants his mother," Sam said. "Nothing will stop him when he gets this way—unless Heidi holds him."

"Give him to me," Claire said. "I'll bring him in to see her."

Claire walked over to the sheriff, explained the urgent situation, and pleaded to be led to Heidi's jail cell. Sheriff Bell took a long look at Ethan.

"She's only allowed one visitor a day, other than her attorney," the officer said. "And only one at a time. But exceptions can be made for cause. Come back with me. If Attorney Wilkes and Ms. Flynn have no objection, I'll allow you to stay with them. We need to find some way to quiet this screaming baby."

The sheriff motioned to a detention officer and requested he accompany the female sleuth and Ethan to Heidi Flynn's cell. Once there, both Attorney Wilkes and Heidi readily agreed to have Claire join them as soon as they heard Ethan's cries of distress.

"I agree to this, Ms. Caswell, but I must insist that you continue to hold the baby," the attorney said, "until I complete this interview. I need Heidi's full attention."

The child stopped crying the moment he saw his mother. Claire sat down next to Heidi so Ethan could see his mother and touch her arm. It seemed to pacify the child for the moment. Claire listened intently to the questioning.

"Heidi, I want you to tell me everything you know in connection with the murder of Blake Helms. Everything. Every tiny detail," Attorney Wilkes said.

"There's not much to tell. I didn't kill him."

"Well, then, please explain to me why your palm prints and fingerprints were found on the inside doorknob of one of the lodge's front doors and also on the check-in desk's countertop the morning of the murder, why an eyelash of yours was found at the scene, and why the bullets that killed Blake Helms came from a gun exactly like yours. I also need to hear about the juvenile burglary incident you had some involvement with." He glanced down at the blue jeans she was wearing. "Also, I need to know about that missing rivet near the front pocket of your Levi's. One just like it was found at the scene of the murder."

Heidi swallowed hard. "I can explain all of it."

"I'm listening," Attorney Wilkes said.

"It's a long story," Heidi said. "You see, that morning—the morning Blake was murdered—my little son couldn't sleep. He cried for hours straight, until I took him to the car and drove him around for an hour or so. I let my husband stay home and rest. He was so tired. Traveling in a car always puts little Ethan to sleep right away, and it worked like a charm that early morning, too."

Attorney Wilkes took notes as she spoke.

"I had seen Blake Helms the afternoon before. He had come in to the lodge for an early dinner. I was working late, and I ran into him. All I said was hello to the man, and he started in on me. Yelled at me in front of the people I work with. He told me my rooms were not being cleaned properly. I couldn't understand it, because I was cleaning them *perfectly.* We had a bad argument."

"And then what happened, Heidi? Did you stop back at the lodge to see him in the early-morning hours when he was on his shift?"

"I did," she said. For the next few minutes, she couldn't talk as she battled tears. She reached for little Ethan's arm and held on to it for a time. "I just wanted to ask him why he always picked on me. I wanted to have a one-on-one conversation with the man, just the two of us, with no one else around. I wanted to tell him how hard I work and always have. I wanted to tell him how well I clean the rooms. I wanted to ask him to stop embarrassing me in front of my coworkers. And I wanted to tell him to back off and leave me alone."

"So you parked your car at the lodge, left little Ethan asleep in his car seat, and went in to confront the man?" the attorney asked. "Then what happened?"

Heidi contorted her face into an ugly expression, and she dropped her head. For a good three minutes, she did not speak.

Ethan had fallen fast asleep in Claire's arms, and the sleuth's attention was riveted on Heidi, awaiting her answer.

"Heidi, take your time. Tell me exactly what happened next," her attorney urged. "This is critical."

Heidi closed her eyes. "I walked a few steps into the lobby and did not see Blake at first. He wasn't standing behind the check-in desk. And blood was spattered across the top of it, the wall behind it, and all over the area. The sofa and chairs had been ripped up and turned over. Pictures were not hanging on the walls. I didn't know what had happened, but I knew it was something horrible. That's when I looked down and saw his feet sticking out from behind the desk. There was blood all over, so I walked around it and over to the far end of the front side of the check-in desk, leaned over it, and looked down to see his body. He was not breathing, and he was not moving. I called out his name, and there was no answer. It was clear to me he was dead. Blake was covered in blood. He'd been shot to death." She trembled convulsively with revulsion, clearly traumatized reliving the incident.

"What did you do next, Ms. Flynn?"

"I panicked. I ran out to the car and drove home as fast as I could. I cried all the way. I put Ethan into his crib, washed my face, and climbed in next to my husband. I never said a word to anyone. I thought they would think that I had done it."

Her attorney scribbled notes. "When you leaned over the check-in desk, did you put your hands on the top of it to brace your body? And did you touch an inside front doorknob when you let yourself out?"

Heidi thought for a moment. "I did. My answer is yes to both of your questions."

"That explains the palm prints on the top of the check-in desk and the palm prints and fingerprints on the inside door knob," Attorney Wilkes said. "Also probably answers why your eyelash was found at the scene, and it even explains the blue jean rivet. That must have popped off when you leaned over the check-in desk and rolled. Now, what about that juvenile burglary charge?"

"I never did time on that," Heidi said. "I was with a group of kids who entered a garage and took some things, and because I was in the car that transported them there, I got charged, too. I had no part of it. I didn't even know they had been planning to do it. I stayed in the car the whole time. But I ended up getting probation. The kids had done some other burglaries in the past, and I got pulled into the whole mess, even though I was innocent. It's not a good memory."

"Another question. Why did you fail to show up for your arraignment on Thursday morning, Ms. Flynn?" the attorney asked. "I need to hear this in your own words."

"I was just plain scared to death, so I hid," Heidi said. "I did that as a child when my father was on a drinking terror. I'd hide until things got better. It's old behavior, and I know it's wrong, but that's what I did. I'm sorry."

"Thank you for being honest with me, Ms. Flynn," her attorney said. "I have a few more questions for you. First, where is your gun?"

"I don't know. I really don't know. I always carried it in my purse. Sam told me to. In case my car would ever break down or some other trouble started and I needed to defend myself. Earlier in the week—the same week Blake was murdered—I noticed it was missing from my bag when I went to leave work one day. I haven't seen it since. And my box of ammo was missing from my purse, too."

"Any thoughts on who might have taken your gun, Ms. Flynn?"

Attorney Wilkes asked.

"No. None."

"Any thoughts on who might have wanted to frame you for the murder of Blake Helms, Ms. Flynn?"

"No."

"Did you ever draw your gun on Rosie Flores?"

"No, I did not."

"Okay, Ms. Flynn. I now have something to work with. I'll see what I can do about getting you out of here. If I can pull some strings, I might be able to make it happen. But don't plan on it. Oh, and by the way, what time did you arrive at the lodge the morning of the murder?"

"Probably about 2:45 a.m.," Heidi said.

The interview had ended, and she leaned over and kissed the still-sleeping Ethan on his cheek. "Goodbye, my little man. Mommy loves you," she said.

ATTORNEY WILKES, Claire Caswell, and little Ethan returned to the others. The attorney filled Sam and Guy in on what Heidi had divulged.

"This is all good, right?" Sam asked. "She's explained everything."

"Not really," Attorney Wilkes said. "In fact, if you want my honest opinion, and I'm sure you do, things just got a whole lot worse." He sighed. "Heidi has now admitted to being at the scene of the crime at or about the time of the murder. Add this admission to the following facts: her palm prints and fingerprints were the only ones found at the scene; her eyelash and a rivet from her Levi's jeans were found at the scene; the bullets used to kill Mr. Helms are the same caliber as those used in Heidi's registered gun, and most likely from her specific gun model, as well; and Heidi and Blake argued regularly."

Attorney Wilkes took on a grave expression. "So, all in all, I'd say the case against her is solidifying nicely for the prosecution. We have only Heidi's word that she didn't kill Blake Helms, and that's not enough. We need more. We need proof that she didn't." He cleared his throat. "If someone used Heidi's gun to kill Blake Helms in an attempt to frame her, they got the added surprise bonuses of her showing up at the scene unexpectedly around the time of the murder and leaving behind her DNA and other evidence. The actual murderer must be out celebrating. He could never have dreamed up anything so perfect as to have all this extra circumstantial evidence piling up against Ms. Flynn." He took in a deep breath and exhaled. "It'll be difficult, if not impossible, to argue Heidi's case successfully without something solid to back it up. So, in answer to your question, Sam, no, this is not good."

No one spoke for a time.

"We'll need to figure out who the real killer is—and fast—if we're going to help her," Claire said.

26

THE INVESTIGATORS DROVE Sam and Ethan home, then returned to their guest room. It was time to look again at the employees who had acquired one or two stars by their name. If there was a discovery to be made that could sway this case away from Heidi Flynn, now was the perfect time to make it.

"Let's look over our list carefully," Claire said. "As far as I'm concerned, and call it investigator instinct if you'd like, Heidi and Sam are not suspects. Or LoLo Whiting, for that matter. So we're left with the lodge employees, and, of course, Jay and Piper."

"And remember," Guy said, "Blake's ex-wife and children all have airtight alibis. I've checked out all three thoroughly. So they're off the suspect list, too, as far as I'm concerned. Looks like we're down to Hazel Schroeder, Chaz Warner, Rosie Flores, Phil Kagan, Darlene Nichols, June Howard, and Charlotte Rodriguez. Jay and Piper, too."

"Let's see if we can't eliminate a few more of these potential suspects today and whittle down our list," Claire said. "We have to concentrate on the ones with the greatest motive for the time being. If we get through all of these people without finding anything helpful, then we'll be forced to spend more time with the other names."

Two hours passed, and after doing extensive background checking through phone calls and Internet searches, the sleuths eliminated June Howard, Charlotte Rodriguez, and Darlene Nichols from the list. Everything about the three checked out flawlessly, and there appeared to be no motive for any of them to murder Blake Helms.

"Okay. Now we have six main suspects," Claire said. "Hazel Schroeder, Chaz Warner, Rosie Flores, Phil Kagan, and Jay and Piper Cantrell. But my investigator instincts tell me Piper didn't do it. And you know my thoughts on Jay. Since we can't talk to Phil until tomorrow, I say we go talk to Hazel and Chaz again—and Rosie, if she's still there. Let's see what more we can learn."

The sleuths walked to the lodge hurriedly and checked at the front desk. All three employees were on duty. They spotted Jay.

"Jay, we'd like to talk to Hazel, Chaz, and Rosie again now. Can you please send them into the interview room, one at a time, like before? Rosie first, before she leaves for the day."

"Sure," Jay said. "What's up?"

"It's part of our investigation, Jay. Thanks," Guy said.

"That folder of employee work applications is at the front desk now, if you want to look through it," Jay said.

ROSIE FLORES was first.

"Rosie, please have a seat," Claire said. "How are you today?"

"Fine, I think," the housekeeper said. "Shouldn't I be?"

"Well, I don't know," Claire said. "Heidi Flynn has been arrested for the murder of Blake Helms. You certainly are aware of that fact, aren't you?"

"Yeah. We all are."

"You made a serious allegation about Heidi Flynn when we first interviewed you, Rosie. And now we're wondering how you feel about Heidi's arrest," Claire said.

The housekeeper's cheeks flushed, and she put a finger in her mouth to pick at her teeth. She didn't respond for a time.

"How do you feel about Heidi's arrest, Rosie?" Claire repeated her question.

"Not sure, I guess," Rosie said.

"I mean, you certainly wanted to point the finger at Heidi for Blake's murder. You told us she had a gun. You told us she pulled it out and threatened you with it. You told us she laughed at you and showed you the gun wasn't loaded," Claire said. "All of those things helped poison the well against Heidi Flynn. So, I'm wondering how you feel about the role you played in all of this—in Heidi's arrest." Claire stared at Rosie without blinking.

Rosie twisted her body from side to side, distorting her shape.

"We're waiting for your answer, Rosie," Claire said.

Rosie refused to talk, and her face grew redder.

"Do you know what I think?" Claire asked.

Rosie shook her head slightly.

"I think you lied to us. I think you made up a story about Heidi. I think you knew she had a gun, so you knew you could make up a tale to get your coworker into serious problems with the law."

Rosie's head dropped.

"How am I doing?" Claire asked.

"I . . . didn't know . . ." Rosie said.

"You didn't know what?" Claire asked.

"I didn't realize . . ." Rosie said.

"You didn't realize *what*?" Claire asked again.

"I never realized it would go this far," Rosie said.

"So, you admit you made up the story?" Claire asked.

The housekeeper murmured an inaudible answer under her breath.

"Was that a yes?" Claire asked.

Rosie nodded.

"I'm at a total loss for words," Claire said.

Rosie looked sheepish. "I'm . . . sorry."

"We cannot accept your apology," Claire said. "You'll need to apologize to Heidi directly. She's the one you wronged, and now she's in a terrible situation."

Rosie started to whimper. "Heidi's so pretty and so thin. She has everything going for her. Even has a boyfriend. And look at me. I'm ugly, overweight, and boys don't ever look at me."

"Did Heidi ever mistreat you?" Claire asked.

"Not really," Rosie said. "I guess I've been really mean to her, though. I even messed up the rooms she cleaned to get her in trouble with Blake, so he'd yell at her when the guests complained."

"So that explains why Blake confronted Heidi about her work, even though she claimed she was cleaning the rooms perfectly," Guy said. "And it also explains why Heidi fought back so adamantly. You baited the two against each other, Rosie. You knew what the result would be."

"You know what you need to do, Rosie. This interview is over," Claire said. The tone of voice told Rosie exactly what Claire thought of the housekeeper's lying and intentional plot to make life miserable for Heidi Flynn. The sleuth shook her head as Rosie shuffled from the room.

"If she had made those willful false statements on the witness stand—under oath, in a court of law—she would be charged with perjury," Guy said.

CHAZ WARNER appeared next.

"Hello, Chaz," Claire said. "Please sit down. We have a few additional questions for you."

"Do I need an attorney?" Chaz asked, sitting down on the edge of the seat and leaning forward.

"I don't know. Do you?" Guy asked. "You let us know if you want one, and the questioning will stop."

Silence filled the air as Chaz twiddled his thumbs. "I have nothing to hide. So ask away. Don't have a lot of time, though. People out there are hungry, and I'm supposed to serve them."

"We now know about your past conviction for assault," Claire said.

"And because of that, I'm automatically a suspect in a *murder*?" Chaz asked.

"I didn't say that," Claire said. "However, you do have an anger problem. That's been well established. Add that to your assault conviction, to the fact that you seemed to go at it verbally with Blake Helms, to the statement in your first interview that you felt like 'punching the hell out of the old sucker,' and to a witness's statement that you allegedly said, 'the man should be dead. He should be put out of his misery.' Because of *that*, of course you become of interest in the investigation."

"So, what do you want from me?" Chaz asked. "What the hell can I do to prove my innocence?"

"Tell us the truth," Claire said. "The truth is how you can prove your innocence. Let's start with the fact that you're related to Sheriff Bell."

He looked stunned. "Okay, so you're really good investigators. I get it. You found that out. What you don't know is that Sheriff Bell, even though he is a relative, is not going to protect me again if I screw up. Is that what you're implying? I know I got off easy on the assault conviction, but Sheriff Bell made it clear to me that he'd help me only one time. Believe me, he's reiterated this over and over. Now I have to walk the high road or pay the price. Next time I screw up, he told me I'd be looking out from behind bars. If he, too, failed to communicate the fact that we're related, believe me, it's because he's doing his own investigation as we speak to see if I was involved in this mess. No way will he protect me if he thinks I killed a man. You can take that to the bank."

"So, are you?" Claire asked. "Walking the high road, that is?"

"I know my temper's a problem. It's just there. It's a part of me. I deal with it the best I can. Sometimes when I get angry, I shout at people. But that's where it starts and stops. It never goes beyond that," Chaz said. He paused. "Only that once."

"Did you ever say, 'the man should be dead. He should be put out of his misery'?" Guy asked.

"Probably. Blake Helms had a grand way of getting under my skin, irritating me to no end. I don't know why I let him get to me, but I did. He acted so superior with that attitude of his. So high and mighty. But did I ever mean I was actually going to harm the man? No. Absolutely not. They were mere words."

"Words are powerful," Claire said.

The Terra Restaurant server stared at her. "I realize that. Now more than ever."

"Did you murder Blake Helms, Chaz?" Claire asked.

"No," he said emphatically. "I did not. Shit, do you think I'd do something that stupid to land myself behind bars for the rest of my life? I don't have another *get-out-of-jail-free card* to play."

"Well, Chaz, we will get to the bottom of this, and soon we'll know who committed the crime," Guy said.

"I thought Heidi Flynn was arrested for the murder," the server said.

"Do you think she committed the crime?" Claire asked.

Chaz shook his head. "Not really."

"Thank you, Chaz. If you come up with anything that could be important to us, please let us know," Guy said.

"Oh, and one more question before you leave," Claire said. "I noticed a huge diamond on Hazel Schroeder's right ring finger the other day. Have you seen it?"

"Have I seen it? Who hasn't? It nearly blinded me! Everybody's whispering about it in the kitchen. She eats up the attention, of course," Chaz said. "Seems she's always doing things to make people look at her—whether it's talking as loud as she can, walking around with her nose in the air, or rudely ordering the staff around. It's all pretty obnoxious, if you ask me."

"Where did she get it?" Claire asked. "The ring."

"No idea. She's always complaining about how little money she makes at the lodge and bitching that she should be paid much more for all the work she does around here. Blah. Blah. Blah. We all work just as hard." He stopped to think for a moment. "Maybe someone in her family died and left her a wad."

HAZEL SCHROEDER, the last of the three, hurried into the room. Claire excused herself and ran out to the lobby to grab the employee work applications folder. She quickly located Hazel Schroeder's application, glanced through it, and zeroed in on one question. She kept the folder with her and returned to the interview room.

"I'm quite busy right now. What is it?" Hazel asked. "I don't have a lot of time to waste."

"Hello, Hazel, thank you for sitting down with us," Guy said. "We have a few more follow-up questions to ask you."

"Well, let's get on with it, then. I have a special event to pull together tonight," Hazel said, "and I have a lot of work to do to get ready for it."

"Hazel, we've interviewed many people and done a substantial amount of research in the matter of the demise of Blake Helms," Claire said. "And several of the people we interviewed told us that you and Blake did not get along very well. In fact, on occasion we understand that the two of you argued loudly enough that others at the lodge couldn't help but overhear the disagreements."

"Yeah? So?" Hazel asked.

"So you made it onto our suspect list," Guy said.

Hazel looked astounded. "I'm a *suspect*?"

"You are," Guy said. "Along with a few others."

Hazel flinched. "I don't understand. What about Heidi Flynn? She was arrested for the murder, wasn't she? Why are you still barraging people with questions and talking about a suspect list?"

"Yes, Heidi was arrested on the charge of murder, and the sheriff's office is convinced that she did it," Claire said. "But we're not. In fact, we believe strongly she did *not* commit the crime."

"I'm shocked!" Hazel said. "And maybe even a little scared. So you're saying the *real* killer may still be out there?" She shifted in her seat.

The investigators ignored her question.

"Hazel, I've noticed you wearing a large diamond ring on your right hand recently," Claire said. "And I do not see it on your finger now. Can you tell us about the ring?"

"Now you want to know about my *jewelry*? What else do you want to know? The color of my underwear?" Hazel asked.

"Well, for starters, when did you get the ring?" Claire asked.

"I . . . I bought it. Recently. But I don't see how that's any of your business," Hazel replied, sharply. "To be painfully candid, I'm actually greatly offended by your question. What are you driving at?"

"We know the kind of salary you earn here at the lodge, and quite frankly, it doesn't support that type of purchase," Guy said.

"It's a cubic zirconia ring set in sterling silver, okay?" Hazel blurted out. "It didn't cost much, but I saved up for it."

"Really? May I see it?" Claire asked. "I'm going to guess it's in your pocket."

"It is not," Hazel said.

"Please stand up," Claire said.

Reluctantly, the supervisor stood. She looked around the room.

"Perhaps you can tell us what that is in your pocket, then," Claire said. "Something in there is sticking out." The female investigator paused. "We'd like to see the ring, Hazel."

Hazel took her sweet time and slowly reached down into her pocket, all the while leering at Claire. "Here it is," Hazel said begrudgingly, handing the ring to the female investigator.

"You didn't have it when we first interviewed you, did you?" Claire asked.

"No. It was a very recent purchase. I told you that." She blinked repeatedly.

"And you didn't wear it into this interview, why?" Claire asked.

"No reason," Hazel said. She squirmed in her seat.

Claire looked carefully at the ring. Then she pulled a loupe—a small jeweler's magnifying glass that she always kept with her—from her purse, and she examined the stone and circular band at close range. She handed the ring to Guy for his perusal and returned it to Hazel.

"Beautiful ring, Hazel," Claire said. "Are you married? I noticed you left that question blank on the lodge application you filled out."

"That is a personal question," Hazel said, "and it's none of your business. But if you must know, no, I am not." She inhaled and exhaled loudly. Her anger level seemed to be growing by the second, and she began to tap her fingers rapidly on the table.

"Engaged?" Claire asked.

Hazel stared at her in disbelief. "You're like a dog on a bone. Absolutely relentless!" She squeezed her lips together, inwardly seething. "No, I am not engaged, either."

"Thank you," Claire said. "That is all."

"What? No more questions? How can this be?" Hazel asked, overwhelming sarcasm dripping from her tone.

"Let me clarify—no further questions for you *at this time*, Hazel," Claire said. "You're free to go."

Hazel got up and stormed from the room.

Guy turned to Claire. "That lady definitely has issues."

"I'd say it's more than issues," Claire said. "Her ring is *not* a cubic zirconia. It's a magnificent, nearly flawless white diamond. And the setting is marked 18 carat. That's 18 carat white gold, not sterling silver."

"So, she's a liar," Guy said.

"She is," Claire said. "A ring like that costs big bucks. It's certainly out of her league. Where did she get the money to buy it?"

Guy raised his brows.

"Well, I think we can remove Chaz Warner from our list—or at least put him on the far back burner. In my opinion, he has too much to lose to commit a murder. And Rosie Flores is off the list totally, if you ask me. But Hazel Schroeder remains on it—and as a strong suspect," Claire said.

"I agree on all counts," Guy said. "And now there are four main suspects in my mind: Hazel Schroeder, Jay Cantrell, Phil Kagan, and Piper Cantrell."

"I can't wait to sit down with Phil tomorrow and ask him the tough questions," Claire said. "For starters, how he thought he could steal our books and get away with it. What he expected to find in the books. Where he lives. What he knows about the recent discovery Blake Helms made just before he was murdered. He needs to answer a lot of questions."

"You've got that right," Guy said. "I'd also like to know if he owns a gun and if he knows how to shoot one."

WHEN THE investigators walked into the lobby, Jay was standing alone behind the check-in desk. When he saw the two approaching, he hastily pushed something back into a large envelope and shoved the packet into the top drawer.

"Care to join us for dinner?" Jay asked.

27

"OKAY, WHAT WAS *that* about?" Guy asked.

"I don't know, but I don't like it," Claire said. "Jay's acting secretive about something, and it makes me question what he's up to."

Once they reached their room, the two changed clothes for dinner. Claire pulled her hair back into a ponytail and touched up her makeup, finishing with a stroke of coral lipstick.

"We've been at this for more than a week now," she said, "and I think we're coming close to identifying the real killer. Narrowing the field of suspects has been difficult with so many potentials, but we've actually done it quite quickly, considering. I'm hoping our interview with Phil Kagan tomorrow will shed some new light on the investigation. Personally, I can't wait to confront the man."

"One thing we do know for sure: he'll try his comedian act again to dilute the seriousness of the matter," Guy said. "Count on it."

"Yeah, well, that act might work on some, but it won't get him far with us."

The investigators sat on the chaise lounge chairs on the balcony for the few minutes they had before dinner. The towering pines swayed ever so gently in the evening breeze, wafting the fresh scent of pine needles their way. The sun, now lower in the sky, reflected off Flathead Lake, causing the water to dance with the brilliance of polished diamonds. The serenity of the setting at once put the investigators' minds at ease, and all of the day's tension seemed to dwindle.

"We've been so busy with this case, there's been little time left over to enjoy all of this," Guy said. "I think I could sit here for a week straight and not tire of it."

Claire exhaled. "I'd have to bring you food." She laughed. Then her expression turned serious. "How are you doing, honey? I mean, with the issues you've been dealing with since we returned from Crete."

"I think I'm better, thanks for asking," Guy said. "Seeing Blake's life cut short makes me remember how precious life is. I'm fighting to return to my old self, and I'm not going to give up."

Claire smiled at the man she loved. "That makes me happy."

Soon it was time to meet Piper and Jay. The sleuths strolled across the parking lot, hungry for a good meal. They walked up the steps to the lodge entrance and met up with the Cantrells. Piper seemed a bit more upbeat.

"I'm glad we can eat dinner together," Piper said. "I'm still feeling incredibly guilty knowing that each day goes by with the two of you buried up to your eyeballs in the investigation. I had so many things planned for us to do together when you visited. But you know what they say, *the best laid plans . . .*"

"Come this way," Jay said. "We reserved a nice spot."

Piper and Jay led the way into the Terra Restaurant. The couples sat down at a table near a large picture window, one offering a stunning view of Flathead Valley and Flathead Lake. Other lodge guests were seated nearby at the surrounding tables.

Chaz Warner approached, shot both investigators a rather icy look, and informed the foursome that he would be their server. He took beverage orders and disappeared into the kitchen. Minutes later, he reappeared with the drinks and set a plate of coconut shrimp with a sweet Thai mango dipping sauce on the table as an appetizer. "Compliments of Chef Nichols," he said in a matter-of-fact sort of way.

"Very nice," Jay said.

"Before you order this evening," the server said, "I'd like to tell you about tonight's special. This evening, Chef Nichols is preparing a special eight-ounce Blue Mesa Ranch tenderloin with forest berry chipotle rub and tarragon butter. It's topped with sautéed mushrooms, and we'll add some blue cheese crumbles, if you'd like. As you know, the steaks are served with fry bread, salad or soup, vegetable, and your choice of garlic mashed potatoes or sweet potato fries." He spoke in a stiff, robotic manner—and without a tinge of friendliness in his tone.

It was clear to the investigators that Chaz had not appreciated another round of questioning in the murder case, and he wanted to make that fact known.

All four ordered the very same thing: the evening's special with salad and sweet potato fries.

"So, what's the word?" Jay asked once Chaz left the table. His expression turned somber. "Why is Chaz upset? Why did you call those three employees in for a second interview?"

"We've narrowed our list of suspects considerably," Claire said, "and there are some remaining issues we needed to clarify. That is all."

"Am I still a suspect?" Jay asked.

"Maybe we should not discuss the investigation and just enjoy our dinner together," Guy said. "Is that possible?"

"You won't answer my question?" Jay asked. "Then I'm going to assume that I am."

"It would put his mind at ease to hear he's no longer on the suspect list," Piper said. "Certainly you can understand that. And me, too, for that matter." She reached over and grabbed his hand.

It was the first sign of affection Claire had seen either Jay or Piper show toward the other since the day the sleuths had arrived. But Jay immediately and covertly pulled his hand away from Piper's. Claire noticed this, too.

"I'd rather we didn't discuss this over dinner," Guy repeated.

"Then, to hell with you," Jay said. He pushed his chair from the table and rushed off.

"Oh, now that wasn't necessary," Claire said. "We have a job to do, Piper, and we're doing it to the best of our ability." She gave Piper a half smile. "Piper, many of the people we interviewed told us that Jay and Blake argued on a regular basis. Some even said Jay and Blake engaged in heated arguing only days before Blake was killed. Jay's on the suspect list, along with several others. We wouldn't be very good at what we do if we ignored the facts, simply because you both are our friends, would we? We must leave no stone unturned. We've told you this from the beginning."

"But you don't seriously believe Jay is capable of *murder*, do you, Claire?" Piper asked. "Or me?"

Claire said. "Look. I believe wholeheartedly that Heidi Flynn was framed. So it's up to us to track down the real killer. That's what we are trying to do."

"This is a tough situation for us," Guy said. "Believe me."

Just then, Chaz Warner appeared to serve the dinners.

"Chaz," Piper said, "keep Jay's warm in the kitchen, will you, please? He had to check on something."

"No problem," the server said.

The food was sumptuous, and in utter silence, the three ate every morsel.

The server returned to the table. "Dessert or coffee, anyone?"

Decaf coffees were ordered all around.

"Piper," Claire said, "did you and Blake . . ."

Just then, Jay returned to the table and slipped into his chair. "I apologize for my behavior. Haven't been myself lately. Being a suspect in a murder case has a way of doing that to a person." His words were apologetic, but his tone was definitely not.

Chaz delivered Jay's dinner to him, and Jay ate without talking.

The evening was awkward and strained, and when goodbyes were exchanged, they could not have come too soon.

CLAIRE AND Guy returned to their room, discussed their inability once again to ask Piper about the allegations of the affair, talked about their plans for the following day, and retired early. The stress of the growing tension between the investigators and their long-time friends ate away at them both throughout the long night.

MORNING ARRIVED and the investigators readied for the day. Just as they were about to lock up the room, Guy's cell phone rang.

"Gaston, it's Jasper Wilkes. Yesterday, I did my best to get Heidi Flynn released on bail pending her trial date. I even claimed special circumstances to get the matter heard on a Saturday. But I had no such luck—even after they heard all the extenuating circumstances. They're playing hardball because she fled prior to her arraignment. Unfortunately for Heidi, Sam, and little Ethan, Heidi will be confined to her detention cell until the trial date. And we're looking at two months. Bad news, I'm afraid."

"Thanks for letting us know, Jasper," Guy said. "Let's keep each other posted on any new developments."

Guy filled Claire in on Heidi's predicament.

"I'm sorry for Heidi. Actions have consequences, and she's learning this the hard way," Claire said.

As the two started walking in the direction of the lodge, Claire said, "Let's walk over to Woods Bay Grill, instead, this morning. The change will do us good."

They reached the neighborhood restaurant in no time. The place was filled with the regular crowd. When LoLo saw the sleuths, she quickly cleared a corner table and waved them over.

"Do you have good news?" LoLo asked, pouring fresh-brewed coffee into two cups. "Did you find out what Blake wanted to show me?"

"Afraid not, but we're narrowing our list of suspects," Claire said. "Still not sure what Blake planned to show you, LoLo." She sighed.

They ordered a light breakfast.

"How's that poor child, Heidi Flynn, holding up at the detention center?" LoLo asked.

"Probably not well," Claire said. "We're doing our best to get her out, but first we need to identify the real killer. We've narrowed the list considerably, as I said, but there's still work to be done."

"I'd ask you who is on the list, but I know you won't tell me." She bustled away to deliver some orders and make the rounds refilling coffees, leaving the pleasant aroma of fresh lilacs wafting in the air behind her—as always.

Claire's mind drifted in a different direction. "I want to call Chief Soderberg in Whitefish and check in on the situation there," Claire said. "It'll be interesting to learn if they've discovered anything new."

"Good idea. We told him we'd assist, and we can't abandon him now," Guy said.

Claire dialed the chief's cell number.

"Chief Soderberg? Claire Caswell calling. I know it's Sunday, but we wanted to check in with you. Gaston and I are curious about the situation in Whitefish."

She listened intently to his response—and his request.

"We could drive up today, if you'd like," she said.

After hearing a bit more from the chief, she commented, "We'll drive up this afternoon and plan on sticking around into the evening."

LoLo delivered the breakfasts, and while Claire filled Guy in on the Whitefish situation, the investigators enjoyed the repast.

"It should work out fine," Claire said. "We need to go to the lodge and interview Phil Kagan first. Then we can drive to the Lake County Detention Center and visit Heidi Flynn. After that, we can head up to Whitefish."

LoLo brought the check, refilled the coffees, and reminded them to keep her posted on everything. "You find his murderer!" she said. "And find out what he wanted to show me, too!" She scurried off.

Claire and Guy left money on the table for the bill and included a generous tip. They walked with a steady pace back to the lodge. When they arrived, they found Jay in the kitchen and requested he send Phil Kagan into the interview room.

"No can do," Jay said. "The man called in sick again today. Left us in a lurch. Piper and I have been trying to keep the big brunch going this morning, and we're also manning the front desk. Try that sometime."

"You're kidding. Do you have a telephone number for Phil, either home or a cell?" Guy asked.

"He doesn't have a home phone, and he said he's having trouble with his cell phone. Said he had to drive to a gas station to call in sick from a payphone. Told me he has some kind of a bad flu bug."

"So we have no home number, no cell number to reach him, and no home address?" Guy asked. "Is that correct?"

"Apparently so," Jay said.

"But we need to talk to Phil Kagan," Guy said. "ASAP."

"Well, until he reports back to work, I don't know how you're going to do that," Jay said. "Is Phil a *suspect*, too?"

"I'm not going there, Jay," Guy said. "Thanks for the information."

Claire and Guy walked to the parking lot and jumped into the green Land Rover Discovery. It was low on gas, and they drove to a nearby station and filled up.

On the drive to the detention center, the investigators seemed sullen.

"I feel like we've hit a giant roadblock," Claire said. "Phil Kagan is really throwing a wrench into the development of our case, and time is of the essence. Especially for Heidi Flynn. It makes me wonder what he's all about."

"He could be genuinely ill, I suppose," Guy said. "Have you considered that possibility?"

"Not on your life," she said. "He stole the books from our room for a reason. And moments later, he went home 'sick' from work, and now he's been missing in action for two days. Something is definitely rotten with that man."

"We have nothing concrete on him," Guy said, "other than the fact that he's got a repellent personality and he took Blake's books from our room."

"He was also a friend of Blake's," Claire said. "And Blake shared his knowledge about the American Indian tribes of this region with Phil." Claire stared straight ahead, and Guy did not disturb her thoughts. "I want to ride back out to the area where I met Running

Cloud, Guy. And I want to do it today, right after we see Heidi Flynn, and before we drive to Whitefish."

"The reason?" Guy asked.

"I need to talk with Running Cloud again. I must."

"I'll call Jay and ask him to have two horses saddled up for us," Guy said.

"Make sure one of them is Whispering Spirit," Claire said. "It can only be Whispering Spirit for me. And you might want to ask for a horse other than Giddy Up." She contorted her face. "One with a little more zip, perhaps?"

As Guy phoned Jay to make the arrangements, she went over the facts of the case in her mind. She was so sure they were on the cusp of learning the identity of the murderer. Claire recalled many times in past investigations when a jumble of seemingly unrelated puzzle pieces had appeared to be piling up and leading nowhere, and then, when least expected, a few pieces fit together, and then several more, and suddenly the big picture came screaming into focus. She had witnessed this so many times before, and she hoped strongly for the same outcome in this case.

She picked up her cell and dialed Sheriff Bell.

"Sheriff Bell, have any of the other paintings stolen on the night Blake Helms was murdered showed up anywhere?"

"Funny you should ask," the sheriff said. "I was just going to call you. Yesterday and again today, we've received calls from galleries in all different directions from here. In two of the cases, the store-owner purchased valuable original paintings at a healthy, but discounted, cost from someone saying an aunt had recently passed away and left him the pieces. Unfortunately, both owners checked with us *after* the fact, wondering if the pieces they acquired were among those stolen from Mountain Lake Lodge—those on the theft alert they received. We had sent that alert about these pieces so they would know not to purchase them, but people do not always take heed. Now the purchasers will have to turn the pieces over to us and deal directly with their insurance companies for reimbursement."

"You said *him*?" Claire asked. "It was a *man* offering to sell the artwork to the galleries? Was he alone?"

"Yes. That's what we were told," the sheriff said. "It was a man, and no one else was with him."

"Did you get the man's description?"

"Yeah. They all said the same thing: the man was big in stature and had a thick mustache that was heavily waxed on each end to turn up into a curl. It looked like he was perpetually smiling, they all reported."

"I'll bet," Claire said. "All the way to the bank. I think I know who it probably was, sheriff. Phil Kagan. Are you planning to check the lodge employees' bank accounts when the banks open in the morning? A tip-off would be an unusually large deposit."

"I've already asked one of my major case team detectives to do just that. He'll check every bank within an hour's drive of here."

"Sheriff, thanks for keeping an open mind," Claire said. "I'm sure we can both agree that we want the actual killer to be convicted in this case."

Silence predominated for a long minute.

"I want to do the right thing, Ms. Caswell. Perhaps we acted too hastily in arresting Ms. Flynn. We'll scan a photo of Phil Kagan to each gallery that contacted us and ask if he's the man offering the pieces for sale. We can use his driver's license photo on file with the DMV."

"Tell the galleries to imagine the man with a mustache. Or better yet, ask the storeowners to draw a similar mustache on the image you send them. This might give them a better idea. Keep us posted, please," Claire said. "This is heating up. And thank you, Sheriff

Bell, for your help and cooperation. We're close to catching the real perpetrator." She paused. "If we don't, Heidi Flynn will go to prison for a crime she didn't commit."

28

AT THE LAKE County Detention Center, the sleuths asked to see Heidi Flynn. They signed the registration log, showed identification, and were taken to her cell.

"Ms. Caswell, Mr. Lombard," Heidi said. "Thank you for coming to see me. I don't like being locked in here. I feel like a caged animal. Like I'm suffocating."

"I can only imagine," Claire said. "We stopped by to check on you and to ask if you've remembered anything else that might be of help to us and to your attorney. Heidi, we're convinced you did not murder Blake Helms. And we're trying our hardest to come up with evidence of who did."

"Thank you. Thank you," she said. She reached her fingers through the bars and touched their hands. "And, no, I don't remember anything else. I've told you and Attorney Wilkes everything."

"All right," Guy said. "Notify your attorney immediately if you come up with *anything*, and ask him to call and fill us in, as well."

"Of course I will," Heidi said. "Things have spun out of control so quickly. I've been accused of a crime I didn't commit, and I'm locked up while the killer is out there, walking around free, probably having a good laugh that I'm taking the fall."

"We're trying to correct that, Heidi," Guy said.

"Give us a little more time. We're close," Claire said. "Keep your spirits up. Be strong."

Heidi sighed deeply. "Sam and Ethan are supposed to stop by today. That will help. I miss them so much." Her eyes filled with tears, and she started to whimper. "I'm afraid . . ."

"What is it, Heidi?" Claire asked.

"I'm afraid Ethan will forget his momma."

"That will never happen," Claire said. "*Never.*"

THE INVESTIGATORS drove back to the lodge; ran to their room; changed into jeans, comfortable shirts, and boots; and headed to the farm property owned by Jay at the top of the hill.

Jay's employee was there, and he'd already saddled up two horses for their ride: Whispering Spirit and Giddy Up.

"When I checked with Jay, he told me to get these two horses ready to go," the man said. When he noticed Guy's disappointment, he added, "Jay thought it best if you stuck with Giddy Up, sir. It's better to ride a horse that remembers you."

Claire and Guy spent a few minutes getting reacquainted with the horses. When the timing was right, they mounted from the left and tried to recall everything Jay had instructed them to do on the first ride.

"How long will you be?" the man asked.

"A couple hours, tops," Claire said.

"I'll be here. Have a good ride," the employee said.

The sleuths gently kicked their horses in the side and made a clucking sound with their tongues. "Let's go," they both called out. The horses took off simultaneously, Whispering Spirit assuming the lead.

After a short time, Claire leaned over and talked to Whispering Spirit. "Take me to Running Cloud, boy. Find him. I need to see him again." Before she had even fully settled back into her saddle, Whispering Spirit bolted gently, whinnied loudly, and took off in a full gallop.

Guy yelled to Giddy Up, "Follow that horse!" Giddy Up picked up his trot minimally but refused to gallop, and within minutes, Claire and Whispering Spirit were no longer in sight.

Once again, Claire held on for dear life, but this time she knew what to expect. She knew it would come to an end, eventually—if she could only stay centered. The wind cut into her face, her eyes filled with water, her body slid on the leather saddle, and she rode in apprehension that the reins would slip through her fingers. *Hold on!* she shouted to herself. *Hold on!* Staying centered on the runaway horse became a punishing challenge, but she stayed with it admirably.

In due course, Whispering Spirit slowed, suddenly veered to the left, and eventually curved to the right. He trotted down the pine-lined path where he had taken her the last time, and then he stopped cold.

Claire slid off. "Good boy! You rest now," she said, stroking Whispering Spirit's long face.

She turned in place, closed her eyes, and said, "Running Cloud, are you nearby?" She waited in anticipation. Nothing happened. She said again, louder this time, "Running Cloud, are you nearby?" All of a sudden, the gelding threw his head back in the air and whinnied with a great deal of volume. As before, an eagle soared overhead.

"Easy, boy," Claire said. "Easy." She touched his face.

"I'm here." The voice came from behind.

Claire swung around, and there stood Running Cloud.

"What is your need on this occasion, white woman?" he asked. His eyes exuded kindness, but his facial expression appeared stern.

"I respectfully seek your advice," she said. "You left so quickly last time."

"What is it?" he asked. "What do you need?"

"The sheriff's office arrested a young woman for the murder of the lodge employee, Blake Helms. But I do not believe she did it, so we're continuing to investigate the matter. Our list of suspects is now small, but I need your guidance."

"The young woman taken into custody did not commit the act," he said.

"Then we are in agreement," Claire said. "Last time, you had me shut my eyes to see clearly. You asked me to look anew at the murder scene, using my mind's eye. You instructed me to look at the big picture. I did that. And I did it again back at the lodge where the murder occurred. I sat down and examined the photographs of the lodge lobby prior to the murder, and then I stood up and looked at the crime scene with a fresh outlook. I'm still missing something, however, and I don't know what it is."

"Pale lady, you look with your eyes," Running Cloud said, "but you do not see. Look deeper. Your answer is within reach."

"In the photos?" Claire asked.

He nodded ever so slightly. "You are close. Murderers always leave a trail behind. Follow it."

"Two trails of sapphire gravel were found leading to and from the body," Claire said.

"A clue worthy of your attention," Running Cloud said. He

grabbed the black braid hanging alongside his face and let it drop. "Also think of a braid."

Out of the blue, Claire heard Guy yelling for her in the distance. She turned toward the direction of his voice for a mere split second, and when she turned back around, Running Cloud was gone. Once again, he had vanished in a heartbeat.

Whispering Spirit nudged her gently and blinked his sizable olive eyes. She placed her left foot into the left saddle stirrup and hoisted her body up and into the saddle.

"Take me back to the open field, boy," she whispered in his ear.

He retraced his steps in and soon delivered Claire out to the spot where he had made the left turn.

"Guy," Claire screamed. "I'm over here." She heard no response, so she yelled out again.

Before long, she heard the sound of approaching hoof beats, and soon Guy rode up to her on Giddy Up.

"I lost you completely," he said. "Did you find him?"

"I did. Whispering Spirit took me back to the same place, and a short time later, Running Cloud appeared."

"Hope it was worthwhile," Guy said.

They rode back in a leisurely trot.

"I'm getting used to this horseback riding," Guy said. "I kind of like it."

Guy was definitely returning to his former self, steps at a time, Claire thought, and that made her elated.

THE SLEUTHS returned to their room and quickly changed back into more appropriate work clothing. They picked up sandwiches at the lodge to eat on the way and jumped into the 4 x 4. It was time to leave for Whitefish.

On the drive, Claire related her meeting with Running Cloud to Guy. For some reason, this time she could remember every part of it clearly.

"What the hell is he talking about?" he asked. "A *braid*?"

"I wish I knew," Claire said. "But there's one thing I'm sure of. The answer lies somewhere in those photos. He said we're close. He said, all murderers leave behind a trail. He told me to consider a braid, too."

Guy remained silent, thinking about her comments.

Whitefish

CLAIRE AND Guy arrived at the police department, made their way through the protesters, and were taken to the meeting room. Chief Soderberg, his assistant, the detective lieutenant, the patrol lieutenant, the sergeant, the detective, and the patrol officers stood when the two entered. They had all come in on a Sunday.

"Please. Sit. Thank you for meeting with us again," Chief Soderberg said. "At your suggestion, we've completed additional background checking on the Iron Horse homeowner we brought in for questioning—Andrew Hoyt."

"Did you do further checking on his son, daughter, and wife, too, as we suggested at the end of our last meeting?" Claire asked.

"We did," the chief said. "But I first want to tell you that Andrew Hoyt's situation has progressed to critical. Both of his homes are heading into foreclosure in ten days. He's at the proverbial end of his rope. Banks will no longer extend loans to the man. Don't know how he sleeps at night."

"Who says he does?" Claire asked. "He's desperate, and he may be taking desperate measures. What did you learn about the son?"

"Now, that's where things get real interesting," the chief said. "His son, Aiden, is twenty. He dropped out of the San Francisco Art Institute a few months ago. I called the school and learned he left because he couldn't afford the tuition. They called him 'a most promising student,' though."

"Is Aiden employed at this time?" Guy asked.

"No. So, I imagine that's an additional pressure on Andrew Hoyt," Chief Soderberg said.

"I assume you ran a criminal check on both Andrew and Aiden?" Guy asked.

"We did," the chief said. "Both are clean. No priors on either."

"Any more on *Mrs.* Hoyt?" Claire asked.

"We learned the Hoyts separated more than a year ago. Mrs. Hoyt—Amy Hoyt—moved into a small apartment in Walnut Creek, just east of San Francisco. The two children live with Andrew Hoyt." The chief referred to his notes as he talked.

"What did you find out about the daughter?" Claire asked.

"Alison Hoyt is a year younger than Aiden, so that puts her at nineteen," the chief said. "She's a waitress at the Iron Horse clubhouse restaurant. It's open seven nights a week during golf season and two nights a week during the winter. That employment gives her enough money to put food on the Hoyt table. When we first looked over the list of Iron Horse employees I had obtained earlier, the name Hoyt was not yet on our radar screen. I checked it now, and she's listed as an employee, clear as day. She's a bright girl academically, according to some people I talked to, and she's had to put her life on hold for the time being. Can't afford to go to college. It's a bad situation all around. And they're not the first family to bottom out in this economy. It takes a toll on the best of them."

"I assume you ran a criminal check on Amy and Alison, as well?"

Claire asked.

"Yep. Both clean. No priors," Chief Soderberg said.

"Those Hoyts are under severe stress," Claire said. "Sounds like the daughter is the only one bringing in any income."

"Did you find any other homeowners in the Iron Horse community in a similar situation?" Guy asked.

"Surprisingly, no," the chief said. "Most of the owners are independently wealthy, and many are retired. So money is not an issue."

The force members listened intently to the conversation.

"Did you chart the occurrences of the burglaries?" Guy asked.

"We did," Chief Soderberg said. "At this point, let me turn it over to Detective Curtis Briggs. I asked him to look into that."

"I recorded each burglary on a master sheet, just as you suggested last time," Detective Briggs said. He unfolded the large, rectangular piece of paper sitting in front of him and turned it to face the investigators. "As you take a look, you'll be able to identify the date, the day of the week, and the time of each occurrence, together with the property owner's name and the property's address. To date, there have been a total of eleven home invasions. For the first nine, we found evidence that he had left the stolen property outside near the houses. After the tenth and eleventh invasions, however, we found no evidence that he had hid the stolen property outside of the homes. You'll see that here." He pointed to a column on his chart.

Guy pulled the chart closer.

"Good work, Detective Briggs," Claire said. "We'd like to have some time to study it. Could we reconvene in one hour? And we'll also need to look at the plat drawing showing the locations of all the Iron Horse residences. Oh, and if we can use the computer again . . ."

"You've got it," the chief said. One of the officers handed the schematic to the sleuths and another set up the computer. "Let's all meet back here in one hour. Check your watches."

The force streamed out, leaving the sleuths alone in the room. The hour passed quickly, but it was ample time for the investigators to find what they were looking for. A pattern had jumped out at them. The chief and his officers filed back into the room and sat down.

"Find anything interesting in all that data?" Chief Soderberg asked.

"We did," Guy said. "There's an order to the burglaries."

"But I looked for a structure to the burglaries. We all did," Detective Briggs said. "We couldn't find one."

"The pattern doesn't jump out easily," Claire said. "But it's there. We concentrated only on the day of the week each crime was committed, the address of the property, and the time of day. And according to what we found, the burglar has struck on one of two days of the week; we believe between the specific hours of midnight and 3:00 a.m. And the culprit has stayed within a certain perimeter of the development that we're guessing provides the easiest escape route. Therefore, it appears that the next hit will occur between midnight and 3:00 a.m. *tonight*. And we can even show you the house that will, in all probability, be hit. It's the only house that has not been burglarized within the perimeter we defined."

Rapt attention fell on the Miami investigators.

"Let us explain further," Guy said.

For the next several minutes, the sleuths charted out the specific pattern they had discovered for the chief and his force members to see firsthand.

"Fascinating," Chief Soderberg said.

Pleasant looks of surprise took over the others' faces.

"We missed it completely," Detective Lieutenant Keller said. "I can't believe it."

"Tonight's the night to nab the intruder," Guy said.

"Tonight's the night," Chief Soderberg repeated. "The night we finally arrest the burglar and restore peace to our community. The night our office regains the respect of the citizens of Whitefish."

"I think using *camouflage* is the way to do this," Claire said. "We'll be with you tonight. I suggest we all wear army fatigues to blend in with the environment. We will hide from sight."

"I'll take care of acquiring the uniforms," the chief said. "Let's meet here at 11:00 p.m. sharp to dress for the caper and go over all the details."

"And chief, I'd have every one of your force working the case tonight," Claire said.

29

THE SLEUTHS RETURNED to their guest room in Bigfork.

"I think we should catch an hour's nap," Guy said. "We could be in for an all-nighter in Whitefish, depending on how it plays out. I'll set the alarm, and put the 'do not disturb' sign on the door."

"Thanks for taking care of that," Claire said. "I'm tired. My lack of sleep has definitely caught up with me."

Claire and Guy crawled in between the soft, freshly laundered sheets. Claire nestled close to Guy, her front to his back and her arm around his torso. With bent knees, their bodies fit together perfectly. She could hear and feel his rhythmic breathing, and sleep came easy for her. Since their arrival in Montana, the sleuths' schedule had been nonstop and demanding, and an unplanned timeout was just what they needed.

It seemed that only minutes had passed when the persistent buzzing of the alarm clock signaled time to get up.

Claire and Guy pulled themselves out of bed, dressed in casual clothing suitable for the evening's caper, and walked to the lodge for dinner. Piper was sitting in the lobby, looking through the photo book, and Jay sat behind the check-in desk, doing bookwork.

"Care to join us for a quick dinner?" Claire asked. She glanced at the page holding Piper's attention and noticed it was a photo of Blake Helms.

Piper closed the album. "Haven't eaten since breakfast, so you won't have to ask me twice."

"Jay?" Guy asked. "What about you?"

"You three go ahead," he said. "I have some work to finish. I'll catch up with you if I can."

The three friends ate a quiet dinner.

"Piper?" Claire said. "How are you holding up?"

"I'm taking one day at a time," Piper said. She forced an insincere smile.

"Piper, were you having an affair with Blake Helms?" Claire inquired, at last asking the tough question.

"Would you care for dessert?" Piper asked.

CLAIRE AND Guy had two hours to kill before driving to Whitefish, so they returned to the room and spent that time researching the remaining suspects. Claire and Guy decided to zero in on Hazel Schroeder and see what they could discover.

After the first hour, the sleuths compared notes.

"I don't like what I'm seeing," Guy said. "Hazel's recent background seems almost nonexistent. Perhaps she's gone by a different name. In fact, I see virtually nothing on the woman for the last five years, except some incomplete social networking gibberish. And even with that, there are no friends or followers listed, no communications with others, and no substantial information about her. Just some old photos of her with blonde hair and blue eyes, which I still find strange. It's as if she joined the sites to get only her name—Hazel Schroeder—and face on the Internet, to create a presence. And that is where it starts and stops."

"Exactly," Claire said. "I'm finding the very same thing. And how long has Hazel worked at the lodge? *Five years!* Why has she been virtually staying under the radar screen for the last five years? Think she's hiding something?"

The next hour was spent looking into Phil Kagan. The sleuths went to work on their laptops and made calls to research the Mountain Lake Lodge daytime chef. Neither Claire nor Guy discovered anything remarkable about the man. He did not have a criminal record.

Claire grabbed the folder of employee work applications and flipped through the sheets. She noted that several employees listed a post office box for their home address. It was not unusual. She looked at the clock. "Time to go," she said.

They put on walking shoes, and each toted a medium-weight jacket. Ten minutes later, they were on the way to Whitefish.

Whitefish

IN THE car, the sleuths rolled down the windows and inhaled deeply the amazingly fresh Montana air.

"That scent of pine needles," Claire said, "I'll miss it when we leave."

On the drive, they discussed the plans for the night.

The evening brought with it a slight chill, and Claire put on her jacket to warm up.

All of a sudden, she shrieked, "Watch out! Deer! On the shoulder! Running onto the road!" She pointed.

Guy hit the brakes and swerved, bringing the vehicle to a screeching stop. "I didn't see them," he said. "That was close."

One creature after another crossed the road in front of them. All together, they counted five. It slowed down their momentum.

"Jay warned us about nighttime driving out here," Guy said. "He said it's very dark, and if you see one deer, there are probably many. He was right. Better stay watchful."

They drove in silence for a time, diligently searching the road and shoulders with their eyes.

"If we're correct about tonight," Claire said, "this happens soon. The infamous Whitefish burglar will at last be nabbed."

Anxiety heightened as they neared Whitefish.

When the sleuths walked into the Whitefish Police Department, they were impressed with Chief Soderberg's preparation and organization. His force had collected, and they were dressing in the fatigues he had obtained. Nervousness about the imminent stakeout was palpable throughout the stationhouse. The staff had waited a long time to corner this criminal, and they'd taken a lot of heat from the townsfolk for not doing so earlier—despite all concerted efforts. But tonight, finally, vindication was within reach. Protests would stop. Life would return to normal.

The members of the Whitefish Police Department greeted the Miami investigators, and the chief handed each of them a set of fatigues.

Soon the team was ready to go.

Chief Soderberg reviewed all details of the pending activities, including the secretive approach to and surveillance of the property in question. "The owners are not at home; they're not in Montana at this time. I checked it out." He paused and looked around his force.

"I want to grab this criminal with stolen property in his hands. Not before. That way, the case against him will be fail proof. We are all to follow procedures exactly as set out. No variations from what we've discussed. Questions?"

There were none. The group's anxiousness to get started and complete the mission was clearly evident.

"Check your weapons. Make sure everything is a go. And make certain you have plenty of ammo," the chief said. "Then load up, and we'll be on our way. Good luck!"

They started out for Iron Horse in numerous dark, unmarked cars. Claire and Guy rode with Chief Soderberg, and the other vehicles carried the assistant chief, the patrol lieutenant, the patrol sergeant, and a slew of patrol officers.

In addition, Detective Lieutenant Keller and Detective Briggs agreed to trail slightly behind in another car. Once they neared the property, they would park out of sight and watch the scene unfold from their vehicle. This way, should the culprit decide to make a run for it, the detectives could pursue him. Or if the others needed further assistance on the property site, the detectives could join them as backup.

The drivers turned the vehicles' headlights off prior to driving into the Iron Horse development. Once inside, they were encompassed by the darkness. The vehicles inched their way along the inky roadways until they neared the subject property. Then, as planned, each drove in a different direction to park off-road. The chief and the sleuths exited their vehicle and crept toward the house. A patrol officer accompanied them. Together, the foursome hid behind some conveniently placed shrubbery near the house to avoid detection and to watch. The others paired off into predetermined two-man teams, planting themselves out of sight at various points along the property sidelines. Soon everyone was securely in place. The camouflage clothing did its intended job, entirely concealing the group from anyone approaching.

The detectives rolled in next with headlights turned off, and they parked off-road where they were not visible, yet they themselves still had a clear view of the house and property.

Waiting became the name of the game. As the participants in the sting crouched motionless, in utter anticipation, they hawkishly eyed their surroundings, ready to pounce at a moment's notice. Time moved slowly.

Two hours passed. And one more. The team members felt impatient. Weary. Was this going to happen or not? Just then, two figures appeared on the driveway, moving stealthily. Dressed in black from head to toe, both wore black caps pulled low onto their faces, and one toted a small canvas bag. Their steps were cautious and light-footed as they made their way to the front door of the stately home. There, the entrance cove cloaked them in darkness. The dim glow of a red light could be seen, and a short while later, the front door opened, and the pair slipped in.

Seconds passed. The alarm did not activate.

Exactly three minutes later, both figures emerged rushing from the front doorway, each with two large paintings in hand. They ran to an area on the property sidelines and stored the pieces in the heavily wooded thicket. Once again, they had reverted to their former pattern. Then they returned for more.

But this time, when the thieves dashed from the house carrying stolen art, the police chief yelled out in a loud, sharp cry, "Move in!"

With guns drawn, the assistant chief, patrol lieutenant, patrol sergeant, and patrol officers appeared from every direction, rapidly surrounding the culprits.

"Set the art down gently, and put your hands in the air!" the chief shouted at the top of his lungs. "It's over! You are both under arrest."

The burglars obeyed.

The force rushed the burglars, cuffed their hands behind their backs, and clamped shackles around their ankles. There was no way these two were going to make a getaway. Simultaneously, the detectives' vehicle roared into the driveway, and the men jumped from the vehicle, ready to offer any assistance necessary.

Detective Briggs threw on gloves and sprinted to the house, returning in no time at all with the canvas tote he had located just inside the doorway. He pulled it open and peered inside. It was filled with an elaborate assortment of lockpicking tools, cloths, various lengths of rope, bags, a laser gun, what looked to be some type of jammer, and several flashlights. "All of their equipment is in this tote," he announced loudly. At once, he tagged it as evidence.

Claire and Guy joined the chief as he approached the two figures dressed in black. As the three neared, they saw that the burglars' faces were covered with black grease paint. The captain yanked the caps from both of their heads.

Claire recognized the perpetrators at once, despite their painted faces. "Meet your burglars," she said. "Aiden and Alison Hoyt."

Certain patrol officers stayed behind to bring the lifted artwork back inside the house and to secure the premises. Chief Soderberg took the evidence tote into his personal possession. The patrol sergeant read the Miranda Warning to Aiden Hoyt and to Alison Hoyt, one at a time. Patrol officers then placed the two into the back of different patrol cars and drove them to the Whitefish jailhouse.

Aiden and Alison Hoyt were locked up in segregated cells, but within shouting distance of each other. The chief, the two detectives, and the investigators arrived at the jail minutes later and stood on the outside of Aiden Hoyt's cell, looking in.

"What do you have to say for yourself?" Chief Soderberg asked Aiden. "Did you really think you'd get away with this forever?"

"We did, didn't we?" Aiden said nastily. "Until today."

Claire glanced at his feet and noticed his shoes. Tennis shoes. *Common sneakers.* And she guessed them to be a size 9. Probably an exact match for the one imprint left behind at a home burglary. She saw Chief Soderberg and the two detectives glaring at Aiden's shoes, as well. Then they glanced up and nodded. Aiden's sneaker would be compared to the impression the police had lifted from the dirt at the burglarized home. If it was a match, as they presumed it would be, it represented additional evidence to be used against him at trial.

Claire and Guy walked over to Alison's cell.

She sat on the bench in her confined quarters. "I didn't want to do it," she said. "Aiden made me. He said it was the only way we could help our father, and we had to do something. Our lives had spun out of control. Dad was losing everything he'd worked so hard for. We couldn't let that happen."

"Shut up, Alison!" Aiden yelled. "Don't say another word. Not until we have a lawyer."

"Aiden told me the owners had insurance. That it was no big deal. That they would get reimbursed for the losses," Alison prattled on. "He made me ask the owners I served at the clubhouse when they'd be leaving town and when they'd be back. That way, we'd never hurt anyone. We'd always go in when no one was home. We'd take the artwork and hide it in the trees. Then we'd go back later when no police were around to retrieve it. It was a slick plan. But then one day when Aiden was driving through Iron Horse, he spotted the Whitefish police snooping around the grounds of one of the houses we had entered. He feared they had discovered our plan. So from that point on—for the last two burglaries, that is—we stole less from the houses and carried everything away with us, rather than leave it in the trees."

"Shut your mouth, Alison. I mean it!" Aiden shouted from his cell.

"I want to tell you everything," Alison said, defying her brother's orders. "I'm glad it's finally over."

"How did you disable the alarm systems?" Guy asked.

"Aiden did that. He worked for a large alarm company evenings and weekends when he was in art school in San Francisco, and he had access to all the various systems. He downloaded the instructions for each operating system and studied how to instantly disarm all of them. He used a laser gun to put a hole in the control panel and short circuit the system so the alarm would not go off, and he has a jammer the size of a remote to jam the cellular backup. I don't understand exactly how it all works, but it does."

"Stop talking, Alison!" Aiden bellowed from his cell.

"Aiden is heavy into Locksport, too," Alison went on. "It's a sport where you learn the art of defeating locking systems. He even belongs to a group where the members meet at bars and network to exchange information and knowledge on lockpicking. They do it for fun, for the challenge. They even have contests to see who can pick a variety of difficult locks the fastest. But Aiden used his knowledge for illegal purposes, and he dragged me into it. Said we *had* to do it to help our father. He gave me no choice but to help him."

"What did you do with the stolen pieces of art, Alison?" Claire asked.

"Aiden met a Canadian guy who worked in Whitefish for the summer. Aiden convinced the guy to secure some pieces under his car every time he drove home across the border for a weekend, and then he fenced the art in Canada. Aiden gave him a percentage of the profit. It worked well, and we've made lots of money."

"I'm going to kill you!" Aiden screamed to Alison.

"I'll even give you the man's name," Alison said.

"Is your father involved in this?" Chief Soderberg asked.

"No. He knows nothing about it. We were saving the money until we had enough to pay down on the mortgages, to save our houses from foreclosure. We planned to surprise him."

"Why did you enter the one property when the owners were at home?" Claire asked. "Tell us about that."

"That was a horrible night," Alison said. "They were supposed to be gone. When I waited on them at the clubhouse restaurant days earlier, they had told me they would be leaving the day before we entered their house. We were totally surprised to find them sleeping in their bed. Aiden thought quickly. He whispered that we had to tie them up, gag, and blindfold them. He made me help. He said I should take care of the woman and he'd take care of the man. We always carried rope and cloth with us to help with the thefts, so we had the supplies we needed. We surprised them in their sleep. Bound their hands first, gagged them almost simultaneously, blindfolded them, and tied their feet together—before they even realized what was happening. We wore tight gloves and used new materials, so no fingerprints would be left behind. We worked in silence, with speed, and in total darkness. The owners never knew there were two of us. They went into shock—groggy from being awakened from deep sleep and frozen with fear. Didn't even fight back. Aiden found the blunt end of a regular dinner knife and held that to their heads. It was metal and cold, and he wanted them to think it was a gun. He never used a gun. He doesn't even own one. But he didn't want the owners to try to escape while we did our work, so he tried to scare them into compliance."

Alison dropped her head low. "It felt awful to participate in something like this, and I will never forgive myself. I feel dirty, and no matter how many showers I take, the feeling doesn't go away. I hate Aiden for involving me in all of this. I'd give anything to take it all back."

"There's one thing I agree with your brother, Aiden, about,"

Detective Briggs said. "You're going to need to hire an attorney to represent you."

"Damn straight," Detective Lieutenant Keller said.

"I demand to call my father!" Aiden boomed from his cell. "Now!"

BACK AT the Whitefish Police Department, Chief Stan Soderberg and his force lined up to extend a heartfelt thank-you to the sleuths. "It's clear. We could not have done this without your help. We are forever indebted to you both," the chief said.

"It was a tough case to break. We're just glad it's over and that Whitefish can finally put the matter to rest," Claire said. "And get back to being the charming little town that it is."

"I'll make sure the paper carries the whole story and gives you two the credit," the chief said.

"Actually, we prefer that your department take full credit for the arrests, Chief Soderberg. You did most all of the work," Guy said. "Our preference is to be left out of it completely."

"In fact, we insist," Claire said. She smiled warmly.

THE SLEUTHS wheeled their way back to Bigfork at four-thirty in the morning.

What a night it had been. The notorious Whitefish burglars had at last been arrested.

Claire and Guy fell onto the bed about ten minutes after they walked into their room, overcome by sheer exhaustion.

MORNING ARRIVED all too soon. Today was another big day. The investigators showered, dressed, and walked to the lodge.

Adrenaline was keeping them going, despite the extreme fatigue they felt. This was day twelve on the case. It was also the morning to confront Phil Kagan, and that prospect alone pushed them onward.

They walked to their usual breakfast table and sat down. Katie Kyle took their order and delivered fresh juice and hot black coffee.

Claire's cell phone rang. She listened to the caller.

"Who is this?" she asked.

The person talked rapidly on the other end of the phone.

"Are you sure?" Claire asked. "*Absolutely* sure?"

She waited for the answer.

"Thank you. Thank you very much," Claire said and ended the call.

She shook her head in disbelief.

"You're not going to believe this," she said. "That was an employee from the Gem Mountain Sapphire Mine. She told me that since our visit, she's been thinking a lot about the photos we showed her. The photo of one person in particular looked vaguely familiar to her that day, but she didn't say anything because she wasn't positive. Well, she saw the person again late yesterday at the mine, and now she's absolutely certain it's the person in one of the photos. But based upon what she just told me, I'm not sure of anything right now."

"Who did she identify?" Guy asked. "Don't keep me in suspense."

Just then, Phil Kagan approached the table and delivered breakfast. "I understand you've been looking for me," he said. He beamed from ear to ear, clasped his hands above his head, and danced a jig.

30

PHIL KAGAN STRUTTED into the interview room and took a seat opposite the investigators.

"Feeling better, Phil?" Claire asked.

"I am. Thank ye," he said. He clapped his hands and made a funny face.

"What was the problem?" she asked.

"The problem?" Phil asked.

"What was wrong with you?" Claire said.

"Oh. That. I guess it was a flu bug," Phil said. "And now it *flew* away." He chortled.

"Phil, why did you take the two books from our room?" Claire asked.

His face indicated he was startled by the question. "Um. I wanted to look at them. Is there a problem?"

"You bet there is," Guy said. "You took those books without our permission. And you didn't tell us that you took them. We had to find out on our own how they mysteriously disappeared from our room."

"Well, excuse the heck out of me. Obviously, most folks in these parts are a lot kinder and more generous than the two of you." Phil furrowed his brow and then broke into inappropriate laughter. "Folks around here don't get bent out of shape when people borrow things."

"Does that include guns?" Claire asked.

Phil's comical expression began to wane, and he looked at her without blinking. "Funny. Real funny. Remind me to laugh."

"Where are the books, Phil?" Claire asked.

"Where are they?"

"That is the question," Claire said.

"Well, they're either in my car or at my place," Phil said. "I guess I'm not sure."

"Where do you live, Phil?" Claire asked.

"What an odd question. Where do you both live?" Phil asked. He made a silly face.

"What is your address, Phil?" Guy asked. "We'd like a street address."

"Well, now, that is something I don't give out," Phil replied. "What could you possibly want with my street address?"

"Phil, we can do this the easy way or the hard way. If you'd prefer, we can get the sheriff involved right now," Guy said. He reached for his cell phone as he stared at the man. "We want an answer to our last question, and we want it now."

"Pushy, pushy, pushy," Phil said.

"Your address. What is it?" Guy thundered.

"Well, I live north and east of Bigfork in an older house."

"The address of the older house?" Guy asked. His anger mounted by the second, and in the worst way, he wanted to grab this Kagan fellow around the neck and force the information out of him.

"Um. I have to think. As I said, I never give it out," Phil said. He placed his index finger under his mouth and started to tap it.

Claire sensed that Guy was close to his breaking point. She reached under the table for his knee and squeezed it tightly, signaling for him to hold tight.

Both investigators stared at the inane-acting man. Neither said a word.

Two minutes passed in utter silence. And then two more.

Phil moved from side to side in his chair. He whistled softly and glanced around the room. He picked at his nails and touched his neck.

Still, the investigators said nothing, using the power of silence to make Phil Kagan increasingly more uncomfortable.

Sweat dripped from Phil's forehead and into his eyes, and he rubbed them. He turned his head upward and squinted his eyes, as if trying to remember. He scratched his head.

Still, Claire and Guy did not speak.

"Shit!" Phil finally boomed. "How long is this show going to last? I need to go out and buy some buttered popcorn if it's going to go on."

"Your address?" Claire asked.

Suddenly, Phil's humor seemed less apparent. "Do you have paper and a pen?"

Claire passed him both.

He jotted down an address and handed it over.

"Whom do you live with, Phil?" Claire asked.

"Whom do I live with?" Phil repeated.

"That's what I asked you," Claire said.

"Well, a couple of other people live there in the house and share the rent. It's a *big* old house," Phil replied.

"Who are these other people?" Claire asked.

"A couple of ladies," Phil replied. "They're both employed, and the rent they pay me helps make ends meet. Is there a law against that?"

"Do you own a gun, Phil?" Guy asked. His question was direct and unexpected.

At this point, the atmosphere of the meeting turned undeniably somber, and the clown part of Phil retreated completely.

"No, I do not," he replied. "I do not own a gun."

"Do you know how to shoot a gun?" Guy asked.

"Yeah, I know how to shoot a gun. Everyone in this state probably does," Phil replied.

"You visited with Blake Helms quite often," Claire said. "You told us that in our previous interview. Other people also shared this information with us. Blake discussed with you many things he read or learned concerning the Native American tribes of this area."

"He was a friend. So yes, we talked," Phil said. "He shared things with me that he had read on the topic. I told you, I found it all fascinating."

"What did Blake talk about in the days immediately preceding his murder?" Claire asked.

"In regards to what?" Phil asked. He looked at the investigators, his already-somber expression turning even graver.

"Anything. What did he talk about? Had he made a discovery about something in the books he was reading? Something perhaps you found intriguing?" Claire asked. "Something that made you take the books from us to look at them for yourself?"

Phil did not respond.

"What had Blake discovered, Phil?" Claire persisted. "Was it something worth killing for?"

Phil leaned back in his chair. "I want a lawyer."

"That's fine, Phil," Guy said. "We won't ask you any more

questions, but we do want the books. And we want them now. We're going to walk to your car with you and see if they're in there."

Phil and the investigators stood up. They trailed the chef to his car in the parking lot. He pulled a ring of keys from his pocket, selected one, and opened the trunk. The books were inside. He handed them to Claire.

"Don't plan on leaving town," Guy said to Phil.

THE SLEUTHS walked back to the lodge and stepped into the lobby. Guy pulled out his cell phone, called Sheriff Bell, and filled him in on the development with Phil Kagan. Claire walked over to the sofa, sat down, put the books next to her, and pulled the photo album to her lap. Guy joined her.

"Let's look at these pictures again," Claire said. She turned to the photos of the lobby area and carefully considered each one of them. Then, unexpectedly, her eyes fell upon the blankets underneath the saddles, and she focused her concentration on them. *Is that a sleeve on the deerskin one? With fringe?* she thought to herself. She was confused. Jay had said they were blankets, and they both looked like blankets at first glance. But why would a blanket have a sleeve? Then, in her mind's eye, Running Cloud's fringed shirt flashed quickly before her, and her thoughts went into a spin.

All at once, it hit her. "We've been going about this all wrong!" Claire shrieked. "I've felt that the answer was here, in front of me, in these photos, in this lobby. Running Cloud said so. I saw with my eyes, but I didn't really see it all." Running Cloud's exact words screamed out in her subconscious. *Pale lady, you look with your eyes, but you do not see.* "We completely forgot to gaze beyond the saddles, because we were told they had so little value."

"Not sure I'm following," Guy said.

"What do you see when you look right here in these photos?" Claire asked. She pointed to particular spots.

"Two saddles, sitting above the lobby, on a railing, in a wall cubbyhole," Guy said.

"What *else* do you see?" Claire said. "Look again. Let your eyes really see." Again, the words of Running Cloud thundered back to her.

"The blankets," Guy said. "Is that it? Jay said the antique store had thrown them in with the saddles to sweeten the deal."

"Yes, in part. One is a blanket. But actually, the other looks like an old, fringed deerskin shirt. See? There's a sleeve. My guess is, it's part of a Blackfoot costume. Look at the porcupine quills and glass beads and painting on it. They're barely visible, but they are there." She remembered vividly the entire outfit worn by Running Cloud.

Claire grabbed one of Blake's books and handed the other to Guy. "I'll bet if we look, we'll find the shirt in one of these two books. I'll bet Blake Helms was reading these books on Blackfoot clothing and recognized that a shirt in an illustration was the one here in the lodge—sitting under one of the old saddles. I'll bet Blake told Phil Kagan about it, and that's what got Blake murdered."

"Slow down, Claire," Guy said. "Let's take this one step at a time." He opened the book Claire had given him and began to browse through the pages.

Claire, likewise, looked through the other book.

The books were thick and contained numerous color illustrations as well as black-and-white sketches, and the two searched for close to an hour before the answer surfaced.

"Is *this* it?" Claire asked. She held her book alongside the photograph, and compared the two shirts. "I think we have a match," she said. "The shirt is part of a ritual costume. Look here. Leggings went with it, too. It had a high price in its day. Apparently in the early 1800s, one scalplock suit—that's what it was called—could be traded for thirty horses. I can only imagine its worth today." Claire looked further at the book text. "It says the stripes and dots painted on the upper portion of the shirt—in the yellow area—are a reminder of the sacred war shirt allegedly handed over to the Blackfoot by bear spirits."

"You just found the real motive for the murder," Guy said. "*Greed.* And all bets are now solidly on Phil Kagan."

"You're right, in part," Claire said. "But there's more to it."

Guy didn't hear her. "Time is of the essence," he said. "If Phil knows we've figured out the motive, he'll hide the shirt where it'll never be found."

Claire pulled her cell phone from her purse and called Sheriff Bell. "We just discovered something you'll want to see, sheriff. Can you meet us at the Bigfork Post Office right away? We need your help. And we'd better move fast."

Claire grabbed both books and the photo album. "Come on, Guy," she said. "Suddenly, it's all coming together—and quickly."

The investigators bolted from the lodge, raced to the green Land Rover Discovery 4 x 4, and tore off. As they exited the parking lot, Jay was just pulling in. He rolled his window down to say hello. They kept going.

Arriving at the post office in record time, the investigators waited for the sheriff in agony. It was a drive for him to come from Polson, and each minute seemed like twenty. When he pulled into the lot, the investigators ran to his car.

"We need to find out whose mail is delivered to Phil Kagan's post office box. And it's imperative we learn this at once. We need your help to do it," Claire said. "Trust us, please. We'll fill you in on everything."

The three rushed into the post office, and the sheriff asked a clerk for the information.

"I'll check," the woman said. "It will be just a moment." She got on her computer. "How do you spell his last name?"

"K-a-g-a-n," Guy said.

"We deliver to three people at that box," the woman said. She listed the names aloud.

"Can you confirm his street address, also?" Guy asked.

The worker wrote down his address on a small sheet of paper and handed it to Guy. It was not the same address Phil had written down for them during his interview that morning. No surprise there. The investigator quickly memorized the correct address and handed the note to the sheriff.

"That's what we needed. Thank you," Claire said.

The three raced from the building.

"Just as I thought!" Claire said. "Sheriff Bell, we need a search warrant for Phil Kagan's house. How fast can you get it?"

"I'll drive to the courthouse and ask for it now," the sheriff said. "I don't have time to draft up an affidavit setting forth probable cause, so I'll have to beg for the court's leniency and argue the case verbally. I'll explain that it's an emergency. I'll try to get to the Kagan residence as soon as possible, but it will take me some time. And I'll bring some patrol deputies with me."

"We'll meet you there," Claire said. "We're heading over now to observe. Please hurry!"

Both cars raced from the lot.

Claire picked up her cell phone and dialed Jay's number.

"What's your policy on married couples, or people from the same family, working at the lodge, Jay?" she asked.

His answer confirmed her suspicions.

Claire then called Sergeant Massey of the Miami-Dade Police Department. He owed her many favors, and she needed a couple right now. She asked him to obtain information on two individuals as quickly as possible, and he readily complied. Impatiently, she waited on the line while he searched his sources. The surprising information he came back with raised her eyebrows. It was crucial to putting the case together.

When Claire and Guy arrived at the Kagan residence, they parked down the street, but within viewing range. From their vantage point, the sleuths could see the two worn-out saddles sitting alongside the house, near the driveway.

"Let's see what they do with those," Guy said. "If they leave them, we'll let the sheriff know so he can pick them up."

They sat, watched, and waited. An hour passed. And then two. While they waited, Claire went over the details of the case.

"Just when you think it may never come together, *boom*!" she said. "It does! Here's what happened: When the employee from the Gem Mountain Sapphire Mine called me and said she remembered it was *Dalia Young*—the Mountain Lake Lodge housekeeper—who had visited the mine recently, it didn't make sense at first. But then a short while later, it all started to click. If Dahlia Young had been the one to traipse sapphire gravel in and out of the lodge on the early morning of the killing, then Dahlia Young could have also been the one who stole Heidi's gun and ammunition. They worked together cleaning the rooms, and Dahlia would have had ample opportunity to purloin the revolver and bullets at any time."

"Go on," Guy said, intrigued.

"But it also didn't make sense to me that she acted alone," Claire said. "What was her motive? Then when we learned about Blake having a recent discovery pertaining to the Blackfoot tribe, Phil Kagan came to mind. Blake would most likely have shared any such news with Phil—even before LoLo. But what was the connection between Phil and Dahlia? Dahlia is a twenty-four-year-old housekeeper. Phil is a fifty-one-year-old chef. The lodge employs both individuals."

"Did Sergeant Massey help make the connection?" Guy asked.

"He did. But hang on," Claire said. "Then Hazel Schroeder entered the picture, wearing that expensive diamond ring. A fifty-two-year-old woman—once blonde, but now sporting auburn-colored hair—and also a lodge employee. Phil Kagan and Hazel Schroeder began their employment at the lodge at almost the same time, five years ago. I checked the dates on their applications. Dahlia joined the staff three years ago."

Guy listened with rapt attention.

"I know now that Mountain Lake Lodge has a policy prohibiting married couples, dating couples, or people in the same family from being employed there at the same time. Jay confirmed it," Claire said. "So, Hazel used her *maiden name* when she filled out her application to work at the lodge. She kept her marriage to Phil Kagan a secret, and he, too, did not disclose his marriage to her when he applied. Then when their daughter Dahlia moved to Montana, the ruse continued. Dahlia had been married and divorced, so she used her *married name* to apply for employment at the lodge, and Jay and Piper were none the wiser. The three did not socialize with other staffers or each other, and the deceit continued unabridged."

"Amazing," Guy said.

"It was when Blake shared his recent discovery of the Blackfoot ritual costume shirt with Phil that things became complicated," Claire continued. "Phil saw a grand opportunity before his eyes. A meal ticket to becoming wealthy and living like a king. A chance to quit his mundane job at the lodge and live the luxurious life of his dreams. It was within his reach. The only roadblock standing in his way was Blake Helms. No one else knew about the found treasure. I'm sure Blake unwittingly confirmed that for Phil. But how could

Phil get away with stealing the shirt and selling it for a huge sum as long as Blake was still alive? He couldn't. So by sharing what he'd learned with Phil, Blake sealed his own fate. Phil concocted the plan, and Hazel and Dahlia became willing participants."

"And Dahlia's involvement?" Guy asked.

"I believe Phil asked Dahlia to steal Heidi's gun and ammo," Claire said. "After all, most of the staff members knew she carried them both in her purse. That was the easy part. Then, I believe Phil, Hazel, and Dahlia all surprised Blake with a visit in the early-morning hours—and killed him. You can only imagine how shocked and bewildered Blake would have been when he saw the three of them walk in at the same time at that hour. He never even knew they were related. It must have been a moment of raw confusion for Blake Helms."

Claire paused as if deep in thought. Her mind raced to the time she looked into the lodge from an aerial perspective, with the help of Running Cloud. She had seen the murderer standing in front of the check-in desk that awful night, cloaked in shadows. Now she realized the shadows had been his accomplices. And she remembered the expression on Blake's face, too.

She continued. "I believe Dahlia tracked the sapphire gravel in on her shoes. And I believe Phil Kagan walked up to Blake, with the others at his sides, lifted the gun out from under his jacket, and pulled the trigger five times. That is why Blake put up no resistance. It was totally unexpected. It was a surprise attack. He thought Phil was his friend."

Guy stared at Claire, taking it all in.

"From there, my guess is that the three of them lifted out paintings—both to throw blame onto the Whitefish burglar and to sell the pieces for quick cash—and then they stole the saddles, blanket, and shirt," Claire went on. "They tore up the lobby to make it look as if the robber were searching for hidden valuables, and then they left under the cover of darkness. It would have taken the three of them—moving rapidly after Blake was murdered—to haul the stolen items out of there and be gone by the time Heidi arrived to confront Blake at 2:45 a.m. My guess is Phil, Hazel, and Dahlia got to the lodge just after 1:00 a.m., which fits, because Blake's time of death was placed between 1:00 a.m. and 4:00 a.m. Their plan was carefully conceived before they carried it out, and the trio worked with great urgency. The paintings were an added bonus, you see, but the *prize* was the Blackfoot fringed shirt."

Guy shook his head, absorbing it all.

"And it was Phil and Hazel who asked the teenage boy in Polson to sell two paintings to the frame shop, and they put that money down to buy Hazel's diamond ring." Claire paused. "It was also Phil and Hazel who asked the frame shop owner all about us the day of the art festival. It was Phil alone who sold other pieces of artwork to various galleries on his 'sick days,' wearing a fake mustache to cover up that irregularly shaped birthmark above his upper lip—something that could easily identify him. I'm sure the shop owners will verify the fact that it was Phil Kagan. Right now, Sheriff Bell's office is working on getting those confirmations."

Guy's eyes darted to the house, as they had every couple minutes since Claire began to wrap it all up for him.

"And I'm sure Phil Kagan is now offering the priceless shirt to collectors on the black market for an unconscionable price," Claire said. "All of this will come out at trial."

Just then, Guy motioned to the house. "They're on the move!"

31

PHIL KAGAN, HAZEL Schroeder, and Dahlia Young walked from the house. Phil carried a long, cylindrical canvas duffel bag over his shoulder and pulled a large suitcase with his hand. The women each dragged a small suitcase behind them. Phil loaded the pieces of luggage and the bag into the cavernous trunk. Then the trio went back into the house and reappeared minutes later, carrying wrapped parcels. From their size and shape, a reasonable person would conclude they were paintings—the ones not yet sold to unwitting galleries or elsewhere. Some were loaded into the trunk, and others were put into one side of the vehicle's backseat.

"They're going to make a run for it," Guy said.

"We've got to stop them," Claire said. "Pull up closer. I want to get the license plate number."

Guy edged the car nearer to the Kagan house.

"A little closer," Claire said, as she jotted down the make and color of the car. "I can't quite read the plate."

Guy slowly edged the 4 x 4 nearer. Phil and Hazel settled into the car's front seat. Just as Dahlia was about to get into its backseat, she looked over and spotted the sleuths. She shrieked loudly and jumped in. Phil put the car in reverse and floored it. The car made a screening sound as it backed down the driveway and out onto the street. Phil shifted the auto into drive and sped off.

"Follow them!" Claire said.

Guy took off after the three, trailing closely behind and honking the 4 x 4's horn continuously.

Claire grabbed her phone and dialed Sheriff Bell.

"Sheriff, they're getting away. They are in Phil's car, and we're tailing them. He just jumped the red traffic light in town." She gave Sheriff Bell the color and make of Phil's car and pinpointed its exact location. Then she quickly filled him in on her latest discoveries.

"We're on our way—only three blocks from there," the sheriff said. "We'll get 'em. And by the way, you'll be happy to know we've heard back from several of the galleries. They've all identified Phil Kagan as the man who offered or sold them the stolen paintings."

The marked squad cars, sirens blazing and lights flashing, quickly zeroed in on the getaway car. The patrol deputies formed a roadblock with their vehicles and cut the trio off before they could leave the outskirts of Bigfork.

Sheriff Bell approached with his Glock pistol drawn. His deputies walked by his side, weapons in hand. Phil, Hazel, and Dahlia were apprehended and handcuffed without incident.

"Phil Kagan, Hazel Schroeder Kagan, and Dahlia Kagan Young, you are under arrest for the premeditated murder of Blake Helms and for felony theft connected to the killing." He read the Miranda Warning separately to each of the three charged.

"Bring them into custody," he ordered his patrol deputies. "We've got a young lady sitting behind bars right now for the crimes these people committed. We need to get her out."

Claire and Guy looked on with interest.

"Before you take them away, sheriff, grab Dahlia's shoes for evidence," Claire said. "If the sapphire gravel is not on that pair, it will be stuck in the soles of another pair either in her luggage or at the house. And if you don't find it on any shoes, check in the cuffs of her slacks. You'll find it somewhere in her clothing."

"We'll take care of it immediately, Ms. Caswell," Sheriff Bell said.

He demanded Dahlia remove her shoes on the spot. As Claire suspected, the grooves on the soles of her shoes were filled with gravel. The lab would have to test the coarse mixture to identify it, but the investigators had no doubt it would be the same sapphire gravel as what was left behind on the floor of the lodge lobby the fateful morning of Blake Helms's death.

"And we're guessing the Blackfoot shirt is in the duffle bag in the car trunk, together with the gun and ammunition," Guy said. "Also, the remaining pieces of stolen art from the lodge should be in there."

Sheriff Bell pulled on a pair of latex gloves, retrieved the keys from Phil Kagan, opened the trunk, and loosened the drawstring on the canvas bag to look inside. "It's all here," he said. "The fringed shirt is rolled up and wrapped in tissue paper, a smaller bag inside contains a .38 Special revolver and a box of ammo—minus five bullets—and the wrapped pieces here look to be the artwork stolen from Mountain Lake Lodge."

"I'm sure that revolver will check out to be Heidi Flynn's gun, stolen by Dahlia Young," Guy said. "The gun used to murder Blake Helms. And the ammo will be Heidi's as well."

"We'll have them checked for prints straightaway, and we'll determine for certain if the bullets that killed Blake Helms were fired from this gun," the sheriff said. "Hopefully Phil Kagan's prints will be all over it, the bullets will match, and it'll be an open-and-shut case. And regardless of which of the three actually pulled the trigger, they're all equally complicit in the murder and theft conspiracy, and thereby equally guilty of the crime." The sheriff continued to look through the trunk. "Oh, and here's a thick pillow with five holes surrounded by powder burn. My guess? It was used to help silence the bullets that killed Blake Helms. We never found any pillow stuffing material at the crime scene, so if there was any, they must have cleaned that up. We'll have the pillow checked out, too."

"Anything else in there, sheriff?" Claire asked.

"Yeah. Three pairs of gloves. No wonder they left no prints behind." He shook his head from side to side. "And a carpenter's knife. Probably used to slash the lobby furniture to make the murder look like a robbery with a violent ending. All of this evidence will be rigorously analyzed."

"We noticed the two stolen saddles sitting on the ground on the side of the Kagan house," Guy said. "Looks like they maybe planned to dump them when they made their getaway, but didn't have time to load them in the car. Make sure your patrol deputies pick them up and return them to the lodge, will you, please? After you examine them for evidence, that is. And you'll no doubt find the blanket taken with the saddles somewhere on their property, too, either inside or out, if it's not in Phil's car."

"We'll take care of it all," Sheriff Bell said. "Thanks for the heads-up."

The investigators watched as the squad cars pulled away, carrying the Kagan family of criminals to the Lake County Detention Center.

"I've got to ask, Claire," Guy said. "How did you put it together that *three* people were involved in the murder? Conspiracies are often tough to crack."

"I thought you'd never ask." She smiled. "It was what Running

Cloud said to me the second time I saw him. He told me to think of a *braid*. Remember? I was puzzled at first by that comment. But I mulled it over until I got it. A braid consists of three strands interlaced together. Three combine to make one. And the one is stronger than the three alone. So that was my clue that three people acted in collusion to commit this crime. We were already suspicious of Phil Kagan and of Hazel Schroeder, but I couldn't figure out who the third accomplice might be. Until, of course, I received the call from the Gem Mountain Sapphire Mine staffer who informed me that Dahlia Young had visited the mine. Dahlia Young, the lodge housekeeper who had totally escaped our scrutiny, who had never even warranted a single star in our opinion—but who had daily access to Heidi's gun."

Claire paused. "So, from there, I just had to figure out how the three were connected. I discovered from Jay that related individuals are not allowed to work at the lodge at the same time. Then I phoned Sergeant Massey in Miami and called in a favor. He did some checking and informed me that Phil Kagan and Hazel Schroeder *Kagan* are married, and that they have one offspring; namely, a daughter named Dahlia. I put it all together real quick and determined the three of them had pulled a fraud on the lodge by intentionally using different last names when applying for employment."

"And all the pieces fell neatly into place," Guy said.

"It's all in the teamwork, counselor. The three of us put this puzzle together much better than any one of us could have done separately."

"The *three* of us?" Guy asked.

"You, me, and Running Cloud. Together, we had the strength of a *braid*." She looked at him and smiled a sweet smile.

Claire pulled out her cell phone and dialed Sam Barlone. "We want you and Ethan to meet us at the Lake County Detention

Center as soon as you can get there. We have good news."

Guy called Attorney Jasper Wilkes and filled him in on all the recent developments as he and Claire walked to the car to head to Polson.

"I'm at a loss for words," Attorney Wilkes said. "And that doesn't happen often." He was silent for a long few seconds, absorbing it all. "Sounds as if you did my job for me. I'll contact the prosecutor and meet you two at the detention center. Let's get Heidi out of there."

The scene at the detention center was bittersweet. Sweet for Heidi Flynn, Sam, and Ethan when she was freed from incarceration and all charges against her were dropped. Bitter for Phil Kagan, Hazel Schroeder Kagan, and Dahlia Kagan Young as they were processed as criminals, a date was set for each one's arraignment, and heavy doors slammed shut on their three separate cells.

Sam passed little Ethan to Heidi's awaiting arms. She squeezed him tightly. "I love you, little one," she said. She kissed him gently on both of his plump cheeks.

"Mommy's coming home."

She passed Ethan back to Sam and took turns giving each of the investigators a hug. "I owe you my life. Thanks for believing in me."

Claire and Guy started the walk toward their car.

Sheriff Bell ran after them. "I didn't get the chance to properly thank you," he said. "So, thank you!" He shook the right hand of both sleuths heartily. "Please stop by and say hello whenever you're in the area."

The sleuths resumed their walk.

"I'm exhausted. Want to take a long nap with me?" Claire asked.

"I had something else in mind first, but then a nap will certainly be what the doctor ordered." He flashed the grin she loved.

"You're back, aren't you?" she asked. "You're back. You've finally put the incident in Crete behind you."

He smiled and winked. "I'm working on it. I'm close."

Lovemaking was impassioned. Afterward, they entered the Land of Nod and slept a hard sleep. Guy was the first to awaken, and he took the opportunity to whisper into Claire's ear while she continued to sleep. "Marry me," he said softly. "Marry me." His hope to one day wed the woman of his dreams had not abated. He kissed Claire gently on her back and nudged her tenderly. "Time to get up, my beauty."

She stirred and opened her eyes.

"It's late. We slept for hours," Guy said. "Let's run over to Riley's Pub and get something to eat. I'm starving."

"Sounds good," Claire said.

They threw on some clothes and walked to the restaurant. Jay and Piper were both there, working late.

"Join us for dinner. It's time to celebrate," Claire said. "We solved the case."

Piper and Jay looked fixedly at the investigators, stunned by the revelation.

Claire and Guy took turns filling their friends in on the day's discoveries and on the ultimate arrests.

"Unbelievable," Jay said. "The *three* of them did it!"

"We had *no* inkling they were related," Piper said. "Not a clue."

"And the fringed Blackfoot shirt," Jay said. "The owner at the antique store had merely thrown it and the blanket in with the saddles to bargain with me. I guess I didn't even really notice it was a shirt. I thought it was just a nice old relic from the past—colorful and decorative, but of no real value. Blake had always thought that, too. I can only imagine his surprise when he learned what it really was and of its true value. We had no idea. It's funny how sometimes things are right before our eyes and we don't see them."

Claire nodded in a knowing way.

"Well, as soon as the sheriff's office is done with the shirt, it'll be returned to you, together with all the artwork taken from the lodge, which has now been recovered, and the saddles. The old blanket, too, if the sheriff's patrol deputies can find it," Claire said. "It's all yours. And the fringed shirt will bring a handsome price from a collector, if you decide to part with it."

"Even though the money could help our business get through this challenging time, I'm inclined to turn it over to the National Museum of the American Indian. Or better yet, return it to the Blackfoot peoples still remaining in Montana," Jay said. "It's where it rightfully belongs."

Piper nodded in agreement. "I wholeheartedly concur."

Dinner was a grand time.

"Now that you've solved the case, we hope you'll stay on a few extra days, so you can actually enjoy Montana together," Piper said.

"Maybe one. Or two," Guy said.

"Or three." Claire laughed. "We'd love to."

"Great," Piper said. "Claire, the two of us can now spend a day on Electric Avenue in our quaint little town of Bigfork. We'll go to S. M. Bradford Co. to look at clothes, and we must stop into Eva Gates Homemade Preserves to buy you some huckleberry jam to take back to Miami with you. We'll browse through the Eric Thorsen Fine Art Gallery, Roma's Gourmet Kitchen Store, and Frame of Reference—an amazing frame shop and gallery. After that, we'll shop at all the other adorable stores on the main street. Then, we'll take a break and stop for a cup of aromatic Montana coffee and a cinnamon roll at Brookies Cookies, and then—"

"I can't wait," Claire broke in. "The two of us out on the town for an entire day of shopping? It's been a while since we've done that." She smiled broadly.

"Guy, we'll play eighteen holes at Eagle Bend Golf Course," Jay said. "You'll like its natural setting."

"Now you're talking," Guy said.

"And one evening we can all attend a play at the Bigfork Summer Playhouse. You'll enjoy that," Piper said. "And we should take you to an Indian trading post while you're here. You can see original trading beads used by Lewis and Clark to obtain buffalo hides when their famous expedition took them through this part of Montana."

The couples seemed to be back on track with each other.

"Oh, and one last question," Jay said. "Does this mean I'm finally off the suspect list?" He looked at Guy.

"You're officially off the list, Jay," Guy said. "As though you were never on it. I hope we can put it behind us and go on."

Both Claire and Guy shared a similar thought at that moment. It had been difficult to investigate a murder where professionalism demanded they treat their own friends like any other suspects. They had managed that hurdle on another case in the past, as well, and they hoped never to be faced with this type of situation again.

The men exchanged a handshake.

"Ah, come here," Jay said. He grabbed Guy and gave him a quick hug. "All is forgiven. I'll admit, I hated you for a time, but now that feeling is gone. I don't want to lose our friendship."

"This whole matter has made Jay and I realize how much we love each other," Piper said. "We've agreed to see a marriage therapist and get things back on the right path." Jay leaned over, and his lips touched Piper's. They embraced.

Piper hesitated before continuing. "And because you never received an answer to this question . . . *no*, I never had an affair with Blake Helms. He was simply a nice man who cared about what I had to say. He was a valued friend. That is all. I know you've been wondering all along, and I've never really answered the question. I guess I was deeply bothered by the insinuation, especially coming from the two of you. I thought you both knew me better than that."

"Believe me, Piper, it was difficult for us as well," Claire said. "But as investigators, we had to ask the question, regardless of the fact we are friends, and regardless of what our personal instincts may have been."

Piper nodded. "I understand that now. You are truly good at what you do." She smiled at both Claire and Guy.

"All's well that ends well," Claire said.

She winked at Guy, and he grinned back in an unrestrained manner. It was his famous grin, the one she hadn't seen in months, and it stayed on his face for some time.

Claire beamed broadly. "I love you," she mouthed.

BACK IN the room that evening, the investigators sat on chairs out on the balcony. Together, they stared up into the star-filled indigo sky. Flathead Lake glistened and danced in the steady glow of the moonlight. The evening air felt brisk. Sweet-tempered breezes brushed their faces in a delightful way, wafting the strong scent of fresh pine needles through the air. A coyote howled briefly in the distance. And an owl hooted. But otherwise, all was still. All was serene. Before long, an incredible sensation of peace fell over Claire and Guy.

"Remind me to call LoLo in the morning and fill her in on today's events," Claire said. "She'll want to know everything."

Guy didn't respond. He seemed preoccupied.

"Maybe we can retire here someday," he said. "I think I'd like that."

"Maybe," she said. She got up, walked over to Guy, and threw her arms around his shoulders. "I love you."

He turned his head and looked up at her. "It's me," he said. "I'm back." He smiled. "And I love you, too. I think I've put the trip to

Crete and the road to Omalos behind me for good. From this point on, I'm only looking forward . . . to our future together. I promise." He flashed his famous grin again and stood up to take her in his arms.

"By the way, when we were walking out after dinner, I asked Jay about the folder we saw him shove into the check-in desk drawer," Claire said. "I had to know what it was."

"You did? And?" Guy asked.

"Jay was having Piper followed. He admitted he had hired a PI more than a week before, and he was looking at photos of her the investigator sent him. Said the investigator proved she wasn't having an affair with Blake, after all. He didn't want us to see the pictures. I think he was deeply embarrassed by what he did. That's why he acted so strangely. He promised me he'd sit down with Piper and let her know what he'd done. He said he wants to start over with everything on the table."

"Again, a good ending, even if things were difficult along the way," Guy said. "Blake's murderers were apprehended, the Whitefish burglars were nabbed, Piper and Jay are working things out, peace and tranquility have returned to Whitefish and Bigfork, and for us . . ." He paused and fumbled for the right words. "For us . . . many adventures lie ahead." He wanted so badly to ask her the question, but once again, the dread and fear of her not saying yes stopped him in his tracks.

THAT NIGHT, Running Cloud visited Claire in her dreams.

"Well done, pale-skinned white woman," he said. The corners of his mouth turned up ever so slightly. "You did good."

But before she could thank him for his insights, in true-to-form fashion, he disappeared suddenly. In the twinkling of an eye.

Whoever is a partner with a thief
  hates his own life;
He swears to tell the truth, but
  reveals nothing.

Proverbs 29:24